Violin

Violin

ANNE RICE

Alfred A. Knopf

NEW YORK · TORONTO

1997

THIS IS A BORZOI BOOK
PUBLISHED BY ALFRED A. KNOPF, INC.,
AND ALFRED A. KNOPF CANADA

http://www.randomhouse.com/

Library of Congress Cataloging-in-Publication Data
Rice, Anne.
Violin / by Anne Rice.—1st ed.
p.   cm.
ISBN 0-679-43302-3
I. Title
PS3568.I265V56   1997
813'.54—dc20   96-38581
CIP

Canadian Cataloguing in Publication Data
Rice, Anne.
Violin
ISBN 0-676-97074-5
I. Title.
PS3568.I22V56   1997   813'.54   C97-930837-2

A limited signed edition of this book has been published by
B. E. Trice Publishing, New Orleans.

Manufactured in the United States of America
First Trade Edition

FOR
Annelle Blanchard, M.D.
FOR
Rosario Tafaro
FOR
Karen
and as always and forever
FOR
Stan and Christopher and Michele Rice,
John Preston,
and
Victoria Wilson
and
in tribute
to the talent of
Isaac Stern
and
Leila Josefowicz

*And the Angel of the Lord declared unto Mary,
and she conceived of the Holy Ghost.*

Violin

Proem

WHAT I seek to do here perhaps cannot be done in words. Perhaps it can only be done in music. I want to try to do it in words. I want to give to the tale the architecture which only narrative can provide—the beginning, the middle and the end—the charged unfolding of events in phrases faithfully reflecting their impact upon the writer.

You should not need to know the composers I mention often in these pages: Beethoven, Mozart, Tchaikovsky—the wild strummings of the bluegrass fiddlers or the eerie music of Gaelic violins. My words should impart the very essence of the sound to you.

If not, then there is something here which cannot be really written.

But since it's the story in me, the story I am compelled to unfold—my life, my tragedy, my triumph and its price—I have no choice but to attempt this record.

As we begin, don't seek to link the past events of my life in one coherent chain like Rosary beads. I have not done so. The scenes come forth in bursts and disorder, as beads tossed helter-skelter to the light. And were they strung together, to make a Rosary—and my years are the very same as the beads of the Rosary—fifty-four—my past would not make a set of mysteries, not the Sorrowful, nor the Joyful or the Glorious. No crucifix at the end redeems those fifty-four years. So I give you the flashing moments that matter here.

See me, if you will, not as an old woman. Fifty-four today is nothing. Picture me if you must as five feet one inch tall, plump, with a shapeless torso that has been the bane of my adult life, but with a girlish face and free dark hair, thick and long, and slender wrists and ankles. Fat has not changed the facial expression I had when I was twenty. When I cover myself in soft flowing clothes, I seem a small bell-shaped young woman.

My face was a kindness on the part of God, but not remarkably so. It is typically Irish-German, square, and my eyes are large and brown, and my hair, cut blunt just above my eyebrows—bangs, if you will—disguises my worst feature, a low forehead. "Such a pretty face" they say of dumpy women like me. My bones are just visible enough through the flesh to catch the light in flattering ways. My features are insignificant. If I catch the eye of the passerby, it's on account of an acuity visible in my gaze, an honed and nourished intelligence, and because when I smile, I look truly young, just for that instant.

It's no uncommon thing to be so young at fifty-four in this era, but I mark it here, because when I was a child, a person who had lived over half a century was old, and now it's not so.

In our fifties, our sixties, it does not matter what age, we all wander as our health will allow—free, strong, dressing like the young if we want, sitting with feet propped up, casual—the first beneficiaries of an unprecedented health, preserving often to the very end of life itself a faith in discovery.

So that's your heroine, if a heroine I am to be.

And your hero? Ah, he had lived beyond a century.

This story begins when he came—like a young girl's painting of the dark and troubled charmer—Lord Byron on a cliff above the abyss—the brooding, secretive embodiment of romance, which he was, and most deservedly so. He was true to this grand type, exquisite and profound, tragic and alluring as a Mater Dolorosa, and he paid for all that he was. He paid.

This is . . . what happened.

❦ 1 ❧

H<small>E CAME</small> before the day Karl died.

It was late afternoon, and the city had a drowsy dusty look, the traffic on St. Charles Avenue roaring as it always does, and the big magnolia leaves outside had covered the flagstones because I had not gone out to sweep them.

I saw him come walking down the Avenue, and when he reached my corner he didn't come across Third Street. Rather he stood before the florist shop, and turned and cocked his head and looked at me.

I was behind the curtains at the front window. Our house has many such long windows, and wide generous porches. I was merely standing there, watching the Avenue and its cars and people for no very good reason at all, as I've done all my life.

It isn't too easy for someone to see me behind the curtains. The corner is busy; and the lace of the curtains, though torn, is thick because the world is always there, drifting by right around you.

He had no visible violin with him then, only a sack slung over his shoulder. He merely stood and looked at the house—and turned as though he had come now to the end of his walk and would return, slowly, by foot as he had approached—just another afternoon Avenue stroller.

He was tall and gaunt, but not at all in an unattractive way. His black hair was unkempt and rock musician long, with two braids tied back to keep it from his face, and I remember I liked the way it hung down his back as he turned around. I remember his coat on account of that—an old dusty black coat, terribly dusty, as though he'd been sleeping somewhere in the dust. I remember this because of the gleaming black hair and the way it broke off rough and ragged and long and so pretty.

He had dark eyes; I could see that much over the distance of the corner, the kind of eyes that are deep, sculpted in the face so that they can be secretive, beneath arching brows, until you get really close and see the warmth in them. He was lanky, but not graceless.

He looked at me and he looked at the house. And then off he went, with easy steps, too regular, I suppose. But then what did I know about ghosts at the time? Or how they walk when they come through?

He didn't come back until two nights after Karl died. I hadn't told anyone Karl was dead and the telephone-answering machine was lying for me.

These two days were my own.

In the first few hours after Karl was gone, I mean really truly gone, with the blood draining down to the bottom of his body, and his face and hands and legs turning very white, I had been elated the way you can be after a death and I had danced and danced to Mozart.

Mozart was always my happy guardian, the Little Genius, I called him, Master of His Choir of Angels, that is Mozart; but Beethoven is the Master of My Dark Heart, the captain of my broken life and all my failures.

That first night when Karl was only dead five hours, after I changed the sheets and cleaned up Karl's body and set his hands at his sides, I couldn't listen to the angels of Mozart anymore. Let Karl be with them. Please, after so much pain. And the book Karl had compiled, almost finished, but not quite—its pages and pictures strewn across his table. Let it wait. So much pain.

I turned to my Beethoven.

I lay on the floor of the living room downstairs—the corner room, through which light comes from the Avenue both front and side, and I played Beethoven's *Ninth*. I played the torture part. I played the Second Movement. Mozart couldn't carry me up and out of the death; it was time for anguish, and Beethoven knew and the Second Movement of the symphony knew.

No matter who dies or when, the Second Movement of the *Ninth Symphony* just keeps going.

When I was a child, I loved the last movement of Beethoven's *Ninth Symphony*, as does everybody. I loved the chorus singing the "Ode to Joy." I can't count the times I've seen it—here, Vienna once, San Francisco several times during the cold years when I was away from my city.

But in these last few years, even before I met Karl, it was the Second Movement that really belonged to me.

It's like walking music, the music of someone walking doggedly and almost vengefully up a mountain. It just goes on and on and on, as though the person won't stop walking. Then it comes to a quiet place, as if in the Vienna Woods, as if the person is suddenly breathless and exultant and has the view of the city that he wants, and can throw up his arms, and dance in a circle. The French horn is there, which always makes you think of woods and dales and shepherds, and you can feel the peace and the stillness of the woods and the plateau of happiness of this person standing there, but then . . .

. . . then the drums come. And the uphill walk begins again, the determined walking and walking. Walking and walking.

You can dance to this music if you want, swing from the waist, and I do, back and forth like you're crazy, making yourself dizzy, letting your hair flop to the left and then flop to the right. You can walk round and round the room in a grim marching circle, fists clenched, going faster and faster, and now and then twirling when you can before you go on walking. You can bang your head back and forth, back and forth, letting your hair fly up and over and down and dark before your eyes, before it disappears and you see the ceiling again.

This is relentless music. This person is not going to give up. Onward, upward, forward, it does not matter now—woods, trees, it does not matter. All that matters is that you walk . . . and when there comes just a little bit of happiness again—the sweet exultant happiness of the plateau—it's caught up this time in the advancing steps. Because there is no stopping.

Not till it stops.

And that's the end of the Second Movement. And I can roll over on the floor, and hit the button again, and bow my head, and let the movement go on, independent of all else, even grand and magnificent assurances that Beethoven tried to make, it seemed, to all of us, that everything would someday be understood and this life was worth it.

Violin

That night, the night after Karl's death, I played the Second Movement long into the morning; until the room was full of sunlight and the parquet floor was glaring. And the sun made big beams through the holes in the curtains. And above, the ceiling, having lost all those headlights of the long night's traffic, became a smooth white, like a new page on which nothing is written.

Once, at noon, I let the whole symphony play out. I closed my eyes. The afternoon was empty, with only the cars outside, the never ending cars that speed up and down St. Charles Avenue, too many for its narrow lanes, too fast for its old oaks and gently curved street lamps, drowning out in their alien thunder even the beautiful and regular roar of the old streetcar. A clang. A rattle. A noise that should have been a racket, and was once I suppose, though I never in all my life, which is over half a century, remember the Avenue ever truly being quiet, except in the small hours.

I lay that day in silence because I couldn't move. I couldn't do anything. Only when it got dark again did I go upstairs. The sheets were still clean. The body was stiff. I knew it was rigor mortis; there was little change in his face; I'd wrapped his face round and round with clean white cloth to keep his mouth closed, and I'd closed his eyes myself. And though I lay there all night, curled up next to him, my hand on his cold chest, it wasn't the same as it had been when he was soft.

The softness came back by midmorning. Just a relaxing of the body all over. The sheets were soiled. Foul smells were there. But I had no intention of recognizing them. I lifted his arms easily now. I bathed him again. I changed everything, as a nurse would, rolling the body to one side for the clean sheet, then back in order to cover and tuck in the clean sheet on the other.

He was white, and wasted, but he was pliant once again. And though the skin was sinking, pulling away from the features of his face, they were still his features, those of my Karl, and I could see the tiny cracks in his lips unchanged, and the pale colorless tips of his eyelashes when the sunshine hit them.

The upstairs room, the western room, that was the one in which he'd wanted us to sleep, and in which he died, because the sun does come there late through the little attic windows.

This is a cottage, this huge house, this house of six Corinthian columns and black cast-iron railings. It's just a cottage really, with grand spaces on one floor, and small bedrooms carved from its once cavernous attic. When I was very little it was only attic then, and smelled so sweet, like wood all the time, like wood and attic. Bedrooms came when my younger sisters came.

This western corner bedroom was a pretty room. He'd been right to choose it, dress it so bountifully, right to fix everything. It had been so simple for him.

I never knew where he kept his money or how much it was, or what would become of it later. We had married only a few years before. It hadn't seemed a proper question to ask. I was too old for children. But he had given so generously—anything I desired. It was his way.

He spent his days working on his pictures and commentaries on one saint, one saint who captured his imagination: St. Sebastian. He'd hoped to finish his book before he died. He had almost won. All that remained were scholarly chores. I would think of this later.

I would call Lev and ask Lev's advice. Lev was my first husband. Lev would help. Lev was a college professor.

I lay a long time beside Karl and as night came, I thought, Well, he's been dead now for two days and you've probably broken the law.

But what does it really matter? What can they do? They know what he died of, that it was AIDS and there was no hope for him, and when they do come, they'll destroy everything. They'll take his body and burn it.

I think that was the main reason I kept him so long. I had no fear of the fluids or any such thing, and he himself had been so careful always in the final months, demanding masks and gloves. Even in the filth after he died, I'd lain there in a thick velvet robe, my unbroken skin closing me in and saving me from any virus that lingered around him.

Our erotic moments had been for hands, skin against skin, all that could be washed—never the daredevil union.

The AIDS had never gotten into me. And only now after the two days, when I thought I should call them, I should let them know— only now, I knew I wished it had gotten me. Or I thought I did.

It's so easy to wish for death when nothing's wrong with you! It's so easy to fall in love with death, and I've been all my life, and seen its most faithful worshipers crumble in the end, screaming just to live, as if all the dark veils and the lilies and the smell of candles, and grandiose promises of the grave, meant nothing.

I knew that. But I always wished I was dead. It was a way to go on living.

Evening came. I looked out the little window for a while as the street lamps came on. As the lights of the florist shop went on, just as its doors to the public were locked.

I saw the flagstones ever more covered with the stiff, curling magnolia leaves. I saw how wretched were the bricks along the side of the fence, which I ought to fix so no one would fall on them. I saw the oaks coated with the dust rising from the roaring cars.

I thought, Well, kiss him goodbye. You know what comes next. He's soft, but then it's decay and a smell that must have nothing, nothing to do with him.

I bent down and kissed his lips. I kissed him and kissed him and kissed—this partner of only a few short years and such considerately rapid decline—I kissed him and though I wanted to go back to bed I went downstairs and ate white bread in slices from the wrapping, and drank the diet soda, hot from the carton on the floor, out of sheer indifference, or rather the certainty that pleasure in any form was forbidden.

Music. I could try it again. Just one more evening alone listening to my disks, all to myself, before they came, screaming. Before his mother sobbed on the phone from London, "Thank God the baby is born! He waited, he waited until his sister's baby was born!"

I knew that's exactly what she would say, and it was true, I guess; he had waited for his sister's baby, but not waited long enough for her to come home, that's the part that would keep her screaming longer than I had the patience to listen. Kind old woman. To whose bedside do you go, that of your daughter in London, giving birth, or that of your dying son?

The house was littered with the trash.

Ah, what license I'd taken. The nurses didn't really want to come during the last days anyway. There are saints around, saints who stay with the dying until the very last, but in this case, I was there, and no saints were needed.

Every day my old-timers, Althea and Lacomb, had come to knock, but I hadn't changed the note on the door: All Is Well. Leave a Message.

And so the place was full of trash, of cookie crumbs and empty cans, and dust and even leaves, as if a window must be open somewhere, probably in the master bedroom which we never used, and the wind had brought the leaves in on the orange carpet.

I went into the front room. I lay down. I wanted to reach out to touch the button and start the Second Movement again, just Beethoven with me, the captain of this pain. But I couldn't do it.

It even seemed all right for the Little Genius, Mozart perhaps, the bright safe glow of angels chattering and laughing and doing back flips in celestial light. I wanted to . . . But I just didn't move . . . for hours. I heard Mozart in my head; I heard his racing violin; always with me it was the violin, the violin above all, that I loved.

I heard Beethoven now and then; the stronger happiness of his one and only *Violin Concerto* which I had long ago memorized, the easy solo melodies, I mean. But nothing played in the house where I lay with the dead man upstairs. The floor was cold. It was spring and the weather wavered in these days from very hot to winter chill. And I thought to myself, Well, it's getting cold, and that will keep the body better, won't it?

Someone knocked. They went away. The traffic reached its peak. There came a quiet. The phone machine told lie after lie after lie. Click and click and click click.

Then I slept, perhaps for the first time.

And the most beautiful dream came to me.

✣ 2 ✤

I DREAMED of the sea by the full light of the sun, but such a sea I'd never known. The land was a great cradle in which this sea moved, as the sea at Waikiki or along the coast south of San Francisco. That is, I could see distant arms of land to left and right, reaching out desperately to contain this water.

But what a fierce and glistening sea it was, and under such a huge and pure sun, though the sun itself I couldn't see, only the light of it. The great waves came rolling in, curling, full of green light for one instant before they broke and then each wave did a dance—a dance—I'd never witnessed.

A great frothy foam came from each dying wave, but this foam broke into great random peaks, as many as six to eight for one wave, and these peaks looked like nothing so much as people—people made of the glistening bubbles of the foam—reaching out for the real land, for the beach, for the sun above perhaps.

Over and over, I watched the sea in my dream. I knew I was watching from a window. And I marveled and tried to count the dancing figures before they would inevitably die away, astonished at how well formed of foam they became, with nodding heads and desperate arms, before they lapsed back as if dealt a mortal blow by the air, to wash away and come again in the curling green wave with a whole new display of graceful imploring movements.

People of foam, ghosts out of the sea—that's what they looked like to me, and all along the beach for as far as I could see from my safe window, the waves all did the same; they curled, green and brilliant, and then they broke and became the pleading figures, some nodding to each other, and others away, and then turning back again into a great violent ocean.

Seas I've seen, but never a sea where the waves made dancers. And even as the evening sun went down, an artificial light flooded the combed sand, the dancers came still, with heads high and long spines and arms flung beseechingly landward.

Oh, these foamy beings looked so like ghosts to me—like spirits too weak to make a form in the concrete world, yet strong enough to invest for a moment in the wild disintegrating froth and force it into human shape before nature took it back.

How I loved it. All night long I watched it, or so my dream told me, the way dreams will do. And then I saw myself in the dream and it was daytime. The world was alive and busy. But the sea was just as vast and so blue I almost cried to look at it.

I saw myself in the window! In my dreams, such a perspective almost never comes, never! But there I was, I knew myself, my own thin square face, my own black hair with bangs cut blunt and all the rest long and straight. I stood in a square window in a white façade of what seemed a grand building. I saw my own features, small, nondescript with a smile, not interesting, only ordinary and totally without danger or challenge, my face with bangs long almost to my eyelashes, and my lips so easily smiling. I have a face that lives in its smiles. And even in the dream I thought, Ah Triana, you must be very happy! But it never took much to make me smile, really. I know misery and happiness intimately!

I thought all this in the dream. I thought of both the misery and the happiness. And I was happy. I saw in the dream that I stood in the window holding in my left arm a big bouquet of red roses, and that with my right arm I waved to people below me.

But where could this be, I thought, coming closer and closer to the edge of wakefulness. I never sleep for long. I never sleep deep. The dreadful suspicion had already made itself known. This is a dream, Triana! You aren't there. You're not in a warm bright place with a vast sea. You have no roses.

But the dream would not break, or fade, or show the slightest tear or flaw.

I saw myself high in the window, waving still, smiling, holding the big floppy bouquet, and then I saw that I waved to young men and women who stood on the sidewalk below—tall children, no more than that—kids of twenty-five years or less—just kids, and I knew that it was they who had sent me the roses. I loved them. I waved and waved and so did they, and in their exuberance they jumped up and down, and then I threw them kisses.

Kiss after kiss I threw with the fingers of my right hand to these admirers, while behind them the great blue sea blazed and evening came, sharp and sudden, and beyond these youthful dancers on the patterned black and white pavements, there danced the sea once more, flocks of figures rising from the foamy waves, and this seemed a world so real I couldn't pronounce it just a dream.

"This is happening to you, Triana. You're there."

I tried to be clever. I knew these hypnagogic tricks that dreams could do, I knew the demons who come face to face with you on the very margin of sleep. I knew and I turned and tried to see the room in which I stood. "Where is this? How could I imagine it?"

But I saw only the sea. The night was black with stars. The delirium of the foamy ghosts ran for as far as I could see.

Oh, Soul, Oh, Lost Souls, I sang aloud, Oh, are you happy, are you happier than in life which has such hard edges to it and such agony? They gave no answer, these ghosts; they extended their arms, only to be dragged back into dazzling sliding water.

I woke. So sharp.

Karl said in my ear: "Not that way! You don't understand. Stop it!"

I sat up. That was a shocking thing, to have so recollected his voice, to have imagined it so close to me. But not a terribly unwelcome thing. There was no fear in me.

I was alone in the big dirty front room. The headlights threw the lace all over the ceiling. In the painted St. Sebastian above the mantel the gilded halo gleamed. The house creaked and the traffic crawled by, a lower rumbling.

"You're here. And it was, it was, it was a vivid dream, and Karl was right here beside me!"

For the first time I caught a scent in the air. Sitting on the floor, my legs crossed, still all filled up with the dream and the strictness of

Karl's voice—"Not that way! You don't understand. Stop it!"—all filled up with this, I caught the scent in the house that meant his body had begun to rot.

I knew that scent. We all know it. Even if we have not been to morgues or battlefields we know it. We know it when the rat dies in the wall, and no one can find it.

I knew it now . . . faint, but filling all of this whole house, all its big ornamented rooms, filling even this parlor, where St. Sebastian glared out from the golden frame, and the music box lay within inches. And the telephone was once more making that click, time for the lie, click. A message perhaps.

But the point is, Triana, you dreamed it. And this smell could not be borne. No, not this, because this wasn't Karl, this awful smell. This was not my Karl. This was just a dead body.

I thought I should move. Then something fixed me. It was music, but it wasn't coming from my disks strewn on the floor, and it wasn't a music I knew, but I knew the instrument.

Only a violin can sing like that, only a violin can plead and cry in the night like that. Oh, how in childhood I had longed to be able to make that sound on a violin.

Someone out there was playing a violin. I heard it. I heard it rise tenderly above the mingled Avenue sounds. I heard it desperate and poignant as if guided by Tchaikovsky; I heard a masterly riff of notes so fast and dexterous they seemed magical.

I climbed to my feet and I went to the corner window.

He was there. The tall one with the shiny black rock musician hair and the dusty coat. The one I'd seen before. He stood on my side of the corner now, on the broken brick sidewalk beside my iron fence and he played the violin as I looked down on him. I pushed the curtain back. The music made me want to sob.

I thought, I will die of this. I will die of death and the stench in this house and the sheer beauty of this music.

Why had he come? Why to me? Why, and to play of all things the violin, which I so loved, and once in childhood had struggled with so hard, but who does not love the violin? Why had he come to play it near my window?

Ah, honey babe, you are dreaming! It's just the thickest yet, the worst most hypnagogic trap. You're still dreaming. You haven't waked at all. Go back, find yourself, find yourself where you know you are . . . lying on the floor. Find yourself.

"Triana!"

I spun round.

Karl stood in the door. His head was wrapped in the white cloth but his face was stone white and his body almost a skeleton in the black silk pajamas I had put on him.

"No, don't!" he said.

The voice of the violin rose. The bow came crashing down on the lower strings, the D, the G, making that soulful agonizing throb that is almost dissonance and became in this moment the sheer expression of my desperation.

"Ah, Karl!" I called out. I must have.

But Karl was gone. There was no Karl. The violin sang on; it sang and sang, and when I turned and looked I saw him again, with his shiny black hair, and his wide shoulders, and the violin, silken and brown in the street light, and he did bring the bow down with such violence now that I felt the chills run up the back of my neck and down my arms.

"Don't stop, don't stop!" I cried out.

He swayed like a wild man, alone on the corner, in the red glow of the florist shop lights, in the dull beam of the curved street lamp, in the shadow of the magnolia branches tangled over the bricks. He played. He played of love and pain and loss and played and played of all the things I most in this world wanted to believe. I began to cry.

I could smell the stench again.

I was awake. I had to be. I hit the glass, but not hard enough to break it. I looked at him.

He turned towards me, the bow poised, and then looking right up at me over the fence, he played a softer song, taking it down so low that the passing cars almost drowned it.

A loud noise jarred me. Someone banging on the back door. Someone banging hard enough to break the glass.

I stood there, not wanting to leave, but knowing that when people knock like that, they are bound to come in, and someone had caught on that Karl was dead, for sure, and I had to go and talk sane. There was no time for music.

No time for this? He brought the notes down low, moaning, loud and raucous again and then high and piercing from the strings.

I backed away from the window.

There was a figure in the room; but it wasn't Karl. It was a woman. She came from the hallway, and I knew her. She was my neighbor. Her name was Hardy. Miss Nanny Hardy.

"Triana, honey, is that man bothering you?" she asked. She went to the window.

She was so outside his song. I knew her with another part of my mind, because all of the rest of me was moving with him, and quite suddenly I realized he was real.

She had just proved it.

"Triana, honey, for two days, you haven't answered the door. I just gave the door a hard push. I was worried about you, Triana. You and Karl. Triana, tell me if you want me to make that horrible man go away. Who does he think he is? Look at him. He's been outside the house, and now listen to him, playing the violin at this time of night. Doesn't he know that a man is sick in this house—"

But these were teeny tiny sounds, these words, like little pebbles dropping out of somebody's hand. The music went on, sweet, and demure, and winding to a compassionate finale. *I know your pain. I know. But madness isn't for you. It never was. You're the one who never goes mad.*

I stared at him and then again at Miss Hardy. Miss Hardy wore a dressing gown. She'd come in slippers. Quite a thing for such a proper lady. She looked at me. She looked around the room, circumspect and gently, as well bred people do, but surely she saw the scattered music disks and empty soda cans, the crumpled wrapper from the bread, the unopened mail.

It wasn't this, however, that made her face change as she looked back at me. Something caught her off guard; something assaulted her. Something unpleasant suddenly touched her.

She'd smelled the smell. Karl's body.

The music stopped. I turned. "Don't let him go!" I said.

But the tall lanky man with the silky black hair had already begun to walk away, carrying in his hands his violin and his bow, and he looked back at me as he crossed Third Street and stood before the florist shop, and he waved at me, waved, and carefully placing his bow in his left hand with the neck of the violin, he raised his right hand and blew a kiss to me, deliberate and sweet.

He blew me a kiss like those young kids had done in the dream, the kids who'd brought me roses.

Roses, roses, roses . . . I almost heard someone saying those words, and it was in a foreign tongue, which almost made me laugh to think a rose by any other tongue is still a rose.

"Triana," Miss Hardy said so gently, her hand out to touch my shoulder. "Let me call someone." It was not a question, really.

"Yes, Miss Hardy, I should make the call." I pushed my bangs out of my eyes. I blinked, trying to gather up more light from the street and see her better in her flowered dressing gown, very neat.

"It's the smell, isn't it? You can smell it."

She nodded very slowly. "Why in God's name did his mother leave you here alone!"

"A baby, Miss Hardy, born in London, a few days ago. You can hear all about it from the machine. The message is there. I insisted that his mother go. She didn't want to leave Karl. And there it was, you see, no one can tell you exactly when a dying man will die, or a baby will be born, and this was Karl's sister's first, and Karl told her to go, and I insisted she go, and then . . . then I just got tired of all the others coming."

I couldn't read her face. I couldn't even imagine her thoughts. Perhaps she didn't know them herself in such a moment. I thought she was pretty in her dressing gown; it was white with pale flowers and pleated at the waist, and she had satin slippers too, such as a Garden District lady might, and she was very rich, they always said. Her gray hair was neatly trimmed in small curls around her face.

I looked back out at the Avenue. The tall lanky man was gone from view. I heard those words again. *You're the one who never goes mad!* I couldn't remember the expression on his face. Had he smiled? Had he moved his lips? And the music, just thinking of it made the tears flow.

It was the most shamefully emotional music, so like Tchaikovsky just saying, Hell with the world, and letting the sweetest, saddest pain gush, in a way that my Mozart and my Beethoven never did.

I looked at the empty block, the far houses. A streetcar came slowly rocking towards the corner. By God, he was there! The violinist. He had crossed to the median and he stood on the car stop, but he didn't get on the car. He was too far away for me to see his expression or know even that he could still see me, and now he turned and drifted off.

The night was the same. The stench was the same.

Miss Hardy stood in frightening motionlessness.

She looked so sad. She thought I was crazy. Or she just hated it, perhaps, to be the one to find me this way, the one to have to do something perhaps. I don't know.

She went away, to find the phone, I thought. She didn't have more words for me. She thought I was out of my mind and not worth another word of sense, and who could blame her?

At least it was true about the baby born in London. But I would have let his body lie there even if they'd all been home and here. It just would have been harder.

I turned around and hurried out of the parlor, and across the dining room. I went through the small breakfast room and ran up the steps. They are small, these steps—not a grand staircase as in a two-story antebellum house, but small delicate curved steps to go to the attic of a Greek Revival cottage.

I slammed his door and turned the brass key. He was always one for every door having its proper key, and for the first time ever I was glad of it.

Now she couldn't get in. No one could.

The room was icy cold because the windows were wide open, and it was full of the smell, but I took deep gulping breath after breath and then crawled under the blankets and beside him for the last time, just one more time, just one more few minutes before they burn each and every finger and toe, his lips, his eyes. Just let me be with him.

Let me be with all of them.

From far off there came the clamor of her voice, but something else from a distance. It was the dim respectful pavane of a violin. *You out there, playing.*

For you, Triana.

I snuggled up against Karl's shoulder. He was so very dead, so much deader than yesterday. I shut my eyes and pulled the big gold comforter over us—he had such money, he loved such pretty things—

in this our four-poster bed, our Prince of Wales–style bed which he had let me have, and now I dreamed for the last time of him: the grave dream.

The music was in it. It was so faint I couldn't tell if I was only remembering it now from downstairs, but it was there. The music.

Karl. I laid my hand on his bony cheeks, all sweetness melted away.

One last time, let me wallow in death and this time with my new friend's music coming to me as if the Devil had sent him up from Hell, this violinist, just for those of us who are so "half in love with easeful Death."

Father, Mother, Lily, give me your bones. Give me the grave. Let's take Karl down into it with us. What matter to us, those of us who are dead, that he died of some virulent disease; we are all here in the moist earth together; we are dead together.

❧ 3 ❧

DIG DEEP, deep, my soul, to find the heart—the blood, the heat, the shrine and resting place. Dig deep, deep into the moist soil all the way to where they lie, those I love—she, Mother, with her dark hair loose and gone, her bones long since tumbled in the back of the vault, as other coffins came to rest in her spot, but in this dream I range them round me to hold as if she were here, Mother, in a dark red dress, with her dark hair and he—my lately dead father, wax probably still, buried without a tie because he had wanted none and I took it off him right there beside the coffin and unbuttoned his shirt, knowing how much he had hated ties, and his limbs were whole and neat with undertakers' fluids or who knows, perhaps within they were alive already with all earth's tender mouths, come to mourn, devour and then depart, and she, the smallest one, my beautiful one, cancer-bald yet lovely as an angel born hairless and perfect, but then let me give her back her long golden hair that fell out because of the drugs, her hair that was so fine to brush and brush, strawberry blond, the prettiest little girl in all the world, flesh of my flesh—my daughter dead so many years now she'd be a woman if she had lived—

Dig deep . . . let me lie with you, let us lie here, all of us together.

Lie with us, with Karl and me. Karl's a skeleton already!

Open lies this grave with all of us so tenderly and happily together. There is no word for union as gentle and total as this, our bodies, our corpses, our bones, so heavily snuggled together.

I know no separation from anyone. Not Mother, not Father, not

Karl, not Lily, not all the living and all the dead as we are one—kin—
in this damp and crumbling grave, this private secret place of our own,
this deep chamber of earth where we may rot and mingle as the ants
come, as the skin is covered over with mold.

That doesn't matter.

Let us be together, no face forgotten, laughter of each one clear as
it ran some twenty years ago or twice that long, laughter lilting as
the music of a ghostly violin, an uncertain violin, a perfect violin,
our laughter our music that blended minds and souls and bound us all
forever.

Fall softly on this great soft secret snuggling grave, my warm
and singing rain. What is this grave without rain? Our gentle southern rain.

Fall soft with kisses not to scatter this embrace in which we are
living—I and they, the dead, as one. This crevice is our home. Let the
drops be tears like song, more sound and lull than water, for I would
have nothing here disturbed, but only lustrous sweet, among you all
forever. Lily, snuggle against me now, and Mother let me burrow my
face in your neck, but then we are one, and Karl has his arms round us
all, and so does Father.

Flowers, come. There is no need to scatter broken stems or the
crimson petals. No need to bring them big bouquets all tied with
shining ribbon.

Here the earth will celebrate this grave; the earth will bring its wild
thin grass, its nodding blooms of simple buttercups and daisies and
poppies, colors blue and yellow and pink, the mellow shades of the
rampant untended and eternal garden.

Let me snuggle against you, let me lie in your arms, let me assure
you that no outward sign of death means anything to me as much as
love and that we lived, you and I, once, all of us, alive, and I would not
be anywhere now but with you here in this slow and damp and safe
corruption.

That consciousness follows me down to this final embrace is a gift!
I am intimate with the dead, and yet I live to know it and savor it.

Let trees bow down to hide this place, let trees form over my eyes a
dense and thickening net, not green but black as if it snared the night,
so shut away the last prying eye, or vantage point, as the grass grows

high—so that we may be alone, just us, you and I, those whom I so adored and cannot live without.

Sink. Sink deep into the earth. Feel the earth enclose you. Let the clods seal our quietude. I want nothing else.

And now, bound up with you and safe, I can say, Hell to all that tries to come between us.

Come, the steps of strangers on the stairs.

Break the lock, yes, break the wood, and pull the tubes away, and pump the air with white smoke. Do not bruise my arms for I am not here, I am in the grave; and it is an angry rigid image of me that you intrude upon. Yes, you see the sheets are clean, I could have told you!

Wind him up, wind him thick, thick in the sheets, it does not matter one whit—you see, there is no blood, there is no virulent thing that can get you from him—he died not from open cankers but he starved inside as those with AIDS are wont to do, so that it hurt him even to draw breath, and what do you have left now to fear?

I am not with you or with those who ask questions of time and place and blood and sanity and numbers to be called; I cannot answer to those who would Help. I am safe in the grave. I press my lips to my father's skull. I reach for my mother's bony hand. Let me hold you!

I can still hear the music. Oh, God, that this lone violinist would come through high grass and falling rain and the dense smoke of imagined night, envisioned darkness, to be with me still and play his mournful song, to give a voice to these words inside my head, as the earth grows ever more damp, and all things alive in it seem nothing but natural and kind and even a little beautiful.

All the blood in our dark sweet grave is gone, gone, gone, save mine, and in our bower of earth I bleed as simply as I sigh. If blood is wanted now for any reason under God, I have enough for all of us.

Fear won't come here. Fear is gone. Jangle the keys and stack the cups. Bang the pots on the iron stove downstairs. Fill the night with sirens if you will. Let the water rush and rush and rush, and the tub fill. I see you not. I know you not.

No petty worry will come here, not to this grave where we lie. Fear is gone—like youth itself and all that old anguish when I watched them commit you to the ground—coffin after coffin, and Father's of such fine wood, and Mother's, I can't remember, and Lily's so small and white, and the old gentleman not wanting to charge us a nickel because she was just a little girl. No, all that worry is gone.

Worry stops your ears to the real music. Worry doesn't let you fold your arms around the bones of those you love.

I am alive and with you now, truly only now realizing what it means that I will have you always with me!

Father, Mother, Karl, Lily, hold me!

Oh, it seems a sin to ask compassion of the dead, those who died in pain, those I couldn't save, those for whom I didn't have the right farewells or charms to drive off panic, or agony, of those who saw in the final careless, dissonant moments no tears perhaps or heard no pledge that I would mourn you forever.

I'm here now! With you! I know what it means to be dead. I let the mud cover me, I let my foot push deep into the spongy side of the grave.

This is a vision, my house. They matter not:

"That music, can you hear it?"

"I think she should get into the shower again now! I think she should be thoroughly disinfected!"

"Everything in that room should be burnt—"

"Oh, not that pretty four-poster bed, that's foolishness, they don't blow up the hospital room, do they, when somebody dies of this."

". . . and his manuscript, don't you touch it."

No, don't you dare touch his manuscript!

"Shhh, not in front of—"

"She's crazy, can't you see it?"

". . . his mother is on the morning plane out of Gatwick."

". . . absolutely stark raving mad."

"Oh, please, both of you, if you love your sister, for God's sake, be quiet. Miss Hardy, did you know her well?"

"Drink this, Triana."

This is my vision; my house. I sit in my living room, washed, scrubbed, as if I were the one to be buried, water dripping from my hair. Let the morning sun strike the mirrors. Toss the peacock's brilliant feathers out of the silver urn and all over the floor. Don't hang a ghastly veil over all things bright. Look deep to find the phantom in the glass.

This is my house. And this is my garden, and my roses crawl on these railings outside and we are in our grave too. We are here and we are there, and they are one.

We are in the grave and we are in the house, and all else is a failure of imagination.

In this soft rainy realm, where water sings as it falls from the darkening leaves, as the earth falls from the uneven edges above, I am the bride, the daughter, the mother, all those venerable titles forming for me the precious claims I lay upon myself.

I have you always! Never never to let you leave me, never never to go away.

All right. And so we made a mistake again. So we played our game. So we nudged at madness as if it were a thick door and then we slammed against it, like they slammed against Karl's door, but the door of madness didn't break, and that uncharted grave is the dream.

Well, I can hear his music through it.

I don't even think they hear it. This is my voice in my head and his violin is his voice out there, and together we keep the secret, that this grave is my vision, and that I can't really be with you now, my dead ones. The living need me.

The living need me now, need me so, as they always need the bereaved after the death, so needy of those who have nursed the most, and sat the longest in the stillness, so needy with questions and suggestions and assertions and declarations, and papers to be signed. They need me to look up at the strangest smiles and find some way to receive with grace the most awkward sympathies.

But I'll come in time. I'll come. And when I do, the grave will hold us all. And the grass will grow above all of us.

Love and love and love I give you—let the earth grow wet. Let my living limbs sink down. Give me skulls like stones to press against my lips, give me bones to hold in my fingers, and if the hair is gone—like fine spun silk, it does not matter. Long hair I have to shroud all of us, isn't that so. Look at it, this long hair. Let me cover us all.

Death is not death as I once thought, when fear was trampled underfoot. Broken hearts do best forever beating upon the wintry windowpane.

Hold me, hold me, hold me here. Let me never never tarry in another place.

Forget the fancy lace, the deftly painted walls, the gleaming inlay of the open desk. The china that they take with such care now, piece by piece, to place now all over the table, cups and saucers ornamented with blue lace and gold. Karl's things. Turn around. Don't feel these living arms.

The only thing important about coffee being poured from a silver spout is the way that the early light shines in it; the way that the deep brown of the coffee becomes amber and gold and yellow, and twists and turns like a dancer as it fills the cup, then stops, like a spirit snatched back into the pot.

Go back to where the garden breaks to ruin. You will find us all together. You will find us there.

From memory, a perfect picture: twilight: the Garden District Chapel; Our Mother of Perpetual Help; our little church within an old mansion. You have only to walk a block from my front gate to reach it. It is on Prytania Street. The tall windows are full of pink light. There are low guttering candles in red glass before a saint with a smiling face whom we love and revere as "The Little Flower." The darkness is like dust in this place. You can still move through it.

Mother and my sister Rosalind and I kneel at the cold marble Altar Rail. We lay down our bouquets—little flowers picked here and there from walls, through iron fences like our own—the wild bridal wreath, the pretty blue plumbago, the little gold and brown lantana. Never the gardeners' blooms. Only the loose tangle no one might miss from a viny gate. These are our bouquets, and we have nothing to bind them with, save our hands. We lay our bouquets on the Altar Rail, and when we make the Sign of the Cross and say our prayers, I get a doubt.

"Are you sure that the Blessed Mother and Jesus will get these flowers?"

Beneath the altar before us, the carved wooden figures of the Last Supper are set in their deep glass-covered niche, and above on the ornate cloth stand the regular bouquets of the Chapel which have such size, authority, giant spear-like flowers with snow-white blooms. These are powerful flowers! Flowers as powerful as tall wax candles.

"Oh, yes," says Mother. "When we leave, the Brother will come and he'll take our little flowers and he'll put them in a vase and he'll put them before the Baby Jesus over there or the Blessed Mother."

The Baby Jesus stands to the far right, dark beside the window now. But I can still see the world He holds in his hands, and the gold that glints on His crown, and I know that His fingers are raised in blessing, and that he is the Infant Jesus of Prague in that statue, with His fancy flaring pink cape and lovely blooming cheeks.

But about the flowers, I don't think it's so. The flowers are too humble. Who will care about such flowers left like that in the gloaming, the chapel now full of shadows that I can feel because my Mother is a little afraid, clutching the hands of her two little girls, Rosalind and Triana, come, as we make our genuflection and then turn to go out. We are wearing Mary Janes that click on a dark linoleum floor. The holy water is warm in the font. The night breathes with light, but not enough anymore to come inside among the pews.

I worry for the flowers.

Well, I worry not anymore for such things.

I cherish only the memory, that we were there, because if I can see and feel it and hear this violin that sings this song, then I am there again, and as I said—Mother, we are together.

I worry not for all the rest. Would she, my child, have lived had I moved Heaven and Earth to take her to a faraway clinic? Would he, my Father, have not died if the oxygen had been adjusted just so? Was she afraid, my Mother, when she said, "I'm dying" to the cousins who cared for her? Did she want one of us? Good God! Stop it!

Not for the living, not for the dead, not for the flowers of fifty years ago, I won't relive the accusations!

Saints in the flicker of the chapel do not answer. The icon of Our Mother of Perpetual Help only gleams in solemn shadow. The Infant Jesus of Prague holds court with a jeweled crown and eyes with no less luster.

But you, my dead, my flesh, my treasures, those whom I have completely and totally loved, all of you with me in the grave now—without eyes, or flesh to warm me—you are with me!

All partings were illusions. Everything is perfect.

"The music stopped."

"Thank God."

"Do you really think so?" That was Rosalind's soft deep voice, my outspoken sister. "The guy was terrific. That wasn't just music."

"He is very good, I'll give him that much." This was Glenn, her husband and my beloved brother-in-law.

"He was here when I came." Miss Hardy speaking. "In fact, if he hadn't come playing his violin, I would never have found her. Can you see him out there?"

My sister Katrinka:

"I think she should leave now for the hospital for an entire battery of tests; we have to make absolutely sure that she did not contract—"

"Hush, I won't have you talk this way!" Thank you, perfect stranger.

"Triana, this is Miss Hardy, dear, can you look at me? Forgive me, dear, for quarreling so with your sisters. Forgive me, dear. But I want you to drink this now. It's just a cup of chocolate. Remember when you came that afternoon, and we drank chocolate and you said you loved it, and there's lots of cream and I'd like you to have this . . ."

I looked up. How fresh and pretty the living room was in the early sun, and how the china shone on the table. Round tables. I have always loved round tables. All the music disks and cookie wrappers and cans had been taken away. The white plaster flowers on the ceiling made their proper wreath, no longer degraded by detritus beneath them.

I got up and went to the window, and lifted back the heavy yellowing curtain. The whole world was outside, right up to the sky itself, and the leaves scuttling on the dry porch right in front of me.

The morning race for downtown had begun. There came the clatter of trucks. I saw the leaves on the oak above shiver with the thunder of so many wheels. I felt the house itself tremble. But it had trembled so for a hundred years or more, and would not fall down. People knew that now. They didn't come to tear down the splendid houses with the white columns now. They didn't vomit out lies about these houses being impossible to keep, or heat. They fought to save them.

Someone shook me. It was my sister Katrinka. She looked so distraught, her narrow face bitter with anger; anger was so much her friend. Anger just jumped up and down in her, waiting any second to get out, and it was out now, and she could barely speak to me she was so furious.

"I want you to go upstairs."

"For what?" I said coldly. I haven't been afraid of you for years and years, I thought. Not since Faye left, I suppose. Faye was the smallest of us all. Faye was the one whom we all loved.

"I want you to wash again, wash all over, and then go to the hospital."

"You're a fool," I said. "You always were. I don't have to."

I looked at Miss Hardy.

At some time or other during this long and cacophonous night, she'd gone home and changed into one of her pretty shirt-waist dresses, and her hair was freshly combed. Her smile was full of comfort.

"They took him away?" I asked Miss Hardy.

"His book, his book on St. Sebastian, I put all of it away, except the last pages. They were on the table near the bed. They—"

My sweet brother-in-law Glenn spoke: "I put them downstairs; they're safe, with the rest."

That's right, I had showed Glenn where Karl's work was stashed, just in case . . . *burn everything in the room.*

Behind me, people quarreled. I could hear Rosalind trying to quiet the younger ever anxious Katrinka's long clench-teeth diatribes. Someday Katrinka will break her teeth in mid-speech.

"She's crazy!" said Katrinka. "And she's probably got the virus!"

"No, now stop it, Trink, please, I'm begging you now." Rosalind didn't know anymore how to be unkind. Whatever she had known in childhood had long ago been weeded out, and replaced.

I turned around, looked at Rosalind. She sat slumped at the table, large and sleepy looking and with her dark eyebrows raised. She made a little gesture and said in her frank deep voice:

"They'll cremate him." She sighed. "It's the law. Don't worry. I made sure they didn't cart out the room board by board." She laughed, a smug, smart-alecky laugh, which was perfect. "You leave it to Katrinka, she'll have the whole city block torn down." She shook with her laughter.

Katrinka began to roar.

I smiled at Rosalind. I wondered if she was afraid about money. Karl had been so generous with money. No doubt everyone was thinking about money. Karl's effortless doles.

There would be some quarrel about funeral arrangements. There always is, no matter what is done before, and Karl had done everything. Cremation. I could not think of this! In my grave, among those I love, are no undifferentiated ashes.

Rosalind would never say it but she *had* to be thinking of money. It was Karl who gave Rosalind and her husband, Glenn, the money to live, to run their small vintage book and record shop which never actually made a dime, not so much as I know. Was she afraid the money would stop? I wanted to reassure her.

Miss Hardy raised her voice. Katrinka slammed the door. Katrinka is one of only two adults I know who actually slams doors when she is angry. The other was miles away, long gone out of my life, and dearly remembered for better things than such petty violence.

Rosalind, our eldest, the heaviest, very plump now with her hair all white yet beautifully curly as it had always been—she had the loveliest richest hair—just sat there still making that shrug, that smirk.

"You don't have to rush to the hospital," she said. "You know that." Rosalind had been a nurse for too long, lugging oxygen tanks and cleaning up blood. "No rush at all," she assured me with authority.

I know a better place than this, I said or thought. I had only to close my eyes and the room swam and the grave came and there was that painful wonder: Which is dream and which is real?

I laid my forehead on the windowpane, and it was cold, and his music . . . the music of my vagabond violinist . . . I called to it. *You're there, aren't you? Come on, I know you didn't go away. Did you think I wasn't listening . . . ?* It came again, the violin. Florid yet low, anguished, yet full of naive celebration.

And behind me Rosalind began to hum in low tune, a phrase or so behind him . . . to hum along, to join her voice to his distant voice.

"You hear him now?" I said.

"Yeah," she said with her characteristic shrug. "You've got some friend out there, like a nightingale. And the sun didn't drive him off. Sure, I hear him."

My hair was dripping water on the floor. Katrinka was sobbing in the hallway and I could not make out the other two voices, except to know that they were women's voices. "Just can't go through this right now, I can't go through this," Katrinka said, "and she's crazy. Can't you see? I can't, I can't, I can't."

It seemed a fork in the road. I knew where the grave was and just how deep, and I could go there. Why didn't I?

His music had moved into a slow but lofty melody, something merging with the morning itself, as though we were leaving the grave-yard together. In a disquieting yet vivid flash I saw our little bouquets on the white marble Altar Rail of the Chapel as I looked back.

"Come on, Triana!" My mother looked so pretty, her hair in a beret, her voice so patient, her eyes so big. "Come on, Triana!"

You're going to die separated from us, Mother. Beautiful and without a gray hair in your head. When the time comes I won't even have the sense to kiss you goodbye the last time I see you. I'll only be glad you're going because you're so drunk and sick and I'm so tired of taking care of Katrinka and Faye. Mother, you will die in a terrible, terrible way, a drunken woman, swallowing her tongue. And I will give birth to a little girl who looks like you, has your big round eyes and lovely temples and forehead, and she'll die, Mother, die before she's six years old, surrounded by machines during the few minutes, the very few minutes, Mother, when I tried as they say to catch some sleep. I caught her death, I—

Get thee behind me, all such torment. Rosalind and I run ahead; Mother walks slowly on the flags behind us, a smiling woman; she's not afraid in the dusk now, the sky is too vibrant. These are our years. The war has not come to an end. Cars passing slowly on Prytania Street look like humpback crickets or beetles.

"I said, Stop it!" I talked to my own head. I put my hands on my wet hair. How dreadful to be in this room with all this noise, and dripping with water. Listen to Miss Hardy's voice. She is taking command.

Outside, the sun fell down on the porches, on the cars streaking by, on the old peeling wooden streetcars as they crossed right in front of me, the uptown car clanging its bell, with all the drama of a San Francisco cable car.

"How can she do this to us?" sobbed Katrinka. But that was beyond the door. The door she had slammed. She was bellowing in the hallway.

The doorbell rang. I was too far over to the edge of the house to even glimpse who had come up the steps.

What I saw were the white azaleas against the fence all the way to the corner and around where the fence turns. How lovely, how sublimely lovely. Karl had paid for all that, gardeners and mulch and carpenters and hammers and nails and white paint for the columns, look, the Corinthian capitals restored, the acanthus leaves rising to hold high the roof, and look, the clean blue for the porch roof so that the wasps thought it was the sky and would not nest up there.

"Come on, honey." This was a man's voice, a man I knew, but not so well, a man I trusted, but couldn't think of his name just now, perhaps because in the background Katrinka was shouting and shouting.

"Triana, honey," he said. Grady Dubosson, my own lawyer. He was all spiffed up, full suit and tie, and didn't even look sleepy at all, and perfectly in command of his serious face as though he knew, like so many people here, just how to deal with death and not to put a false face or a denial on it.

"Don't worry, Triana darlin'," he said in the most natural, confiding voice. "I won't let them touch a silver fork. You come with Dr. Guidry and you go downtown. Rest. There can't be any ceremony till the others are back from London."

"Karl's book, there were some pages upstairs."

Glenn's consoling voice again, deep, southern: "I got them, Triana. I took his papers down and nobody's going to incinerate anything up there—"

"I'm sorry for the trouble I've made," I whispered.

"Absolutely cracked!" That was Katrinka.

Rosalind sighed. "He didn't look to me like he suffered, just like he went to sleep." She was saying that to comfort me. I turned around again and made a small secret of thanks to her. She caught it; she gave me her soft beam.

I loved her utterly. She pushed her thick framed glasses up on her nose. All her young life, my father shouted at her to push her glasses on her nose, but it never really worked because she had, unlike him, a rather small nose. And she looked the way he had always hated her— dreamy and sloppy, and sweet, with glasses falling down, smoking a cigarette, with ashes on her coat, but full of love, her body heavy and shapeless with age. I loved her so.

"I don't think he suffered at all," she said. "Don't pay any attention to the Trink. Hey, Trink, did you ever think about all the beds in the hotels that you and Martin sleep in—like who's been in them, I mean, like you, with AIDS?"

I wanted to laugh.

"Come on, darlin'," Grady said.

Dr. Guidry took my hand in both of his. What a young man he was. I can't get used to doctors now being younger than me. And Dr. Guidry is so blond and so utterly clean, and always, in the top pocket of his coat, is a small Bible. You know he can't be a Catholic if he carries a Bible like that. He must be a Baptist. I feel so ageless myself. But that's because I'm dead, right? I'm in the grave.

No. That never works for very long.

"I want you to follow my advice," said Dr. Guidry as gently as if he were kissing me. "And you let Grady take care of things."

"It's stopped," said Rosalind.

"What?" demanded Katrinka. "What's stopped?" She stood in the hallway door. She was blowing her nose. She wadded up the Kleenex and threw it on the floor. She glared at me. "Did you ever think what this kind of thing does to the rest of us?"

I didn't answer her.

"The violinist," Rosalind said. "Your troubadour. I think he's gone away."

"I never heard any damned violinist," Katrinka said, clenching her teeth. "Why are you talking about a violinist! You think this violinist is more important than what I'm trying to tell you!"

Miss Hardy came in, walking past Katrinka as if Katrinka did not exist. Miss Hardy was wearing the cleanest white shoes. It must be spring then, because Garden District ladies never wear white shoes except at the proper time of year. But I was sure it was cold.

She had a coat and scarf for me. "Now, come darling, let me help you dress."

Katrinka stood staring at me. Her lip trembled and her bulbous reddened eyes ran with tears. How miserable her life had been, always. At least Mother had not been drunk when she was born. Katrinka was healthy and pretty, whereas Faye had barely survived, a tiny smiling thing that they had put in a machine for weeks, who never believed in her own special elfin loveliness.

"Why don't you just leave?" I asked Katrinka. "There are enough people here. Where's Martin? Call him and tell him to come get you." Martin was her husband, a real estate wonder and sometime lawyer of considerable local renown.

Rosalind laughed, smug and smirking and sort of to herself but for me. And then I knew. Of course.

And so did Rosalind, who folded her arms and sat forward, her heavy breasts resting on the table. She pushed her glasses up.

"You belong in the nuthouse," Katrinka said, trembling. "You were crazy when your daughter died! You didn't need to take all that extreme care of Father! You had a nurse here night and day. You had doctors coming and going. You're crazy and you can't stay in this house—"

She stopped; even she was ashamed of her clumsiness.

"I must say, you are one outspoken young woman," Miss Hardy said. "If you'll excuse me . . ."

"Miss Hardy, you must accept my thanks," I said. "I'm so terribly, terribly—"

She gestured for me to be quiet, that it was all forgiven.

I looked at Rosalind and Rosalind was laughing softly still, her head moving from side to side, peering up at Katrinka over her glasses, a big authoritative and beautiful woman in her weight and her age.

And Katrinka, so athletically and fetchingly thin, with her breasts pointed fiercely through the silk of her short-sleeve blouse. Such small arms. In a way, Katrinka had of the four of us gotten the perfect body, and she was only one with blond hair, true blond hair.

A silence. What was it? Rosalind had drawn herself up and lifted her chin.

"Katrinka," Rosalind said now under her breath, filling the whole room by the solemnity of her tone. "You ain't getting this house." She slapped the table. She laughed out loud.

I burst out laughing. Not very loud, of course. It was too funny, really.

"How dare you accuse me of this!" Katrinka turned on me. "You stay here for two days with a dead body and I try to make them realize you're sick, you have to be committed, you have to be checked, you have to be in bed, and you think I want this house, you think I came here at a moment like this, as if I didn't have my own house mortgaged to the hilt, my own husband, my own daughters, and you think, you dare say that to me in front of people we hardly . . ."

Grady spoke to her. It was a low but urgent flow of words. The doctor was trying to take Katrinka by the arm.

Rosalind shrugged. "Trink," she said. "I hate to remind you. It's Triana's house until she dies. It's hers and Faye's if Faye is alive. And Triana may be crazy, but she ain't dead."

And then I couldn't help laughing again, a small mischievous laugh, and Rosalind laughed too.

"I wish Faye were here," I said to Rosalind.

Faye was our youngest sister by my mother and father. Faye was just a little waif of a woman, an angel, born from a sick and starved womb.

No one had seen my beloved Faye in over two years, nor heard even a single word by phone or post from her. Faye!

"But, you know, maybe that was the trouble all along," I confessed, almost crying, wiping at my eyes.

"What do you mean?" asked Rosalind. She looked too sweet and calm to be a normal person. She got up, awkwardly, hoisting her bulk from the chair, and she came to me, and she kissed me on the cheek.

"In times of trouble, we always want Faye," I said. "Always. We always needed Faye. Call Faye. Get Faye to help with this and that. Everybody always needed Faye, wanted Faye, depended on Faye."

Katrinka stepped in front of me. It came as a shock, the full dislike in her expression, the full personal contempt. Would I never, never get used to it? From childhood I had seen this impatient, raging contempt, this intense personal dislike, this distaste! This aversion in her face that made me want to shrivel and give in and turn away and be silent and win no argument or fight or point of discussion.

"Well, Faye might be *alive* right now," Katrinka said, "if you hadn't financed her running off and disappearing without a trace, you and your dead husband."

Rosalind told her plainly to shut up. Faye? Dead?

This was too much. I smiled to myself. Everyone knew it was too much. Faye had disappeared, yes, but dead? And still, what did I feel, the big sister? A protective fear for Trink, that she'd indeed gone way too far, and they'd really insult her now, poor Katrinka. She'd cry and cry and never understand. They'd all despise her for this and she'd be so wounded.

"Don't—" I started to say.

Dr. Guidry made motions to hurry me from the room. Grady took my arm.

I was confused. Rosalind was at my side.

Katrinka wailed on and on. She was going to pieces in there. Somebody had to help her. Maybe it would be Glenn. Glenn always helped people, even Katrinka.

The implication of the words struck me again—"might be alive."

"Faye's *not* dead, is she?" I asked. If I'd known for sure after these agonizing years of waiting for Faye, well, then I could have invited her down into the wet grave with us, and we could have been there, Faye and Lily and Mother and Father and Karl, Faye included in my litany. But Faye couldn't be dead. Not my precious Faye.

It made a lie of all my eccentricity, my seemingly excessive wisdom and high-toned feeling. "Not Faye."

"There's no word on Faye at all," said Rosalind next to my ear. "Faye's probably drinking tequila in a truck stop in Mexico." She kissed me once more. I felt her heavy tender arm.

We stood in the front door, Grady and I—the mad widow and the kindly elderly family lawyer.

I love the front door of my house. It's a big double door, right in the middle of the house, and you go out on the wide front porch and you can walk to the left or the right, and the porch wraps all the way around the sides of the house. It's so pretty. Not a day of my life has ever passed that I have not thought of this house and thought of it as pretty.

Years ago, Faye and I used to dance on the porch of this house. Eight years younger than me, she was small enough to be in my arms, like a monkey, and we would sing, "Casey, he waltzed with the girl he adored and the band played on—"

And look at the azaleas in the patches by the steps, blood red, and so thick! Of course it was spring. Everywhere they bloomed, these pampered plants—a real Garden District house with its snow-white columns.

And look, Miss Hardy didn't have on white shoes at all. They were gray.

Back inside the house, Rosalind roared at Katrinka. "Don't talk about Faye, not now! Don't talk about Faye."

And Katrinka's words came in one of those long dramatic drawn-out growls . . .

Someone had lifted my foot. It was Miss Hardy, putting a slipper on my foot. The gate stood open below. Grady had my arm.

Dr. Guidry stood beside an open ambulance.

Grady spoke again, telling me if I would go to Mercy Hospital, I could walk out just as soon as I wanted to. Just let them get some fluids and nourishment into me.

Dr. Guidry came to take my hand. "You're dehydrated, Triana, you haven't eaten. Nobody's talking about committing you anywhere. I want you to go into the hospital, that's all. I want you to rest. And I promise you, no one will do anything or test for anything."

I sighed. Everything was getting brighter.

"Angel of God," I whispered, "my guardian dear, to whom God's love commits me here . . ."

Suddenly I saw them clearly around me.

"Oh, I'm sorry," I said, "I'm so so sorry . . . I am so very sorry for all this, I . . . I'm sorry." I cried. "You can test. Yes, test. Do what has to be done. I'm sorry . . . I'm so sorry . . ."

I stopped on the front walk.

There were my beloved Althea and Lacomb at the gate, and they were so concerned. Maybe all these white people—doctor, lawyer, lady in gray shoes—held them back.

Althea made a lip as if she would cry, her heavy arms folded, and she tilted her head.

Lacomb said in his deep voice, "We're here, boss."

I was about to answer.

But I saw something across the street.

"What is it, honey?" Grady said. Lovely touch of Mississippi in his accent.

"That's the violinist." Just a distant figure in black, far across both sides of the Avenue, and half his way down the Third Street block towards Carondelet, glancing back.

Now he was gone.

Or at least the traffic and the trees had made him seem to disappear. I'd caught him though, distinct for a second, holding his instrument, this strange watchman of the night, glancing back and walking with those great even strides.

I got into the ambulance and lay down on the stretcher, which is not apparently the normal way it is done, because it was rather awkward, but we did it that way, obviously because I began to climb in the ambulance before anyone could stop me. I covered up with the sheet and closed my eyes. Mercy Hospital. All my aunts who had been nuns there for so many years were gone. I wondered if my vagabond fiddler would be able to find Mercy Hospital.

"You know that man's not real!" I woke with a shock. The ambulance was moving into traffic. "But then . . . Rosalind, and Miss Hardy. They heard him."

Or was that too a dream in a life where dream and reality had woven themselves so tight that one inevitably triumphs over the other?

✺ 4 ✺

IT WAS three days of sleepless hospital sleep, thin and filled with annoyances and horrors.

Had they cremated Karl yet? Were they absolutely sure he was dead before they put him in that horrible furnace? I couldn't get this question out of my mind. Was my husband ashes?

Karl's mother, Mrs. Wolfstan, back from England, cried and cried by my bed that she had left me with her dying son. Over and over I told her that I had loved taking care of him, and that she must not worry. There was a beauty in the birth of the new child, so close to Karl's death.

We smiled at pictures of the new baby born in London. My arms ached with needles. A blur.

"You'll never never have to worry about anything again," Mrs. Wolfstan said.

I knew what she meant. I wanted to say thank you, that Karl had once explained it all, but I couldn't. I started to cry. I would worry again. I would worry about things that Karl's generosity could not alter.

I had sisters to love and lose. Where was Faye?

I had made myself ill—a person drifting for two days with no more than gulps of soda and occasional slices of bread could create in herself an irregular heartbeat.

My brother-in-law Martin, Katrinka's husband, came and said she was so concerned, but just couldn't set foot in a hospital.

The tests were run.

In the night I woke sharply, thinking, This is a hospital room, and Lily is in the bed. I'm sleeping on the floor. I have to get up and see if my little girl is all right. And there came one of those broken-glass-shard memories so abrupt it drew all my blood—I had come in out of the rain drunk and looked at her lying there on the bed, five years old, bald, wasted, almost dead, and burst into tears, a flood of tears.

"Mommie, Mommie, why are you crying? Mommie, you're scaring me!"

How could you have done that, Triana!

Some night, high on Percodan and Phenergan and other opiates to make me calm and make me sleep, and to make me stop asking stupid questions as to whether the house was locked and safe, and what had become of Karl's study of St. Sebastian, I thought the curse of memory is this: *Everything is ever present.*

They asked if they could call Lev, my first husband. Absolutely not, I said, don't you dare bother Lev. I'll call him. When I want to.

But drugged I couldn't really go down.

The tests were run again. I walked and walked one morning in the hall until the nurse said, "You must go back to bed."

"And why? What is wrong with me?"

"Not a damned thing," she said, "if they'd stop shooting you full of tranquilizers. They have to taper them off."

Rosalind put a small black disk player by my bed. She put the earphones on my head, and softly came the Mozart voices—the angels singing their foolishness from *Così Fan Tutte.* Sweet sopranos in unison.

I saw a movie in my mind's eye. *Amadeus.* A vivid marvelous film. I saw this movie in which the evil composer Salieri, admirably played by F. Murray Abraham, had driven to death a laughing, childlike Mozart. There had been a moment when, in a gilded, velvet-lined theater box, Salieri looked down upon Mozart's singers and the little cherubic and hysterical conductor himself, and the voice of F. Murray Abraham had said: "I heard the voice of the angels."

Ah, yes, by God. Yes.

Mrs. Wolfstan didn't want to leave. But all was done, the ashes in the Metairie Mausoleum, and every test on me had been negative for HIV, for anything really. I was the picture of health and had lost only five pounds. My sisters were with me.

"Yes, do go on, Mrs. Wolfstan, and you know I loved him. I loved him with all my heart, and it never had anything to do with what he gave me or anyone."

Kisses, the smell of her perfume.

Yes, said Glenn. Now, stop going over it. Karl's book was in the hands of the scholars Karl had designated in his will. Thank God, no need to call Lev, I thought. Let Lev be with the living.

Everything else was in Grady's hands, and Althea, my beloved Althea, had gone right to work on the house, and so had Lacomb, polishing silver for "Miss Triana." Althea had my old bed on the first floor in the big northerly room all full of nice pillows the way I liked it.

No, the Prince of Wales marriage bed upstairs had not been burnt! No, indeed. Only the bedding. Mrs. Wolfstan had had the charming young man from Hurwitz Mintz come out with new pillows of watered silk and comforters of velvet and create a new band of scalloped moiré from the wooden canopy.

I'd go home to my old room. My old rice bed, with the four-posters carved with rice, the symbol of fertility. The first-floor bed-room was the only real bedroom the cottage had.

Whenever I was ready.

One morning I woke up. Rosalind slept nearby. She dozed in one of those big sloping, dipping wooden-handled chairs they give in hos-pital rooms for the vigilant family.

I knew four days had passed, and that last night I'd eaten a full meal and the needles felt like insects in my arm. I pulled back the tape, removed the needles, got out of bed, went to the bathroom, found my clothes in the locker and dressed completely before I woke Rosalind.

Rosalind woke dazed, and dusted the cigarette ashes off her black blouse.

"You're HIV negative," she said at once, as if she'd been just dying to tell me and couldn't remember that everyone already had, staring wide eyed through her glasses. Dazed. She sat up. "Katrinka made them do everything but remove one of your fingers."

"Come on," I said. "Let's get the hell out of here."

We hurried down the hall. It was empty. A nurse passed who didn't know who we were or didn't care.

"I'm hungry," Rosalind said. "You hungry, for real food I mean?"

"I just wanna go home," I said.

"Well, you'll be very pleased."

"Why, what do you mean?"

"Oh, you know the Wolfstan tribe; they bought you a stretch limousine and hired you a new man, Oscar, and this one can read and write, no offense to Lacomb—"

"Lacomb can write," I said. This is something I'd said a thousand times because my man Lacomb can write, but when he talks it's a deep black jazz musician's dialect that almost no one can understand a word of.

"—and Althea's back, and jabbering away and calling the hired cleaning lady names and telling Lacomb not to smoke in the house. Can anyone understand what she says? Do her kids understand what she says?"

"Never figured it out," I said.

"But you should see that house," said Roz. "You'll love it. I tried to tell them."

"Tell who?"

The elevator came; we went inside. Shock. Hospital elevators are always so immense, big enough to hold the living or the dead stretched out full length and two or three attendants. We stood alone in this vast metal compartment gliding down.

"Tell who what?"

Rosalind yawned. We moved rapidly to the first floor.

"Tell Karl's family that we always go home after a death, that we always go back, that you wouldn't want some fancy condominium downtown or a suite in the Windsor Court. Are the Wolfstans really so rich? Or just crazy? They've left you cash with me, cash with Althea, cash with Lacomb, cash with Oscar. . . ."

The elevator doors opened.

"You see that big black car? You own that damn thing. That's Oscar out there, you know the type, old-guard chauffeur; Lacomb raises his eyebrows behind Oscar's back, and Althea has no intention of cooking for him."

"She won't have to," I said with a little smile.

I did know the type, caramel skin not quite as light as Lacomb's, a voice like honey, grizzled hair, and sparkling silver-framed glasses. Very old, too old perhaps to be driving, but so fine, and so traditional.

"You just get right in, Miss Triana," said Oscar, "and you rest yourself and let me take you home."

"Yes, sir."

Rosalind relaxed as soon as the door was closed. "I'm hungry." The privacy panel had gone up between us and Oscar in the front. I liked that. It would be nice to own a car. I couldn't drive. Karl would not. He had always rented limousines, even for the smallest thing.

"Roz," I asked as gently as I knew how. "Can't he take you to eat after I'm settled in?"

"Gee, that would be nice. You sure you want to be alone there?"

"Like you said, we always go home afterwards, don't we? We don't run. I'd sleep in that upstairs bed, except that was never mine. That was our bed, Karl's and mine, in sickness and in health. He wanted to be where the afternoon sun hit the windows. I'd curl right up in his bed. I want to be alone."

"I figured it," said Roz. "Katrinka's silenced for a while. Grady Dubosson produced a paper that said everything Karl had ever given you was yours, and he had signed away any possible claim on your house the day he moved into it, and so that shut her up."

"She thought Karl's family would try to take the house?"

"Some crazy thing like that, but Grady showed her the quick claim or the quitclaim. Which is it?"

"I honestly don't remember."

"You know what she really wants, of course."

I smiled. "Don't worry, Rosalind. Don't worry at all."

She turned to me, hunched forward and took on her most grave manner, a hand both rough and soft as she held mine. The car moved up St. Charles Avenue.

"Look," she said, "Don't worry about the money Karl was giving us. His old lady laid a pile in my lap, and besides it's time that Glenn and I tried to make a go of the shop, you know, to actually sell books and records????" She laughed her deep throaty laugh. "You know Glenn, but we are going to be on our own, if I have to go back to nursing, I don't care what it takes."

My mind drifted. It was irrelevant. It had only been one thousand a month to keep them afloat. She didn't know. Nobody knew how much Karl had really left, except Mrs. Wolfstan perhaps, if she had changed all of it.

Over a hidden speaker there came a polite voice.

"Miss Triana, ma'am, you want to drive by the Metairie Cemetery, ma'am?"

"No, thank you, Oscar," I said, seeing the small speaker above.

We have our grave, he and I, and Lily and Mother and Father.

"I'm just going to go home now, Roz. You are my darling, always. You call Glenn. Go get him, close up shop, and go to Commander's Palace. Eat the funeral feast for me, will you? Do that for me. Do the eating for both of us."

We had crossed Jackson Avenue. The oaks were fresh with spring green.

I kissed her goodbye and told Oscar to take her on, do whatever she said, stay with her. It was a nice car, a big gray velvet-lined limousine such as they used at funeral parlors.

"And so I got to ride in it after all," I thought as they pulled away. "Even though I missed the funeral."

How radiant my house looked. My house. Oh, poor poor Katrinka!

Althea's arms are like black silk, and when we hug, I don't think anything in the world can hurt anybody. No use trying to write here what she said, because she's no more understandable than Lacomb and says perhaps one syllable of every multisyllable word that she speaks, but I knew that it was Welcome home, and worried, missed you so, and would have done anything in those last days, should have called me, washed them sheets, not afraid to wash them sheets, just you lie down, you let me make you some hot chocolate, you, my baby.

Lacomb skulked in the kitchen door, a short bald man who'd pass for white anyplace but in New Orleans, and then the voice, of course, was always the dead giveaway.

"How you doing, boss? You looking thin to me, boss. You better eat something. Althea, don't you dare cook this woman any of your food. Boss, I'll go out for it. What you want, boss? Boss, this house is full of flowers. I could sell them out front, make us a few dollars."

I laughed: Althea read him some rapid form of the riot act with appropriate rises and falls of tone, and a few good gestures.

I went upstairs just to make sure the Prince of Wales four-poster bed was still there. It was, and with its new fine satin trimmings.

Karl's mother had put a framed picture of him by the bed—not the skeleton they carted away, but the brown-eyed frank-hearted man who had sat with me on the steps of the uptown library, talking about music, talking about death, talking about getting married, the man who took me to Houston to see the opera and to New York, the man who had every picture of St. Sebastian ever done by an Italian artist or in the Italian mode, the man who had made love with his hands and his lips and would brook no argument about it.

His desk was clean. All the papers gone. Don't worry about this now. You have Glenn's word, and Glenn and Roz have never failed anyone.

I went back down the stairs.

"You know, I could have helped you with that man," Lacomb said. And Althea replied that he had said it enough, and I was back and go be quiet, or mop a floor, just shoo.

My room was clean and quiet, the bed turned down, the most tender and fragrant Casablanca lilies in the vase. How had they known? Or of course, Althea told them. Casablanca lilies.

I climbed into the bed, my bed.

As I have said, this bedroom is the master bedroom of the cottage and the only real bedroom, and it is on the first floor on the morning side of the house, an octagonal wing extending out into the deep dark grove of cherry laurels that hide the world away.

It is the only wing which the house has, which is otherwise a rectangle. And the wraparound galleries, our deep deep porches that we so love, come round and out along this bedroom, whereas on the other side of the house, they merely stop before the kitchen windows.

It's nice to walk from your bed out a tall window onto a porch, back away from the street, and look through the ever glossy leaves of cherry laurels at a comforting commotion that doesn't take note of you.

I wouldn't give the Avenue for the Champs Elysées, for the Via Veneto, for the Yellow Brick Road, for the Highway to Heaven. But it's nice sometimes to be way back here in this easterly bedroom or to stand at the railing, too far from the street to be noticed, and peer out at the cheerful lights as they go by.

"Althea, honey, pull back my curtains so I can look out my window."

"It's too cold for you to open it now."

"I know, I only want to see. . . ."

"—no chocolate, no books, you no want your music, your radio, I got your disks off the floor, I got all that put away, Rosalind come and put all that in order, she say Mozart with Mozart, Beethoven with Beethoven, she show me where . . ."

"No, just to rest, kiss me."

She bent down and pressed her silky cheek to mine. She said: "My baby."

She covered me with two big comforters, all silk, and no doubt filled with down, Mrs. Wolfstan's style, Karl's style, that everything be real goose down, loving the weightless weight. She pushed them around my shoulders.

"Miss Triana, why you never call Lacomb and me when that man was dying, we woulda come."

"I know. I missed you. I didn't want you to be frightened."

She shook her head. Her face was very pretty, much darker than Lacomb's, with big lovely eyes, and her hair was soft and wavy.

"You turn your head to the window," she said, "and you sleep. Ain't nobody coming in this house, I promise you."

I lay on my side looking straight out the window, through twelve shining clean panes at the distant trees and oaks, the color of traffic.

I loved again to see the azaleas out there, pink and red and white, crowded everywhere so luxuriantly along the fence, and the delicate iron railing painted so freshly black and the porch itself so shining clean.

So wonderful that Karl should give this to me before he died, my house restored. My house with every door to properly click, and lock to work, and every faucet to run the proper temperature of water.

Perhaps five minutes I looked dreaming out the window, perhaps longer. The streetcars passed. My lids grew heavy.

And only out of the corner of my eye did I make out a figure standing there on the porch, my tall gaunt one, the violinist, with his silky hair hanging lank down on his chest.

He hung about the edge of the window like a vine himself, dramatically thin, almost fashionably cadaverous yet very alive. His black hair hung so straight and glossy. No tiny braids tied back this time. Only hair.

I saw his dark left eye, the strong sleek black eyebrow above it. His cheeks were white, too white, but his lips were alive, smooth, very smooth, living lips.

I was scared for a minute. Just a minute. I knew this was wrong. No, not wrong, but dangerous, unnatural, not a possible thing.

I knew when I dreamed and when I did not, no matter how hard the struggle to move between the two. And he was here, on my porch, this man. He stood there looking at me.

And then I was scared no more. I didn't care. It was a lovely burst of utter indifference. I don't care. Ah, it is such a divine emptiness that follows the desertion of fear! And this was a rather practical point of view, it seemed at the moment.

Because either way . . . whether he was real or not real . . . it was pleasing and beautiful. I felt the chills on my arms. So hair does stand on end, even when you are lying, all crushed in your own hair on a pillow, with one arm flung out, looking out a window. Yes, my body went into its little war with my mind. Beware, beware, cried the body. But my mind is so stubborn.

My voice, interior, came very strong and determined, and I marveled at myself, how one can hear a tone in one's head. One can shout or whisper without moving the lips. I said to him:

Play for me. I missed you.

He drew closer to the glass, all shoulders for a moment it seemed, so tall and narrow, and with such torrential and tempting hair—I wanted so to feel it and groom it—and he peered down at me through the higher windowpanes, no angry glaring fictional Peter Quint searching for a secret beyond me. But looking right at what he sought. At me.

The floorboards creaked. Someone trod the path right to the door.

Althea came again. As easily as if it were any common moment.

I didn't turn over to look at her. She merely slipped into the room as she always did.

I heard her behind me. I heard her set down a cup. I could smell hot chocolate.

But I never took my eyes off him with his high shoulders and dusty tailored wool sleeves, and he never took his deep brilliant eyes off me as he stared without interruption through the window.

"Oh, Lord God, you there again," Althea said.

He didn't move. Neither did I.

I heard her words in a soft near unintelligible rush. Forgive this translation. "You here right at Miss Triana's window. Some nerve you got. Why, you like to scare me to death. Miss Triana, he be waiting all this time, night and day, saying he would play for you, saying he couldn't get near to you, that you loved his playing, that you can't do without him, he say. Well, what's you gonna play now that she come home, you think you can play something pretty for her now, the way she is, look at her, you think you gonna make her feel all right?"

She came strolling around the foot of the bed, portly, arms folded, chin stuck out.

"Come on now, play something for her," she said. "You hear me through that glass. She home now, she so sad, and you, look at you, you think I'm going to clean that coat for you, you got another think coming."

I must have smiled. I must have sunk a little deeper into the pillow. She saw him!

His eyes never moved from me. He paid her no respect. His hand was on the glass like a great white spider. But there at his side in the other hand was the violin, with the bow. I saw the dark elegant curves of wood.

I smiled at her without moving my head, because now she stood between us, boldly, facing me, blotting him out. Again, I translate what is not a dialect so much as a song:

"He talk and talk about how he can play and he play for you. How you love it. You know him. I ain't seen him come up here on the porch. Lacomb should have seen him come. I ain't scared of him. Lacomb can run him off right now. Just say so. He don't bother me none. He played some music here one night, I tell you, you never heard such music, I thought, Lord the police will be here and nobody here but Lacomb and me. I told him, You hush now, and he was so upset, you never saw such eyes, he looked at me, he say, You don't like what I play, I say, I like it, I just don't want to hear it. He say all kind of crazy things like he know all about me and what I got to bear, he talk like a crazy man, he just jabbering on and on, and Lacomb say, If you're looking for a handout we gonna feed you Althea's red beans and rice and you gonna die of poison! Now, Miss Triana, you know!"

I laughed out loud but it didn't make very much noise. He was still there; I could see only a little of the big lanky darkness of him behind her. I hadn't moved. The afternoon was deepening.

"I love your red beans and rice, Althea," I said.

She marched about, straightened the old Battenburg lace on the night table, glared at him, apparently, and then smiled down at me, one satin hand touching my cheek for a moment. So sweet, my God, how can I live without you?

"No, it's perfectly fine," I said. "You go on now, Althea. I do know him. Maybe he will play, who knows? Don't bother about him. I'll look out for him."

"Look like a tramp to me," she muttered under her breath, arms folded tight again most eloquently as she started out of the room. She went on talking, making her own song. I wish I could better render for posterity in some form her rapid speech, with so many syllables dropped, and above all her boundless enthusiasm and wisdom.

I nestled into my pillow; I crooked my arm under the pillow and snuggled against it, staring right up at him, his figure in the window, peering over the top of the sash through the double panes of glass.

Songs are everywhere you look, in the rain, in the wind, in the moan of the suffering, songs.

She shut the door. Double click, which means, with a New Orleans door, invariably warped, that she really closed it.

The quiet came back over the room as if it had never been mussed in the slightest. The Avenue gave forth a sudden crescendo of its continued rumble.

Beyond him—my friend peering at me with his black eyes and showing me only a smileless mouth—the birds sang in a late-afternoon spurt that comes each day by their clock and always surprises me. The traffic made its cheerful dirge.

He moved his tall unkempt form into the full window. Shirt white and soiled and unbuttoned; dark hair on his chest like a shadow or fleece. An opened vest of black wool because its buttons were all gone.

This is what I think I saw, at least.

He leaned very close against the twelve-paned frame. How thin he was, sick perhaps? Like Karl? I smiled to think it might all unfold once more. But no, that seemed very far away now, and he so vivid as he looked down at me, so very remote from the real weakness of death.

There came a chiding look from him, as if to say, You know better.

And then he did smile, and his eyes gave a brighter ever more secretive gleam, as he gazed at me possessively.

His forehead was pale and bony above his lids, but it gave the eyes their lovely sly shadowy depth, and his black hair grew so thick from his beautiful hairline with its widow's peak and well-proportioned temples that it lent him a hefty beauty even in his thinness. He did have hands like spiders! He stroked the upper panes with his right hand. He made prints that I saw in the dust, as the light made tiny inevitable shifts, as the garden beyond him with its dense cherry laurels and magnolias moved and breathed with breeze and traffic.

The thick white cuff of his shirt was soiled, and his coat gray with dust.

A slow change came over his expression. The smile was gone, but there was no animosity there and I realized now that there had never been. An air of superiority, of secretive superiority, had marked him before, but this expression was unguarded and spontaneous.

A baffled tender feeling passed over his face, held it and then released it to what seemed anger. Then he became sad, not publicly or artificially sad, but deeply, privately sad, as if he might lose his grip on this little spectacle of spookdom on the porch. He stepped back. I heard the boards. My house proclaims any movement.

And then he slipped away.

Just like that. Gone from the window. Gone from the porch. I couldn't hear him beyond the shutters at the far corner end. I knew he wasn't there. I knew he had gone away, and I had the most pure conviction that he had in fact vanished.

My heart thudded too loudly.

"If only it wasn't a violin," I thought. "I mean, thank God it's a violin, because there isn't any other sound on earth like that, there's . . ."

My words died away.

Faint music, his music.

He hadn't gone very far. He'd just chosen some dark distant part of the garden way out in the back, near to the rear of the old Chapel Mansion on Prytania Street. My property meets the Chapel property. The block belongs to us, to the Chapel and to me, from Prytania to St. Charles along Third Street. Of course there is another side to the block, where other buildings stand, but this great half of the square is ours, and he had only retreated perhaps as far as the old oaks behind the Chapel.

I thought I would cry.

For one moment, the pain of his music and my own feeling were so perfectly wedded that I thought, I cannot be expected to endure this. Only a fool would not reach for a gun, put a gun in the mouth and pull the trigger—an image that had haunted me often when I was, in younger years, a hopeless drunk, and then again almost continuously until Karl came.

This was a Gaelic song, in the Minor Key, deep and throbbing and full of patient despair and ambitionless longing—he had the Irish fiddle sound in it, the hoarse dark harmony of the lower strings played together in a plea that sounded more purely human than any sound made by child, man or woman.

It struck me—a great formless thought, unable to take shape in this atmosphere of slow lovely embracing music—that that was the power of the violin, that it sounded human in a way that we humans could not! It spoke for *us* in a way that we ourselves couldn't. Ah, yes, and that's what all the pondering and poetry has always been about.

It made my tears flow, his song, the Gaelic musical phrases old and new, and the sweet climb of notes that tumbled inevitably into an endless testimony of acceptance. Such tender concern. Such perfect sympathy.

I rolled over into the pillow. His music was wondrously clear. Surely all the block heard it, the passersby, and Lacomb and Althea at it at the kitchen table with their playing cards or epithets; surely the birds themselves were lulled.

The violin, the violin.

I saw a day in summer some thirty-five years ago. I had my own violin in my case, between me and Gee, who rode his motorcycle, as I clung to him from the back, keeping the violin safe. I sold the violin to the man on Rampart Street for five dollars.

"But you sold it to me for twenty-five dollars," I said, "and that was just two years ago."

Away it went in its black case, my violin; musicians must be the mainstay of pawnshops. Everywhere there hung instruments for sale; or maybe music attracts many bitter dreamers such as me with grandiose designs and no talent.

I had only touched a violin two times since—was that thirty-five years? Almost. Save for one blazing drunken time and its hangover aftermath, I never even picked up another violin, never never wanted to touch the wood, the strings, the resin, the bow, no, not ever.

But why did I bother to think of this? This was an old adolescent disappointment. I'd seen the great Isaac Stern play Beethoven's *Violin Concerto* in our Municipal Auditorium. I'd wanted to make those glorious sounds! I'd wanted to be that figure, swaying on the stage. I wanted to bewitch! To make sounds like these now, penetrating the walls of this room. . . .

Beethoven's *Violin Concerto*—the first classical piece of music I came to know intimately later from library records.

I would become an Isaac Stern. I had to!

Why think of it? Forty years ago, I knew I had no gift, no ear, could not distinguish quarter tones, hadn't the dexterity or the discipline; the best teachers told me as kindly as they could.

And then there was the chorus of the family, "Triana's making horrible noises on her violin!" And the dour advice of my father that the lessons cost too much, especially for one so undisciplined, lazy and generally erratic by nature.

That ought to be easy to forget.

Hasn't enough common tragedy thundered down the road since then, mother, child, first husband long lost, Karl dead, the toll of time, the deepening understanding—?

Yet look how vivid the long ago day, the pawnbroker's face, and my last kiss to the violin—my violin—before it slid across the dirty glass countertop. Five dollars.

All nonsense. Cry for not being tall, not being slender and graceful, not being beautiful, not having a voice either with which to sing, or even enough determination to master the piano sufficiently for Christmas carols.

I had taken the five dollars and added fifty to it with Rosalind's help and gone to California. School was out. My mother was dead. My father had found a new lady friend, a Protestant with whom to have an "occasional lunch," who cooked huge meals for my neglected little sisters.

"You never took care of them!"

Stop it, I won't think on those times, I won't, or of little Faye and

Katrinka on that afternoon when I went away, Katrinka scarcely interested, but Faye smiling so brightly and throwing her kisses . . . no, don't. Can't. Won't.

Play your violin for me, all right, but I will now politely forget my own.

Just listen to him.

It's as if he were arguing with me! The bastard! On and on went the song, conceived in sorrow and meant to be played in sorrow and meant to make sorrow sweet or legendary or both.

The world of now receded. I was fourteen. Isaac Stern played on the stage. The great concerto of Beethoven rose and fell beneath the chandeliers of the auditorium. How many other children sat there rapt? Oh, God, to be this! To be able to do this! . . .

It seemed remote that I had ever grown up and lived a life, that I'd ever fallen in love with my first husband, Lev, known Karl, that he'd ever lived or died, or that Lev and I had ever lost a little girl named Lily, that I had held someone that small in my arms as she suffered, her head bald, her eyes closed—ah, no, there is a point surely where memory becomes dream.

There must be some medical legislation against it.

Nothing so terrible could have happened as that golden-haired child dying as a waif, or Karl crying out, Karl who never complained, or Mother on the path, begging not to be taken away that last day, and I, her self-centered fourteen-year-old daughter utterly unaware that I would never feel her warm arms again, could never kiss her, never say, Mother, whatever happened, I love you. I love you. I love you.

My father had sat straight up in the bed, rising against the morphine and saying, aghast: "Triana, I'm dying!"

Look how small Lily's white coffin in the California grave. Look at it. Way out there where we smoked our grass, and drank our beer and read our poetry aloud, beats, hippies, changers of the world, parents of a child so touched with grace that strangers stopped—even when the cancer had her—to say how beautiful was her small round white face. I watched again over time and space, and those men put the little white coffin inside a redwood box down in the hole, but they didn't nail shut the boards.

Lev's father, a hearty gentle Texan, had picked up a handful of earth and dropped it into the grave. Lev's mother had cried and cried.

Then others had done the same, a custom I'd never known, and my own father solemn, looking on. What had he thought: Punishment for your sins, that you left your sisters, that you married out of your church, that you let your mother die unloved!

Or did he think more trivial things? Lily was not a grandchild he had cherished. Two thousand miles had separated them, and seldom had he seen her before the cancer took her long golden streams of hair and made her little cheeks soft and puffy, but there was no potion known to man that could ever dull her gaze or her courage.

He doesn't matter now, your father, whom he loved and did not love!

I turned over in the bed, grinding the pillow under me, marveling that even with my left ear buried in the down, I could still hear his violin.

Home, home, you are home, and they will all someday come home. What does that mean? It doesn't have to mean. You just have to whisper it . . . or sing, sing a wordless song with his violin.

And so the rain came.

My humble thanks.

The rain came.

Just as I might have wished it, and it falls on the old boards of the porch and on the rotting tin roof above this bedroom; it splashes on the wide windowsills and trickles through the cracks.

Yet on and on he played, he with his satin hair and his satin violin, playing as if uncoiling into the atmosphere a ribbon of gold so fine that it will thin to mist once it's been heard and known and loved, and bless the entire world with some tiny fraction of glimmering glory.

"How can you be so content," I asked myself, "to lie right between these worlds? Life and death? Madness and sanity?"

His music spoke; the notes flowed low and deep and hungering before they soared. I closed my eyes.

He went into a ripping dance now, with zest and dissonance and utter seriousness. He played so full and fierce, I thought surely someone would come. It's what people call the Devil's kind of music.

But the rain fell and fell and no one stopped him. No one would.

Like a shock it came to me! I was home and safe and the rain surrounded this long octagonal room like a veil, but I wasn't alone:

I have you, now.

I whispered aloud to him, though of course he wasn't in the room.

I could have sworn that far away and near at hand, he laughed. He let me hear it. The music didn't laugh. The music was bound to follow its hoarse, perfectly pitched, driving course as if to drive a band of meadow dancers weary mad. But he laughed.

I began to fall into sleep, not the deep black beginningless sleep of hospital drugs, but true, deep, sweet sleep, and the music rose and tightened and then gave forth a monumental flood as if he had forgiven me.

It seemed the rain and this music would kill me. I would die quiet without a protest. But I only dreamed, sliding down down into a full-blown illusion as if it had been waiting for me.

❧ 5 ❧

I⟨T WAS⟩ that sea again, that ocean clear and blue and frothing wild into the flopping prancing ghosts with every wave that hit the beach. It had the spell of the lucid dream. It said, Yes, you couldn't be dreaming, you are not, you're here! That's what the lucid dream always says. You turn around and around it and you can't wake up. It says, You cannot have imagined this.

But we had to leave now from the soothing breeze off the sea. The window was closed. The time has come.

I saw roses strewn across a gray carpet, roses with long stems and each tipped with a sealed vial of water to keep it fresh, roses with petals darkened and soft, and voices spoke in a foreign tongue, a tongue I ought to know but didn't know, a language made up, it seemed, just for this dream. For surely I was dreaming. I had to be. But I was here, imprisoned in this, as if transported body and soul into it, and something in me sang, Don't let it be a dream.

"That's right!" said the beautiful dark-skinned Mariana. She had short hair, and a white blouse that didn't cover her shoulders, a swan's neck, a purring voice.

She opened the doors of a vast place. I could not believe my eyes. I could not believe that solid things could be as lovely as the sea and sky, and this—this was a temple of polychrome marble.

It's not a dream, I thought. You couldn't dream this! You haven't the visions in you to make such a dream. You're here, Triana!

Look at the walls inlaid with a creamy deep-veined Carrara

marble, panels framed in gold and the skirting of darker brown stone, no less polished, no less variegated, no less wondrous. Look at the square pilasters with their golden scrolled capitals.

And now as we come to the front of the building, this marble moves to green, in long bands along the floor, the floor itself an ever changing and intricate mosaic. Look. I see the ancient Greek key design. I see the patterns dear to Rome and Greece for which I don't remember names, but I know them.

And now, turning, we stood before a staircase such as I have never seen anywhere. It is not merely the scale and the loftiness, but again, the color: behold, O Lord, the radiance of the rose Carrara marble.

But attend first these figures, these bronze faces standing at attention, bodies of deeply carefully carved wood, curving into lion's legs and paws on their plinths of onyx.

Who built this place? For what purpose?

I'm caught suddenly by the glass doors opposite, there is so very much to see, I'm overcome, look, three great Classical Revival doors of beveled glass and semicircular fanlights, mullions black and spoked above, such portals for light, though the day or the night, whichever it is, is locked out beyond them.

The stairs await. Mariana says, Come. Lucrece is so kind. The balustrade is green marble, green as jade, and streaked like the sea, with balusters of a lighter shade, and every wall paneled in rose or cream marble that is framed in gold.

Look up to these smooth, rounded columns of pink marble, with their gilded capitals of double rich acanthus leaf, and high high above, see the broken arches of the cove, and between each a painted figure; see the paneled frame around the high stained-glass window.

Yes, it is day. This is the light of day streaming through the stained glass! It shines on the artfully painted nymphs in panels high above, dancing for us, dancing too in the glass itself. I close my eyes. I open them. I touch the marble. Real, real.

You are here. You can't be awakened or taken from this place; it's true, you see it!

We climb these stairs, we move up and up amid this palace of Italian stone and stand on a mezzanine floor and face three giant stained-glass windows, each with its own goddess or queen, in diaphanous robes, beneath an architrave, with cherubs in attendance and flowers drawn in every border, festooned, garlanded, held in out-stretched hands. What symbols are these? I hear the words, but I see; that is what makes me tremble.

And at each end of this long dreamy space there is an oval chamber. Come look. Look at these murals here, look at these paintings that reach so high. Yes, richly narrative, and once again the bold classical figures dance, heads are wreathed in laurel, contours full and lush. It has the magic of the pre-Raphaelites.

Is there no end to combination here, to beauty woven into beauty? No end to cornices and friezes, moldings of tongue and dart, of proud entablatures, to walls of boiserie? I must dream.

They spoke in the angel language, Mariana and the other, Lucrece, they spoke that soft singing tongue. And there, I pointed: the gleaming golden masks of those I loved. Medallions set high upon the wall: Mozart, Beethoven; others . . . , but what is this, a palace to every song you've ever heard and been unable to endure without tears? The marble shines in the sun. Such richness as this can't be made by human hands. This is the temple of Heaven.

Come down the stairs, down, down, and now I know, with heart sinking, that this must be a dream.

Though this dream can't be measured by the depths of my imagination, it is improbable to the point of impossible.

For we have left the temple of marble and music for a great Persian room of glazed blue tile, replete with Eastern ornament that rivals the beauty above in its sumptuousness. Oh, don't let me wake. If this can come from my mind, then let it come.

That this Babylonian splendor should follow on that bold Baroque glory cannot be, but I so love it.

Atop these columns are the sacrificial ancient bulls with their angry faces, and look, the fountain, in the fountain Darius slays the leaping Lion. Yet this is no shrine, no dead memorial to things lost.

Behold, the walls are lined in shining étagères that hold the most elegant glassware. A café has been made within these decorative reliefs. Once again I see a floor of incomparable mosaic. Small graceful gilded chairs surround a multitude of little tables. People talk here, move, walk, breathe, as if this magnificence were something they have taken utterly for granted.

What place is this, what country, what land, where style and color could so audaciously come together? Where convention has been overrun by masters of all crafts. Even the chandeliers are Persian in design, great silver metal sheets with intricate patterns cut out of them.

Dream or real! I turn and strike the column with my fist. Goddamn it, if I'm not here, let me wake! And then comes the assurance. You are here, most definitely. You are here body and soul in this place, in the Babylonian room beneath the marble temple.

"Come, come." Her hand is on my arm. Is it Mariana or the other lovely one—with the round face and large generous eyes—Lucrece? They commiserate, the two in a singing Latinish tongue.

Our darkest secret.

Things shift. I'm here all right, because this I'd never dream.

I don't know how to dream it. I live for music, live for light, live for colors, yes, true, but what is this, this rank, soiled white-tiled passage, the water on the black floors, so filthy that they are not even black, and look, the engines, the boilers, the giant cylinders with screwed-on caps and seals, so ominous, covered in peeling paint, amid a din of noise that's almost silence.

Why, this is like the engine room of an old ship, the kind you wandered aboard when you were a child and New Orleans was still a living harbor. But no, we are not on board a ship. The proportions of this corridor are too massive.

I want to go back. I don't want to dream this part. But by now, I know it's no dream. I've been brought here somehow! This is some punishment I deserve, some awful reckoning. I want to see the marble again, the pretty rich fuchsia marble against the side panels of the stairs; I want to memorize the goddesses in the glass.

But we walk in this damp, rank, echoing passage. Why? Foul smells rise everywhere. Old metal lockers stand here, as if left behind by soldiers in some abandoned camp, battered, stuck with cutout magazine girls from years before, and once again we view this vast Hell of machines, churning, grinding, boiling with noise as we walk along the steel railing.

"But where are we going?"

My companions smile. They think it a funny secret, this, this place to which they are taking me.

Gates! Great iron gates lock us out, but lock us out of what? A dungeon?

"A secret passage," confesses Mariana with undisguised delight. "It goes all the way under the street! A secret underground passage . . ."

I strain to see through the gates. We can't go in. The gates are chained shut. But look, back there, where the water shimmers, look.

"But someone's there, don't you see? Good God, there's a man lying there. He's bleeding. He's dying. His wrists are slashed and yet his hands are laid together. He's dying?"

Where are Mariana and Lucrece? Flown up again into the domed ceilings of the marble temple where the Grecian dancers make their easy graceful circles in the murals?

I am unguarded.

The stench is unbearable. The man's dead! Oh, God! I know he is. No, he moves, he lifts one of his hands, his wrist dripping blood. Good God, help him!

Mariana laughs the softest sweetest laugh and her hands stroke the air as she speaks.

"Don't you see him dead, good God, he's lying in filthy water . . ."

". . . secret passage that used to go from here to the palace and . . ."

"No, listen to me, ladies, he's there. He needs us." I grabbed the gates. "We have to get to that man there!" The gates that bar our way are like everything here—immense. They're heavy iron, fitted from floor to ceiling, hung with chains and locks.

"Wake up! I will not have it!"

A torrent of music crashed to silence!

I sat up in my own bed.

"How dare you!"

✺ 6 ✺

I SAT up in the bed. He sat beside me, his legs so long that even on this high four-poster, he could sit in manly fashion, and he stared at me. The violin was wet. He was wet, his hair soaked.

"How dare you!" I said again. I reared back, bringing my knees up. I reached for the covers, but his weight held them.

"You come into my house, my room! You come into this room and tell me what I will and will not dream!"

He was too surprised to answer. His chest heaved. The water dripped from his hair. And the violin, for God's sake, had he no concern at all for the violin?

"Quiet!" he said.

"Quiet!" I spat at him. "I'll rouse the city! This is my bedroom! And who are you to tell me what to dream! You . . . what do you want?"

He was too astonished to find words. I could feel his groping, his consternation. He turned his head to the side. I had a chance to look at him close, to see his gaunt cheeks and smooth skin, the huge knuckles of his hands and the delicate shaping of his long nose. He was by any standards—and even filthy and dripping wet—very handsome to look at. Twenty-five. That was the age I calculated, but no one could tell. A man of forty could look so young, if he took the right pills and ran the right miles and visited the right cosmetic surgeon.

He jerked his head round to glare at me!

"You think of trash like that as I sit here?" His voice was deep and strong, a young man's voice. If speaking voices have names, then he was a forceful tenor.

"Trash like what?" I said. I looked him up and down. He was a big man, thin or not. I didn't care.

"Get out of my house," I said. "Get out of my room and out of my house now, until such time as I invite you here as my guest! Go! It puts me in a perfect fury that you dare come in here without my bidding! Into my very room!"

There came a banging on the door. It was Althea's panic-stricken voice. "Miss Triana! I can't open the door! Miss Triana!"

He looked at the door beyond me and then back at me and shook his head and murmured something, and then ran his right hand back through his slimy hair. When he opened his eyes fully they were large, and his mouth, now that was the prettiest part, but none of these details cooled my anger.

"I can't open this door!" Althea screamed.

I called out to her. It was all right. Leave it be. I needed some time alone. It was the musician friend. It was all right. She should go now. I heard her protests, and Lacomb's sage grumbles beneath them, but all of this on my insistence finally died away, and I was alone again.

The creaking boards had charted their retreat.

I turned to him. "So did you nail it shut?" I asked. I meant the door of course, which neither Lacomb nor Althea could force.

His face was still, and this stillness perhaps resembled whatever God and his mother might have wanted it to be: young; earnest; without vanity or slyness. His big dark eyes moved searchingly over me, as if he could discover in all the unimportant details of my appearance some crucial secret. He didn't brood. He seemed an honest, questing being.

"You aren't afraid of me," he whispered.

"Of course I'm not. Why should I be?" But this was bravado. I did for one second feel fear; or no, it wasn't fear. It was this. The adrenaline in my veins had slacked, and I felt an exultation!

I was looking at a ghost! A true ghost. I knew it. I knew it, and nothing would ever take the knowledge away. I knew it! In all my wanderings amongst the dead, I'd talked to memories and relics and fed their answers to them as if they were dolls I held propped in my hand.

But he was a ghost.

Then came a great coursing relief. "I always knew it," I said. I smiled. There was no defining this conviction. I meant only that I knew at last there was more to life, and something we couldn't chart, and couldn't dismiss, and the fantasy of the Big Bang and the Godless Universe were no more substantial now than tales of Resurrection from the Dead or Miracles.

I smiled. "You thought I would be afraid of you? Is that what you wanted? You come to me when my husband is dying upstairs and you play your violin to frighten me? Are you the fool of all ghosts? How could such a thing frighten me? Why? You thrive off fear—"

I paused. It wasn't only the vulnerable softness of his face, the seductive quiver of his mouth; and the way his eyebrows met to frown but not to condemn or forbid; it was something else, something analytical and crucial that had occurred to me. This creature did thrive off something, and what was that something?

A rather fatal question, I realized. My heart lost a beat, which always frightens me. I put my hand to my throat as if my heart were there, which it always seems to be, doing these dances in my throat rather than in my breast.

"I'll come into your room," he whispered, "when I wish." His voice gained strength, young and masculine and sure of itself. "There's no way you can stop me. You think because you spend every waking hour doing the Danse Macabre with all your murdered crew—yes, yes, I know how you think you murdered them all—your Mother, your Father, Lily, Karl, such stupid monstrous egotism, that you were the cause of all these spectacular deaths, and three of them so ghastly and untimely—you think because of that, you can command a ghost? A true ghost, a ghost such as I am?"

"Bring my Father and Mother to me," I said. "You're a ghost. Bring them over to me. Bring them back over the divide. Bring me my little Lily. Bring them in ghostly form if you are a ghost and such a ghost! Make them ghosts, give Karl back to me without pain, just for a moment, one single solitary sacred moment. Give me Lily to hold in my arms."

This wounded him. I was quietly amazed, but adamant.

"Sacred moment," he said bitterly.

He shook his head, and looked away from me as if disappointed but mainly disrupted by the remark, but then again he seemed thoughtful and looked back. I found myself riveted by his hands, by the delicacy of his fingers and the hollow-cheeked yet flawless youth of his face.

"I can't give you that," he said thoughtfully, considerately. "You think God listens to me? You think my prayers count with saints and angels?"

"And you do pray, I'm to believe?" I asked. "What are you doing here! Why are you here? Why have you come! Never mind that you sit here, lazily and defiantly on the side of my bed. Why are you here at all—within my sight, within my hearing?"

"Because I wanted to come!" he said crossly, looking for a second rather painfully young and defiant. "And I go where I would go and do what I would do, as perhaps you noticed. I walked your hospital corridor until a gaggle of mortal idiots made such a riot there was nothing to do but retreat and wait for you! I could have come into your room, into your bed."

"You want to be in my bed."

"I am!" he declared. He leaned forward on his right hand. "Oh, don't even consider it. I'm no incubus! You won't conceive a monster by me. I want something far more critical to your life than the plaything between your legs. I want you!"

I was speechless.

Furious, yes, still furious, but speechless.

He sat back and looked down before him. His knees looked quite comfortable on the side of the high bed. His feet actually touched the floor. Mine never have. I am a short woman.

He let his greasy black hair fall down around him, in streaks across his white face, and when he looked at me again, it was a quizzical look.

"I thought this would be much easier," he said.

"What's that?"

"To drive you mad," he said. He affected a cruel smile. It was unconvincing. "I thought you mad already. I thought it would be . . . a matter of days at most."

"Why the hell should you want to drive me mad?" I asked.

"I like doing such things," he said. The sadness flashed over him, knitted his brows before he could brush it away. "I thought you were mad. You're almost . . . what some people would call mad."

"Yet painfully sane," I said. "That's the problem."

I was now utterly enthralled. I couldn't stop studying all the details of him, his old coat, the wet dust that had made mud on his shoulders, the way his big dreamy eyes sharpened and then mellowed with his thoughts, the way his lips were moistened with his tongue now and then as if he were a human being.

Suddenly a thought came to me. It came crashingly clear.

"The dream! The dream I had of the—"

"Don't talk of it!" he said. He leaned forward, menacingly, so close now his wet hair fell down on the blanket right by my hands.

I pushed back against the headboard for leverage and then with the full strength of my right hand I slapped him. I slapped him twice before he could get his wits! I pushed the covers back.

He rose and moved awkwardly away from me, looking down at me in pitiful bewilderment.

I reached out. He didn't flinch. I knotted my hand into a fist and struck him full in the chest. He moved back a few steps, no more concerned with such a weak blow than a human man might have been.

"The dream came from you!" I said. "That place I saw, the man with . . ."

"I warn you, don't." He cursed, his finger flying out to point in my face even as he backed up and drew himself up like a great bird. "Silence on that. Or I'll wreak such havoc on your little physical corner of the world you'll curse the day you were ever born. . . ." The voice faded out. "You think you know pain, you're so proud of your pain. . . ."

He looked up and away from me. He drew the violin up to his chest and crossed his arms around it. He had said something that displeased himself. His eyes searched the room as if they could really see.

"I do see!" he said angrily.

"Ah, I meant as a mortal man, that's all I meant."

"And that is all I mean, too," he answered.

The rain outside slackened, grew soft and light, so that the various leaks and trickles gained in volume. We seemed in a wet world, wet but warm and safe, he and I.

I knew, knew as clearly as I knew he was there, I knew that I had seldom been so alive in my life as I was now, that the very sight of him, his being here, had brought me back to a fire in life I hadn't known in decades. Long, long ago, before so many defeats, when I'd been young and in love, perhaps I'd been this alive, when I'd wept over my failures and losses in those early energetic years, when everything had been so very bright and hot to touch, maybe then I'd been this alive.

In the maddest grief there was not this kind of vitality. It was more akin to joy, dance, the sheer penetrating and hypnotic power of music.

And there he stood, looking lost, and suddenly looking at me as if he would ask something, and then looking away, his dark brows knitted.

"Tell me what you want," I said. "You said you wanted to drive me mad? Why? For what reason?"

"Well, you see," he said quickly in response, though his words were slow, "I'm at a loss." He spoke frankly with raised eyebrows and a cool poised manner. "I don't know myself what it is I want now! Driving you mad." He shrugged. "Now that I know what you are, or how strong you are, I don't know what words to put it in. There's perhaps something better here than merely driving you out of your mind, assuming of course that I could have done it, and I see you feel superior in this regard, having held so many deathbed hands and watched your lost young husband, Lev, dance on drugs with his friends while you merely sipped your wine, afraid to take the drugs, afraid of visions! Visions like me! You amaze me."

"Vision?" I whispered.

I wrapped my left hand around the bedpost. My body was shaking. My heart did pound. All these symptoms of fear reminded me that there was indeed something here to fear, but then again, what in God's name could be worse than so much that had happened? Fear the supernatural? Fear the flicker of candles and the smiles of saints? No, I think not.

Death is plenty to fear. Ghosts, what are ghosts?

"How did you cheat death?" I said.

"You flippant, cruel woman," he whispered. He spoke in a rush. "You look angelic. You, with your veil of dark hair, and your sweet face and huge eyes," he whispered. He was sincere. He was stung, and his head bent to the side. "I didn't cheat anything or anyone." He looked desperately to me. "You wanted me to come, you wanted—"

"You thought so? When you caught me thinking about the dead?

Is that what you thought? And you came to what? Console? Deepen my pain? What happened?"

He shook his head, and took several steps backwards. He looked out the back window, and in so doing, let the light unveil the side of his face. He seemed tender.

He turned on me in an angry flash.

"So very pretty still," he said, "and at your age, and plump, even so. Your sisters hate you for your pretty face, you know it, don't you? Katrinka, the beautiful one with the shapely body and smart husband, and before him the string of lovers she cannot count. She thinks you have a prettiness that she can never earn or produce or paint or claim. And Faye, Faye loved you, yes, as Faye loved all, but Faye couldn't forgive you your prettiness either."

"What do you know of Faye?" I asked before I could stop myself. "Is my sister Faye still alive?" I tried to stop myself, but I couldn't. "Where is Faye! And how can you speak for Katrinka, what do you know about Katrinka or any of my family?"

"I speak what you know," he said. "I see the dark passages of your mind, I know the cellars where you yourself have not been. I see there in those shadows that your father loved you too much because you resembled your mother. Same brown hair, brown eyes. And that your sister Katrinka cheerfully bedded your young husband, Lev, one night."

"Stop this! What? Have you come here to be my personal Devil? Do I rate such a thing? I? And you tell me in the same breath that I'm not half so responsible as I seem to think for all those deaths. How are you going to drive me mad, I'd like to know? How? You're not sure of yourself at all. Look at you. You quake and you're the ghost. What were you when you were alive? A young man? Maybe even kind by nature, and now all twisted out of—"

"Stop," he pleaded. "Your point is clear."

"Which is what?"

"That you see me clearly, as I see you," he answered coldly. "That memory and fear aren't going to make you waver. I was so very wrong about you. You seemed a child, an eternal orphan, you seemed so . . ."

"Say it. I seemed so weak?" I asked.

"You're bitter."

"Perhaps," I said. "It's not a word I favor. Why do you want me to feel either pain or fear? For what? Why! What did the dream mean? Where was that sea?"

His face was blank with shock. He raised his eyebrows, and then again tried to speak but changed his mind, or couldn't find the words for it.

"You could be beautiful," he said softly. "You almost were. Is that why you fed on trash and beer and let your God-given shape go to waste? You were thin when you were a child, thin like Katrinka and Faye, thin by nature. But you covered yourself with a concealing bulk, didn't you? To hide from whom? Your own husband, Lev, as you handed him over to younger and more beguiling women? You pushed him into bed with Katrinka."

I didn't respond.

I felt an ever-increasing strength inside me. Even as I shuddered, I felt this strength, this grand excitement. It had been so long since any emotion such as this had visited me, and now I felt it, looking at him in his bewilderment.

"You are perhaps even a little beautiful," he whispered, smiling as if he meant quite deliberately to torment me. "But will you grow as large and shapeless as your sister Rosalind?"

"If you know Rosalind and can't see her beauty, you're not worth my time," I said. "And Faye walks in beauty that is beyond your comprehension."

He gasped. He sneered. He looked stubbornly at me.

"You can't recognize the power of one as pure as Faye in my memory. But she's there. As for Katrinka, I have sympathy. Faye was young enough to dance and dance, no matter how deep the dark. Katrinka knew things. Rosalind I love with all my heart. What of it?"

He looked at me as though seeking to read my deepest thoughts, and said nothing.

"Where does this lead?" I asked.

"Little girl at heart," he said. "And wicked and cruel as little girls can be. Only bitter now, and needing of me, and yet denying it. You drove your sister Faye away, you know."

"Stop it."

"You . . . when you married Karl, you made her leave. It wasn't the painful pages in your Father's diaries that she read after his death. You brought a new lord into the house that you and she had shared—"

"Stop it."

"Why?"

"But what's all this to you, and why do we talk of it now? You're dripping from the rain. But you're not cold. You aren't warm either, are you? You look like a teenage rock tramp, the kind that follows famous bands around with a guitar in his hand, begging for quarters at the doorways of concert halls. Where did you get the music, the incredible, heartbreaking music—?"

He was furious.

"Spiteful tongue," he whispered. "I'm older than you can dream. I'm older in my pain than you. I'm finer. I learnt to play this instrument to perfection before I died. I learnt it and possessed a talent for it in my living body such as you never will even understand with all your recordings and your dreams and fantasies. You were asleep when your little daughter Lily died, you do remember that, don't you? In the hospital in Palo Alto, you actually went to sleep and—"

I put my hands up to my ears! The smell, the light, the entire hospital room of twenty years ago surrounded me. I said No!

"You revel in these accusations!" I said. My heart beat too hard, but my voice was under my command. "Why? What am I to you and you to me?"

"Ah, but I thought *you* did."

"What? Explain?"

"I thought *you* reveled in these accusations. I thought you so accused yourself, you so gloried in it, mixing it up with fear and cringing and chills and sloth—that you were never lonely, ever, but always holding hands with some dead loved one and singing your poems of contrition in your head, keeping them around, feeding their remembrance so as not to know the truth: the music you love, you'll never make. The feeling it wrings from your soul will never find fulfillment."

I couldn't answer.

He went on, emboldened.

"You so sated yourself on accusations, to use your own word, you so fed on guilt that I thought it would be nothing to drive you out of your mind, to make it so that you . . ." He stopped. He did more than stop. He checked himself, and stiffened.

"I'm going now," he said. "But I'll come when I please, you can be sure of it."

"You have no right. Whoever sent you must take you back." I made the Sign of the Cross.

He smiled. "Did that little prayer do you any good? Do you remember the miserable California funeral Mass of your daughter, how stiff and out of place everything was—all those clever intellectual West Coast friends forced to attend something as patently stupid as a real funeral in a real church—do you remember? And the bored, toss-it-off priest who knew you never went to his church before she died. So now you make the Sign of the Cross. Why don't I play a hymn for you? The violin can play plainsong. It's not common, but I can find the *Veni Creator* in your mind and play it, and we can pray together."

"So it hasn't done you any good," I said, "praying to God." I tried to make my voice strong but soft, and to mean what I said: "Nobody sent you. You wander."

He was nonplussed.

"Get the hell out of here!"

"But you don't mean it," he said with a shrug, "and don't tell me your pulse isn't ticking like an overwound clock. You're in tireless ecstasy to have me! Karl, Lev—your Father. You've met a man in me such as you've never seen, and I'm not even a man."

"You're cocky, rude and filthy," I said. "And you are not a man. You are a ghost, and the ghost of someone young and morally uncouth and ugly!"

This hurt him. His face showed a cut much deeper than vanity.

"Yes," he said, struggling for self-possession, "and you love me, for the music, and in spite of it."

"That may be true," I said coldly, nodding. "But I also think very highly of myself. As you said, you miscalculated. I was a wife twice, a mother once, an orphan perhaps. But weak, no, and bitter? Never. I lack the sense that bitterness requires . . ."

"Which is what?"

"One of entitlement, that things ought to have been better. It is life, that's all, and you feed on me because I'm alive. But I'm not so worm-eaten with guilt that you can come in here and push me out of my wits. No, not by any means. I don't think you fully understand guilt."

"No?" He was genuine.

"The raging terror," I said, "The 'mea culpa, mea culpa' is only the first stage. Then something harder comes, something that can live with mistakes and limitations. Regret's nothing, absolutely nothing . . ."

Now I was the one who let the words trail off because my most recent memories came back to sadden me, of seeing my mother walk away on that last day, Oh, Mother, let me take you in my arms. The graveyard on the day of her burial. St. Joseph's Cemetery, all those small graves, graves of the poor Irish and the poor Germans, and the flowers heaped there, and I looked at the sky and thought it will never, never change; this agony will never go away; there will never be any light in this world again.

I shook it off. I looked up at him!

He was studying me, and he seemed himself almost in pain. It excited me.

I went back to the point, seeking deeply for it, pushing everything else aside but what I had to realize and convey.

"I think I understand this now," I said. A spectacular relief soothed me. A feeling of love. "And you don't, that's the pity. You don't."

I let my guard down utterly. I thought only of what I was trying to fathom here and not of pleasing or displeasing. I wanted only to be close to him in this. And this he would want to know; he might, he surely would understand, if only he would admit it.

"Please do illuminate me," he said mockingly.

A terrible pain swept over me; it was too vast and total to be piercing. It took hold of me. I looked up imploringly at him, and I parted my lips, about to speak, about to confide, about to try to discover out loud with him what it was, this pain, this sense of responsibility, this realization that one has indeed caused unnecessary pain and destruction in this world and one cannot undo it, no, it will never be undone, and these moments are forever lost, unrecorded, only remembered in ever more distorted and hurtful fashion, yet there is something so much finer, something so much more significant, something both overwhelming and intricate that we both knew, he and I—

He vanished.

He did most obviously and completely vanish, and he did it with a smile, leaving me with my outstretched emotions. He did it cunningly to let me stand alone with that moment of pain and worse, alone with the awful appalling need to share it!

I gave a moment to the shadows. The soft sway of the trees outside. The occasional rain.

He was gone.

"I know your game," I said softly. "I know it."

I went to the bed, reached under the pillow and picked up my Rosary. It was a crystal Rosary with a sterling silver cross. It was in the bed because Karl's mother had always slept in the bed when she came, and my beloved godmother, Aunt Bridget, always slept in it, after the marriage with Karl, when she came, or the Rosary was actually in the bed because it was mine and I had absently put it there. Mine. From First Communion.

I looked down at it. After my mother's death Rosalind and I had had a terrible quarrel.

It was over our Mother's Rosary, and we had literally torn apart the links and the fake pearls—it was a cheap thing but I had made it for Mother and I claimed it, I, the one who made it, and then after we tore it apart, when Rosalind came after me, I had slammed the door so hard against her face that her glasses had cut deep into her forehead. All that rage. Blood on the floor again.

Blood again, as if Mother had been living still, drunk, falling off the bed, striking her forehead as she had twice on the gas heater, bleeding, bleeding. Blood on the floor. Oh, Rosalind, my mourning, raging sister Rosalind! The broken Rosary on the floor.

I looked at this Rosary now. I did the childlike unquestioning thing that came to my mind. I kissed the crucifix, the tiny detailed body of the anguished Christ, and shoved the Rosary back under the pillow.

I was fiercely alert. I was like prepared for battle. It was like an early drunk in the first year, when the beer went divinely to my head and I ran down the street with arms outstretched, singing.

The pores of my skin tingled and the door opened with no effort whatsoever.

The finery of the alcove and the dining room looked brand new. Do things sparkle for those on the verge of battle?

Althea and Lacomb stood far across the length of the dining room, hovering in the pantry door, waiting on me. Althea looked plain afraid and Lacomb both cynical and curious as always.

"Like if you was to scream one time in there!" said Lacomb.

"I didn't need any help. But I knew you were here."

I glanced back at the wet stains on the bed, at the water on the floor. It wasn't enough to bother them with it, I thought.

"Maybe I'll walk in the rain," I said. "I haven't walked in the rain for years and years."

Lacomb came forward. "You talking about outside now tonight in this rain?"

"You don't have to come," I said. "Where's my raincoat? Althea, is it cold outside?"

I went off walking up St. Charles Avenue.

The rain was only light now and pretty to look at. I hadn't done this in years, walk my Avenue, just walk, as we had so often as children or teenagers, headed for the K&B drugstore to buy an ice cream cone. Just an excuse to walk past beautiful houses with cut-glass doors, to talk together as we walked.

I walked and walked, uptown, past houses I knew and weedy barren lots where great houses had once stood. This street, they ever tried to kill, either through progress or neglect, and how perilously poised it always seemed—between both—as though one more murder, one more gunshot, one more burning house would set its course without compromise.

Burning house. I shuddered. Burning house. When I'd been five a house had burned. It was an old Victorian, dark, rising like a nightmare on the corner of St. Charles and Philip, and I remember that I'd been carried in my Father's arms "to see the fire," and I had become hysterical looking at the flames. I saw above the crowds and the fire engines a flame so big that it seemed it could take the night.

I shook it off, that fear.

Vague memory of people bathing my head, trying to quiet me. Rosalind thought it a wonderfully exciting thing. I thought it a revelation of such magnitude that even to learn of mortality itself was no worse.

A pleasant sensation crept over me. That old horrific fear—this house will burn too—had gone with my young years, like many another such fear. Take the big lumbering black roaches that used to race across these sidewalks: I used to step back in terror. Now that fear too was almost gone, and so were they, in this age of plastic sacks and icebox-cold mansions.

It caught me suddenly what he had said—about my young husband, Lev, and even younger sister, Katrinka, that he, my husband whom I loved, and she, my sister whom I loved, had been in the same bed, but I'd always blamed myself for it. Hippie marijuana and cheap wine, too much sophisticated talk. My fault, my fault. I was a cowardly faithful wife, deeply in love. Katrinka was the daring one.

What had he said, my ghost? *Mea culpa.* Or had I said it?

Lev loved me. I loved him still. But then I had felt so ugly and inadequate, and she, Katrinka, was so fresh, and the times were rampant with Indian music and liberation.

Good God, was this creature real? This man I'd just spoken with, this violinist whom other people saw? He was nowhere around now.

Across the Avenue from me as I walked, the big hired car crept along, keeping pace, and I could see Lacomb muttering as he leant out the rear window to spit his cigarette smoke into the breeze.

I wondered what this new driver, Oscar, thought. I wondered if Lacomb would want to drive the car. Lacomb doesn't do what Lacomb doesn't like.

It made me laugh, the two of them, my guards, in the big crawling black Wolfstan car, but it also gave me license to walk as far as I wanted.

Nice to be rich, I thought with a smile. Karl, Karl.

I felt as if I were reaching for the only thing that could save me from falling, and then I stopped, "absenting myself from this dreary felicity a while" to think of Karl and only Karl, so lately shoved into a furnace.

"You know it's not at all definite that I will even become symptomatic." Karl's voice, so protecting. "When they notified me regarding the transfusion, well, that was already four years, and now another two—"

Oh, yes, and with my loving care you will live forever and ever! I'd write the music for it if I were Handel or Mozart or anyone who could write music . . . or play.

"The book," I said. "The book is marvelous. St. Sebastian, shot full with arrows, an enigmatic saint."

"You think so? You know about him?" How delighted Karl had been when I told the stories of the saints.

"Our Catholicism," I had said, "was so thick and ornamented and rule-ridden in those early days, we were like the Hasidim."

Ashes, this man! Ashes! And it would be a coffee table book, a Christmas gift, a library staple that art students would eventually destroy by cutting out the prints. But we would make it live forever. Karl Wolfstan's *St. Sebastian*.

I sank to dreariness. I sank to the sense of the small scope of Karl's life, a fine and worthy life, but not a great life, not a life of gifts such as I had dreamed up when I tried so hard to learn the violin, such as Lev, my first husband, still struggled to maintain with every poem he wrote.

I stopped. I listened.

He wasn't about, the fiddler.

I could hear no music. I looked back and then up the street. I watched the cars pass. No music. Not the slightest dimmest sound of music.

I deliberately thought of him, my violinist, point by point, that with his long narrow nose and such deep-set eyes he might have been less seductive to someone else—perhaps. But then perhaps to no one. What a well-formed mouth he had, and how the narrow eyes, the detailed deepened lids gave him such a range of expression, to open his gaze wide, or sink in cunning secret.

Again and again, old memories threatened, the most agonizing and excruciating bits of recollection drifted at me—my Father, crazed and dying, tearing the plastic tube from his nose, and pushing the nurse away . . . all these images came as if flung in the wind. I shook my head. I looked around me. Then the full fabric of the present wanted to enwrap me.

I refused it.

I thought again very specifically of him, the ghost, refurbishing in my imagination his slender tall figure and the violin which he had held, and trying as best as my unmusical mind could do to recall the melodies he'd played. A ghost, a ghost, you have seen a ghost, I thought.

I walked and walked, even though my shoes were wet and finally soaked, and the rain came heavy again, and the car came round, and I told it to go away. I walked. I walked because I knew as long as I walked, neither memory nor dream could really take hold of me.

I thought a lot about him. I remembered everything that I could. That he had worn the common formal clothes you pick up in the thrift shops more easily than casual or fashionable clothes; that he was very tall, at least six foot three I calculated, remembering how I had looked up at him, though at the time I had not been very dwarfed or in any way intimidated.

It must have been after midnight when I finally came back up the front steps, and heard, behind me, the car sliding before the front curb.

Althea had a towel in her hands.

"Come in, my baby," she said.

"You should have gone to bed," I said. "You seen my fiddler? You know, my musician friend with his violin?"

"No, ma'am," she said, drying my hair. "I think you run him off for good. Lord knows, Lacomb and I were ready to break down that door, but what you got to do you did. He's gone!"

I took off the raincoat and entrusted it to her, and went up the stairs.

Karl's bed. Our upstairs room, ever illuminated by the red light of the florist across the street through lace and lace and lace.

A new mattress and pillows, of course, no indent of my husband here, no last bit of hair to find. But the delicate carved wooden frame in which we'd made love, this bed he'd bought for me in those happy days when buying things for me had been such pleasure for him. Why, why, I had asked, was it so much fun? I had been ashamed that fine carved furniture and rare fabric had made me so happy.

I saw the fiddler ghost distinctly in my mind, though he was not here. I was alone in this room as a person can be.

"No, you're not gone," I whispered. "I know you're not."

But then why shouldn't he be? What debt had he to me, a ghost I'd called names and cursed? And my late husband burnt up even three days ago. Or was it four?

I started to cry. No sweet smell of Karl's hair or cologne lingered in this room. No smell of ink and paper. No smell of Balkan Sobranie, the tobacco he would not give up, the one my first husband Lev always sent him from Boston. Lev. Call Lev. Talk to Lev.

But why? What play did it come from, that haunting line?

"But that was in another country; And besides, *the wench is dead*."

A line from Marlowe that had inspired both Hemingway and James Baldwin and who knows how many others. . . .

I began to whisper a line from *Hamlet* to myself, ". . . 'the undiscover'd country from whose bourn no traveler returns.' "

There came a welcome rustling in the room, the mere stir of the curtains and then those creaks and noises in the floor of this house which can be brought merely by a shift of the breeze against the dormers of this attic.

Then quiet came. It came abruptly, as if he'd come and gone, dramatically, and I felt the emptiness and the loneliness of the moment unbearably.

Every philosophical conviction I'd ever held was laid waste. I was alone. I was alone. This was worse than guilt and grief and maybe was what . . . no, I couldn't think.

I lay down on the new white satin spread and searched for an utter blackness of body and soul. Shut out all thoughts. Let the night be for once the ceiling above, and beyond that a simple untroubled sky, with meaningless and merely tantalizing stars. But I could no more stop my mind than my own breath.

I was terrified my ghost had gone away. I'd driven him away! I cried, sniffling and wiping my nose. I was terrified that I'd never see him again, never, never, never, that he was gone as certainly as the living go, that I'd cast this monstrous treasure to the wind!

Oh, God, no, not so, no, let him come back. If the others you have to keep to yourself for all Time, I understand and always have, but he's a ghost, my God. Let him return to me. . . .

I felt myself drop below the level of tears and dreams. And then . . . what can I say? What do we know when we know and feel nothing? If only we would wake from these states of oblivion with some certain sense that there was no mystery to life at all, that cruelty was purely impersonal, but we don't.

For hours, that was not to be my concern.

I slept.

That's all I know. I slept, moving as far away from all my fears and losses as I could, holding one desperate prayer. "Let him come back, God."

Ah, the blasphemy of it.

❧ 7 ❧

THE FOLLOWING day, the house was full of people. All doors were opened so that the two front parlors flanking the wide front hall were in clear view of the long dining room, and people could flow easily over the varied carpets, talking in cheerful voices as New Orleans people do after a death, as if it were what the dead person wanted.

A little cloud of silence surrounded me. Everybody thought I was mentally taxed, shall we say, having spent two days with a dead body, and then there was the question of slipping out of the hospital without a word, for which Rosalind was being blamed again and again by Katrinka, as if Rosalind had in fact murdered me when nothing could have been further from the truth.

Rosalind, in her deep drowsy voice, asked repeatedly if I was all right, to which I said repeatedly yes. Katrinka talked about me, pointedly, with her husband. Glenn, my beloved brother-in-law and husband of Rosalind, seemed a broken thing, hurt deep by my loss yet unable to do anything but stand rather close to me. I thought musingly to myself of how much I loved them, Rosalind and Glenn, childless, the keepers of Rosalind's Books and Records, where you could find Edgar Rice Burroughs in paperback or a song on a 78 disk recorded by Nelson Eddy.

The house was warm and sparkling, as only this house could sparkle, with its many mirrors and windows and a view in all directions. That was the great genius of this cottage, that, standing in the dining room as I did, you could look through open doors and windows to all four points of the compass, though they were tangled up with trees and the gusty afternoon. It was so lovely to have made a house of such openness.

A big supper was ordered. Caterers came, whom I knew. Some woman famous for a chocolate pie. And there was Lacomb with his hands behind his back looking sneeringly at the black bartender in his suit. Lacomb would make friends with him, however. Lacomb made friends with everybody, at least everybody who could understand him.

At one point, he slid up to me so silently I was startled. "You want something, boss?"

"No," I said, throwing him a little smile. "Don't get drunk too soon."

"Boss, you're no fun anymore at all," he said, slipping away with his own sly smile.

We gathered around the long narrow oval table.

Rosalind, Glenn, as well as Katrinka, her two daughters and her husband, and many of our cousins ate lustily, carrying their plates about, because there were far too many for the chairs. My people mingled easily with the gregarious Wolfstan family.

Karl had begged these relatives not to visit him during his final months. Even when we married, he knew he was sick, and he had wanted it to be private. And now with his mother already gone back again to England, and everything settled and done, these Wolfstans— all of them rather shiny-faced agreeable people of clear German descent—looked a bit surprised at things—a dazed kind of surprise as when you are awakened out of deep sleep, but nevertheless they were at home among all the fine furniture Karl had bought for me—the cabriole-legged chairs, the pearl-inlay tables, the desks and chests of intarsia made up of tortoiseshell and brass, and the timeworn genuine Aubusson rugs, so thin beneath our feet that they seemed sometimes made of paper.

It was all Wolfstan style, this luxury.

They all had money. They had always owned houses on St. Charles Avenue. They were descended from the rich Germans who migrated to New Orleans before the Civil War, and made big money in cigar factories and in beer, long before all the ragged Potato Famine crew hit our shores, the starving Irish and Germans who were my ancestors. These Wolfstan people had blocks of property in key places, and owned the leases on old stores and businesses.

My cousin Sarah sat staring at her plate. She was the youngest grandchild of Cousin Sally, in whose arms my mother had died. I had no mental picture of it. Sarah hadn't even been born then. Other Becker cousins, and those of mine with Irish names, looked a bit baffled among this careful splendor.

The house seemed poignantly beautiful to me all during the afternoon. I kept turning to catch the reflection of the entire crowd of us in the big mirror along the dining room wall, the mirror which is in a direct line with the front door, and does embrace for all practical purposes the entire party.

The mirror was old; my Mother had loved that mirror. I couldn't stop thinking about her, and it occurred to me several times that she had been the first person I'd really hurt and failed, not Lily. I'd made an error in calculation, a terrible error, the error of a lifetime.

I sat deep in thought, sometimes whispering absolute nonsense to people just to make them stop talking to me.

I couldn't get it out of my mind, my Mother leaving this house on that last afternoon—taken by my Father against her will to stay with her Irish godmother and cousin. She hadn't wanted to be shamed. She'd been drunk for weeks and weeks, and we couldn't stay with her then because Katrinka, a child of eight, had suffered a burst appendix and was, technically, though I never knew it then, dying at Mercy Hospital.

Katrinka didn't die of course. I wonder sometimes if the fact that she missed our Mother's death completely—that it happened during such a long illness when she was locked away—I wondered if that alone didn't make her warped, and eternally doubtful of everything. But I couldn't think about Katrinka. Katrinka's insecurities I wore around always like a heavy necklace. I knew what she was whispering about in the corners of the rooms. I didn't care.

I thought of my Mother, being taken down the side path out to Third Street by my Father, and begging him not to make her go to these cousins. She hadn't wanted her beloved Cousin Sally to see her as she was. And I had not even gone to tell her goodbye, to kiss her, to say anything to her! I'd been fourteen. I don't even know why I was walking up the path at that moment when he took her out. I couldn't get it straight, and the horror of it kept thudding in on me, that she'd died with Sally and Patsy and Charlie, her cousins, and though she loved them and they loved her, there had not been one single one of us with her!

I felt I was going to stop breathing.

People meandered about the sprawling cottage. They went out the open windows onto the porches. It seemed a lively and lovely thing, this delayed coming together for my sake, because that is what I supposed it was. I rather enjoyed the glow of the polished highboys and velvet high-back chairs which Karl had strewn everywhere.

Karl had bequeathed a highly polished surface to the old parquet, with coats and coats of lacquer, beneath the overwhelming Baccarat chandeliers that my Father had refused to sell in the old days, even when "we had nothing."

Karl's silver had been brought out for the meal. Our silver, I suppose I should say, as I was his wife, and he had bought this pattern for me. It is called Love Disarmed and was first made by Reed & Barton sometime very early in the century. An old company. An old pattern. Even the new pieces were finely etched because it had fallen from grace with brides somewhere along the line. You could buy it new or old. Karl had trunks of it that he had collected.

It is one of the few silver patterns that features an entire figure, in this instance a beautiful nude woman on each item, no matter how small or how large, of sterling.

I loved it. We owned more of it than we had ever used, because Karl collected it. I wanted to say something to them—about perhaps each taking a piece in remembrance of Karl, but I didn't.

I ate and drank only because when you do this, you have to talk less. Yet to take food at all seemed a monstrous betrayal.

I'd felt that keenly after my daughter Lily's death. After we'd buried her in Oakland, in St. Mary's Cemetery, a faraway and unimportant place, way away from here, we'd gone with my Mother- and Father-in-Law, Lev's parents, to eat and drink and I had almost choked on the food. I remembered distinctly, the wind had begun to blow, and trees to thrash, and I couldn't stop thinking of Lily in her coffin.

Lev seemed the strong one then, brave and beautiful with his long flowing hair, the wildman-poet-professor. He had told me to eat and be quiet, and he carried the conversation along with the bereaved grandparents, and included as well my somber Father, who said little or nothing.

Katrinka had loved Lily. I remembered that! How could I forget? It seemed wretched to have forgotten! And how Lily had loved her beautiful blond Aunt Katrinka.

Katrinka had suffered Lily's death as bad as anyone could. Faye had been frightened by the whole affair of Lily's sickness and death, generous sweet Faye. But Katrinka had been there, there with a knowing heart, in the hospital room, in the corridors, always ready to come. Those were the California years, encapsulated by the fact that we had all eventually returned.

We'd all left our California life in the cities by the Bay, and drifted either home or away. Faye was gone now, no one knew where, and perhaps forever.

Even Lev had left California finally, long after he had married Chelsea, his pretty girlfriend and my close friend. I think they'd had the first child before he went to teach in a college in New England.

I felt a sudden happiness thinking of Lev, that he had three children, boys, that even though Chelsea called frequently and complained that he was unbearable, he really wasn't, and even though he called sometimes and cried, and said we should have stuck it out, I felt no regret, and I knew he really didn't. I liked to look at the pictures of his three sons, and I liked to read Lev's books—slim, elegant volumes of poetry, which were published about every two to three years, to accolades.

Lev. My Lev was the boy I'd met in San Francisco and married in the courthouse, the rebellious student and wine drinker, and the singer of madly improvised songs and the dancer under the moon. He had only started to teach university classes when Lily got sick, and the truth was he never got over Lily's death. Never, never was he ever the same, and what he had sought with Chelsea was consolation, and with me a sisterly approval of the warmth from Chelsea and the sexuality that he desperately needed.

But why, why think of all this? Is this so different from the tragedies of any other life? Is death more rampant here than in any other sprawling family?

Lev was a full professor, tenured, happy. Lev would have come had I asked him to. Why, last night when I'd been walking on the Avenue in the rain, stupid and crazy, I might have called Lev. I hadn't told Lev that Karl died. I hadn't talked to Lev in months, though a letter from Lev was lying on a desk now in the living room unopened.

I couldn't shake all this. It was like tremors. The deeper I fell into these thoughts, of Mother, of Lily, of my lost spouse Lev—the more I began to recall *his* music again, the desperate violin, and I knew I was remembering all these utterly unbearable things compulsively, like one forced to look on the wounds of one's own murder victims. This was a trance.

But maybe such trances would always follow death now, as death piled upon death. In grieving for anyone, I grieved for all. And again, I thought, how foolish to think that Lily had been my first awful crime—letting her die. Why, it was perfectly clear that years before Lily ever died, I'd forsaken my Mother!

Five o'clock came. It was shadowy outside. The Avenue became noisier. All the big rooms had about them a more festive look, and people had drunk plenty enough wine that they were talking freely, as people do in New Orleans after a death, as if it would be an insult to the dead to go around whispering like they do in California.

California. Lily out there on a hill, why? There was no one to visit that grave. Dear God, Lily! But every time I thought of bringing Lily's body home, I had this horrible notion—that when the coffin arrived here in New Orleans, I would have to look in it. Lily, dead before her sixth birthday, had been buried for over twenty years. I couldn't imagine such a sight. An embalmed child covered in green mold?

I shuddered. I thought I was going to scream.

Grady Dubosson had arrived, my friend and lawyer, trusted advisor to Karl and Karl's mother. Miss Hardy was here, had been here for the longest time, and so were several other women from the Preservation Guild, all of them elegant and refined creatures.

Connie Wolfstan said, "We want something, just some little thing, you know, that you wouldn't mind us keeping, to remember him by . . . I don't know . . . just the four of us."

I was so relieved. "The silver," I said. "There's so much of it, and he loved it. You know, he corresponded with silver dealers all over the country to buy up Love Disarmed. Look, see that, that little fork, that's actually what you call a strawberry fork."

"You really wouldn't mind if we each took—"

"Oh, God, I was afraid, afraid that you would be afraid because of his illness. There is so much of it. There's enough for all of you."

A loud noise disturbed us. Someone had fallen over. I knew this cousin was one of those few that was kin to both the Beckers of my family and the Wolfstans of Karl's, but I couldn't remember his name.

He was drunk, poor guy, and I could see his wife was furious. They helped him up. There were long wet stains on his gray trousers.

I wanted to speak, to form words about the silver. I heard Katrinka say, "What are they trying to take?" and it came out of my mouth to Althea as she passed, "His silver, you know all that silverware, let his family all take a piece of it."

I felt my face color as Katrinka glared at me. She said that it was community property, the silver.

For the first time I realized that sooner or later all these people would be gone and I'd be alone here and maybe *he* wouldn't come back, and I saw desperately how his music had comforted me, how it had guided me through memory after memory, and now I was bedeviled, and shaking my head, and obviously looking odd.

What was I wearing? I looked down. A long full silk skirt and a frilly blouse, and a velvet vest that disguised my weight—Triana's uniform, they called it.

There was quite a commotion in the pantry. The silver had been brought out. Katrinka was saying something biting and terrible to poor sad Rosalind, and Rosalind, with her dark eyebrows pointing up and her glasses sliding down her nose, looked lost and in need of help.

My cousin Barbara leaned down to kiss me. They had to go. Her husband couldn't drive anymore after dark, at least he really shouldn't. I understood. I held her tightly for a moment, pressing my lips into her cheek. When I kissed her, it was like I kissed her mother, my long gone great-aunt, and my grandmother who had been that woman's sister.

Katrinka suddenly turned me around, hurting my shoulder. "They're sacking the pantry!"

I got up and made a gesture for her to be quiet, my finger to my lips, which I knew, positively knew, would make her boilingly furious. It did. She backed away. One of Karl's aunts came to kiss me and thank me for the small teaspoon she held.

"Oh, it would make him so happy—" I said. He was always sending Love Disarmed to people as gifts and writing, "Now, be sure to tell me if you do not like this pattern because I may inundate you with it." I think I tried to explain that, but clear words were so difficult for me to utter. I moved away, using this person in a way as a means of escape, escorting her to the door, and though others waved as they went down the steps, I went off along the porch and looked out over the Avenue.

He wasn't there. *He* probably had never existed. With a crashing force, I thought of my Mother, but it wasn't the day before she died. It was another time when I'd given a birthday party for one of my friends. My mother had been drunk for weeks, locked up in the side bedroom, sort of, dead drunk the way she always got, only becoming conscious in the very late hours to roam around, and somehow she'd come wandering out at this party!

She'd come wandering onto the porch, deranged and looking for all the world like Jane Eyre's strange rival, the mad woman in Rochester's attic. We'd taken her back inside, but was I kind, did I kiss her? I couldn't remember. It was too disgusting to think of being that young and that thoughtless, and then it hit me again with a mighty force that I'd let her go, let her die of drunkenness alone, with cousins before whom she was ashamed.

What was the murder of Lily, the failure to save Lily, compared to this?

I gripped the railing. The house was emptying.

The fiddler had been a piece of madness, music imagined! Crazy, lovely, comforting music, spun out of the subconscious by a desperate ordinary talentless person, too pedestrian in every respect to enjoy a fortune left to her.

Oh, God, I wanted to die. I knew where the gun was, and I thought, If you wait just a few weeks, everyone will feel better. If you do it now, then everyone will think it was his or her fault. And then what if Faye is alive somewhere and she comes home and finds her big sister has done such a thing; what if Faye were to take that blame on herself? Unthinkable!

Kisses, waving hands. A sudden rain of delicious perfume—Karl's Aunt Gertrude, and then her husband's soft, crinkled hand.

Karl had whispered to me when he could no longer turn over without help, "At least I'll never know what it means to be old, will I, Triana?"

I turned and looked down over the side lawn. The lights of the florist blazed on the wet grass and the wet bricks beyond, and I tried to calculate where the path had been down which my mother walked on that last day that I saw her. It was gone. During the years in California, when my father was married to his Protestant wife—out of the church, saying his Rosary every night nevertheless, a damned soul, making her perfectly miserable, no doubt—they'd built a garage. The vogue of the automobile had descended even on New Orleans. And there was no old wooden gate now to be Mother's shrine, her gateway to eternity.

I was choking, trying to catch my breath. I turned around. I looked down the long porch. People everywhere. But I could picture my Mother the night she wandered out, perfectly. My Mother had been beautiful, much more good-looking in every respect than any of her daughters, it seemed; she'd had such a wild expression on her face, lost among all these partying teenagers, awakened from a drunken sleep, not knowing where she was, friendless, only weeks from death.

I tried to catch my breath.

"—all you did for him." A voice spoke.

"For whom?" I said. "Daddy," said Rosalind, "and then to take care of Karl."

"Don't talk about it. When I die I want to wander off into the woods alone." Or use the gun shortly.

"Don't we all?" Rosalind said. "But that's just it. You fall and break a hip like Dad and someone slaps you in bed with needles and tubes, or like Karl, they tell you one more go-round of drugs and maybe—"

She went on, being Rosalind, the nurse and the sharer with me of morbid things as we are two sisters both born in different years but in the month of October.

So vividly I saw Lily in a coffin, imagined now with green mold, her small round face, her lovely tiny hand, plump and beautiful on her breast, her country dancing dress, the last dress that I had ever ironed for her, and my Father saying, They will do that at the funeral parlor, but I had wanted to iron it myself, the last dress, the last dress.

Lev said later of his new bride, Chelsea, "I need her so much, Triana, I need her. She's like Lily to me again. It's like I have Lily."

I had said I understood. I think I was numb. Numb is the only way to describe how I'd feel when I sat in the other room and Chelsea and Lev made love, and then they'd come in and kiss me and Chelsea would say I was the most unusual woman she'd ever known.

Now that really is funny!

I was going to start to cry. Disaster! There were car doors closing, dark shadows against the florist shop of people waving farewell.

Grady called from inside the house. I could hear Katrinka. So the moment had come.

I turned and walked down the length of the wet porch, past the rocking chairs that were dappled with drops of rain, and I turned and looked into the wide hall. It was the most lovely view, because the great mirror at the far end, on the dining room wall, reflected both chandeliers, the small one of the hallway and the large one of the dining room, and it did seem you were looking down a truly grand corridor.

My Dad had made such speeches about the importance of those chandeliers, how my mother had loved them, how he'd never sell those chandeliers! Never, never, never. Funny thing was, I couldn't remember who asked him to do it, or when or how. Because after my Mother's death, and with all of us gone eventually, he had done very well, and before that, my Mother would never have let anyone touch those treasures.

The house was almost empty.

I went inside. I was not myself. I was frozen inside an alien form and the voice that came out could not be trusted. Katrinka was crying and had made her handkerchief into a knot.

I followed Grady into the front room where the high-top desk stood, between the front windows.

"I keep remembering things, such things," I said. "Maybe it's to chase away the present, but he died at peace, he didn't suffer as much as we feared, he, we all . . ."

"Darlin', you sit down," said Grady. "Your sister here is determined to discuss this house here and now. Seems she was indeed piqued by your Father's will, just as you said, and feels she's entitled to a portion of the sale of this house."

Katrinka looked at him in amazement. Her husband, Martin, shook his head and glanced at Rosalind's sweet-hearted husband, Glenn.

"Well, Katrinka is entitled," I said, "when I die." I looked up. The words had silenced everybody. Slinging the word "die" with such abandon, I guess.

Katrinka put her hands to her face and turned away. Rosalind had only flinched. And declared in her low stentorian voice, "I don't want anything!"

Glenn made some sharp low remark to Katrinka, to which Katrinka's husband, Martin, violently objected.

"Look, ladies, let's come to the point," said Grady. "Triana, you and I have discussed this moment. We are prepared for it. Indeed, we are well prepared."

"We have?" I was dreaming. I wasn't there. I could see them all. I knew there was no danger of anyone selling this house. I knew it. I knew things that none of them knew except Grady, but it wasn't that that mattered; it was that my violinist had consoled me when I thought of all the dead in the soft earth, and I'd imagined the thing, imagined it!

There had been some conversation—surely the evidence of madness. And it was madness that he'd said he wanted, but that was a lie. It was a balm he brought to me, a salve, a covering of kisses. His music knew! His music didn't lie. His music—.

Grady touched my hand. Katrinka's husband, Martin, said this wasn't a good time, and Glenn said that it wasn't a good time, and these words made no impression.

Lord God, to be born with no talent is bad enough, but to have a macabre and febrile imagination as well is a curse. I stared at the big picture of St. Sebastian over the fireplace. One of Karl's most treasured possessions—the original of the print that would be put on the cover of his book.

The suffering saint was marvelously erotic, tied to the tree, pierced with so many arrows.

And there on the other wall, over the couch, the big painting of flowers. So like Monet, they said.

It was a painting Lev had done for me and sent from Providence, Rhode Island, when he'd been teaching at Brown. Lev and Katrinka. Lev and Chelsea.

Katrinka had been only eighteen. I should never, never have let it all come to that; it was my fault getting Katrinka into that with Lev, and he was so ashamed, and she, what did she say afterwards, that when a woman was as pregnant as I was, that these things—no. I had said that to her, to tell her it was all right, that I was sorry, that I, that he—

I looked up at her. She was so distant, this slender anxious woman, from my solemn and silent little sister Katrinka. Katrinka when she was little had come home once with my Mother, and my Mother, drunk, had passed out on the porch, with the keys to the house in her purse, and little Katrinka, only six, had sat there five hours waiting for me to come home, ashamed to ask anyone to help, sitting there, beside this woman lying on the porch, a little child just sitting there waiting. "She fell down when we got off the streetcar, but she got up."

Shame, blame, maim, pain, vain!

I looked down on the surface of the table. I saw my hands. I saw the checkbook lying there, blue vinyl, or some other slimy and fiercely strong and ugly material like that, a long rectangular checkbook of the simplest kind, with checks in one side, and in the other tucked a thin-lined ledger.

I am a person who never bothers to enter a check into a ledger. But that was of no importance anymore at all. No talent for numbers, no talent for music. Mozart could play backwards. Mozart probably was a mathematical genius, but then Beethoven, he was nothing as sharp, a wholly different kind of . . .

"Triana."

"Yes, Grady."

I tried to pay attention to Grady's words.

Katrinka wanted the house sold, he said, the inheritance divided. She wanted me to sign over my right to remain in the house until death—"usufruct," as it is called under the law—the use of the house until my death, a right in fact shared by me and Faye. Now, how was I supposed to do that, with Faye utterly gone, I thought, and Grady was addressing this in a long drawn out, beautifully drawling way, saying that various attempts had been made to reach Faye, just as if Faye was really all right. Grady's accent was part Mississippi and part Louisiana and always melodious.

One time Katrinka told me that Mother put Faye in the bathtub. Faye was not even two years old, just able to sit up. Mother went "to sleep," which meant drunk, and Katrinka found Faye sitting in the tub, and the tub was full of excrement, turds floating in the water, and Faye was happily splashing, well, that happens, doesn't it, and Katrinka so little at the time. I came home, I was tired. I slammed my school books down. I didn't want to know! I didn't. The house was so dark and so cold. They were too little, either of them, to turn on the gas heaters in this house then, which were without pilot lights and on the open hearths and so dangerous they could anytime set the house on fire. There was no heat! Don't! The danger of fire with them alone and her drunk—. Don't.

It's not like that now!

"Faye is alive," I whispered. "She is . . . somewhere."

No one heard.

Grady had written the check already.

He placed it in front of me. "Do you want me to say what you asked me to say?" he said. This was confidential and kind of him.

Suddenly it jolted me. Of course. I had planned it, in angst and coldness, on a dark shadowy day when Karl was hurting with every breath, that if she ever tried this, my sister, my poor lost orphaned sister, Katrinka, that I would do this to her. We had planned it. I had told Grady, and Grady had had no choice but to follow my advice, and thought it most prudent besides, and he had a small statement to read.

"How much do you calculate this house is worth, Mrs. Russell?" he asked Katrinka. "What would you say?"

"Well, at least a million dollars," Katrinka answered, which was absurd because there were many larger more beautiful houses in New Orleans for sale for less than that. Karl used to marvel at it. And Katrinka and her husband, Martin, who sold real estate, knew this better than anyone, as they were fabulously successful uptown; they had their own company.

I stared at Rosalind. Back then, in the dark years, she had read her

books and dreamed. She had taken one look at Mother drunk on the
bed and then gone into her room with her books. She read Edgar Rice
Burroughs, *John Carter of Mars*. She had been so beautifully proportioned then. Her dark curly hair was lovely. We were not a bad lot,
and each with a different shade of hair.

"Triana."

My mother was beautiful till the moment she died. The funeral
home called. They said, "This woman has swallowed her tongue."
What did that mean? The cousins with whom she'd died had not even
seen her for years, and in their arms she died, with all her long brown
hair still brown, not a single gray strand, I remember that, her high
forehead—it is not easy to be beautiful with a high forehead, but she
was. That last day, as she went down the path, her hair was brushed
and pinned. Who had done it for her?

She had cut it short only once. But that had been years before. I
had come home from school. Katrinka was a baby still, running
around the flagstones in pink panties as children did then, all day in
the southern heat. No one thought to outfit them in name-brand
suits. And my Mother told me quietly that she had cut her hair, that
she had sold it.

What had I said to her? Had I reassured her that she was pretty,
that it was fine? I couldn't remember her with short hair at all. And
only years later did I understand; she sold her hair, sold her hair, to
buy the liquor. Oh, God!

I wanted to ask Rosalind what she thought, if it had been a sin
unforgivable not to say goodbye to our Mother. But I couldn't do
such a selfish thing! There sat Rosalind in torment, looking from
Grady to Katrinka.

Rosalind had her own terrible memories that hurt her so bad she
drank and cried. Once, before our Mother had died, Rosalind had run
into Mother coming up the front steps. Our Mother had a package of
liquor in her hand, a flat flask wrapped the way they did then at
"package liquor stores," in brown paper, and Rosalind had called her a
"drunk," and later confessed to me sobbing, and I had said over and
over, "She didn't know, she forgave, she understood, Rosalind, don't."
My Mother, never in her life at a loss for words, had in this sad story
only smiled at the young Rosalind who was then seventeen, only two
years older than me.

Mother! I'm going to die!

I sucked in my breath.

"Do you want me to read the statement?" Grady asked. "You wanted closure. Do you want perhaps to . . ."

"A modern word, that, closure," I said.

"You're crazy," said Katrinka. "You were crazy when you let Lev go—you just gave your own husband to Chelsea and you know it—you were crazy when you nursed Father, you didn't have to have all that medicine for Father, you didn't have to have the oxygen machines and the nurses and use up every cent he had, you didn't have to do that, you did it out of guilt and you know you did, plain guilt because of Lily . . ." At Lily's name her voice broke.

Look at her tears.

She could hardly bear to say Lily's name even now.

"You drove Faye away," she said, her face red, swollen, childlike, frantic, "and you were crazy to marry a dying man! To bring a dying man in here, I don't care if he did have money, I don't care if he did fix up the house, I don't care if . . . You have no right, no right to do these things . . ."

A roar of voices came to shut her up. She looked so defenseless! Even her husband, Martin, was angry with her now, and he intimidated her; she couldn't bear his disapproval. How small she looked; she and Faye were eternal waifs. I wished that perhaps Rosalind would get up, go hug her, hold her. I couldn't . . . couldn't touch her.

"Triana," said Grady. "Do you want to go ahead and make this statement now, as we planned it?"

"What statement?" I looked at Grady. It was something mean and cruel and terrible. I remembered now. The statement. The all-important statement; the drafts and drafts I'd written of the statement.

Katrinka had no idea how much money Karl had left me. Katrinka had no idea how much money I might one day share with her and Rosalind and Faye, and I had made the vow that if she did this thing, this unspeakable thing, if she did this, we would hand her a check, the very impressive check for a million dollars and no cents, even, and that I would demand with her endorsement the promise that she would never speak to me again. A plot hatched in the dark unforgiving part of the heart.

She'd know then, how penny-wise and pound-foolish she'd been.

Yes, and I would look her straight in the eye for all the cruel things she'd ever said to me, the mean things, the little hateful sister things, and her affection for Lev, her "comforting" Lev while Lily died, as surely as Chelsea . . . but no.

"Katrinka," I whispered. I looked at her. She turned to me, red faced, spurting tears like a baby, all the color washed out of her face but the red, so like the child. Imagine it, a child that little sitting in the school yard with her mother, and her Mother drunk and everyone knowing it, knowing it, knowing it, and that child clinging to her, and then coming home with that drunken woman on the streetcar and . . .

In the hospital one time I came in and Katrinka was like this, this red, this crying. "They told Lily twenty minutes before that blood test that they were going to do it. Why did they do that! This place is a torture chamber. They should have never told her so long before they didn't have to—." For my daughter, how she had cried!

Lily's face had been turned to the wall, my tiny five-year-old child, almost dead, within weeks. Katrinka had loved her so much.

"Grady, I want you to give her the check," I said quickly, raising my voice. "Katrinka, it's a gift. Karl arranged it for you. Grady, there's no speech, there's no point, there's no question now, just give her the gift that he wanted her to have."

I could see that Grady gave a huge heaving sigh of relief that there would be no acrimonious and melodramatic words, even though he knew full well that Karl had never laid eyes on Katrinka and had never arranged such a gift—

"But don't you want her to know it's your gift?"

"I do not," I whispered to him. "She couldn't accept it, she wouldn't. You don't understand. Give Rosalind her check, please," I said. That one had carried no conditions, meant only as a splendid surprise, and Karl had loved Rosalind and Glenn greatly, and leased for them their little shop, Rosalind's Books and Records.

"Say it's from Karl," I said. "Do it."

Katrinka held the check in her hand. She came towards the table. Her tears were still a childish flood, and I noticed how thin she had become, struggling now against age as we all did. She looked so like our Father's family, the Beckers, with her large slightly protruding eyes and her small pretty but hooked nose. She had the touch of the Semite beauty in her, a gravity to her tear-stained face. Her hair was fair and her eyes were blue. She trembled and shook her head. Her eyes were squeezed shut, and the tears oozed out of her eyes. My father had told us countless times that she was the only one of us who was truly beautiful.

I must have lost my balance.

I felt Grady steady me. And Rosalind murmured something that was lost for lack of enough self-confidence. Poor Roz, to endure this.

"You can't write a check like this," Katrinka said. "You can't just write a check for a million dollars!"

Rosalind held the check Grady had put in her hands. She appeared stupefied. So did Glenn, who stood over her, peering down at it as if it were a wonder of the world, a check for a million dollars.

The statement. The speech. All those words rehearsed in anger for Katrinka, "that you never seek my company again, that you never cross this threshold, that you never . . ." They all died and blew away.

It was the hospital corridor. Katrinka cried. In the room the strange California priest baptized Lily with water from a paper cup. Did my beloved atheist Lev think I was a perfect coward? And Katrinka was crying then as she cried now, real tears for my lost child, our Lily, our Mother, our Father.

"You were always . . ." I said, "so good to her."

"What are you talking about?" Katrinka said. "You don't have a million dollars! What is she saying? What is this? Does she think that—"

"Mrs. Russell, if you will allow," Grady began. He looked to me. He rolled on even before I nodded.

"Your sister has been left most comfortable by her late husband, with all arrangements made before his death and with the knowledge of his mother, arrangements which do not involve any will, or any such instrument, which can on any grounds be contested by any of his family.

"And indeed Mrs. Wolfstan signed numerous papers some time before Karl's death, that this arrangement would not in any way be questioned upon the loss of her son, Karl Wolfstan, and could and would be most speedily transacted."

He went on.

"There is no question as to the validity or the integrity of the check that you hold in your hand. This is your sister's gift to you which she would like you to accept, as your portion of whatever this house might be worth, and I must say, Mrs. Russell, I do not think even this house, charming as it is, would sell for one million dollars, and of course you have in your hand a check for the entire sum, though you also, as you well know, have three sisters."

Rosalind gave a little moan. "You don't have to," she said.

"Karl," I said. "Karl wanted me to be able to—"

"Ah, yes, to make it possible," said Grady, stumbling now to fulfill my last commission to him, realizing that he had failed to carry out my whispered instructions and now off the beat and for the moment lost. "It was Karl's wish that Triana be able to provide a gift to each of her sisters."

"Listen," said Roz. "How much is there? You don't have to give anything to us. You don't have to give anything to her or me or anyone. You don't . . . Look, if he left you . . ."

"You have no idea," I said. "Really, there is plenty. There's so much it's purely simple."

Rosalind sat back, drew in her chin, raised her eyebrows and peered through her glasses at the check. Her tall willowy husband, Glenn, was at a loss for words, touched, amazed, confused by what he saw around him.

I looked up at the wounded and quivering Katrinka. "Don't worry anymore, Trink," I said. "Don't worry ever again . . . about anything."

"You're insane!" Katrinka said. Her husband reached out to take her hand.

"Mrs. Russell," said Grady to Katrinka, "let me recommend you take the check to the Whitney Bank tomorrow and endorse and deposit it as you would any check, and I am certain you will be happy to discover that your funds are readily available to you. It is a gift and carries no tax penalty for you. No tax whatsoever. Now, I would appreciate some statement with regard to this house, that you will not in future—"

"Not now," I said. "It doesn't matter."

Rosalind leant towards me again. "I want to know how much. I want to know what this costs you to do this for me and for her."

"Mrs. Bertrand," said Grady to Rosalind, "believe me, your sister is amply provided for. In addition, and perhaps this will make my point as delicately as possible, the late Mr. Wolfstan had also endowed a new hall in the city museum to be entirely devoted to paintings of St. Sebastian."

Glenn in great distress shook his head. "No, we can't."

Katrinka narrowed her eyes as if she suspected a plot.

I tried to form words. They were just beyond my reach. I gestured to Grady and mouthed the word "explain." I made an open shrugging gesture.

"Ladies," said Grady, "let me assure you, Mr. Wolfstan left your sister very well off. These checks really, to be quite literal and frank with you, do not make a particle of difference."

And so the moment was over.

Just like that. It was over.

The terrible speech had *not* been made to Katrinka, take this million and never . . . and there had been no stunning realization for her that she had forfeited forever in hate the possible share of something much larger.

The moment was gone. The chance was gone.

Yet it was ugly, uglier even than I could have planned it because she stood now, furious with hate, and she wanted to spit in my face and there was no way in the world she was going to risk losing one million dollars.

"Well, Glenn and I are grateful for this," said Roz in her low, earnest voice. "I honestly never expected one thin dime from Karl Wolfstan, it's kind, it's kind that he would even, but are you sure, Grady? Are you telling us the real truth?"

"Oh, yes, Mrs. Bertrand, your sister is well off, very well off—"

I saw a vision of dollar bills. A true vision of them flying towards me, each dollar bill with tiny wings on it. The most insane vision, but I think for the very first time in my life there was a relaxed realization of what Grady was saying, that that type of worry was no longer required, that that type of misery was no longer part of the larger picture, that the mind could turn now in perfect peace and quiet upon itself, Karl had seen to that, and his people, it had been nothing to them to see to it, the mind could turn to finer things.

"So that's how it was, then," Katrinka said, looking at me, her eyes tired and dull the way eyes get after hours of fury.

I didn't answer.

Katrinka said:

"It was just all a dry financial arrangement between you and him, and you never even had the decency to tell us."

No one spoke.

"With him dying of AIDS, you might have had the decency to let us know."

I shook my head. I opened my mouth, I started to say, no, no, that's abomination, what you're saying, I . . . but it struck me suddenly as just the perfect thing that Katrinka would do, and I began instead to smile and then to laugh.

"Honey, honey, don't cry," said Grady. "You're going to be all right."

"Oh, but you see, it's perfect, it's . . ."

"All this time," said Katrinka, her tears returning, "You let us worry and tear our hair out!" Katrinka's voice carried over Rosalind's pleas for quiet.

"I love you," Rosalind said.

"When Faye comes home," I whispered to Roz as if the two of us, sisterlike, had to hide from all the rest, at this round table in this front room. "When Faye comes home, she'll love the way the house looks now, don't you think, all of this, all that Karl did, it's so beautiful."

"Don't cry."

"Oh, I'm not, am I? I thought I was laughing. Where is Katrinka?" Several people had left the room.

I got up and left the room. I went into the dining room, the heart and soul of the house, the room in which so long ago Rosalind and I had had that terrible fight with the Rosary. Good Lord, it is a surfeit of memory that drives people to drink, I think so sometimes. Mother must have remembered such terrible, terrible things. We'd torn Mother's Rosary to pieces! A Rosary.

"I have to go to bed," I said. "My head aches, I keep remembering. I'm remembering bad things. I can't get them out of my mind. I must ask you something. Roz, my love . . ."

"Yes," she said at once, both hands extended, her dark eyes fixed firmly on me with utter sympathy.

"The violinist, do you remember him, the night that Karl died. There was a man out there on St. Charles Avenue and—"

The others crowded under the small chandelier in the hall. Katrinka and Grady were in a furious discussion. Martin was being stern with Katrinka, and Katrinka was almost screaming.

"Oh, him," said Roz, "that guy with the violin." Rosalind laughed. "Yeah, I remember him. He was playing Tchaikovsky. Of course he was really, you know, doing it up, as if anybody had to improvise on Tchaikovsky, but he was—" She cocked her head. "He was playing Tchaikovsky."

I moved further with Rosalind across the dining room. She was talking . . . and I couldn't understand. In fact, it was so strange I thought she was making it up, and then I remembered—. But it was a wholly different kind of recollection, with none of the sting and heat of these other memories; it was pale and long ago released and generally let to slide away, or deliberately veiled under dust. I didn't know. But now I didn't fight it.

"That picnic, out there in San Francisco," she said, "and you know all you beatniks and hippies were there, and I was scared to death we were all gonna get busted and dumped in San Francisco Bay, and you took that violin and just played and played and Lev danced! It was like the Devil came into you, that time and the other time when you were little and you got a hold of that little three-quarter violin up at Loyola, remember that? And you just played and played and played but—"

"Yes, but I could never make it happen again. I tried and tried, after both those times . . ."

Rosalind shrugged and hugged me close.

I turned and saw us in the mirror—not the hungry, thin, bitter girls fighting over the Rosary. I saw us now. Rubensesque women. Rosalind kissed my cheek. I saw us in the mirror, the two sisters, she with her beautiful white curly hair bouffant and natural around her face, her large soft body in flowing black silk, and I with my bangs and straight hair and ruffled blouse and thick hateful arms, but it didn't matter, the flaws of our bodies, I just saw us, and I wanted so to be here on this spot with her, in relief, to feel the glorious flow of relief, but I couldn't.

I just couldn't.

"Do you think Mother wants us in this house?" I stared to cry.

"Oh, for the love of God," said Rosalind. "Who gives a damn! You go to bed. You should have never stopped drinking. I'm going to drink a six-pack of Dixie beer. You want us to stay upstairs?"

"No." She knew the answer to that.

In the doorway of the bedroom I turned and looked at her.

"What is it?"

My face must have frightened her.

"The violinist, you do remember him, the one playing out there on the corner when Karl . . . I mean when everybody . . ."

"I told you. Yes. Of course." She said again that it was definitely Tchaikovsky, and I could tell by the way that she lifted her head that she was very proud she could identify the music, and of course she was right, or so I thought. She looked so dreamy and sympathetic and sweet and gentle to me, as if nothing of meanness had survived in her at all, and here we were—and we were not old.

I felt no older today than any other day. I didn't know what it meant to feel old. Old. Fears go. Meanness goes. If you pray, if you are blessed, if you try!

"He kept coming here, that guy with the violin," Rosalind said, "while you were in the hospital. I saw him this evening out there, just watching. Maybe he doesn't like playing for crowds," she said. "He's damned good, if you ask me! I mean the guy's as good as any violinist I ever heard in person or on any record."

"Yes," I said. "That he is, isn't he?"

I waited until the door was shut to cry again.

I like to cry alone. It felt so marvelously good, to cry and cry, totally removed from any hint of censure! No one to tell you yes or no, no one to beg for forgiveness, no one to intervene.

Cry.

I lay down on the bed and cried, and listened to them out there, and felt so tired suddenly, as if I had carried all those coffins to the grave myself . . . Think of it, scaring Lily like that, coming into the hospital room and bursting into tears and letting Lily see it, and Lily saying, "Mommie, you're scaring me!" And at that moment, when I'd come back late from the bar, I'd been drunk, hadn't I? I'd spent those years drunk, but never too drunk, never so that I couldn't . . . and then that awful, awful moment of seeing her small white face, her hair all gone, her head cancer-bald yet lovely like the bud of a flower, and my stupid, stupid, ill-timed bursting into tears. Cruel, cruel. Dear God.

Where was that brilliant blue sea with its ghostly foam?

When I realized he'd been playing, it must have been after a long while.

The house had gone quiet.

He must have started low, and it did have the pure Tchaikovskian sweetness this time, the civilized eloquence, one might say, rather than the raw horror of the Gaelic fiddlers that had so enthralled me last night. I sank deep into the music, as it came nearer and grew more distinct.

"Yes, play for me," I whispered.

I dreamed.

I dreamed of Lev and Chelsea, of us fighting in the café and Lev saying, "So many lies, lies," and realizing what he meant, that he and Chelsea—and she so distraught, so basically kind, and naturally loving him, and wanting him, and my friend, and then the most terrible things came tumbling back, memories of Father's angry speeches and Mother crying in this house, crying in this very house, for us, and I not coming to her, but all this was wedded with sleep. The violin sang and sang and pressed for the pain, pressed as only Tchaikovsky might, deep into agony, into its ruby red sweetness and vividness.

Drive me mad, not a chance, but why do you want me to suffer, why do you want me to remember these things, why do you play so beautifully when I remember?

Here comes the sea.

The pain was wedded with drowsiness; Mother's poem of night from the old book: "The flowers nod, the shadows creep, a star comes over the hill."

The pain was wedded to sleep.

The pain was wedded to his exquisite music.

❧ 8 ❧

MISS HARDY was in the parlor. Althea was just setting down the coffee when I came into the room.

"Ordinarily I wouldn't think of disturbing you at this time," Miss Hardy said, half rising as I bent to kiss her cheek. She wore a peach-colored dress, very becoming to her, her silver hair combed back into a perfect frame of disciplined yet yielding curls.

"But you see," she said, "he's requested it. He asked us specifically if we would invite you because he respects you so, your taste for music and your kindness to him."

"Miss Hardy, I'm sleepy and dull-witted. Bear with me. Who is this we're talking about?"

"Your violinist friend. I had no idea you even knew the man. As I said, to ask you to come out at a time like this is not something I would do, but he said you would want to come."

"And where is that, I mean, I'm not clear, forgive me."

"The Chapel around the block, tonight. For the little concert."

"Ah." I sat back.

The Chapel.

With a shock I saw all the familiar objects of the Chapel, as if a sudden discharge of memory had let loose details irretrievable until now—the Chapel. I saw it, not as it was now after the Vatican Council II and a radical remodeling, but as it had been in the old days, when we went there to Mass together. When Mother took us, Roz and me, hand in hand.

I must have looked perplexed. I heard the singing in Latin.

"Triana, if this upsets you, I'll simply tell him that it's too soon for you to be going out."

"He's going to play in the Chapel?" I asked. "Tonight." I nodded with her in confirmation. "A little concert? A recital, sort of."

"Yes, for the benefit of the building. You know how bad the building is. It needs paint, it needs a new roof. You know all that. It was all rather astonishing. He simply walked into the Preservation Guild office and said he was willing to do it. Have a concert with all proceeds for the building. We'd never heard of him. But how he plays! Only a Russian could play like that. Of course he says he is an émigré. He never lived in Russia as it is now, which is quite obvious, he's quite the European, really, but only a Russian could play like that."

"What is his name?"

She was surprised. "I thought you knew him," she said, softening her voice, knitting her brows with concern. "Excuse me, Triana. He told us that you knew him."

"I do, I know him very well. I think it's wonderful that he'll play at the Chapel. But I don't know his name."

"Stefan Stefanovsky," she said carefully. "I memorized it, I wrote it down, went over the spelling with him. Russian names." She repeated it, said it in a simple unadorned way, with the accent on the first syllable of Stefan. The man had an undeniable charm, with or without the violin. Very distinctive dark eyebrows, very straight across, eccentric hair, at least in these days, for a classical musician.

I smiled. "It is all changed now. The longhairs are the rock stars, not the longhairs anymore, how odd. And you know the strange thing is when I look back on all the concerts I've ever attended—even the very first—it was Isaac Stern, you know—I don't remember longhairs having any long hair."

I was worrying her.

"I'm delighted," I said gathering my thoughts. "So you thought him handsome?"

"Oh, everyone swooned when he walked in the door! Such a dramatic demeanor. And then the accent, and when he just raised the violin and bow and began to play. I think he stopped traffic outside."

I laughed.

"It was something very different he played for us," she said, "from what he played—" Politely she stopped, and lowered her eyes.

". . . on the night you found me here, with Karl," I said.

"Yes."

"That was beautiful music."

"Yes, I suppose it was, and I really didn't hear it, so to speak."

"Understandable."

She was suddenly confused, doubtful about the propriety or wisdom of this.

"After he played, he spoke very highly of you, said you truly were the rare person who understood his music. And this to a room of fainting women of all ages, including half the Junior League."

I laughed. It wasn't merely to put her at ease. It was the image of the women, young and old, being swept off their feet by this phantom.

My, but this was a stunning shock, this turn of events. This invitation.

"What time tonight, Miss Hardy?" I asked. "What time will he play? I don't intend to miss this."

She stared at me for a moment in lingering discomfort and then with great relief plunged into the details.

I left for the concert at five minutes before the time.

It was dark, of course, it being the season for darkness at eight o'clock, yet there was no rain tonight and only a friendly, gentle air, almost warm.

I walked out my own gate, turned left at the corner of Third and walked slowly all the way back to Prytania Street on the old, broken brick sidewalks, treasuring every bump, every hole, every hazard. My heart was thumping. In fact, I was so full of anticipation I could scarcely stand it. The last few hours had dragged and I had thought only of him.

I'd even dressed for him! How stupid. Of course for me that only meant a better white ruffled blouse with more and finer lace, and a better black silk skirt to the ankles and a light sleeveless tunic of black velvet. The better Triana Uniform. That's all it meant. And my hair loose and clean. That's all.

A dim street lamp burned ahead of me as I approached the end of the block, making the darkness all the more oppressive around me, and for the first time I realized there was no oak any longer on the corner of Third and Prytania!

It must have been years since I had walked back this block, stood here. There had been an oak, surely, because I could remember the streetlamp shining through it, down on the high black iron fence and on the grass. Strong, hefty, black oak branches, twisted and not so very thick, not so heavy as to fall down.

Who has done this to you? I spoke to the earth, the broken place in the bricks. I saw it now, where the oak had been, but all roots were gone. It was only earth, the inevitable earth. Who took this tree that might have lived for centuries?

Ahead, across Prytania, the deeper regions of the Garden District seemed hollow and black and empty, their mansions folded up and latched.

But to the left of me, on Prytania, before the Chapel there were bright lights, and I could hear a very agreeable mingling of cheerful voices.

Only the Chapel occupied this corner lot, just as my house occupied the corner lot facing St. Charles Avenue far away and directly behind, past cherry laurels and oaks and wild grass, past bamboo and oleander.

The Chapel was the bottom floor of a great house, much larger and finer than my own. It was a house just as old as mine, and born infinitely more grand, of masonry and trimmed in very fancy ironwork.

It had had once—most certainly—the classic center hall with parlors on either side, but that had all been changed long before I was born. The whole first floor had been hollowed out, dressed with statues and holy pictures and a gorgeous white trimmed altar. A tabernacle of gold. What else? Our Lady of Perpetual Help, a Russian icon.

That was the Blessed Mother to whom we had brought our flowers.

Ironic, that, but absolutely of no significance.

Of course, he knew how much I had loved this place, this building, this garden, this fence, the Chapel itself, and he knew all about the little wilting handful of flowers on the Altar Rail, stems broken by our

little hands, the little bouquets that we would leave during our evening walks, Rosalind and Mother and I, before the war ended, before
Katrinka and Faye came, before the drinking came. Before Death
came. Before Fear came. Before Sorrow.

He knew. He knew how it had been—this great massive house
which still looked on the outside like a grand home, its front porches
parallel and broad, its colonnettes made of iron, its twin chimneys
straight and firm atop the high gable of the third floor in that unmistakable New Orleans pattern.

Chimneys floating together under the stars. Chimneys for fire-
places long gone, perhaps.

In those upstairs rooms, my Mother had gone to school as a girl. In
the Chapel itself, my Mother's coffin had lain on the bier. In the
Chapel alone, I had played the organ in the dark, on summer nights,
when the priests let me lock up, and no one was there. I tried and tried
to make music.

Only the Blessed Sacrament could have been so patient with the
miserable broken bits of song I played, the chords, the hymns I tried
to learn with some vague promise that I could one day play if and
when the organ lady would allow, but which never happened because
I never got good enough and was never brave enough even to
attempt it.

The Garden District ladies always wore such pretty hats to Mass. I
think we were the only ones who wore kerchiefs like peasants.

It didn't take a death to make me remember, a funeral to make me
cherish, or even the sweet twilight visits with flowers in our hands, or
the picture of Mother with only a few other girls, rare high school
graduates for that time—bobbed hair and white stockings—standing
with their bouquets to the left of this very gate.

Who ever prayed in that old Chapel who didn't remember it?

That old Catholicism was never without the scent of pure beeswax
candles, and the incense that lingered forever in any church where the
Monstrance had been held high, and there had been sweet-faced
saints in the shadows then, artists of pain like St. Rita with the wound
in her forehead, and Christ's dreadful journey to Calvary marked in
the Stations on the walls.

The Rosary wasn't rote prayer, but a chant through which we

pictured the suffering Christ. The Prayer of Quiet meant to sit very still in the pew, clear the mind, let God speak directly to you. I knew the Latin of the Ordinary of the Mass by heart. I knew what the hymns meant.

All that had been swept away. Vatican II.

But a Chapel still it was, for Catholics who prayed now in English.

I had come to it only once in its modern style—for a wedding three or four years ago. Everything I held dear had been taken away. The Little Infant Jesus of Prague in his golden crown was no more.

Ah, but you have a motive in this. How you honor me. A concert for my benefit in this, of all places where I'd come before I killed her, or any of them, worrying about flowers on the Altar Rail.

I smiled to myself, leaning against the fence for a moment. I glanced back to see Lacomb keeping watch over me. I'd told him to hang around. I was as scared of real people in the dark streets as anybody else.

After all, the dead can only do so much to you, until you meet a ghost, that is, a ghost who can play music out of God's mind, and a ghost who has a name: Stefan.

"Some plan you have," I whispered. I looked up and envisioned the oak branches surrounding and obscuring this light, only it wasn't this light then.

Light streamed out of the unadorned windows of the Chapel—windows like my own, to the floor, with many panes and some still with the old glass, wavery, melting, though I couldn't see such a thing from here. I just knew it and thought of it, beholding the house, beholding the time, beholding all of this to anchor my thoughts to the clever design of this stunt, this drama.

So he was going to play the violin for everybody, was he? And I must be there.

I turned to the left on Prytania and walked down towards the gates. Miss Hardy and several other classic Garden District ladies stood there to greet those coming.

Cabs stopped in the street. I saw the all too familiar uniformed policeman looking on—for this dark paradise was now too dangerous at evening for the old ones to come out, and they had indeed come out to hear him.

I knew some names; some faces; some I'd never known; some I simply didn't place. But it was a good crowd, perhaps one hundred, lots of gentlemen in light wool suits, and almost every woman in a dress, southern style, except for a few very modern young people who wore genderless clothes, and a flock of college students, or so they appeared, probably from the Conservatory uptown, where I had once struggled so wretchedly at fourteen to become a violinist.

My, how your fame has spread.

As I took Miss Hardy's hand and greeted Renee Freeman and Mayteen Ruggles, I peered inside and realized that he was already there, the main attraction.

The *thing* itself, as Henry James's brave governess would have said of Quint and Miss Jessel without a qualm, the very *thing*—standing in the aisle, before the altar, which had been demurely covered for this occasion, and he was clean and properly dressed and his lustrous hair combed as well as mine. He wore his two small braids again, knotted in back, to keep his hair from falling too much into his face.

He was distant, but unmistakable, and I watched him talking to them.

For the first time . . . for the first time since it had begun . . . I thought, I am going out of my mind. I don't want to be sane. I don't want to be present or aware or alive. I don't. I don't. He's there, among the living, just as if he were one of them, just as if he were real and alive. He was talking to students. He was showing them the violin.

And my dead are gone! Gone! What charm could make Lily rise? A wretched story came to mind, Kipling, "The Monkey's Paw," the three wishes, you don't want the dead to come back, no, you don't pray for that.

But he had penetrated the walls of my room, and then vanished. This I'd seen. He was a ghost. He was dead.

Look at the living people for once, or start screaming.

Mayteen wore the loveliest perfume. She was my mother's oldest living friend. She said words which I strained to understand. My heart filled my ears.

". . . just to touch such an instrument, an actual Stradivarius."

I squeezed her hand. I loved the perfume. It was something very old and simple, something not very expensive, that came in pink bottles and the powder came in pink flowered boxes.

My head was buzzing with the sound of my heart. I made a few simple words, just about as bland as an amnesiac could possibly conjure, then I hurried up the marble steps, steps that were always slippery when it rained and I walked into the harshly lighted modern Chapel.

Forget the details.

I am a person who always sits in the front row. What was I doing now, going into the back pew?

But I couldn't go closer. And this was a small place, this, very small, and from this corner of the back pew I could see him perfectly.

He bowed to the woman beside him, his partner in conversation—What kind of things do ghosts say at such moments?—and he held the violin out for the young girls to examine. I saw the deep luster, the seam down the back. He held the violin without ever letting go of it or the bow, and he didn't look up at me as I sank back against the oak of the pew and looked at him.

People shuffled in. I nodded several times at those who whispered greetings. I didn't hear anything that was said.

You're here, among the living, as solid as they are, and they will hear you.

He looked up suddenly, without fully raising his head, and his eye fixed me.

Others have always seen and heard me.

Several figures moved between us. The little building was all but full. Two ushers stood in the back, but they had chairs they could use—if they wanted them.

The lights were dimmed. A single well-placed spot covered him in a dusty tarnished haze. How finely he had dressed for this, how white his shirt, and how clean his hair, and the braids holding his hair back—so simple.

Miss Hardy had risen to her feet. She spoke soft words of explanation and introduction.

He stood calm and collected, his clothes formal, yet rather timeless, a coat that could have been two hundred years old or made yesterday, long and shaped a bit, and he wore a pale tie with his shirt. I couldn't tell if the color was violet or gray, the color of the tie.

He was dashing, no doubt of it. "You're insane," I whispered to myself, barely moving my lips. "You want a highborn ghost out of novels charged with significant romance. You dream."

I wanted to cover my face. I wanted to leave. And to never leave. I wanted to stay and to run. I wanted at least to get out of my purse something, a paper handkerchief, anything, something to somehow blunt the force of this, rather like putting your hands up over your eyes during a film, and watching through slatted fingers.

But I couldn't move.

With admirable poise, he thanked Miss Hardy, and thanked us all. Even, accented, but quite understandable, it was the voice I'd heard in my bedroom—a young man's voice. He looked half my age.

He lifted the instrument to his chin, and raised the bow. The air quivered. No one stirred or coughed or rumpled a program.

I deliberately pictured the blue sea, the blue sea of the dream and the dancing ghosts; I saw them, I closed my eyes and saw the radiant sea beneath the invisible but nearby moon, and the distant arms of the land reaching out.

I opened my eyes.

He had stopped. He glared at me.

I don't think people knew what his expression meant, or in what direction he looked or why. He had all the license of the eccentric on his side. And he was so fine to look at, fine, fine, thin and imperial as Lev had been, yes, not at all unlike Lev, only his hair was so dark and his eyes so black, and Lev, like Katrinka, had been fair. Lev's children were fair.

I shut my eyes. Damn it to hell, I had lost the image of the sea, and as he began to play, I saw those old trivial and horrible things, and turned slightly to the side. Someone beside me touched my hand as if in sympathy.

A widow, a madwoman, I thought quite consciously, having stayed in a house with a body for two days. Everybody must have known. Everybody in New Orleans knew anything that was worth knowing, and something that peculiar was probably worth knowing.

Then his music cut to the quick.

He brought the bow down and went immediately into the rich dark of the lower chords, the Minor Key, a hint of dreaded things to come. The tone was so refined and so controlled, the pitch so perfect, the rhythm so spontaneous that I thought of nothing, absolutely nothing but this.

There was no need for tears, no need to hold them back either. There was only this richly unfolding song.

Then I saw Lily's face. Twenty years brushed by. Lily lay dying in her bed this very minute. "Mommie, don't cry, you're scaring me."

9

I SENT the vision flying. I opened my eyes and let them rove over the peeling plaster ceiling of this neglected place, over the indifferent metal decorations that were so modern and so utterly meaningless. I understood the battle now, even as the music flooded me and Lily's voice was right by my ear, intermingled with the music, and part of it.

I looked directly at him, and I thought only of him. I focused on him and refused to think of anything else. He couldn't stop his playing. Indeed, he was energized, he was brilliant, his tone was beyond description it was so controlled yet so relaxed, and the pitch so poignant.

Yes, Tchaikovsky's concerto it was, which I knew by heart from my disks, with the orchestral parts woven right into it, so that it became a rich solo piece of his own making, with the heavy solo thread and all the other threads completely balanced.

Music to tear you to pieces.

I tried to breathe slowly, to relax and not clench my hands.

Suddenly something changed. It was total, like when the sun goes behind a cloud. Only this was night and this was the Chapel.

The saints! The old saints were back. The old décor of thirty years ago surrounded me.

The pew was old and dark with a scrolled arm beneath the fingers of my left hand and beyond him stood the traditional and venerable high altar, with the fully carved and fully painted figures of the Last Supper beneath it, set in their glass case.

I hated him. I hated him for this, because I couldn't stop looking at these lost saints, at the painted plaster Infant Jesus of Prague holding his tiny globe, at the old dusty yet vibrant pictures of Christ carrying his cross down one side of the room and up the other between the darkling windows.

You are cruel.

And that is what they were, the windows of evening time, darkling, full of lavender light, and he stood in softened shadows, and the old ornate Communion Rail crossed in front of him, which had been taken away a long time ago with everything else. He stood fixed in this perfect rendering of everything I remembered, but which I couldn't have recalled in detail a moment before!

I was transfixed. I stared at the Icon of Our Lady of Perpetual Help that hung behind him, over the altar, over the blazing golden tabernacle. Saints, the smell of wax. I could see the red glass candles. I could see everything. I could smell it, the wax and incense again, and he played on, varying the concerto, dipping his slender body into the music and drawing gasps from the crowd that listened to him, but who were they?

This is evil. It is beautiful, but it is evil, because it is cruel.

I closed and opened my eyes. See what is here now! For an instant I did.

Then the veil came down again. Was he going to bring her back? Mother? Was she coming, to lead me and Rosalind up the aisle, in old-fashioned safety in the shadowy evening Chapel? No, the memory overrode his inventions.

The memory was too hurtful, too awful. The memory of her not here in this sacred place in the happy times before she was poisoned like Hamlet's mother, no, the memory of her drunk and lying on a burnt mattress, her head only inches from the burning hole. That is what I saw, and Rosalind and I running back and forth with the pots of water, and beautiful Katrinka, with her yellow curls and huge blue eyes, only three years old, staring mutely at Mother, as the room filled with smoke.

You will not get away with this

He was deep into the concerto. I deliberately filled the Chapel with lights, I deliberately envisioned the audience till it was the people, had to be, the very people I now knew. I did this and I stared at him, but he was too strong for me.

I was a child in my mind, approaching the Altar Rail. "But what do they do with our flowers after we leave them?" Rosalind wanted to light a candle.

I stood up.

The crowd was magnetized by him; they were so totally in his thrall that I went unnoticed. I moved out of the pew, and turned my back on him and walked down the marble steps and out and away from his music, which never slackened but grew all the more heated, heated, as if he thought he could burn me up with it, damn him.

Lacomb, cigarette in hand, rose from his gateside slouch and we walked almost side by side, fast down the flags. I could hear the music. I looked deliberately at the flags. If my mind veered, I saw that sea again, that foam. I saw it in sudden crashes of wild color; this time I heard it.

Even as I walked, I heard the sea and saw it and saw the street before me.

"Slow down, boss, you gonna trip and break my neck!" Lacomb said.

Such a clean smell. The sea and the wind together give birth to the cleanest finest scent, and yet everything that lurks below the surface of the sea can give off the stench of death if dragged up to the sandy bank.

I walked faster and faster, looking carefully at the broken bricks and weeds growing among them.

We reached my light, thank God, my garage, but there was no gate open there. Mother's gate was gone, taken away, that old green painted wooden gate fitted into the brick arch through which she had walked right into death.

I stood motionless. I could still hear the music, but it was far away. It was tuned for human ears that were near to him and he seemed bound to that by some rule of his nature that I was very pleased to discover, though I wanted better to understand what it meant.

We walked up to the Avenue, and towards the front gate. Lacomb opened it for me, and held it, this heavy gate that always fell forward, that could slam on you and knock you right down on the pavement. New Orleans abhors a plumb line.

I went up the steps, and into the house. Lacomb must have unlocked the door, but I didn't notice. I told him I would listen to music in the front room. Shut all the doors.

He knew this pattern.

"You don't like your friend over there?" he asked in a deep voice, the words so run together like syrup that it took me a brief second to interpret this.

"I like Beethoven better," I said.

But *his* music came like a hiss through the walls. It had no eloquence now, no compelling meaning. It was the strum of the bees in the graveyard.

The doors were shut to the dining room. The doors were shut to the hall. I went through the disks which had been put in perfect alphabetical order.

Solti, Beethoven's *Ninth*, Second Movement.

In an instant I had it in the machine and the kettle drums had put him completely to rout. I turned the volume loud as it would go, and there came the familiar trudging march. Beethoven, my captain, my guardian angel.

I lay down on the floor.

The chandeliers of these parlors were small, not decorated with gold like the Baccarats of the hall and dining room. These chandeliers had only crystal and glass. It was nice to lie on the clean floor and look up at the chandelier which had only dim candle bulbs in it.

The music blotted him out. On and on went the march. I hit the button which told the machine to repeat, but to repeat only this band of the disk. I closed my eyes.

What do you yourself want to remember? Trivia, nonsense, humor.

In my young years I daydreamed incessantly to music; I always saw his brand of images! I saw people and things and drama, and was worked up almost to making fists as I listened.

But not now; now it was just the music, the driving rhythm of the music, and some vague commitment to the idea of climbing the eternal mountain in the eternal forest, but not a vision, and safe within this thundering insistent song I closed my eyes.

He didn't take too long.

Maybe I had lain there an hour.

He came right through the locked doors, materializing instantly, the doors quivering behind him, the grand violin and bow choked in his left hand.

"You walk out on me!" he said.

His voice rose over the sound of Beethoven. Then he walked towards me in loud menacing steps. I climbed up on my elbows, then sat up. My vision was blurred. The light shone on his forehead, on the dark neat brushed brows that made such a distinct line, as he glared down at me, narrowing his eyes, looking perhaps as hostile as any creature I've ever seen.

The music moved on over him and over me.

He kicked the machine with his foot. The music faltered and roared. He tore the plug out of the wall.

"Ah, clever!" I said before the silence came down. I could scarcely keep from smiling in triumph.

He panted, as if he'd run some distance, or maybe it was only the effort of being material, of playing for spectators, of passing invisible through walls and then coming alive in lurid flaming splendor.

"Yes," he said contemptuously and spitefully, looking at me, his hair falling down dark and straight on both sides. The two small braids had come undone and mixed now with the longer locks, loose and shining.

He bore down on me with all his powers to frighten. But it only brought some old actor's beauty to my mind, yes, with his sharp nose and enthralling eyes, he had the dark beauty of Olivier of years gone by, in a filmed play by Shakespeare, Olivier as the humpback and deformed and evil King Richard III. Irresistible, a lovely trick in paint, to be both ugly and beautiful.

An old film, an old love, old poetry never to be forgotten. I laughed.

"I'm not humpbacked and I'm not deformed!" he said. "And I'm not a player of a part for you! I'm here with you!"

"So it seems!" I answered. I sat up straight, pulling my skirt down over my knees.

"Seems?" He used Hamlet's speech to mock me. " 'Seems, madam! Nay, it is; I know not "seems." ' "

"You overtax yourself," I said. "Your talent's for music. Don't wax desperate!" I said, using words more or less from the same play.

I grabbed hold of the table and climbed to my feet. He stormed towards me. I almost flinched, but held fast to the table, looking at him.

"Ghost!" I said. "You had a whole living world looking at you! What do you want here when you can have that? All those ears and eyes."

"Don't anger me, Triana!" he said.

"Oh, so you know my name."

"As much as you know it," he turned to the left and then to the right. He walked towards the windows, towards the eternal light dance of the traffic behind the lace birds.

"I won't tell you to go away," I said.

His back to me still, he lifted his head.

"I'm too lonely for you!" I said. "Too fascinated!" I confessed. "When I was young, I might have run screaming from a ghost, run screaming! Believing it with a total superstitious Catholic heart. But now?"

He only listened.

My hands shook badly. I couldn't tolerate this. I pulled out the chair from the table. I sat down and rested against the back. The chandelier was reflected in a blurred circle in the polish of the table, and all around it, the chairs with their Chippendale wings sat at attention.

"Now I'm too eager," I said, "too despairing, too careless." I tried to make my voice firm, yet keep it soft. "I don't know the words. Sit here! Sit down and lay down the violin and tell me what you want. Why do you come to me?"

He didn't answer.

"You know what you are?" I asked.

He turned around, furious, and came near to the table. Yes, he had the very magnetism of Olivier in that old film, all made up of dark contrasts and white skin and a dedicated evil. He had the long mouth, but it was fuller!

"Stop thinking of that other man!" he whispered.

"It's a film, an image."

"I know what it is, you think I'm a fool? Look at me. I'm here! The film is old, the maker dead, the actor gone, dust, but I am with you."

"I know what you are, I told you."

"Tell me what precisely, then, if you will?" He cocked his head to the side, he gnawed his lip a little, and he wrapped both his hands around the bow and the neck of the violin.

He was only a few feet away. I saw the wood more distinctly, how richly lacquered it was. Stradivarius. They had said that word, and there he held it, this sinister and sacred instrument, he just held it, letting the light catch it and race up and down its curves as if the thing were real.

"Yes?" he said. "Do you want to touch it or hear it? You know damned good and well that you can't play it. Even a Strad wouldn't mend your miserable faults! You'd make it shriek or even shatter in outrage if you tried."

"You want me to . . ."

"No such thing," he said, "only to remind you that you have no gift for this, only a longing, only a greed."

"A greed, is it? Was it greed you meant to implant in the souls of those who listened in the Chapel? Greed you meant to nourish and feed? You think Beethoven . . ."

"Don't speak of him."

"I will and I do. Do you think it was greed that forged—"

He came to the table, consigned the violin to his left hand and laid down his right hand as near to me as he could. I thought his long hair hanging down would touch my face. There seemed no perfume to his clothes, not even the smell of dust.

I swallowed and my vision blurred. Buttons, the violet tie, the flashing violin. It was all a ghost, the clothes, the instrument.

"You're right on that. Now what am I? What was your pious judgment upon me—about to be pronounced—when I interrupted you?"

"You are like the human sick," I said. "You need me in your suffering!"

"You whore!" he said. He backed up.

"Oh, that I've never been," I said. "Never had the courage. But you are diseased and you need me." I continued, "You're like Karl. You're like Lily in the end, though God knows—" I broke off, switched. "You're like my Father when he was dying. You need me. Your torment wants a witness in me. You're jealous and eager for that, aren't you, as eager as any human who is dying, except in the last moments perhaps when the dying forget everything and see things we can't see—"

"What makes you think they do?"

"You did not?" I asked.

"I never died," he said, "properly, I should explain. But you know that. I never saw comforting lights or heard the singing of angels. I heard gunshots and shouts and curses!"

"Did you?" I asked. "Such drama, but then you are very fancy, aren't you?"

He drew back as if he'd let me pick his pocket.

"Sit down," I said. "I've sat beside many a deathbed, you know I have. That's why you chose me. Maybe you're ready to end your little ghostly wandering."

"I am not dying, lady!" he declared. He pulled back the chair and sat opposite. "I grow stronger by the minute, by the hour, by the year."

He relaxed in the chair. That put four feet of polished wood between us.

His back was to the blinkering window curtains, but the dull mist of the chandelier revealed his whole face, too young to have ever been an evil king in any play, and too full of hurt suddenly for me to enjoy it.

I wouldn't glance away, however.

I watched. He revealed it.

"So what's it about?" I asked.

He seemed to swallow as surely as a human being, and to chew on his lip again, and then he pressed his lips together for discipline.

"It's a duet," he said.

"I see."

"I am to play and you are to listen, and you are to suffer and to lose your mind or do whatever my music drives you to do. Become a fool if you like, become mad like Ophelia in your favorite play. Become as cracked as Hamlet himself. I don't care."

"But it's a duo."

"Yes, yes, that's your proper word, a duo, not a duet, for I alone make the music."

"That's not so. I feed it and you know. In the Chapel you feasted on me and everyone there, and everyone else there was not enough, and you turned again to me, and mercilessly you made images come that meant absolutely nothing to you, and you tore my heart with the abandon of some common ignorant criminal in your desire to make suffering. Suffering you know nothing about but need. That's a duet as well as a duo. That's music by two, such a thing."

"My God, but you have speech, don't you, even if you are a musical idiot, and always were, and like to swim in the deep waters of other people's talent. Wallowing on the floor with your Little Genius, and the Maestro, and that Russian maniac, Tchaikovsky. And how you feed on death, yes, you do, you do, you know you do. You needed them all, all those deaths, you did."

He was genuinely passionate, glaring at me, letting the deep eyes widen at the perfect moments to emphasize his words. He was or had been far younger than the Olivier as Richard III.

"Don't be so stupid," I said calmly. "Stupidity doesn't become a being that doesn't have mortality for an excuse. I learned to live with death and smell it and swallow it and clean up after its slow progress, but I never needed it. My life might have been a different thing. I didn't—"

But hadn't I hurt her? It seemed entirely true. My Mother had died at my hands. I couldn't go out there now and stop her from leaving by the side gate that didn't exist. I couldn't say, "Look Father, we can't do this, we must take her to the hospital, we must stay with her, you and Roz go with Trink and I'll stay with Mother. . . ." And for what would I have done that, so she could have gotten out of the hospital as she had once before, talking her way out, playing sane and clever, and charming, and come home to lie again in a stupor, to fall again on the heater and gash her head so that the blood spread in a pool on the floor?

My father spoke, "She's set the bed on fire twice, we can't leave her here. . . ." Was that then? "Katrinka's sick, she's going into surgery now, I need you!"

Me?

And what did I want? For her to die, my Mother—for it to end, her sickness, her suffering, her humiliation, her misery. She was crying.

"Look, I won't!" I said. I shook myself all over. "It's vile and cheap, what you do, you raid my mind for things you don't need."

"They're always swimming in your ken," he said. He smiled. He looked so brightly, frankly young, unlined and unworn. Struck down surely in youth.

He glowered. "That's nonsense," he said. "I died so long ago there is nothing in me that is young. I passed into this, this 'thing,' as you so described me in your own mind earlier this evening, when you couldn't endure the grace or the elegance that you saw, I became this 'thing,' this abomination, this spirit, when your guardian, your magnificent symphonic master, was alive and was my teacher."

"I don't believe you. You speak of Beethoven. I hate you."

"He was my teacher!" he raged. And he meant it.

"That's what brought you to me, that I love him?"

"No, I don't need you to love him, or mourn your husband or dig up your daughter. And I'll drown out the Maestro, I'll drown him out with my music before we're finished, until you can't hear him, not by machine, not through memory, not through dreams."

"Oh, how kind. Did you love him as much as you love me?"

"I simply made the point that I am not young. And you will not speak of him to me with any possessive superiority, and what I loved I will tell you not."

"Bravo," I said. "When did you cease to learn, when you threw off the flesh? Did your skull thicken even as it became a phantom skull?"

He sat back. He was amazed.

And so was I, a little, but then my own riffs of words often frightened me. That's why it had been years and years since I drank.

I made such speeches often when I drank. I couldn't even remember the taste of wine or beer, and craved neither. I craved consciousness, and even my lucid dreams, dreams in which I roamed like the dream of the marble palace, knowing that I dreamt, yet there, and dreaming still, the best of both worlds.

"What do you want me to do?" he asked.

I looked up. I was seeing other things, other places. I fixed right on his face. He looked as solid as anything in the room, though totally animated, lovable, enviable, fine.

"What do I want you to do?" I asked, mockingly. "And what does the question mean? What do I want?"

"You said you were lonely for me. Well, I am for you. But I *can* let you go. I can move on—"

"No."

"I didn't think so," he said with a little flash of a smile that faded at once. He looked very serious and his eyes grew large as they relaxed.

His eyebrows were perfect and heavily black, lifted above the ridge so that they made a beautiful and commanding expression.

"All right, you've come to me," I said. "You come like something I would conjure. A violinist, the very thing I once wanted with all my heart to be, perhaps the only thing I ever tried with all my heart to be. You come. But you're not my creation. You're from somewhere else and you are hungry and needy and demanding. You're furious that you can't drive me mad, yet drawn to the very complexity that defeats you."

"I admit it."

"Well, what do you think is going to happen if you remain? You think I'm going to let you spellbind me and drag me back to every grave on which I've strewn flowers? You think I'll let you fling my lost husband, Lev, in my face, oh, I know you've forced my thoughts to him, often in these last hours, as if he were as dead as all the others, my Lev—him and his wife, Chelsea, and their children. You think I will permit this? You must want a terrible struggle. You must prepare for defeat."

"You could have kept Lev," he said softly, thoughtfully. "You were too proud. You had to be the one to say, 'Yes, go marry Chelsea.' You couldn't be betrayed. You had to be gracious, sacrificing."

"Chelsea was carrying his child."

"Chelsea wanted to kill it."

"No, she didn't, and neither did Lev. And our child had already died, and Lev wanted the child and wanted Chelsea and Chelsea wanted him."

"And so you proudly gave away this man you'd loved since he was a boy, and felt the winner, the controller, the director of the play."

"So what?" I said. "He's gone. He's happy. He has three sons, one very tall and blond and a pair of twins, and they're in pictures all over this house. Did you see them in the bedroom?"

"I did. I saw them in the hallway, too, along with the old sepia photograph of your sainted Mother, when she was a beautiful girl of thirteen with her graduation flowers and her flat chest."

"All right, so what do we do? I won't have you do this to me."

He turned to the side. He made a little humming sound. He drew up the violin from his lap, and laid it very carefully on its back on the table, and the bow beside it, and held the violin's neck with his left hand. His eyes moved slowly up to Lev's painting of the flowers on the wall above the couch, Lev's gift, my husband, the poet and painter and the father of a tall blue-eyed son.

"No, I will not think about it," I said.

I stared at the violin. A Stradivarius? Beethoven his teacher?

"Don't mock me, Triana!" he said. "He was, and so was Mozart when I was very young, a little child, so that I don't even remember him. But the Maestro was my teacher!"

His cheeks flamed. "You know nothing of me. You know nothing of the world from which I was torn. Your libraries are filled with studies of that world, its composers, its painters, the builders of its palaces, yes, even my father's name, patron of the arts, generous patron of the Maestro and yes, the Maestro was my teacher."

He broke off, and turned away.

"Ah, so I am to suffer and remember, but not you," I said. "I see. You brag as men so often do."

"No, you don't see anything," he said. "I only want you, you of all people, you who worship these names as if they were household saints—Mozart, Beethoven—I want you to know I knew them! And where they are now, I know not! I'm here, with you!"

"Yes, it is so," I said, "as you've said and I've said, but what are we to do? You know you can catch me unawares a thousand times, but I won't sink again into it. And when I dream, of the surf, of the sea, do I dream what you . . ."

"We won't speak of that, your dream."

"Oh, why, because it's a doorway to your world?"

"I have no world. I'm lost in your world."

"You had one, you have a history, you have a series of connected events behind you, trailing, don't you, and that dream comes from you because I've never seen those places."

He tapped his right fingers on the table, and tipped his head down, thinking.

"You remember," he said maliciously, smiling up at me, though he was much taller, letting his brows do the work of being ominous while his voice was naive and his mouth sweet. "You remember, after your daughter's death you had a friend named Susan."

"I had many friends after my daughter's death, good friends, and as a matter of fact there were four of them named Susan or Suzanne, or

Sue. There was Susan Mandel, who had gone to school with me; there was Susie Ryder, who came to give me solace, and then became an ally to me. There was Suzanne Clark . . ."

"No, not any of those. It's true, what you say, you've often known your women in clusters of names. Remember the Annes of your college years? The three of them, and how they joked about you being Triana, which meant three Annes. But I don't want to talk about them."

"Why would you? The memories are only pleasant."

"Then where are they now, all these friends, especially the fourth . . . Susan?"

"You're losing me."

"No, madam, I have you locked to me." He smiled broadly. "Just as tightly as when I play."

"Sensational," I said. "You know it's an old word."

"Of course."

"And that's what you are, producing all these hot sensations in me! But come now, why not talk straight, what Susan do you mean, I don't even . . ."

"The one from the south, the one with the red hair, the one that knew Lily . . ."

"Oh, that was Lily's friend, that Susan, she lived right upstairs, she had a daughter Lily's age, she—"

"Why don't you simply talk of it to me? Why should it drive you mad? Why don't you tell me? She loved Lily, that woman. Lily loved to go up to her apartment and sit with her and draw pictures, and that woman, that woman wrote to you years after Lily's death, when you were here in New Orleans; and that woman Susan who had so loved your daughter, Susan told you that your daughter had been reborn, reincarnated, you remember this?"

"Vaguely. It's a pleasure to think of that rather than the time when they were both together, since one's dead and I thought the letter was absurd. Are people reborn? Are you going to tell me such secrets?"

"Never, and furthermore I don't know. My existence is one continuous strategy. I only know that I am here and here and here, and it never ends, and those I love, or come to hate, they die, but I remain. That's what I know. And no soul has ever leapt up bright before me declaring to be the reincarnation of anyone who hurt me, hurt *me*—!"

"Go on, I'm listening."

"You remember that Susan and what she wrote."

"Yes, that Lily had been reborn in another country. Ah!" I stopped with shock. "That's what you make me see in the dream, a country to which I've never been where Lily is, that's what you would have me believe?"

"No," he said, "I only want to throw it in your face that you never went to look for her."

"Oh, pranks again, you have a thousand. Who hurt you? Who fired these guns you heard when you died? Don't you want to tell me?"

"The way Lev told you about his women, how all during Lily's illness he had had one after another young girl to comfort him, the father of a dying daughter . . ."

"You are one filthy devil," I said. "I won't match words with you. For myself, I say, he did have his girls briefly and without love, and I drank. I drank. I grew heavy? So be it. But this is pointless, or is it what you want? There is no Judgment Day. I don't believe in it. And with my faith in that, went any faith I had in Confession or Self-Defense. Go away. I'll turn the music box back on. What will you do? Break it? I have others. I can sing Beethoven. I can sing the *Violin Concerto* from memory."

"Don't dare to do that."

"Why, is there recorded music waiting for you in Hell?"

"How would I know, Triana?" he asked with sudden softness. "How would I know what they have in Hell? You see for yourself the terms of my perdition."

"Seems a lot better than eternal fire, if you ask me. But I'll play my guardian Beethoven anytime I please, and sing what I can remember even if I mangle pitch and key and melody—"

He leant forward and timidly; before I could gather my strength I dropped my gaze. I looked at the table and felt a huge misery in me, a misery rising so that I couldn't breathe. The violin. Isaac Stern in the auditorium, my childish certainty that I could attain such greatness—.

No. Don't.

I looked at the violin. I reached out. He didn't move. I couldn't cover the four feet of table. I got up and came round to the chair next to him.

He watched me the whole time, keeping his pose deliberately, as if he thought I meant to do some trick to him. Perhaps I did. Only I didn't have any tricks yet, nothing really worth trying, did I?

I touched the violin.

He looked superior and smoothly beautiful.

I sat right in front of it now, and he moved back his right hand, out of the way, so that I could touch the violin. Indeed, he moved the violin a little towards me, still gripping its neck and bow.

"Stradivarius," I said.

"Yes. One of many I once played, just one of many, and it's a ghost with me now, as surely as I am a ghost, it's a specter as I am a specter. But it's strong. It is itself as I am myself. It is a Stradivarius in this realm as truly as it was in life."

He looked down on it lovingly.

"You might say after a fashion I died for it." He glanced at me. "After Susan's letter," he asked, "why didn't you go looking for your daughter's reborn soul?"

"I didn't believe the letter. I threw it away. I thought it was foolish. I felt sorry for Susan but I couldn't answer."

He let his eyes brighten. His smile was cunning. "I think you lie. You were jealous."

"Of what on earth would I be jealous, that an old friend had lost her mind? I hadn't seen Susan in years; I don't know where she is now . . ."

"But you were jealous, consumed with rage, more jealous of her than ever of Lev and all his young girls."

"You're going have to explain this to me."

"With pleasure. You were in an agony of envy, because your reincarnated daughter revealed herself to Susan and not to you! That was your thought. It couldn't be true, because how could the link between Lily and Susan have been stronger! That's what you felt, outrage. Pride, the same pride that let you give away Lev when he didn't know his left hand from his right, when he was sick with grief, when—"

I didn't answer him.

He was absolutely right.

I had been tormented by the very idea that anyone would claim such intimacy with my lost daughter, that Susan in her seemingly addled brain would imagine that Lily, reincarnated, had confided in her instead of me.

He was right. How perfectly stupid. And how Lily had loved Susan. Oh, the bond between those two!

"So, you play another card. So what?" I reached for the violin. He didn't loosen his grip. Indeed, he tightened it.

I fondled the violin but he wouldn't allow me to move it. He watched me. It felt real; it was magnificent; it was lustrous and material and gorgeous in its own right, without a note of music coming forth from it. Ah, to touch it. To touch such a fine and old violin.

"It's a privilege, I take it?" I asked bitterly. Don't think about Susan and her story of Lily being reborn.

"Yes, it is a privilege . . . but you deserve as much."

"And why is that?"

"Because you love the sound of it perhaps more than any other mortal for whom I've ever played it."

"Even Beethoven?"

"He was deaf, Triana," he said in a whisper.

I laughed out loud. Of course. Beethoven had been deaf! The whole world knew that, as well as they knew that Rembrandt was Dutch, or that Leonardo da Vinci had been a genius. I laughed freely, kind of softly.

"That is very funny, that I should forget."

He was not amused.

"Let me hold it."

"I will not."

"But you just said—"

"So what of what I said? The privilege does not extend that far. You can't hold it. You can touch it, but that's all. You think I'd let a creature like you ever so much as pluck the string? Don't try it!"

"You must have died in a rage."

"I did."

"And you, the pupil, what did you think of Beethoven, though he couldn't hear you play, what was your estimation of him?"

"I adored him," he whispered. "I adored him as you do in your mind without ever having known him, only I did, and I was a ghost before he died. I saw his grave. I thought when I came into that old cemetery that I would die again of grief, of horror, that he was dead, that a marker stood there for him . . . but I couldn't."

He totally lost the look of spite.

"And it came so quick. That's how it is in this realm. Things are quick. Or lingering and seemingly eternal. Years had passed for me in some haze. Later, so much later, I heard of his great funeral, from the chatter of the living, of how they had carried Beethoven's coffin through the streets. Ah, Vienna loves grand funerals, loves them, and now he has his proper monument, my Maestro." His voice fell almost to silence. "How I wept at that old grave." He looked off, wondering, but his hand never relaxed on the violin.

"Remember when your daughter died, you wanted the whole world to know?"

"Yes, or to stop or to take one second to reflect or . . . something."

"And all your California friends didn't know how to sit through a simple Mass for the Dead, and half of them lost the trail of the hearse on the freeway."

"So what?"

"Well, the Maestro you so love had the funeral you so desired."

"Yes, and he is Beethoven, and you knew him and I know him. But what is Lily? Lily is what? Bones? Dust?"

He looked tender and regretful.

My voice wasn't strident or angry.

"Bones, dust, a face, I can recall perfectly—round, with a high forehead like my mother's, not like mine, oh, my mother's face," I said. "I like to think of her. I like to remember how beautiful she was . . ."

"And when Lily's hair fell out and she cried?"

"Beautiful still. You know that. Were you beautiful when you died?"

"No."

The violin felt silky and perfect.

"Sixteen ninety was the year in which it was made," he said. "Before I was born, long before. My father bought it from a man in Moscow, where I've never been, not even since, nor would I go on any account."

I looked lovingly at it. I really didn't care much about anything in the world then but it, ghost or fake or real.

"Real and spectral." He corrected me. "My father had twenty instruments made by Antonio Stradivari, all of them fine, but none as fine as this, the long violin."

"Twenty? I don't believe you!" I said suddenly. But I didn't know why I said it. Rage.

"Jealousy, that you have no talent," he said.

I studied him; he had no clear direction. He didn't know whether or not he hated me or loved me, only that he desperately needed me.

"Not you," he countered, "just someone."

"Someone who loves this?" I asked. "This violin and knows it's 'the long Strad' that the elder Stradivari made near the end of his life?" I asked. "When he had broken away from the influence of Amati?"

His smile was soft and sad, no—worse than that, deeper than that, full of hurt, or was it thanks?

"Perfect F holes," I said softly, reverently, running my fingers over them on the belly of the violin. Don't touch the string.

"No, don't," he said. "But you can . . . you can keep touching it."

"You are the one weeping now? Real tears?"

I meant it to be mean but it lost its power. I just looked at the violin and I thought how exquisite, how unexplainable. Try to tell someone who hasn't heard a violin what the sound is like, this voice of this instrument, and think—how many generations lived and died without ever hearing anything quite like it.

His tears were becoming to his long deep-set eyes. He didn't fight them. For all I knew, he made them, made them like he made the whole image of himself.

"If only it were that simple," he confided.

"A dark varnish," I said looking at the violin. "That tells the date, doesn't it, and that the back is jointed—two pieces, I've seen that, and the wood is from Italy."

"No," he said. "Though many of the others were." He had to clear his throat, or the semblance of it, in order to speak.

"It's the long violin, yes, you are right on that; they call it *stretto lungo.*"

He spoke sincerely and almost kindly. "All that knowledge in your head, all those details you know of Beethoven and Mozart, and your weeping as you listen to them, clutching your pillow—"

"I follow you," I said. "Don't forget the Russian madman as you so unkindly call him. My Tchaikovsky. You played him well enough."

"Yes, but what good did any of it do you? Your knowledge, your desperate reading of Beethoven's or Mozart's letters and the endless study of the sordid detail of Tchaikovsky's life? Look, here you are, what are you?"

"The knowledge keeps me company," I said, slowly and calmly, letting my words speak to him as much as to me, "rather like you keep me company." I leant forward, and came as close to the violin as I could. The light from the chandelier was poor. But I could see through the F hole the label, and only the round circle and the letters AS and the year, perfectly written as he had said: 1690.

I didn't kiss this thing, that seemed a wanton vulgar thing even to think of. I just wanted to hold it, put it in place on my shoulder, that much I knew how to do, to wrap my left fingers around it.

"Never."

"All right," I said with a sigh.

"Paganini had two by Antonio Stradivari when I met him, and neither was as fine as this—"

"You knew him as well?"

"Oh, yes, you might say he unwittingly played a heavy role in my downfall. He never knew what became of me. But I watched him through the dark veil, I watched him once or twice, that was all I could bear, and time had no natural measure anymore. But he never had an instrument as fine as this . . ."

"I see . . . and you had twenty."

"In my father's house, I told you. Profit by your reading. You know what Vienna was in those days. You know of princes who had private orchestras. Don't be stupid."

"And you died for just this one?"

"I would have died for any of them," he said. He let his eyes move over the instrument. "I almost did die for all of them. I . . . But this one, this was mine, or so we always said, though of course I was only his son, and there were many and I used to play all of them." He seemed to be musing.

"You did truly die for this violin?"

"Yes! And for the passion to play it. If I'd been born a talentless idiot like you, an ordinary person like you, I would have gone mad. It's a wonder you don't!"

Instantly he seemed sorry. He looked at me almost apologetically.

"But few have ever listened like you, I'll give you that."

"Thank you," I said.

"Few have ever understood the sheer language of music as you do."

"Thank you," I whispered.

"Few have ever . . . longed for such a broad range." He seemed puzzled. He looked almost helplessly at the violin before him.

I said nothing.

He became flustered. He stared at me.

"And the bow," I said, suddenly frightened that he would go, go again, disappear out of vengeance. "Did the great Stradivari make the bow too?"

"Perhaps, it's doubtful. He didn't much bother with bows. But you know that. This one could be his, it could, and of course you know the wood." His smile came again, intimate and a little wondering.

"I do? I think I don't," I said. "What wood is it?" I touched the bow, the long broad bow. "It's wide, very wide, wider than our modern bows, or those used today."

"To make a finer sound," he said, looking at it, "Oh, you do notice things."

"That is obvious. Anyone would have noticed that. I'm sure the audience in the Chapel noticed that it was a wide bow."

"Don't be so certain of what they noticed. Do you know why it is so wide?"

"So that horsehair and wood don't touch so easily, so that you can play more stridently."

"Stridently," he repeated, with a smile. "Strident. Ah, I never thought of it in that way."

"You attack often enough, you come crashing down. A slightly concave bow is necessary for that, isn't it? What is the wood of the bow, it's some special wood. I can't remember. I used to know these things. Tell me."

"I would like to," he said. "The maker I don't know, but the wood I do know and did when I was alive, and the wood is pernambuco." He studied me as if expecting something. "Does that ring no chords in your memory, pernambuco? Does it have no resonance for you?"

"Yes, but what is pernambuco? I don't—"

"Brazilwood," he said. "And it was only from Brazil that it came at the time this bow was made. Brazil."

I studied him. "Ah, yes," I said.

Suddenly, the wide sea appeared, the brilliant sparkling sea, and the moonlight flooding it, and then a great course of waves. The image was so strong it blotted him out and caught me, but then I felt him lay his hand on my hand.

I saw him. I saw the violin.

"You don't remember? Think."

"Of what?" I asked. "I see a beach, I see an ocean, I see waves."

"You see the city where your friend Susan told you your child was reborn," he said sharply.

"Brazil—." I looked at him. "In Rio, in Brazil, oh, yes, that's what Susan wrote in the letter, Lily was . . ."

"A musician in Brazil, just what you always sought to be, a musician, remember? Lily was reincarnated a musician in Brazil."

"I told you, I threw the letter away. I've never seen Brazil, why do you want me to see it?"

"I don't!" he said.

"But you do."

"No."

"Then why do I see it? Why do you wake me when I see the water and the beach? Why did I dream of it? Why did I see it just now? I didn't recall that part of Susan's letter. I didn't know the meaning of the word 'pernambuco.' I've never been—"

"You're lying again, but you're innocent," he said. "You really don't know it. Your memory has a few merciful rips in it, or places where the weave is too worn. St. Sebastian, he is the patron saint of Brazil."

He looked up at Karl's Italian masterpiece of St. Sebastian above the fireplace. "Remember that Karl wanted to go, to complete his work on St. Sebastian, to gather the Portuguese renderings of St. Sebastian that he knew were there, and you said you'd rather not."

I was hurt and unable to answer. I had said this to Karl, I'd disappointed him. And he had never been well enough again to make the trip.

"Ah, she faults herself, so naturally," he said. "You didn't want to go because it was the place that Susan had mentioned in her letter."

"I don't remember."

"Oh, yes, you do, because I wouldn't know it if you didn't."

"I can't make any sea pounding on a beach in Brazil. You're going to have to find something worse, something more specific. Or disentangle it from yourself, because you don't want me to see it, which can only mean—"

"Stop your stupid analysis."

I sat back.

Pain had for the moment won out. I couldn't speak. Karl had wanted to go to Rio, and there had been many a time when I was very young that I had wanted to go—south to Brazil and Bolivia and Chile and Peru—all those otherworldly places, and Susan had said it in the letter, that Lily had been reborn in Rio, and there was something else, some fragment, some detail . . .

"The girls," he said.

I remembered.

In our building in Berkeley, in the apartment above Susan, the beautiful Brazilian woman and her two daughters and how they said when they left, "Lily, we'll never forget you." University people from Brazil. There had been several families. I went to the bank and got silver dollars for them and gave them each five, those beautiful girls with the deep, throaty voices, and soft . . . oh, yes, those were the accents of the speech in the dream! I looked at him.

The language of the marble temple was Portuguese.

He stood up in rage. He drew back the violin.

"Give in to it, suffer it, why don't you? You gave them the silver dollars, and they kissed Lily and they knew she was dying but you thought Lily didn't. It was only after Lily died that her friend, her motherly friend Susan, told you that Lily had known all along she was going to die."

"I won't, I swear I won't." I stood up. "I'll exorcise you like some cheap demon before I'll let you do this to me."

"You do it to yourself."

"You go too far, much too far, and for your own purposes. I remember my daughter. That's enough. I . . ."

"What? Lie with her in an imaginary grave? What do you think my grave is like?"

"You have one?"

"I don't know," he said. "I never looked. But then they would never have put me in consecrated ground, or given me a stone."

"You look as sad and broken as I feel."

"Never," he said.

"Oh, we are some pair."

He drew back, as if he were afraid of me, clutching the violin to his chest.

I heard the dull stroke of a clock—one of several, the loudest perhaps coming from the dining room. Hours had passed, hours as we sat here sparring.

I looked at him and a terrible malice grew in me, a vengeance that he even knew my secrets, let alone drew them out and played with them. I reached for the violin.

He drew back. "Don't."

"Why not? Will you fade if it leaves your hands?"

"It's mine!" he said. "I took it with me into death and with me it remains. I don't ask why anymore. I don't ask anything anymore."

"I see, and if it is broken, shattered, smashed in any sense?"

"It can't be."

"Looks to me like it could."

"You're stupid and mad."

"I'm tired," I said. "You've stopped crying and now it's my turn."

I walked away from him. I opened the back doors of the room to the dining room. I could see straight through it and out the back windows of the house, and there the tall cherry laurels were lighted against the fence of the Chapel priest house, bright leaves in a flash of electric lights, moving as if there were a wind, and I hadn't—in this big house, creaky as it might be—hadn't even noticed the wind. Now I heard it tapping the panes, and creeping beneath the floors.

"Oh God," I said. I had my back to him and I listened as he walked towards me, cautiously, as if he just wanted to be close.

"Yes, cry," he said. "Why is that wrong?"

I looked at him. He seemed for the moment very human, almost warm.

"I prefer other music!" I said. "You know I do. And you have made this a hell for both of us, this little affair."

"Do you think some better bond is possible?" He sounded sincere. He looked sincere. "That I at this advanced stage, so alienated from life, could be won over to something like love, perhaps? No, there isn't heat enough in love for me. Not since that night, not since I left the flesh and took this instrument with me."

"Go on, you want to cry too. Do it."

"No," he said, backing up.

I looked back out at the green leaves. Suddenly the lights went off.

That meant something. It meant an hour of the clock and such an hour had just struck, and at that time, the lights went off automatically in one place, and on automatically somewhere else.

I heard no sound in the house. Althea and Lacomb slept. No, Althea had gone out tonight and wouldn't be back till morning, and Lacomb, he'd gone down to the basement room to sleep so that he could smoke where he knew the smell of it wouldn't sicken me. The house was empty.

"No, we two are here," he whispered in my ear.

"Stefan?" I said. I pronounced it as Miss Hardy had, with the weight on the first syllable.

His face smoothed and brightened. "You live a brief life," he said. "Why don't you pity me that this is my misery forever?"

"Well, then, play for me. Play for me, and let me dream and remember without begrudging you. Or do I have to hate it? Will pure misery given up to you be enough, for once?"

He couldn't bear this. He looked like a lacerated child. I might as well have slapped him. And when he did look up, his eyes were glassy and pure and his mouth quivered.

"Very young when you died," I said.

"Not as young as your Lily," he said bitterly, spitefully, but he could hardly make the words audible. "What did the priests tell you? She had not even reached 'The Age of Reason'?"

We looked at one another, I holding her in my arms and listening to precocious talk, the clever wit and irony born out of pain and tongue-loosening drugs like Dilantin. Lily, my shining one with a glass lifted among all the friends to toast, her head perfectly bald, her smile so lovely that even I was grateful, grateful to see this so vividly in retrospect. Oh, yes, please, the smile. I want to see it, and hear her laugh like something tumbling merrily downhill.

Memory of talking to Lev. "My son Christopher laughs the same way, that belly laugh, that effortless laugh!" Lev had told me on some long-distance call two children ago, when Chelsea and he were both on the wire and we all cried for the happiness of it.

I walked slowly through the dining room. The lights of the house had all been properly turned out for the night. Only the sconce by my bedroom door remained lighted. I drifted past it. I went into my room.

He followed every step I took, soundlessly but there, there as distinct as a great shadow following me, a great cloak of pure darkness.

But then I looked at his vulnerable face, and his helplessness, and I thought to myself, And please, God, don't let him know, but he is like all the rest, dying and needing me. It's no mere insult to sting him. It's true.

Perplexed, he watched me.

I had an urge to take off these clothes, the velvet tunic I wore, the silk skirt, I wanted to remove all that bound me. I wanted a loose gown, and to slide beneath the covers and dream, dream of the dream graves and the dream dead, and all that. I was warm and mussed but not weary, no, not for one second weary.

I was poised for battle as if for once I might win! But winning, what would that be like, and would he suffer? Could I want this, even from someone so rank and unkind and literally out of this world?

But I didn't brood on him, this young thing, except to know again with a thudding heart that he was truly there, that if I was mad, I was safely mad where no one could reach me but him. We stood together.

I began to remember something, something so dreadful that not a month of my life passed that I didn't think of it, something that came like a big slice of glass into me, and yet I'd never described it to anyone, not a soul, ever, ever, in my life, not even Lev.

I shivered. I sat on the bed, easing myself back, but it was so high my feet wouldn't touch the ground. I climbed off it and walked, and he stepped back to let me pass.

I felt the wool of his coat. I even felt his hair. I reached back in the door of the alcove, right before the dining room and I grabbed his long hair.

"Now, that's cornsilk, but it's black," I said.

"Ah, stop it," he said. He freed himself. It felt slippery and it glittered, the hair, as it left my hand. But then my hand was already open.

He made a dodge into the dining room and darted a long way from me. And then he lifted the bow. No need to tighten the horsehair of the pernambuco spectral bow, it seems, to play now.

I closed my eyes on him and on the world but not on the past and not on this memory. This was for him, this one . . . and so small and so hard to gather and face, like slicing one's hand with glass. . . .

But I was driven to it. What would be lost? Not even this trivial and ugly and unconfessed thing was going to push me to the end of all reason. If I could still make lucid dreams, and phantoms too, well, then let him come after me.

✒ 10 ✑

We began together. I let myself drift; this particular torment is private, heated with shame, so debased that one can't even connect it with sadness.

Sadness.

It was the same house in which we stood now. He played a sonata for me in the lower pitch, drawing his bow with such skill on the deep notes that it seemed my eyes saw an earlier time as visibly as my mind.

But I was on the other side of the long dining room.

I smelled the summer before machines had come to cool houses such as this, when wood took on that special baked smell, and the stench of the kitchen's common foods, cabbage and ham, lingered for eternity. Was there a house then that I knew that didn't smell of boiled cabbage? But I was thinking of little houses then, the small gingerbread shotgun houses in the Irish-German waterfront whence my people came—well, some of them—and where often I went with my Mother or Father, hand held tight, gazing on narrow barren sidewalks, wishing for trees, wishing for the soft jumbled mansions of the Garden District.

This after all was a big house; a cottage yes, of only four great rooms on its main floor, with children sleeping in small bedchambers beneath a dormered attic. But each of those four rooms was large, and on that night, the night I remembered, or could never privately forget, the unsharable night, the ugly night, the dining room that lay between me and the master bedroom seemed so vast that surely I was no more than eight years old, if that.

Yes, eight, I remembered, because Katrinka had been born, and somewhere upstairs she slept, a baby who knew how to crawl, and I had become frightened in the night and wanted my mother's bed, which wasn't all that uncommon. I had just come down the stairway.

My Father, long home from the war, had begun his nighttime jobs, as had his brothers, all of them working feverish hours to keep their families, and was gone where on this evening it didn't matter.

Only that she had begun to drink, that's what mattered, and that my Grandmother was dead, and fear had come, the dull terrible misery of dread; I knew it, knew the gloom that threatened to consume all hope, as I had come creeping down the stairs and into this dining room, hoping for the light in her bedroom, because even if she was "sick," as we called it then, and had that sour taste (read liquor) on her breath, and slept so soundly that one could shake her head and nothing would happen, still, she'd be warm, the light would burn; she hated the dark, she was afraid of it.

There was no electric light, none that I could see. *Let your music speak of fear, overwhelming child's fear, fear that the entire fabric of things is rent and will never be whole.* It was possible even then to wish I'd never been born; I just didn't have the words to explain it.

But I knew I'd been launched on an awful existence of anguish and peril, of wandering beyond the range of comfort again and again, closing my eyes, wishing only for the morning sun, for the company of others, seeking solace in the sight of the headlamps of the passing cars, which each had such a distinct shape.

Down the narrow curving stairs I had come and into this dining room.

Look, that was the black oak buffet we had in those days, carved by machines, bulbous and grand. That was the one Father gave away when she died, saying he had to give her furniture to "her family" as if we, her daughters, were not her family. But this, this particular night, was long before her death. The buffet was an eternal landmark on the map of dread.

Faye was yet to come, tiny, starved out of the black water of the rotten womb, beloved tiny Faye had not yet come like something sent from Heaven to make warmth, to dance, to distract, to make us all laugh, Faye who walked in beauty like the day and would forever, no matter what pain was thrust upon her, Faye who could lie for hours watching the movements of the green trees in the wind, Faye, born in poison and offering everyone only boundless sweetness forever.

No, this was just before Faye, and this was cheerless, and without safety; this was as dark as the world would ever get, perhaps, even more nearly hopeless than the realizations that come with age, because there was no wisdom to help me. I was afraid, afraid.

Maybe Faye was in Mother's womb that night, already. Could have been. Mother bled all the time she carried Faye. If so, Faye was floating in the drunken contaminated sightless world, penetrated perhaps with misery? Does a drunken heart beat as strong as any other heart? Is a drunken mother's body just as warm to a tiny speck of a being like that, floating, waiting, groping towards a consciousness of dark and chilled rooms where fear stands on the threshold? Panic and misery hand in hand in one timid guilty child peering across a dirty room.

Behold, the intricately carved fireplace, roses in the reddish wood, a painted frame of stones, a dead gas heater that could scorch the mantel. Behold the moldings above, the lofty framework of grand doors, shadows flung hither and thither by the gliding traffic.

Filthy house. It was then, who could deny it? It was before vacuum cleaners or washing machines, and the dust was always in the corner. The iceman lugged his shining magical load up the steps each morning, a man always on the run. The milk in the icebox stank. Roaches crisscrossed the white enameled metal of the kitchen table. Knock, knock before you sat down, to make them flee. Always a glass was rinsed before it was used.

Barefoot, we were dirty all summer long. Dust hung in the window screens that rusted to a dark black color after a while. And when the window fan was turned on in summer, it brought the dirt itself right into the house. The filth flew through the night, hung safe from every curlicue and brace as natural as moss from the oaks outside.

But these were normal things; after all, how could she keep such huge rooms clean? And she with all her dreams of reading poetry to us, and that we must not be troubled with chores, her girls, her geniuses, her perfectly healthy children; she would leave the mounds of dirty laundry on the bathroom floor, reading to us, laughing. She had a beautiful laugh.

The scope of things was overwhelming. Such was life. I remember my Father atop the ladder reaching all the way with his arm to paint the fourteen-foot ceilings. Talk of plaster falling. Rotted beams in the attic; a house sinking, sinking year after year ever deeper into the earth, an image that strangled my heart.

It was never all clean or finished, the house, never all straight; flies crawled on dirty plates in the pantry, and something had burnt on the stove. Sour, dank, that was the motionless night air through which I moved, barefoot, disobedient, out of bed, downstairs, terrified.

Yes, terrified.

What if a roach came, or a rat? Or what if the doors were unlocked and someone had broken in, and there she was, drunk in there, and I couldn't wake her? Couldn't lift her? What if the fire came, oh, yes, that terrible, terrible fire of which I was in some delirious fear that I could never stop thinking of it, fire like the fire that had burned that old Victorian house on Philip and St. Charles, fire that had seemed in my earlier mind, earlier than this memory, born of the very darkness and wrongness of the burned house itself, our world itself, our tee-tering world in which kind words were followed by stupor and cold-ness, and rank neglect; where things accumulated eternally and made for a universe of disorder—oh, that any place should be so shadowy and cheerless as that old Victorian house, a hunkering monster on the corner of that block, which went up into the greatest flames I'd ever seen.

But what was to stop such a thing from happening here, in these more spacious rooms, behind white columns and iron railings? Look, her heater burned. Her fat-legged gas heater burned, a little blazing flame of ornamented iron squatting at the end of its gas pipe, too near the wall. Too near. I knew. I knew the walls got too hot from all the heaters in this house. I knew already.

It couldn't have been summer then, and it wasn't winter, or was it? It was knowledge that made my teeth chatter.

In the memory and now, as Stefan played and I let this old child-hood misery unfold, my teeth chattered.

Stefan played a slow, walking music, like the music of the Second Movement of Beethoven's *Ninth*, only more somber than that, as if he walked with me over this parquet which had no shine then and was thought to be hopeless, given the chemical and mechanical possibili-ties of that era—was it 1950 yet? No.

I saw the gas heater in her room, even the sight of the orange flames making me wince and cover my eyes, though I stood a full room and alcove away; think of fire, fire and trying to get Katrinka out, and her drunk, and Rosalind, where was she? She didn't figure in memory or in phobia. I was alone there, and I knew how old the wiring was; they spoke of it carelessly enough at dinner tables:

"This place is so dried out," my Father said once. "It would burn like kindling."

"What did you say?" I had asked.

She had come with the lying reassurances. But every dull 60-watt bulb of those days blinked when she ironed, and when she was drunk, she could drop her cigarette, or forget a hot iron, cords were frayed, sparks flew from old plugs, and what if the fire burned and burned and I couldn't get Katrinka out of the baby bed, and Mother would be coughing, coughing in the smoke but unable to help, coughing as Mother was now.

And eventually, as we both know, I did murder her.

That night, I heard her struggling with that endless, hacking smoker's cough that never stopped for too long, but it meant to me that she was awake beyond the dark length of this room, awake enough to clear her throat, to cough, perhaps to let me under the covers to curl up beside her, even though all day she'd slept in her drunken trance, yes, now I knew it had been that way, that she had— because she had never dressed—merely lain there under the covers in her underwear, pink panties, and braless, her breasts small and empty, though she had nursed Katrinka for a year, and her naked legs down over which I'd pulled the covers were so ropy with swollen veins in back that I couldn't dare look at them. It looked like pain, calves that were clusters of swollen veins, from "carrying three children," she'd said to her sister Alicia on the phone long distance once, once. . . .

Walking across this floor, I feared disintegration, that something so terrible would come out of the dark that I would scream and scream. I had to get to her. I had to ignore the orange flames and the constant thump thump thump fear of fire, the images that recurred and went round and round, the house filled with smoke as I'd seen it when she'd set the mattress on fire and put it out herself, once, and I had to get to her. Her coughing was the only sound in the house, the house rendered all the more empty by its immense black oak furniture—the table with its five bulbous legs—this grand old buffet with its thick lower carved doors and high spotted mirror.

Rosalind and I had crawled inside the buffet when we were small, amongst the china left and even a glass or two from her wedding. That was when she let us write or draw on the walls, and break everything. She wanted her children to be free. We pasted our paper dolls to the wall with glue from the five-and-dime on Canal. We had a dream world of many characters, Mary, Madene, Betty Headquarters, and later came Katrinka's favorite, Doan the Stone, over whom we laughed and laughed for the sheer tickle of the sound, but that was later.

There was no one in this memory but Mother and I . . . and she coughed in the bedroom and I came tiptoeing towards her, frightened that she might be so drunk, her head would swing and smack the wood of the door, and her eyes would swim like cow's eyes in pictures, big and dumb, and it would be ugly, but I didn't really care that much, I mean it would be worth it, if I could just reach her, and sneak into the bed beside her. I didn't mind her body, with the potbelly and the varicose veins and the sagging breasts.

She often wore nothing but her underpants and a man's shirt around the house; she liked to be free. There are things you never, never, never tell anyone.

Just ugly awful things, like that when she sat on the toilet to have a bowel movement, she kept the bathroom door wide open, and her legs wide apart and liked us to be there with her as she read, a display of pubic hair, white thighs, and Rosalind would say, "Mother, the smell, the smell," as this defecating went on and on, and Mother with the *Reader's Digest* in one hand and the cigarette in the other, our beautiful Mother of the high domed forehead and the big brown eyes would laugh at Rosalind, who wanted to bolt, and then our Mother would read us one more funny story from the magazine, and we would all laugh.

All my life I knew people had their favorite comfort modes for the working of their bowels—that all doors be locked, that no one be near; or that there be no windows to the small room; and some like her, that wanted someone to be near, someone to be talking. Why?

I didn't care. If I could just get to her I could take any ugly sight. Never in the midst of any state had she herself seemed anything but clean and warm, her shining hair growing from a white, white scalp, through which I'd run my fingers, her skin smooth. Perhaps the filth accumulating around her could smother her but never corrupt her.

I crept to the door of the alcove. Her bedroom, which was now mine, had only an iron bed then with a naked coiled spring beneath the striped mattress, and she would put a thin white spread over it now and then, but mostly only sheets and blankets. It seemed the normal course of life, big thick white cups for coffee, always chipped; frayed towels; shoes with holes; the green scum on our teeth, until our Father said, "Don't any of you ever brush your teeth?"

And there might be a toothbrush for a while or even two or three and even some powder with which we could brush our teeth, but then those things would fall on the floor, or get lost or go away, and on went the pace of life, covered with a thick gray cloud. In the kitchen tubs, my Mother washed by hand as our grandmother had done till she died.

Nineteen forty-seven. Nineteen forty-eight. We carried the sheets out into the yard in a big wicker basket; her hands were swollen from wringing them out. I liked to play with the washboard in the tub. We hung the sheets on the line, and I carried the end so it didn't fall in the mud, I love it, running through clean sheets.

She had said once to me right before she died, and mark, I'm jumping now ahead some seven years, she said that she had seen a strange creature in the sheets in the yard, two small black feet, she hinted of a demonic thing, her eyes wide. I knew she was going crazy. She'd die soon. And she did.

But this was long before I thought she could die, even though our grandmother had. At eight, I thought people came back; death hadn't struck the deep fear in me. It was she who struck the fear, perhaps, or my Father gone on his nighttime jobs, delivering telegrams on a motorbike after his regular hours at the post office, or sorting mail at the American Bank. I never fully understood the extra things he did, only that they kept him away, only that he had two jobs, and on Sunday, he went with the Holy Name Men who went through the parish and gave to poor children, and I remember that because one Sunday he took my crayons, my only crayons, and gave them to a "poor child" and was so bitterly disappointed in me for my selfishness that he sneered as he turned and left the house.

Where was the certain source of crayons in such a world? Way way off over the stony field of lassitude and sloth, in a dime store to which I might never drag anybody for years and years again, to get more crayons!

But he wasn't there. The heater was the light. I stood in the door of her room. I could see the heater. I could see something by it, something white, indistinct, white and dark, and glittering. I knew what it was but not why it was glittering.

I stepped into the room; the warm air hung there imprisoned by the door and the transom shut above it, and on the bed to my left, its head to the wall nearest me, she lay; the bed was where it was now, only it was old and iron and sagged and creaked and when you hid under it, you could see such dust in the coils of springs; it seemed quite fascinating.

Her head was raised, her hair, not yet shorn or sold, was long and dark all over her naked back and she shook with the cough, the light of the heater showing the thick ropy veins collected on her legs, and the pink panties over her small bottom.

What *was* that lying by the heater, dangerously, oh, God, it would catch fire like the legs of the chairs that were charred black when someone pushed them up against the heater and forgot about them and there was that smell of gas in the room, and the flames burnt orange, and I shrank up against the door.

I didn't care now if she was angry that I'd come down, if she told me to go back to bed, I wouldn't go, I couldn't go, I couldn't move.

Why did it glitter?

It was what they called a Kotex, a pad of soft white cotton fibers that she wore in her panties with a safety pin when she bled, and it was pinched in the middle from being worn and all dark with blood, of course, yet the glitter, why the glitter?

I stood at the head of her bed, and saw her, in the corner of my eye, sit up. Her coughing was now so bad, she had to sit up.

"Turn on the light," she said in her drunk voice. "Pull the shade, Triana, turn on the light."

"But that," I said, "but that." I moved closer to it, pointing, the Kotex white cotton pad creased in the middle and clotted with blood. It was swarming with ants! That's why it glittered! Oh, God, look at it, Mother! Ants, ants everywhere over it, ants, you know, the way they could come and take over a plate left outdoors, swarming, devouring, tiny, impossible to kill.

"Mother, look, it's covered with ants, the Kotex!"

Now if Katrinka saw that, if Katrinka crawled and found something like that, if anyone saw—I went closer and closer. "Look," I said to her.

She coughed and coughed. She waved her right arm as if to say, Leave it alone, but you couldn't leave something like this alone, it was a Kotex covered with ants, just thrown in the corner. It was near the heater. It could catch fire, and the ants, you stop ants. Ants could get all over everything. You locked up the old world of 1948 or '49 tight from ants, you never let them get a head start; they ate the dead birds as soon as they fell in the grass; they made a line creeping under the door and up the kitchen counter to find the one spill of molasses.

"Ah," I made some noise of disgust. "Look at it, Mother." Oh, I didn't want to touch it.

She stood up, wobbling, coming behind me. I bent down pointing at it, crinching up the features of my face.

Behind me she struggled to speak, to say, Stop, Stop. She said, "Leave it alone," and then coughed so hard she seemed to strangle. She grabbed my hair, slapped me.

"But Mother," I said. I pointed at it.

Again, she slapped, and again, so that I cowered, arms up, slap after slap coming down on my arm. "Stop it, Mother!"

I went down on my knees on the floor, where the heater made a flaming reflection even in the dusty boards with their old shellac, and I smelled the gas and saw the blood, the thick collection of blood covered with ants.

She slapped me again. I put out my right hand. I screamed. I broke my fall, but my hand almost touched it, and the ants swarmed, the ants went into a frenzy, racing at ant speed over the thick blood. "Mamma, stop!"

I turned around; I didn't want to pick it up, but somebody had to pick it up.

She stood looming over me, unsteady, the thin pink panties stretched high over her little belly, her breasts sagging and brownnippled, and her hair a big tangle over her face, coughing and waving furiously for me to get away, to go out, and then she lifted her knee and her naked foot and she kicked me, hard in the stomach. Hard.

Hard, hard.

Never in all my living life had I known this!

This wasn't pain. This was the end of everything.

I couldn't breathe. I couldn't breathe. I wasn't alive. I couldn't reach or find my breath. I felt the pain in my stomach and chest and I had no voice to scream and I thought I will die, I would die, I would die. Oh, God, that she did that, you kicked me, I wanted to say, you kicked me, you didn't mean to do it, you couldn't mean it, Mother! But I couldn't breathe, let alone speak, I was going to die and my arm brushed the hot heater, the burning iron of the heater.

She grabbed for my shoulder. I did scream. I did. I panted and panted and screamed and screamed—and I screamed now, as I had then, but now—that Kotex glittering with the swarming ants and the pain in my stomach and the vomit coming up in my scream, that was all there was, You didn't mean, you didn't . . . I couldn't get up.

No. Put an end to it!

Stefan.

His voice. Ethereal and loud.

The cold house of present time. Any less haunted?

He stood crumpled beside the four-poster bed. It was now, forty-six years later after that moment, and all of them gone to the grave, but me and the baby upstairs who grew up to be so full of dread, and so full of hatred of me that I couldn't save her from these things, and didn't—and he, our guest, my ghost—bent double, grabbing the fancy carved post of the mahogany bed.

Yes, please let it all come back, my counterpanes of lace, my curtains, my silk, I never, my Mother, she didn't mean, she couldn't . . . that pain, absolutely unable to breathe, then hurt, hurt, hurt and nausea, can't move!

Vomit.

No! No more, he said.

And he hooked his right arm around the post of the bed, and let go of the violin safely on the big soft mattress of the bed, atop the feathered counterpane. With both hands, he held the bedpost and he cried.

"Such a little thing," I said, "She didn't cut me with a knife!"

"I know, I know," he cried.

"And think of her," I said, "naked like that, how ugly she looked, and she kicked me, she kicked hard with her naked foot, she was drunk, and my arm got burned on the heater!"

"Stop it!" he pleaded with me. "Triana, stop." He lifted both hands to his face.

"Can't you make music of that," I said drawing near. "Can't you make high art of something so private and shameful and vulgar as that, as that!"

He cried. Just like I must have cried.

The violin and the bow lay on the counterpane.

I rushed at the bed, grabbed both of them—violin and bow—and stepped back away from him.

He was astonished.

His face was wet and white. He stared at me. For a moment, he couldn't grasp what I'd done, and then his eyes fixed on the violin and he saw it and he understood.

I lifted the violin to my chin; I knew how; I lifted the bow and I began to play. I didn't think on it or plan or dread to fail; I began to play, to let the bow, barely grasped between two fingers, fly against the strings. I smelled the horsehair and the resin of the bow, I felt my left fingers stomping up and down the neck of it, damping down the throbbing strings, and I tore at the strings wildly with the bow, and in the stroking and in the pound of my fingers, it was a song, a coherent song, a dance, a drunken frenzied dance, with note following too fast upon note for the mind to direct, a devil's dance, like that long ago drunken picnic, when Lev had danced and I'd played and played, and could let the bow and my fingers move without stopping. It was like that, and more, and it was a song, a crazed, plunging discordant rural song, wild, wild, like the songs of the Highlands and the dark mountain places, and grim weird dances in memory and in dreams.

It had come into me . . . *I love you, I love you, Mamma, I love you, I love you, I love you.* It was a song, a real true bright and shrieking and throbbing song coming out of his Stradivarius, unbroken, streaming out as I rocked back and forth, the bow sawing wildly and my fingers prancing. I loved it, loved it, this untutored dark and rustic song, my song.

He grabbed for the violin.

"Give it back to me!"

I turned my back on him. I played. I went motionless, then drew the bow down in a long low mournful wail; I played the saddest slowest phrase, dark and sweet, and in my eyes I dressed her and made her pretty and saw her in the park with us, her brown hair combed, her face so beautiful; we never, any of us, ever had her beauty.

Years and years wrapped round all this and meant nothing as I played.

I saw her crying in the grass. She wanted to die. During the war, when we were so small, Rosalind and I, we always walked beside her, holding her hands, and one evening, we were locked by mistake in the dark museum of the Cabildo. She wasn't afraid. She wasn't drunk. She was full of hope and dreams. There was no death. It had been an adventure. Her smiling face as the guard came to our rescue.

Oh, draw the bow out long and let the notes go deep, so deep that they scare you that anything could make this sound. He reached for me. I kicked him! I kicked him as sure as she had kicked me, only my knee came up and he went whirling back.

"Give it to me!" he demanded, struggling to regain his balance.

I played and played so loud I couldn't hear him, turning away from him again, seeing nothing but her, *I love you, I love you, I love you.*

She said she wanted to die. We were in the park, and I was a young girl and she was going to drown herself in the lake. Students had drowned themselves in the lake of the park—it was deep enough. The oaks and fountains hid us from the world of the Avenue, the streetcars. She was going to go down into that slimy water and drown.

She wanted to, and desperate Rosalind, pretty Rosalind of fifteen years old, with her glossy perfect frame of curls, begged her and begged her not to do it. I had breasts under my dress but no brassiere. I had never even put one on.

Forty years later or more, I stood here. I played. I slashed and slashed at the strings with the bow. I stamped my foot. I drew out the sound, I made it scream, this violin, twisting this way and that.

In the park, near the filthy gazebo where the old men made urine and would always stand, leering, near there, eager to show a limp penis in a hand, pay them no mind, near there I had Katrinka and little Faye in the swings, those small wooden swings they had for the little little kids with the slide bar in front so they wouldn't fall out, but I could still smell the urine, and I was pushing both of them in the swings, taking turns, one push for Faye, one push for Katrinka, and these sailors wouldn't leave me alone, these boys, who were hardly any older than me, just the teenager sailor boys who were always in port in those days, English boys maybe or boys from up north, I don't know, boys walking along Canal Street, smoking their cigarettes, just boys.

"Is that your mother? What's wrong with her?"

I didn't answer. I wanted them to go away. I didn't think anything even in answer. I just stared and pushed at the swings.

He had forced us out, my Father; he had said, You have got to get her out of this house, I have to get her out of here and clean this place, I can't stand it, you're taking her out, and we knew she was drunk, stinking drunk, and he made us take her; Rosalind said, I will hate you till the day I die, and we had all together gotten her on the streetcar and she had nodded and wagged, drunken and half asleep as the streetcar rocked uptown.

What did people think of her then, this lady with her four girls; she must have worn some respectable dress, yet all I can recall is her hair, prettily combed back from her temples and her lips pursed and the way she shook herself awake and straightened up, only to wag forward again, eyes glazed, little Faye clinging tight to her, tight, tight.

Little Faye, head against her Mother's skirts, little Faye, unquestioning, and Katrinka, solemn and shamed and mute and staring with numbed eyes already at that tender age.

When the streetcar came to the park, she said, "Here!" We all went with her to get off the streetcar by the front door, because we were nearer to the front. I remember. Holy Name Church across the street and on the other side the beautiful park with its balustrades and fountains and the green, green grass where she used to take us all the time, years before.

But something was wrong. The streetcar stood still. The people in the wooden seats stared. I stood on the pavement looking up at her. It was Rosalind. Rosalind sat in a back seat looking out the window pretending that she wasn't one of us, ignoring Mother, as Mother said so ladylike you would have never dreamt she was drunk, "Rosalind, dear, come on."

The driver waited. The driver stood there as they did at that time, in the front window of the car, with the controls, the two knobs, and waited, and everyone on the streetcar stared. I grabbed Faye's hand. She almost wandered into the traffic. Katrinka, sullenly, sucking her thumb, round-cheeked and blond, and lost, stared dully at all that took place.

My mother walked back down the length of the car. Rosalind couldn't hold out. She had to get up, and she came.

And now, in the park, as Mother threatened to drown herself, as she fell back on the grass sobbing, Rosalind begged her and begged her not to do it.

The sailor boys said, "How old are you? Is that your Mother? What's wrong with her? Here, let me help with that little girl."

"No."

I didn't want their help! I didn't like the way they looked at me. Thirteen. I didn't know what they wanted! I didn't know what was wrong with them, to crowd around me like that, and two little children, and over there, she lay on her side, her shoulders shaking. I could hear her sobs. Her voice was lovely and soft as the pain perhaps grew less sharp, the prick of it that Rosalind had tried to stay on the car, that Mother was drunk, that my Father had forced her out, that she was drunk, that she wanted to die.

"Give it back to me!" he roared, "give me the violin."

Why couldn't he take it? I didn't know. I didn't care.

I went on and on with the chaotic dance, the jig, my feet moving, prancing like the feet of the deaf mute Johnny Belinda in the movie, to the vibrations of the fiddle she could only feel, dancing feet, dancing hands, dancing fingers, wild, mad, Kerry rhythm, chaos. Dancing on the bedroom floor, dancing and playing and letting the bow dip to the left then bringing it down, fingers choosing their own path, bow its own time, yes, jam, jam, as they said at the picnic, let it go, jam.

Blow it out, let it go. I played and played.

He grabbed at me, clutching me. He wasn't strong enough to overpower me.

I backed up against the window, and wrapped my arms over the violin and the bow against my chest.

"Give it back," he said.

"No!"

"You can't play it. It's the violin that's doing it; it's mine, it's mine."

"No."

"Give it to me, it's my violin!"

"I'll crush it first!"

I crunched my arms tight against it, I didn't want to make the bridge collapse, but he couldn't tell how hard I held it. I must have been all elbows and huge eyes to him, holding it.

"No," I said. "I played it, I played it that way before, I played my song, my version of it."

"You did not, you lying whore! Give me the violin now, damn you, I tell you, it's mine! You can't take such a thing."

I shivered all over staring at him. He reached for me, and I shrank in the corner and tightened my grip.

"I'll smash it!"

"You wouldn't do that."

"Why should it matter? It's a spectral thing, is it not? It's a ghost as you are ghost? I want to play it again. I want . . . just to hold it. You can't take it back . . ."

I lifted it and put it under my chin again. His hand came out and I kicked him again. I kicked at his legs as he tried to get away. I put the bow to the strings and played a wild cry, a long awful cry and then slowly, with eyes closed, ignoring him, holding tight to it with every finger and every fiber of my being, I played, I played soft and slow, a lullaby perhaps, for her, for me, for Roz, for my wounded Katrinka and my fragile Faye, a song of twilight like Mother's old poem, her soft voice reading to us before the war ended and Father came home. I heard the tone rise, the rich and rounded tone; ah, this was the touch, this was the very touch—the way to bring the bow down with no conscious thought of pressure on the strings, and then it was just one phrase following another. *Mother, I love you, I love you, I love you.* He'll never come home, there is no war, and we'll always be together. These higher notes were so thin and pure, so bright yet sad.

It weighed nothing, the violin, it hurt my shoulder bone only a little, and I felt a dizziness, but the song was the compass. I knew no notes, no tunes. I knew only these wandering phrases of melancholy and grief, these sweet Gaelic laments without ending, one twining into the next, but it flowed, dear God, it flowed, it flowed like—what, like blood, like blood on the filthy rag on the floor. Like blood, the never ending flow of blood from a woman's womb and a woman's heart, I don't know. In her last year, she bled month in and month out, and so had I at the end of my fertile life, and now childless, no more ever to be born out of me at this age now, like the living blood, let it go.

Let it go.

It was music!

Something brushed my cheek. It was his lips. My elbow rose and I threw him over, past the bed. He was awkward, hopeless, grabbing for the bedpost and glowering at me as he struggled to stand.

I stopped, the last notes shimmering. Good God, we had spent the long night in our wanderings, or was it just the moon, yes, the moon in the cherry laurels and the big obliterating darkness of that building next door, a wall of the modern world that could shadow but never destroy this paradise.

The sorrow I felt for her, the grief, the grief for her in that moment when she had kicked me, the eight-year-old girl here in this room, the grief I felt was flowing with the resonance of the notes in the air. I had only to lift the bow. It was *natural*.

He stood in fear of me against the far wall.

"You either give it back, or I warn you, I'll make you pay for this!"

"Did you cry for me? Or for her?"

"Give it back!"

"Or was it the sheer ugliness? What was it?"

Was it a little girl unable to breathe, in panic, clutching at her belly, her arm brushing the hot iron of the open heater, oh, this is such small sorrow in a world of horrors, and yet of all memories there had been nothing more secret, more awful, more untold.

I hummed. "I want to play." I began softly now, realizing how simple it was to glide the bow gently on the A string and the G, and to make a song all on that one lower string if I wanted, and let the soft grinding sound come up and into it; oh, weep, weep for the wasted life, I heard the notes, I let them surprise and express my soul in stroke after stroke, yes, come to me, let me know, let my mind reach out through this to find my mind; she did not live another year after she cried in the park, not even another year, her hair was long and brown, and on that last day no one went with her to the gate.

I think I sang as I played. Whom did you cry for, Stefan, I sang. Was it for her, was it for me, was it for shabbiness and ugliness? How good this felt to my arm, my fingers so flexible and exact, as if my fingers were tiny hooves stomping on the strings, and the music building upon my ear without a bass or treble clef, such poor script for sound, such ancient inadequate code for this, I could command this tone, yet be astonished and swept up by it as I'd always been swept up in the song of the violin, only it was in my hands!

I saw her body in the coffin. Rouged like a whore. The undertaker said, "This woman has swallowed her tongue!" My father said to us, "She was so malnourished that her face turned black and collapsed, he's had to put on too much makeup. Oh, no, look, Triana, this isn't right, look, Faye won't recognize her."

And whose dress was that? That was a dark red dress, a magenta dress. She never had such a dress. Aunt Elvia's dress, and she did not like Aunt Elvia. "Elvia said she couldn't find anything in her closet. Your Mother had clothes. She must have had clothes. Didn't she have clothes?"

It was so light, the instrument itself, so easy to keep in place, to tap, tap, tap for the flood of sound, familiar, embraced, easy as it was to the men and women of the hills who pick it up and dance with it in childhood before they can read or write, or even speak perhaps, I had yielded to it, and it to me.

Aunt Elvia's dress, but that seemed an abomination, not so very great, only unforgettable, a final disgusting irony, a bitter, bitter figure of neglect.

Why didn't I buy her dresses, wash her, help her, get her on her feet? What was so wrong with me? The music carried the accusation, and the punishment, in one unbroken and coherent current.

"*Did* she have clothes?" I'd said coldly to my Father. A black silk slip I remember, yes, when she sat under the lamp with her cigarette in her hand, a black silk slip on summer nights. Clothes? A coat, an old coat.

Oh, God, to let her die like that. I was fourteen. I was old enough to have helped her, loved her, restored her.

Let the words melt. That's the genius of it, let the words go; let the great rounded sound tell the tale.

"Give it back to me!" Stefan cried. "Or, I warn you, I'll take you with me."

Dazed, I stopped.

"What did you say?"

He didn't speak.

I began humming, holding the violin still so easily between shoulder and chin. "Where?" I asked, dreamily, "where will you take me?"

I didn't wait for his answer.

I played the soft song that needed no conscious goad at all, just sweet and tumbling notes following as easy as kisses to a baby's hands and throat and cheeks, as if I held little Faye in my hands and kissed her and kissed her, so tiny, good God, Mother, Faye's slipped through the slats of the baby bed, look! I have her. But this was Lily, wasn't it? Or Katrinka alone in the dark house with tiny Faye when I came home.

Vomit on the floor.

And what has become of us?

Where had Faye gone?

"I think . . . I think perhaps you should start calling," Karl had said. "Two years your sister Faye has been gone. I don't think . . . I don't think she's coming back."

"Coming back." Coming back, coming back, coming back.

That's what the doctor had said when Lily lay still beneath the oxygen mask. "She's not coming back."

Let the music cry this, and boil, and ease the fit of all this grief by giving it a new form.

I opened my eyes, playing on, seeing things, the world shining, strange and wondrous, but not naming the things as I saw them, merely seeing their shapes as inevitable and brilliant in the glow from the windows, the skirted dressing table of my life with Karl, and the picture there of Lev, and his beautiful son, the tall oldest boy with the light hair like Lev's and Chelsea's, the one named Christopher.

Stefan rushed at me.

He grabbed on to the violin, and I held it firm. "It's going to break!" I said, and then I whipped it free. Solid, light, a shell of a thing, as full of vibrant life as a cricket's shell before it was detached, was left behind, and could be crushed quicker than glass.

I backed up to the windowpanes. "I'll smash it, and who will be the worse off when I do!"

He was frantic.

"You don't know what a ghost is," he said. "You don't know what death is. You mutter about death as though it were a rocking cradle. It's stench and it's hate and it's rot. Your husband is ashes now, Karl. Ashes! And your daughter, her body bloated by gases and . . ."

"No," I said. "I have it, this violin, and I can play it."

He came towards me. He drew himself up, face soft with wondering but only for a moment. His dark smooth eyebrows were clear of any frown, and his long, darkly lashed eyes peered at me.

"I warn you," he said, voice deepening, hardening, though his eyes had never been so open and full of pain. "You have a thing that comes from the dead," he said to me. "You have a thing that comes from my realm which is not yours. And if you don't give it back, I'll take you with me. I'll take you into my world and my memories and my pain, and you'll know what pain is, you wretched fool, you worthless bitch, you thief, you greedy, brooding, desperate human; you hurt all those who loved you, you let her die, and Lily, you hurt her, remember that, her hip, the bone, you remember that, her face as she looked up, you were drunk and you laid her down on the bed and she was . . . !"

"Take me into the realm of the dead? And that's not Hell?"

Lily's face. I'd thrown her too roughly on the bed; the drugs had eaten up all her bones. I'd hurt her in haste, she had looked up, did look up, saw me, bald, hurt, afraid, candle flame of a child, beautiful in sickness and in health; I had been drunk, dear God, for this I will burn in Hell, forever and ever because I myself will fan the flames of my own perdition. I sucked in my breath. I didn't do that, I didn't.

"But you did, you were rough with her that night, you pushed her, you were drunk, you who swore you'd never let a child suffer what you had with a drunken mother—"

I lifted the violin, and brought the bow down in a searing cry over the E string, the high string, the metal string, maybe all song is a form of crying out, an organized scream; a violin as it reaches for a magic pitch is as sharp as a siren.

He couldn't stop me, simply wasn't strong enough; his hand fluttered on top of mine, he couldn't. Haunt, specter, the violin's stronger than you!

"You've broken the veil," he swore. "I warn you. The thing you hold in your hands belongs to me and neither it nor I are of this world and you know it. To see it is one thing, to come with me is another."

Violin

"And what will I see when I come with you? Such pain that I will give it back? You come in here, offering me desperation rather than despair, and you think I'll weep for you?"

He gnawed his lip, and he hesitated, not to cheapen what he meant to say.

"Yes, you will see that, you will see . . . what distinguishes pain . . . what, it's . . . they . . ."

"And who were they? Who were they that were so terrible they could propel you right out of life with a shape and taking this violin with you so that you come to me, in the guise of comforter, and cast me down, to see those weeping faces, my Mother, oh, you, I hate you—my worst memories."

"You reveled in tormenting yourself, you made your own grave-yard pictures and poems, you sang out for death with a greedy mouth. You think death is flowers? Give me my violin. Scream with your vocal cords, but give me my violin."

Mother in a dream two years after her death, "You saw flowers, my girl."

"You mean you're not dead?" I had cried out in the dream, but then I knew this woman was a fake, not her, I knew by the crooked smile, not my Mother, my Mother was really dead. This imposter was too cruel when she said, "The whole funeral was a sham," when she said, "You saw flowers."

"Get away from me," I whispered.

"It's mine."

"I did not invite you!"

"You did."

"I do not deserve you."

"You do."

"I made up prayers and fantasies, as you said. I laid the tributes on the grave, and they had petals, these tributes. I dug graves that were cut to my size. You took me back, you took me to the raw and the unframed, and you made my head sick with it. You kicked the breath out of me! And now I can play, I can play this violin!"

I turned away from him and I played, the bow rising and falling with ever greater grace, song. My hands knew! Yes, they did.

"Only because it's mine, because it's not real, you shrew, give it up!"

I stepped back, playing the melody down deep and harsh, ignoring the repeated thrust of his desperate hands. Then I broke off, shivering.

The magical link was made between my mind and my hands, between intent and fingers, between will and skill; God be praised, it had happened.

"It's coming from my violin because it's mine!" he said.

"No. The fact that you can't snatch it back is clear enough. You try. You can't. You can pass through walls. You can play it. You brought it with you into death, all right. But you can't get it away from me now. I'm stronger than you. I have it. It stays solid, look. Listen, it sings! What if it was destined somehow for me? Did you ever think of that, you evil predatory creature, did you ever love anyone before or after death yourself, enough to think that perhaps—"

"Outrageous," he said. "You are nothing, you are random, you are one in hundreds, you are the very epitome of the person who appreciates all and creates nothing, you are merely one—"

"Oh, you clever thing. You make your face so full of pain, just like Lily, just like Mother."

"You do this to me," he whispered. "It's not right, I would have moved on, I would have gone if you had asked me. You tricked me!"

"But you didn't move on, you wanted me, you tormented me, you didn't go until it was too late and I needed you; how dare you tear at wounds that deep, and now I have this and I'm stronger than you! Something in me has claimed it and won't let it go. I can play it."

"No, it's part of me, as much as my face or my coat or my hands, or my hair. We're ghosts, that thing and I, you can't begin to imagine what they did, you have no authority, you cannot come between me and that instrument, you don't begin to understand this perdition, and they . . ."

He bit his lip; his face gave the illusion of a man who might faint, so white it went, all the blood that wasn't blood rushing from it. He opened his mouth.

I couldn't bear to see him hurt. I couldn't. It seemed the final error, the ultimate wrong, the last defeat, to see him hurt, Stefan, whom I scarcely knew and had robbed. But I would not give the violin back to him.

I let my eyes mist. I felt nothing, the great cool blankness of nothing. Nothing. I heard music in my mind, a replay of the music I'd made. I bowed my head and shut my eyes. Play again—.

"All right, then," he said. I waked from this blankness, and looked at him, and my hands tightened on the violin.

"You've made your choice," he said, eyebrows lifted, face full of wonder.

"What choice?"

❦ *11* ❧

THE LIGHT dulled in the room; glossy leaves beyond the curtains lost their shape. The smells of the room and the world weren't the same.

"What choice?"

"To come with me. You're in my realm now, you're with me! I have strengths and weaknesses, no power to strike you dead, but I can bind you with spells and plunge you into the true past as surely as an angel could do it, as surely as your own conscience can. You drive me to this, you force me."

A stinging wind swept my hair back. The bed was gone. So were the walls. It was night and the trees loomed and then vanished. It was cold, bitter, biting cold, and there was a fire! Look, a great and lurid blaze against the clouds.

"Oh, God, you wouldn't take me there!" I said. "Not to that! Oh, God, that burning house, that fear, that old child fear of fire! Ah. I will smash this violin to tinder—"

People shouted, screamed. Bells rang. The whole night was alive with horses and carriages and people running to and fro and the fire, the fire was huge.

The fire was in a great long rectangular house five stories high, with all windows of the upper floor belching flames.

This was the crowd of a time past, women with their hair pinned up and in great flowing skirts that flared from beneath their breasts, and men in frock coats, and all in terror.

"Good God!" I cried. I was cold, and the wind lashed my face. The cinders flew over me, the sparks striking my dress. People ran with buckets of water. People screamed. I saw tiny figures in the window of the huge house; they threw things out to the dark crowds leaping below. A huge painting tumbled down like a dark postage stamp against the fire, as men ran to catch it.

The whole great square was filled with those who watched and cried and moaned and sought to help. Chairs were tossed from the high stories. A great tapestry was heavily flung out of one window in awkward heaps.

"Where are we? Tell me."

I looked at the clothes of those who ran past us. The soft flowing gowns of the last century before corsets had come, and the men, the men in big-pocketed coats, and look! Even the shirt of the filthy man who lay on the stretcher, burnt and covered with blood, it had great soft wrinkled ballooned sleeves.

Soldiers wore their hats big-brimmed, turned-up, and sideways. Big lumbering and creaky carriages pulled as close as they could to the very fire itself, and the doors flopped open and men jumped out to assist. It was an assault of common men and gentlemen.

A man near me removed his heavy coat and put it over the shoulders of a sagging, weeping woman whose gown was like a long inverted lily of wilted silk, her bare neck looking so cold as the big coat came down to cover it.

"Don't you want to go inside!" Stefan said. He glared at me. He trembled. He wasn't immune to what he'd called up! He trembled but he was in a fury. I held the violin still, I would never let it go. "Come on, don't you want to! Look, you see?"

People jostled him, pushed us, didn't seem to notice us, yet bumped us as if we had weight and space in their world, though obviously we had none; it seemed the nature of the illusion: a seductive solidity, as vital as the roar of the fire itself. People ran to and from the fire and then a remarkable man, a small man, a man pockmarked and gray-haired yet full of authority and easy glowering anger approached, a sloppy yet powerful man approached, staring hard through small round black eyes at Stefan.

"Dear God," I said, "I know who you are." He was in shadow for a second against the blaze, then shifted so that the light laid bare his full frown.

"Stefan, why are we here?" demanded the man. "Why this again?"

"She's taken my violin, Maestro!" Stefan said, struggling to modulate his fragile words. "She's taken it."

The little man shook his head; the crowd swallowed him up as he stepped back, disapproving, silk tie filthy, my guardian angel, my Beethoven.

"Maestro!" Stefan cried. "Maestro, don't leave me!"

This is Vienna. This is another world, and the wind, this is not the sharp dimensions of the lucid dream, this is vast unto the clouds, and look, the water being pumped, the buckets, the huge wet pavement reflecting the flicker of the fire, they are throwing water, and out of the windows above comes a desperate and hurly-burly succession of mirrors, and even chandeliers, distantly clattering, handed down ladders by man to man to man.

Fire bursts from a lower window. A ladder is toppled. Screams. A woman doubles over and roars.

Hundreds of people rush forward only to be driven back when the same fire spurts from all the lower windows. The building is going to explode with fire. The high fifth-story roof is eaten up with fire! A gust of soot and sparks strikes my face.

"Maestro," Stefan called in panic. But the figure was gone.

He turned, enraged, grief-stricken, beckoning for me to come. "Come, you want to see it, don't you, the fire, you want to see, you should see the first time I almost died for what you stole from me, come. . . ."

We stood inside.

The high-ceilinged hall was filled with smoke. The chain of arches was ghostly above us, on account of that, but otherwise real, real as the sooted air that choked us.

The painted pagan heaven above, broken by arch after arch, was full of deities, struggling to be seen again, to flash color and muscle and wing. The staircase was immense, marble, white, with bulbous balusters, Vienna, the Baroque, the Rococo, nothing as delicate as the realm of Paris, nothing as severe as the realm of England, no, it was Vienna—almost Russian in its excess. Look, the statue that has been knocked to the floor, the twisted marble garments, the painted wood. Vienna on the very frontier of Western Europe, and this as grand a palace as any ever built in it.

"Yes, you have it right. You know," he said. His mouth quivered. "My home, my house! My father's house." His whisper was lost suddenly in the crackling, the stampede of feet.

All this around us would blacken too, these high parterres of blood red velvet, this fringe of twisted gold, and everywhere I looked I saw Boiserie—wood, wood painted white and gold and carved in the heavy Viennese style, wood that would burn with the smell of trees, as if no one had strewn all these preciously detailed walls, with murals of domestic bliss or wartime victory, in rectangular frames on perishable material.

The heat blasted the throng living in the painted walls, the fluted columns, the Roman arches. Look, even the arches are wood, wood painted to look like marble. Of course. This is not Rome. This is Vienna.

Glass shattered. Glass flew through the air, swirling and descending and mingling with the sparks around us.

Men thundered down the steps, legs bowed, elbows out, hefting a huge cabinet of ivory and silver and gold, nearly dropping it, then lifting it with shouts and curses again.

We came into the great room. Oh, Lord, it is too late for this magnificence. It's too far gone, the flame is too passionately hungry.

"Stefan, come on, now!" Whose voice was that?

Coughing, everywhere, men and women were coughing the way she had coughed, my Mother, only the smoke was here, the true dense terrifying smoke of a conflagration. It was moving down, down from its natural hovering place beneath the ceilings.

I saw Stefan—not the one by my side, not the one with his hard, cruel hand on my shoulder, not my ghost who held tight to me, as close as a lover. I saw a living Stefan, memory expressed in flesh and blood, in fancy high collar and vest and ruffled white shirt, all this smeared with soot, as across the giant room he smashed the glass of the huge étagères and grabbed out the violins and passed them to the man who then passed them to another and then down out of the windows.

Even the air was the enemy here, gusting, ominous. "Hurry."

Others stooped to gather what they could. Stefan thrust a fiddle before a fancy gilded chair. He shouted and cursed. Others backed out of the windows, carrying what they could, even sheets and sheets of music. Sheets broke loose and tore up in the gust—all that music.

On the high-coved ceiling above the arches, the painted gods and goddesses blackened and wrinkled. A painted forest was peeling from the walls. Sparks rose in a great artful and beautiful spume against the crusted white wooden medallions.

A great gash was blown through the ceiling plaster as if by a gun, and the naked fire let through its hideous light.

I clutched at his arm, pressed against him, pressed us both back against the wall, staring at this searching tongue of flame.

Everywhere, paintings, huge, framed, fitted into the wall, white-wigged men and women staring helplessly and coldly at us, and at time; look at them, that one begins to curl loose from its frame, there comes a loud snapping sound, and look, even the chairs themselves so artfully fashioned with their curved and ever ready legs, it's all ruined, and the smoke belching from this hole above, belching and curling and seeking to rise again, spreading out beneath the ceiling to blot out the Rococo Elysian Fields forever.

Men ran to gather the cellos and violins that lay strewn on the rose-patterned carpet, instruments all tossed about as if dropped by those who had only lately fled. A table askew. A ballroom, yes, the floor, and displays of food, still shining as if someone might come and take from them. The smoke descended like a veil around a groaning banquet table. Silver and silver and fruit.

The candles of the rocking chandelier were fountains of hot pouring wax, flowing down onto the carpets, the chairs, the instruments, even onto the face of a boy who cried out and looked up and then fled with a golden horn in his hand.

Outside the crowd roared as if for a parade.

"For God's sake, man," someone cried. "The walls are bursting into flame, the very walls!"

A hooded figure, dripping wet, rushed past us, the wetness touching the back of my right hand, flash of shining boots, into the room, heaving the big wet sheet at Stefan to cover and protect him, and then snatching up one lute from the floor, he ran for the window and its ladder.

"Stefan, come now!" he called out.

The lute was gone, passed down. The man turned, eyes watering, face red, reaching back, his arms out for the cello Stefan lifted up and pushed at him.

A great crash echoed through the building.

The light was unbearably bright, as if it were the Last Day. Fire raged beyond a distant left-side door. The farthest window gave up its draperies in a whoosh of flame and smoke, rods falling crooked to the floor like lances.

Look at these fine instruments, these musical miracles so brilliantly crafted that no one ever after, with all the technology of an electronic world, would ever match their perfection. Someone had stepped on that violin. Someone had crushed that viola, ah, sacred thing, broken.

And all this here to burn!

The chandelier swayed dangerously in the noxious mist as above it the entire ceiling visibly trembled.

"Come now!" said the other. Another man grabbed up a small violin, a child's instrument perhaps, and escaped from another sill, and another one with a high folded collar and bushy hair fell down on his knees on the herringbone wood floor, one hand on the carpet. He coughed, he choked.

The young Stefan, hair mussed, princely frock coat covered all over with tiny sparks, dying sparks of real flame, threw the bright wet cloth over the coughing man. "Get up, get up! Joseph, come, you're going to die in here!"

A roar filled my ears. "It's too late!" I screamed. "Help him! Don't leave him!"

Stefan my ghost stood beside me, laughing, his hand on my shoulder. The smoke made a veil between us, a cloud in which we stood, ethereal and safe and monstrously set apart, his beautiful face not a day older than the other image, sneering down at me, but a poor mask for its own suffering, an innocent mask in a way for all its intolerable grief.

Then he turned and pointed to this distant and active image of himself, wet, bawling, being dragged from the room by two who had come in from the window, the lost one still groping in the dark, scratching at the carpet, I know, I know, you can't breathe. He was going to die. The one you called Joseph. He's dead, too late for him. Dear God, look. A rafter had fallen between us.

The glass flew in splinters from the doors of the étagères. I saw everywhere the fiddles and gleaming bright trumpets left behind. A great French horn. A tumbled tray of sweets. Goblets sparkling, no, flaming in the light.

The young Stefan, irreparably tangled in the moment, fought his rescuers, reaching out, demanding to be allowed to save one more, one more from the shelf of the étagère, let me go!

He reached for one more, for this, this Strad, the long Strad; glittering glass swept off the shelf, as he pulled it with his free right hand, as he was dragged past it. He had it, and he had the bow.

I could hear my ghost beside me draw in his breath; was he turning away from this his own magic? I couldn't turn away.

A sudden crackling was consuming the ceiling above. Someone screamed in the great hallway behind us. The bow, Stefan had to have that too, and yes, the violin, and then a huge, muscular man, in fury and fright, took Stefan in his grip, and flung him over the windowsill.

The fire rose up, just like it had from that awful Avenue house when I was a child, that dark place of simpler arches and more pedestrian shadows, faint common American echo of this grandeur.

The fire fed and gulped and rose to make a sheet of itself. The night was red and brilliant, and nobody was safe, nothing was safe; the man in the smoke coughed and died, and the fire came closer and closer. The fancy gilded sofas near to us burst into flame, the very tapestry igniting as if from within. All draperies were torches, all windows featureless portals to a black and empty sky.

I must have been screaming.

I stopped, still clutching the ghost violin, the image of which he'd just saved.

We were no longer in the house. Thank God for this.

We stood in the crowded square. How the horror illuminated the night.

Ladies in their long gowns scurried, wept, embraced each other, pointed.

We stood before the long blazing façade of the house, invisible to the weeping frantic men who still ran to drag objects to safety. The wall would come down on all those velvet chairs. It would come down on the couches thrown out, helter skelter, and the paintings, look at them, frames broken, smashed, great portraits.

Stefan slipped his arm around me as if he were cold, his white hand covering my hand which covered the violin, but not trying to tear it loose. He trembled against me. He was lost in the spectacle. His whisper was mournful and carried over any envisioned tumult.

"And so you see it fall," he whispered in my ear. He sighed. "You see it fall, the last great Russian house in beautiful Vienna, a house which had survived Napoleon's guns and soldiers, and plots of Metternich and his ever vigilant spies, the last great Russian house to keep its own full orchestra, like so many waiters for the table, ready to play the sonatas of Beethoven as soon as the ink was dry, men who could play Bach while yawning, or Vivaldi with the sweat on their foreheads, night after night, and all this until one candle, mind you, one candle touched a bit of silk, and drafts from Hell came up to guide it through fifty rooms. My Father's house, my father's fortune, my father's dreams for his Russian sons and daughters who, dancing and singing on this border between East and West, had never seen their own Moscow."

He pressed close to me, struggling, and clutching at my shoulder with his right hand, the left still over my hand and violin and heart.

"See, look around you, the other palaces, the windows with their architraves. You see where you are? You are in the center of the musical world. You are where Schubert would soon make his name in little rooms and die like the snap of fingers without ever finding me in my own gloom, I can assure you, and where Paganini had not yet dared to come for fear of censure. Vienna, and my Father's house. Are you afraid of fire, Triana?"

I didn't answer him. He hurt himself as he hurt me. He hurt so much that it was like the heat.

I wept, but then weeping with me now was so common that perhaps I should forget to take note of it here or anywhere else as we continue. I cried. I cried, and watched the carriages coming to take the grieving ones away, women in loose fur waving from the carriage windows, the wheels big and slender and delicate, and the horses noisy and unruly in the pandemonium.

"Where are you, Stefan? Where are you now? You did get out of the room, where are you? I don't see you, the living you!"

I was dazed, yes, but apart with him, and what he could point out were only images of things past. I knew it, but in my childhood such a fire would have had me helplessly screaming. Well, childhood was no more and this was a nightmare for a mourning woman, this was a thing for soft sobs and a crumbling within of all strength.

The icy wind whipped the flames; one wing of the house did fly apart, walls unhinged, and windows cracking open and the roof exploding with torrents of black smoke. The great bulk looked like a grand lantern. The crowd was swept backwards. People fell. Screamed.

One last doomed figure leapt from the roof, a little cutout of black limbs tossed in the yellow fiery air. People cried out. Some rushed towards this tiny falling black stick-thing that was a man, a helpless, doomed man, only to fall back, driven by the gusting of the blinding blaze. The windows of the lower floor burst open into blazing flowers.

Another great shower of sparks caught us up, sparks touching my eyelids and my hair. I shielded the spectral violin. The sparks flew against us, heavy and stinking of destruction, as they rained down on all those around us, and on us, on this vision and this dream.

Break this vision. This is a trick. You've broken these lucid dreams before that folded you up so tight you thought you'd died and gone on. Break this one.

I stared down hard at the filthy paving stones. Reek of horse manure. My lungs hurt from the bitter air, the smoke. I looked at the high multistoried long rectangular palaces around us. Real, real, these Baroque façades, and the welkin above, dear God, look at the fire on the clouds, this is the worst measure of its catastrophe—either that or one single victim, and how many had there been here. I breathed the stench of the fire in as I cried. I caught the sparks with my hands that died in the frigid wind. The wind hurt my eyelids more than the sparks.

I looked at Stefan, my Stefan the ghost, staring past me, as if he too were riveted by this hellish vision, his own eyes glazed, his mouth tender, the delicate muscles of his face moving as though he struggled desperately against what he saw—Couldn't this be changed, Couldn't that be changed, Did that have to be destroyed?

He whipped around and looked at me, caught in this moment of preoccupation. Only sorrow. Some question in his eyes to me, Do you see?

The crowd continued to tumble over us, yet never saw us; we were not a part of the frenzy, no obstacle, only two figures that could feel and see all that this world contained, in perfect empathy.

A flash caught my eye, a familiar figure.

"But there you are," I cried. It was the living Stefan, far off, I saw him, the young Stefan of life in the flaring fancy coat with the high collar, safely away from the fire, the instruments strewn about him. An old man leant to kiss Stefan's cheek, stop his tears.

The living Stefan held the violin, the rescued violin, a young Stefan, in dirty bedraggled finery. A woman now came, cloaked in fur-trimmed green silk, and lifted her drapery around him.

Young men gathered the precious salvage.

A hard blast struck me, like a wind not of this vision. Dream, yes, wake. But you can't. You know you can't.

"Of course not, and would you?" Stefan whispered, his hand cold on my hand, which held the true violin. And what had become of that, the toy the young man had saved? How were we propelled to this?

But something brightened fiercely in the corner of my eye.

There stood the Maestro, not alive in this world at all any more than we were. Apart from the crowd; and horrifyingly intimate with us, coming close so that I could see the tufts of his gray-black hair growing from his low brow and his keen black eyes dancing over us, and the pout of his colorless mouth, my God, my guardian, without whom I cannot even imagine life itself.

I wanted no protection from this.

"Stefan, *why* this *now*!" said Beethoven, the little man I knew, the man all the world knew from scowling statuettes and dramatic wind-blown drawings, pockmarked and ugly yet fierce and a ghost as surely as we were. His eyes fixed me, fixed the violin, fixed his tall spectral pupil.

"Maestro!" Stefan pleaded, tightening his embrace, even as the fire burnt on and the night thickened with cries and bells. "She stole it! Look at it. Look. She stole my violin! Make her give it back to me, Maestro, help me!"

But the little man glared, shook his head as he had before, and then turned, sneering, grunting, disgusted, and once again walked away, the crowd eating him up again, the black confusion of jabbering and crying people all chaos around us, and the infuriated Stefan clutching me, trying to close his hand over the violin.

But I had it.

"Turn your back on me?" he said. "Maestro!" he wailed. "Oh, God, what have you done to me, Triana, where have you led me! What have you done! There I see him and he leaves me—"

"You opened this door yourself," I said.

Such a stricken face. Defenseless. No emotion could have made him anything but beautiful. He stepped back, frantic, wringing his hands, truly wringing them, look at his white fingers as he wrings his hands, and he stared with wild tormented eyes at the great crashing collapsing shell of the house.

"What have you done?" he cried again. He stared at me and the violin. His lips shook, and his face was wet. "You cry for what? For me? For it? For you? For them?"

He looked from right to left, and back again.

"Maestro!" he called out, eyes searching the night. He stood back, lip jutting, sobbing. "Give it back," he hissed at me. "Give it back. In two centuries, I have never seen a shade as sure as myself, never and now! And this shade is the Maestro and this shade turns its back on me! Maestro I need you, I need you—"

He moved away from me, not deliberately; it was only the idle dance of his desperate gestures, his searching gazes.

"Give it to me, you witch!" he said. "You're in my world now. These things are phantoms and you know it."

"And so are you and so was he," I said, my voice small, broken, even lost, but insisting. "The violin is in my arms, and no, I won't give it up. I will not."

"What do you want of me?" he cried. His fingers outstretched, his shoulders hunched, the dark straight eyebrows expressionless, themselves giving the eyes beneath them all the more expression.

"I don't know!" I said. I cried. I gasped for breath and found it and didn't need it and it wasn't enough and didn't matter. "I want the violin. I want the gift. I played it. I played it in my own house, I felt myself give in to it."

"No!" he roared, as if he would go mad in this realm where he and I alone stood, ignored by all these fleshly beings rushing and calling.

He came head on, and threw his arms around me. His head came down on my shoulder. I looked up, even as he held me, as I felt all the silky hair of his head falling down wild over my face. I looked up and past him and saw the young Stefan, and there with him a living Beethoven, surely it was, a gray-haired living Beethoven, stooped and belligerent and full of love, hair a fright, clothes snaggled, taking his young pupil by the shoulders as the pupil wept and gestured with the violin as if it were a mere baton, while others sank down to their knees or to sit on the cold stones in their weeping.

The smoke filled my lungs, but it didn't touch me. The sparks made their ceaseless whirl around us but had no fire to burn us. He held me, shivering, and careful not to crush this precious thing. He held me, blindly, burrowing his forehead against me.

Clutching the violin tight, I lifted my left hand to hold his head, to feel a skull beneath his thick, soft, velvet hair, and his sobs were a muffled vibrant rhythm against me.

The fire paled, the crowd faded; the darkness became cool, not cold, and fresh with the salt air of the sea.

We stood alone, or at a great distance.

The fire was gone. Everything was gone.

"Where are we?" I whispered in his ear. He seemed in a trance, as he held me. I smelled the earth; I smelled old and molding things, I smelled . . . I smelled the stench of the newly dead, and the old dead, but above all of clean salt air blowing it all away, even as I caught it.

Someone played a violin exquisitely. Someone brought sheer enchantment out of the violin. What was this facile eloquence?

Was this my Stefan? This was a prankster at the instrument, with an immense power and confidence, tripping and tearing through a song more likely to make fear than tears.

But it pierced the night like the sharpest blade. It was crisp and originless in the gloom.

It was mischievous, gleeful, even full of anger, this song.

"Stefan, where are you? Where do we stand now?" My ghost only held tight to me as if he himself didn't want to see or know. He sighed heavily, as though this frantic song didn't touch his blood, didn't galvanize his spectral limbs, as though it could not ensnare him now in death as it ensnared me.

Soft winds off the sea came again over us, and again the air was full of the damp of the sea, I could smell the sea, and far off I realized what I saw:

A great crowd with candles in their hands, cloaked figures, figures with gleaming black top hats, and long dresses, full skirts gently sweeping the earth, dark gloved fingers protecting tiny quivering flames. Here and there the lights clustered to illuminate a whole gathering of attentive and eager faces. The music was fragile then bursting with strength, a deluge, an assault.

"Where are we?" I asked. This smell, it was the smell of death, of the rotting dead. We were crowded amongst mausoleums and stone angels. "Those are graves, look, marble graves!" I said. "We stand in a cemetery. Who is playing? And who are these people?"

He only cried. Finally he lifted his head. Dazzled, he stared at the distant crowd, and only now did the music seem to strike him, to awaken him.

The distant solo violin had broken into a dance, a dance for which there was a name but I couldn't recall it, a country dance which always carries with it in any land some warning of the destruction inherent in abandon.

Not turning away, only releasing me a little, and looking over his shoulder, he spoke.

"We are in the cemetery, true," he said. He was tired and worn from crying. He held me close again, carefully regarding the violin, not to hurt it, and nothing in his poise or manner suggested he would try to snatch it.

He stared as I did at the distant crowd. He seemed to inhale the power of the leaping music.

"But this is Venice, Triana," he kissed my ear. He gave some soft moan like a wounded thing. "This is the graveyard of the Lido. And who do you think plays there, for effect, for praise, for whim? And the city under Metternich all full of spies for the Hapsburg State which will never let another Revolution come or another Napoleon, a government of censors and dictators; who plays here, taunting God as it were, on sacred ground with a song no one would consecrate."

"Yes, on that we do agree," I whispered. "No one would consecrate it." The notes brought the inevitable chills. I wanted myself to play, to take up my violin and join as if it were a country dance and fiddlers could step forward. What arrogance!

It came like steel, this song, but such dexterity, such swiftness, such boundless and tender power, and now it did glide into its appeal. I felt my heart shrink as if the violin were begging me, begging me as Stefan had for the violin I still held, for something else far more precious, for everything, for all things.

I tore my eyes off the scattering of candles and faces. Marble angels protected no one in the dripping night. I reached out with my right hand and touched a marble grave with pediment and doorway. This is no dream. This is as solid as was Vienna. This is a place. The Lido, he had said, the island off the city of Venice.

I looked up at him and he down at me, and he seemed sweet, almost, and wondering. I think he smiled, but I couldn't be sure. The candles gave a poor light and it was far away. He bent and kissed my lips. The sweetest shiver.

"Stefan, poor Stefan," I whispered, kissing him still.

"You hear him, don't you, Triana?"

"Hear him! He's going to take me prisoner," I said. I wiped at my cheek. The wind was far less cold than that in Vienna. It had no bite, this wind, only its freshness, and the deep corruption of the sea and the cemetery carried lightly on it. In fact, the stench of the sea seemed to fold into it the stench of the grave and declare that both were only natural.

"Who is the virtuoso?" I asked. I deliberately kissed him again. There was no resistance. I reached up and touched the bone of his forehead under his satin eyebrows, the ridge across which they were so straightly and thickly drawn. Soft, brushed hair. Very thin and flat and dark, wide but not thick, that is, and his eyelashes danced willingly against the palm of my hand.

"Who plays like this?" I asked him. "Is it you, can we move through the crowds? Let me see you."

"Oh, not I, my darling, no, though I might have given him a little sport, you'll soon see that, but come, look for yourself, look. There I stand, see? A spectator. A worshiper. Candle in hand, listening and shivering with all the rest as he plays, this genius, for the love of the thrill he makes in us, for the love of the spectacle of the cemetery and its candles, who do you think he is, whom would I come to hear, so far from Vienna, on dangerous Italian roads—see my dirty hair, my worn coat. For whom would I come this long way?—if not the man they called the Devil, the possessed one, the Master, Paganini."

The living Stefan came into focus, cheeks flushed, eyes catching two identical candle flames, though he himself held none, gloved hands twisting, right fingers around the left wrist, listening.

"Only you see . . ." said the ghost beside me. He turned my face away from the living. "Only, you see . . . there's a difference."

"I understand," I said. "You really want me to see these things, you want me to understand."

He shook his head as if this was too harsh and too horrifying, and then faltering, he said, "I've never looked at them."

The music went soft; the night closed, opened on a different shade of light.

I turned. I tried to see the graves, the crowd. But something else altogether had taken its place.

We two, ghost and traveler—lover, tormentor, thief, whatever I was—we two were invisible spectators, without locus, though I felt the violin safely in my hands as ever, and my back firmly against his chest, and my breasts, with the violin held reverently between them, covered by his arms. His lips were on my neck. It felt like words spilling out against the flesh.

I looked forward.

"Want me to see—?"

"God help me."

✑ 12 ✑

THIS WAS a narrow canal; the gondola had turned from the Canale Grande into the strip of dark green reeking water between the rows of shoulder-to-shoulder palaces, windows of Moorish arches, all color bled out in the darkness. Great overbearing façades of clustered splendor rooted in water, an arrogance, a glory, this: Venice. Its walls on either side were so drenched and glazed with slime in the lamplight that Venice might have likely risen from the depths, bringing up nocturnal rot into the moon's light with sinister ambition.

Now I understood for the first time the sleekness of the gondola, the sly black facility of this long, high-prowed boat for striving swift between these stony banks, beneath these rocking feeble lanterns.

Young Stefan sat in the gondola, talking frantically to Paganini.

The man himself, Paganini, seemed enraptured. Paganini, with the large hooked nose and giant protuberant eyes given him in many a painting, a burning presence in which drama has surpassed ugliness effortlessly to make pure magnetism.

In our invisible window on this world, the ghost beside me shuddered. I kissed the fingers curled on my shoulder.

Venice.

From a high flapping shuttered window that opened out like a perfect square of yellow in the night, a woman threw flowers, shouting in Italian, the light spilling down on the blooms as they tumbled onto the virtuoso, her sentence ringing in a peculiarly Italian crescendo: "Blessed Paganini, that he would play without recompense for the dead!" Like a necklace with the very mid-phrase flung out the farthest and then breath drawn back on the word for the dead.

Others echoed the same cry. Shutters opened above. From a rooftop, running figures heaved roses from baskets onto the green water ahead of the boat.

Roses, roses, roses.

Laughter shot up the damp crawling stones; the doors were alive with hidden listeners. Shapes hovered in the alleyways, and a man darted over the bridge just above as the gondola went under it. A woman in the very middle of the bridge leant down to bare her breasts in the light of the passing lantern.

"To study with you, I came," said Stefan, in the gondola, to Paganini. "I came with the clothes on my back, and without my father's blessing. I had to hear you with my own ears, and it was not the Devil's music, curse those who say that, it was the enchantment yes, ancient, most likely true, but not the Devil in this."

A great rip of laughter came from the more hunched figure of Paganini, whites of his eyes bright in the dark. Beside him, a woman clung to him, like a hump growing all over his left side, with only a handful of red curls snaking down his coat.

"Prince Stefanovsky," said the great Italian, the idol, the Byronic fiddler par excellence, the romantic love of little girls, "I've heard of you and your talent, of your house in Vienna, where Beethoven himself presents his work, and that once Mozart came there to give you lessons. I know who you are, you rich Russians. You take your gold from a bottomless coffer in the hands of the Czar."

"Don't mistake me," Stefan said, gentle, respecting, desperate. "I have money to pay you well for these lessons, Signore Paganini," said Stefan. "I have a violin, my own, my cherished Stradivarius. I didn't dare to bring my violin, traveling the post roads, days and nights to get here, I came alone. But I have money. I had to hear you first, to know that you would accept me, that you see me as worthy—"

"Oh, but Prince Stefanovsky, must I school you on the history of Czars and their Princes? Your father is not going to permit you to study with the peasant Niccolò Paganini. Your destiny is the service of the Czar, as it has always been with your family. Music was a pastime in your house, oh, don't take offense, I know that Metternich him-self"—he leant forward to whisper to Stefan—"the happy little dic-

tator himself, plays the violin and well, and I have played for him. But
for a Prince to become what I have become. Prince Stefanovsky, I live
by this, my violin!" He gestured to the instrument in its case of polished wood, which seemed ever so much like a tiny coffin. "And you
my handsome Russian youth must live by Russian tradition and Russian duty. The military awaits you. Honors. Service in the Crimea."

Cries of praise from above. Torches at the dock. Women in
rustling clothes rushing up against a new and steeper bridge. Pink
nipples in the night, bodices laid back like wrapping to display them.

"Paganini, Paganini."

Roses again, falling down on the man as he brushed them away and
looked intently at Stefan. The great cloaked hump of the woman
beside him flashed a white hand down in the dark between Paganini's
legs, fingers playing as if his private parts were a lyre, if not a violin.
He seemed not even to notice.

"Believe me, I want your money," Paganini said. "I need it. Yes, I
play for the dead, but you know of my stormy life, the lawsuits, the
entanglements. But I am a peasant, Prince, and I will not give up my
itinerant victories to prison myself up in Vienna in a drawing room
with you—ah, the critical Viennese, the bored Viennese, the Viennese
who did not even give Mozart his bread and butter; did you know
him, Mozart? No, and you cannot remain with me. Already, no doubt,
Metternich, at your father's behest, has sent someone to look for you.
I'll become accused of some nasty treason in all this."

Stefan was crushed, head bowed, cheeks so tender with pain, and
deep-framed eyes glittering with the reflected light from the torpid
but shiny water.

An interior:

A Venetian room, unkempt and blistered from the damp, chalky
dark walls and soaring yellow ceiling with only faded remnants of a
pagan swarm that had burnt so new and bright before its death in
Stefan's rich Viennese palace. A long drape, a slash of dark dusty burgundy velvet and a deep green satin tangled with it, hung from a high
hook, and out the narrow window, I saw the ochre colored wall of the
palace opposite so close that one could reach across the alley if one
wished and knock upon the solid wood green shutters.

The unmade bed was heaped with tapestried robes and crumpled
linen shirts with costly Reticella lace, the tables stacked with letters,

wax seals broken, and here and there lay the stubs of candles. Everywhere bouquets of dead flowers.

But, look:

Stefan played! Stefan stood in the middle of the room, on the shiny
Venetian oiled floor, playing not this, our spectral violin, but another
undoubtedly by the same master. And round Stefan, Paganini danced,
playing variations that mocked Stefan's theme, a contest, a game, a
duet, a war perhaps.

It was a somber *Adagio* Stefan played, by Albinoni, in G minor for
strings and organ, only he had made it his solo, moving from part to
part, his grief encompassing his fallen house, and through the music I
could see the burning palace faintly in the Vienna cold and all the
beauty turned to kindling. The music, slow, steady, unfolding, held
Stefan himself so in thrall he seemed not to see the cavorting figure
near him.

Such music! It seemed the very maximum of pain that could be
declared with perfect dignity. It bore no accusation. It spoke of
wisdom and deepening sadness.

I felt my tears come, my tears which are like hands to applaud, the
signal of the empathy in me for him, this boyman standing there, as
the Italian genius made his Rumpelstiltskin circle about him.

Thread after thread from the *Adagio* Paganini pulled loose to race
it into a caprice, a frolic of fingers darting too swiftly along the strings
even to be traced, and then he would with perfect accuracy descend to
catch the very phrase which Stefan at his somber pace had only just
reached. Paganini's dexterity seeming sorcery, as it was always said,
and in all this—this lone imperially slim figure played immune in his
pain, and Paganini, the dancer who mocked or tore the shroud for
its gleaming threads—there was nothing discordant but something
wholly new and splendid.

Stefan's eyes were closed, his head tilted. His full sleeves were
stained from rain perhaps, the fine *punto in aria* lace torn at the cuffs,
his boots streaked with dried mud, but his arm was perfect in its mea-
sures. Never had his dark straight eyebrows looked so smooth and
beautiful, and as he took the organ part of this famous music now, I
thought my heart would break for him, and even Paganini drew in,
slipping into this most tortured of moments merely to play with
Stefan, to echo him, to cry above him and below but with honor.

The two stopped, the tall boyish one looking down with utter wonder at the other.

Paganini laid down his violin carefully on the tasseled covers and pillows of the jumbled bed, all golden and midnight blue. His big pop eyes were generous and his smile demonic. The man seemed embraceable in his exuberance. He rubbed his hands.

"Yes, gifted, yes, you are! Gifted!"

You'll never play like that! That was my ghost captain whispering in my ear, even as his whole body clung to mine and pleaded with me for solace.

I didn't answer. Let the picture roll.

"You'll teach me then," said Stefan in flawless Italian, the Italian of Salieri and all his like, the wonder of the Germans and the English.

"Teach you, yes, yes, I will. And if we must get out of this place, then we shall, though you know what you do to me in these times, with Austria so bent on keeping my Italy under her thumb, you know. But tell me this."

"What?"

The little man with the huge eyes laughed; he walked up and down; his heels clicked on the oiled floor, his shoulders were almost humped, his eyebrows long and curling at the ends as if he'd enhanced them with stage paint when he hadn't.

"What, dear Prince, am I to teach you? For you know how to play, yes, that you can do. You can play. What is it that I must bring to a pupil of Ludwig van Beethoven? An Italian levity perhaps, an Italian irony?"

"No," said Stefan in a whisper, eyes fastened on the pacing man. "Courage, Maestro, to throw all else aside. Oh, it is sad, sad to me that my teacher will never hear you."

Paganini paused, lips puckered. "Beethoven, you mean."

"Deaf, too deaf now even for the high notes to pierce, too deaf," said Stefan softly.

"And so he can't give you the courage?"

"No, you misunderstand!" Stefan held the gift violin that he had played, looked at it.

"Stradivari, yes, a present to me, fine as your own, no?" said Paganini.

"Indeed, perhaps better, I don't know," said Stefan. He took up the former point. "Beethoven could teach anyone courage. But he is a composer now, deafness forced this on him as you know, boxed the ears of the virtuoso until he couldn't play, and left him locked up with pen and ink as the only means of making music."

"Ah," said Paganini, "and we are the richer for it. I would so like just once to see him from a distance perhaps or have him watch me play. But if I *make an enemy of your father, I'll never even enter Vienna.* And Vienna is . . . well, after Rome, there is . . . Vienna." Paganini sighed. "I cannot risk it, to lose Vienna."

"I'll see to all this!" Stefan said under his breath. He turned and looked out the narrow window, eyes roving the stone walls. How squalid this place looked compared to the confectionery corridors that had gone up in smoke, but it was perfectly Venetian. Russet velvet piled on the floor, fancy satin shoes thrown about—a peach cut open and all the romance squeezed out here.

"I know," said Paganini now. "I understand. Had Beethoven been playing still in the Argentine and the Schönbrunn and gone to London, and been chased by women, he might be as I am, not much for the composing but always for the center of the stage, for the man alone with the music, for the playing."

"Yes," said Stefan, turning. "You see, and it is playing that I want to do."

"Your father's palace in St. Petersburg is a legend. He'll soon be there. You can turn your back on such comforts?"

"I never saw it. Vienna was my cradle, I told you. I dozed on a couch once as Mozart played keyboard games; I thought my heart would burst. Look. I am alive within this sound, the sound of the violin, and not—like my great teacher—in writing notes for myself or others."

"You have the nerve to be a vagabond," said Paganini, his smile chilling just a little. "You do, but I cannot picture it. You Russians. You I will not . . ."

"No, don't dismiss me."

"I don't. Only resolve this thing at home. You must! This violin you speak of, yours which you took out of the fire, go home for it and take with it your father's blessing, otherwise they'll hound us, these merciless rich, that I've seduced from his duties to the Czar as ambassador's son. You know they can do it."

"I must have my father's permission," said Stefan, as if to make a memorandum of it.

"Yes, and the Strad, the long Strad of which you spoke. Bring that. I don't seek to take it from you. Look, you see what I have. But I want to play on that instrument too. I want to hear you play it. Bring that and your father's blessing, and the gossips we can handle. You can travel with me."

"Ah!" Stefan sank his teeth into his lip. "You promise me this, Signore Paganini? My money is adequate but no fortune. If you dream of Russian coaches and . . ."

"No, no, little boy. You're not listening. I say I will let you come with me and be where I am. I do not seek to be your minion, Prince. I am a wanderer! That is what I am, you see. A virtuoso! Doors open to me for what I play; I needn't conduct, compose, dedicate, mount productions with screaming sopranos and bored fiddlers in the pit. I am Paganini! And you shall be Stefanovsky."

"I'll get it, I'll get the violin, I'll get my Father's word!" Stefan said. "An allowance will be nothing to him."

He smiled openly, and the little man advanced and covered his face with kisses, in an Italian style perhaps, or one that was purely Russian.

"Brave, beautiful Stefan," he said.

Stefan, flustered, handed back to him the precious gift violin. Looking down at his own hands, he saw his many rings, all jeweled. Rubies, emeralds. He removed one and held it out.

"No, son," said Paganini. "I don't want it. I have to live, to play, but you need no bribe to have my promise."

Stefan clamped Paganini's shoulders in his hands and kissed his face. The little man rumbled with a laugh.

"And that violin, you must bring it. Ah, I have to see this long Strad as they call it, I have to play it."

Vienna once more.

The cleanliness was the dead giveaway, every chair gilded or painted with white and gold, and parquet floors immaculate. Stefan's father, I knew him at once, as he sat in the chair by the fire, a blanket of Russian bear fur over his lap, looking up at his son, and in this room, the violins all there in cases as before, though this was not the splendid palace that had burned but some more temporary quarters.

Yes, where they had put up until we could make the move to St. Peters-burg. I had come dashing back. I washed and sent for clean clothes before I came into the city gates. Look, listen.

He did cut a different figure, spruced in the bright fashions of the time, a smart black coat with fine buttons, crisp white collar and silk tie, no pigtail anymore or any of that, hair lustrous and still long from his journey as though it were a badge of his coming detachment from all this, like the hair of rock singers in our day and age that shouts the words Christ and Outcast with equal power.

He was afraid of his father, the elder glowering up at him from the fire:

"A virtuoso, a wandering fiddler! You think I brought the great musicians into my house to teach you this, that you should run off with that cursed bedeviled Italian! That, that trickster that does pranks with his fingers instead of playing notes! He hasn't the nerve to play in Vienna! Let the Italians eat him up. They who invented the castrato so he could sing volleys of notes, arpeggios and endless crescendos!"

"Father, only listen to me. You have five sons."

"Ah, you will not do this," said the Father, his white hair Lenten as it tumbled to the shoulders of his satin robe. "Stop! How dare you, my eldest." But the tone was gentle. "You know that the Czar will soon command your first military service; we serve the Czar! Even now, I depend upon him for our restoration in St. Petersburg!" He cut the tone, softening it with compassion, as though the years between them had given him a wisdom that made him sorry for his son. "Stefan, Stefan, your duty is to the family and to the Emperor; you don't take the toys I gave you for delight and make them your mania!"

"You never thought them toys, our violins, our pianofortes, you brought the finest here for Beethoven when he could still play . . ."

The father leant forward in the big white-framed French chair, too broad and squat to be anything but Hapsburg. He turned his shoulder to a great ornamented stove that climbed the wall to the inevitably painted ceiling, the fire enclosed beneath gleaming glazed enameled white iron and dizzying gold curlicues.

I felt it, I felt it as if I and my ghostly guide were in the room, very near to those we saw so completely. Pastry smells rising; grand broad windows; the dampness here was clean, as fog is clean off the sea.

"Yes," said the Father, obviously struggling to reason, to be kind. "I did bring the greatest of all musicians to teach you and delight you and make your childhood bright." He shrugged. "And I myself, I liked to play the violoncello with them, you know this! For you and your sister and brothers, I gave everything, as it had been done for me . . . great portraits hung on my walls before they burned, and you have always had the best of clothes, and horses in our stables, yes, the best of poets for you to read, and yes, Beethoven, poor, tragic Beethoven, I keep him near for you and for me and for what he is.

"But that is not the point, my son. The Czar commands you. We are not Viennese merchants! We don't seek taverns and coffeehouses full of gossip and slander! You are Prince Stefanovsky, my son. They'll send you to the Ukraine, first, as they did me. And you will pass the necessary years before you go into the more intimate governmental service."

"No." Stefan backed up.

"Oh, don't make it so painful for yourself," said his father wearily. His gray mane hung down around his wobbling cheeks. "We have lost so much, so very much; we have sold all that was saved, it seems, to leave this city, and it was only here that I was ever happy."

"Father, then learn from your own pain. I can't, I won't give up the music for any Emperor near or far. I wasn't born in Russia. I was born in rooms where Salieri played, where Farinelli came to sing. I beg you. I want my violin. Just give me that. Give it to me. Release me penniless and let it out you couldn't stop my headstrong ways. No disgrace will fall on you. Give me the violin and I will go."

There came a subtle threatening change into the Father's face. It seemed there were steps nearby. But neither figure acknowledged any but each other.

"Don't lose your temper, my son." The Father rose to his feet, the bear rug falling to the carpeted floor. He was regal in his satin robe, with furs beneath it, his fingers covered with brilliant jewels.

He was as tall as Stefan, no peasant blood here it seemed, only the Nordic mixed with the Slav to make giants of the ilk of Peter the Great perhaps, who knows, but these were true princes.

His father came close to him, then turned to survey the bright, lacquered instruments that rested all along the sideboards with their rampant painted Rococo gardens on every cabinet door. Silk paneling in the walls, the long streaks of painted gold rising to the muraled cove above.

It was a string orchestra. It made me shiver just to look at it. I didn't know this violin from any other there.

The Father sighed. The son waited, schooled obviously not to weep as he might have done with me, as he did now with me in this invisibility from which we watched. I heard him sigh, but then the vision overwhelmed again and held firm.

"You can't go, my son," the Father said, "to chase around the world with this vulgar man. You cannot. And you cannot take your violin. It breaks my heart to tell you. But you dream, and a year from now you will come to beg forgiveness."

Stefan could scarcely control his voice, looking at this heritage.

"Father, even if we dispute, the instrument is mine, I took it out of the burning room, I . . ."

"Son, the instrument is sold, as are all the Stradivari instruments, and the pianofortes and the harpsichord on which Mozart played, sold, all, I assure you."

Stefan's face wore the shock I felt as I looked on. The ghost in the featureless dark beside me was too sad himself to mock, but only closed tighter to me, trembling as if all this were too much for him, this boiling cloud, and he couldn't clamp it back down into his magic cauldron.

"No . . . No, not sold, not the violins, not the . . . not the violin I—" He blanched and twisted his mouth, and the straight dark eyebrows came together in a challenge of a frown. "No, I don't believe you, why, why do you lie to me!"

"Curb your tongue, my favorite son," said the tall gray-haired man, keeping one hand on the chair. "I sold what I had to sell to get the hell out of here and into our home in St. Petersburg. Your sister's jewels, your mother's jewels, paintings, God knows what, so as to salvage what I could for all of you, of what we had and must retain. To the merchant, Schlesinger, I sold the violins four days ago. He'll take them when we leave. He was kind enough to—"

"No!" Stefan cried out. His hands went up to the sides of his head. "No!" he roared. "Not my violin. No, you cannot sell my violin, you cannot sell the long Strad!"

He turned, eyes frantic, searching the tops of the long, painted credenzas where instruments lay carefully on silken pillows, cellos propped against chairs, paintings set as if to be moved.

"I tell you it's done!" the Father cried out. Turning right to left, he found his silver cane and lifted it in his right hand, first by the knob and then the middle.

Stefan had found the violin with his eye. He rushed towards it. I saw it.

With all my heart, I thought, yes, get it, take it, save it from this awful injustice, this stupid turn of fate, it's yours, yours . . . Stefan, take it!

And you take it from me now. In the fathomless dark he kissed my cheek, but he was too heartbroken to oppose me. *Watch what happens.*

"Don't touch it, don't pick it up," the Father said, advancing on the son. "I warn you!" He swung the cane around so that its ornamented knob was poised like a club.

"You don't dare smash it, not the Strad!" said Stefan.

A fury broke in the Father. It broke at these words, it broke as if over the stupidity of the assumption, the depth of misunderstanding.

"You, my pride," he said, lowering his head as he took one firm step after another. "Your Mother's favorite and Beethoven's cherub, you, you think I'll smash that instrument with this! Touch it, and you'll see what I do!"

Stefan reached for the violin, but the cane came down on his shoulders. He staggered under the blow, bent nearly double, backing up. Again the silver cane struck him, this time on the left side of his head and the blood gushed from his ear.

"Father," he cried.

I was wild in our invisible refuge, wild to hurt the Father, to make him stop, damn him, don't you hit Stefan again, you will not, you will not.

"It is not ours, I told you this," the Father cried. "But you are mine, my son, Stefan!"

Stefan threw up his hand, and the cane whipped through the air.

I must have screamed, but this was far beyond any intervention. The cane so bashed Stefan's left hand that Stefan gasped and whipped the hand to his chest with his eyes closed.

He didn't see the blow descending on his right hand that came to cover the wounded one. The cane struck his fingers.

"No, no, not my hands, my hands, Father!" he screamed.

Rushing feet in the house. Shouts. A young woman's voice, "Stefan!"

"You defy me," said the old man. "You dare." With his left hand he grabbed the lapel of his son's coat, the son so shocked with pain he grimaced, unable to defend himself, and thrusting his son forward so that his hands fell on the credenza, he brought down the cane again on Stefan's fingers.

I shut my eyes. *Open them, look what he does. There are instruments made of wood, and those that are made of flesh and blood and see what he does to me.*

"Father, stop it!" cried the woman. I saw her from behind, slender, tentative creature, with a swan neck and naked arms in her Empire gown of gold silk.

Stefan stood back. He broke the dazzle and the agony. He backed up further and stared down at the blood streaming from his crushed fingers.

The Father stood with the cane poised to strike again.

And now it was Stefan's face that changed; all compassion gone as if it were never possible in such a mask of rage and vengeance.

"You do this to me!" he cried. He waved his useless bleeding hands in the air. "You do this to my hands!"

Stunned, the Father took a backward step, but his face grew hard and stubborn. The doors of the room were filled with those who watched, brothers, sisters, servants, I didn't know.

The young woman tried to come forward, but the old man ordered her: "Back away, Vera!"

Stefan flew at his father, and used what was left to use, his knee, kicking the man back hard against the hot enameled stove, then lifting the tip of his boot to kick the Father's crotch as the old man's hands let loose the cane, and the old man fell to his knees and struggled to protect himself.

Vera screamed.

"You do this to me!" said Stefan, "You do this to me, you do this to me," the blood pouring from his hands.

The next kick caught the old man beneath his chin and sent him down in a spineless slump onto the rug. Again Stefan kicked, and this time the boot struck the side of his father's head, and then again.

I turned around. I didn't want to look, I didn't. *No, watch with me please.* It was so soft, so imploring. *He's dead, you know, dead there on the floor, but I didn't know it then. See, I kicked him again. Look. His knee doesn't rise, though the blow strikes him right where your mother's blow struck you, in the stomach I kick him, see . . . he was dead already from the kick to his chin perhaps, I never knew.*

Parricide, Parricide, Parricide.

Men rushed forward, but Vera swung around, stretching out her hands to block the path. "No, you will not touch my brother!"

It gave Stefan an instant to look up, hands still dripping blood, and in that instant he ran to the nearest door, knocking stunned servants out of his path, clattering down the marble staircase.

The streets. Is this Vienna?

From somewhere he'd procured a greatcoat, and bandages for his hands. He was a secretive figure, clinging to the walls. The street was old and crooked.

O gentle whore, what do you think, I had some gold left. But the news had electrified Vienna. I had killed my father. I had killed my father.

This was the Graben, now gone in reality; I knew it by its twists and turns, the place where Mozart lived, this neighborhood of eternal liveliness by day. But this was night, late night. Stefan waited in the shadows until a man emerged, with a sudden eruption of noise, from a tavern.

He shut the door on the warm world within, so full of smoking pipes, and the smell of malt and coffee, and the sound of talk and laughter.

"Stefan!" he whispered. He crossed the street and took Stefan's arm. "Get out of Vienna. You are to be shot on sight. The Czar himself has given Metternich the written permission. The city's full of Russian soldiers."

"I know, Franz," said Stefan, crying like a child, "I know."

"And your hands," said the young man, "what's been done?"

"Oh, not enough, not nearly enough, they're bound and twisted and broken and not set, it's all done, it's finished." He stood still, looking up at the tiny strip of Heaven. "Oh, Lord God, how could this happen, Franz, how? How could I have come to this when a year ago we were all in the ballroom and we were playing and even the Maestro was there, saying he enjoyed watching the movement of our fingers! How!"

"Stefan, tell me," said the young man called Franz. "You didn't really kill him. They lie, they paint a picture. Something happened, but Vera says that they have unjustly . . ."

Stefan couldn't answer. His eyes were squeezed shut, his mouth drawn back. He didn't dare to answer. He broke loose from his friend and ran, cloak billowing behind him, boots clattering on the rounded cobblestones.

He ran and he ran and we followed him, and he became tiny in the night, and the stars arched over all, and the city vanished.

This was a dark wood, but a young wood, tender, with small leafed trees, and crunching leaves beneath Stefan's boots. The Vienna Woods I knew so well from one college glimpse and so many books and so much music. A town lay ahead, and down into the town Stefan crept, hugging the bloody filthy bandaged hands, grimacing now and then at the pain, but fighting it off, as he entered the main street and a small square. It was late, the shops were all shut up, and the little streets looked picture-book to me in their quaintness. He hurried on his errand. He found a small, gated courtyard, but there were no locks here, and unseen he came inside.

How miniature this rural architecture after the palaces in which we'd witnessed horrors.

In the cool night air, full of the scent of pines and sweet burning stoves, he looked up at a lighted window.

A strange singing came from within, an awful bawling singing, but very happy and full of glee. A deaf man singing.

I knew this place, I knew it from drawings, I knew it was a place where Beethoven had once lived and written, and as we drew closer now, I saw what Stefan saw, as he climbed the little steps—the Maestro inside, swaying at his desk, dipping his pen and wagging his head and stomping his foot, and scratching out the notes, delirious it seemed in his own precious and safe corner of the universe where sounds might be combined as those with ears would never recommend or even tolerate.

The great man's hair was soiled, shot through with gray I hadn't seen before, the pockmarked face was very red, but his expression was relaxed and pure, with no scowl for anyone. He rocked back and forth again; he wrote. He sang that yammering stomping song that surely confirmed a path for him.

Young Stefan came to the door, opened it and stepped inside, peering down on the Maestro, the bandaged hands behind his back, then coming forward, went on his knees at Beethoven's arm.

"Stefan!" he cried out, his voice rough and loud. "Stefan, what is it?"

Stefan bowed his head and broke into tears, and suddenly, not meaning to, he raised his reddened bandaged hand as if to reach out and touch the Maestro.

"Your hands!" the Maestro went frantic. He stood up, throwing over the ink as he reached about on his desk. The conversation book, no, the blackboard, that was what he looked for, the companions of his deaf years, through which he spoke to everyone.

But then he looked down in horror and saw that both of Stefan's hands were useless for a pen as the younger knelt there, stricken, pleading with shakes of his head and shudders for mercy.

"Stefan, your hands, what have they done to you, my Stefan!"

Stefan raised his hand for quiet, raised it, desperate. But it was too late. In his protective panic Beethoven had brought others running.

Stefan had to escape. He clutched the Maestro for one moment, kissing him hard on the mouth, and then went to a farther door just as the one beside him sprang open.

Once again, he fled, Beethoven roaring in pain.

A small room: a woman's bed.

Stefan lay curled up in his tight pants, and a clean shirt, his profile sunk into the pillow, mouth open, face wet but still.

She, a thick and girl-faced woman, squarish and not unlike myself but young, bound fresh bandages around his hands. She doted on him, his still countenance, the battered hands she held, scarcely able to avoid tears. A woman who loved him.

"You must get out of Vienna, Prince," she said in the German of the Viennese, smooth and cultured. "You have to!"

He didn't stir. His eyes let in a little light perhaps or only gave away a tiny bit of white, which looked like death itself, except he breathed.

"Stefan, listen to me!" She took the intimate turn. "They bury your father in state tomorrow. His body will rest in the Van Meck tomb, and do you know what they mean to do, they mean to bury the violin with it."

He opened his eyes first, staring at the candle behind her, staring at the terra-cotta dish in which it rested, the dish that had already caught a pool of wax. Then he looked at her, turning, the wooden headboard plain and thick behind him. Surely this was the poorest place to which he'd ever taken us. A simple place, perhaps over a shop.

His dull eyes looked at her. "Bury the violin. Berthe . . . you said . . . ?"

"Aye, until his murderer is found and they can take the Father's remains home to Russia. It is winter now; you know they cannot make the journey anyway to Moscow. And Schlesinger, the merchant, he has given them the money for the thing, in spite of this. You know they set a trap for you, they think you will come for it."

"That's stupid," said Stefan. "That's mad." He sat up, his knee rising, his stockinged foot pushing into the lumpy mattress. His hair fell down as it was now, satin, undone. "A trap for me! To bury the violin in a coffin with him!"

"Shhh, don't be such a fool. They think you will come to steal it before it is sealed up. If not, it remains in the grave until you come, and they pounce on you. Or forever it lies with your Father until such time as you are found and executed for your crime. It is a grim affair; your sister and brothers are distraught, and not all of them so cruel of heart towards you, by the way."

"No . . ." he murmured, musing, remembering possibly his escape. "Berthe!" he whispered.

"And from your father's brothers comes the vengeful speech— these men, how they huff and puff—that the violin shall be buried with him whom you killed, so that you may never, never play it again. They picture you, a fugitive, who would steal it from Schlesinger."

"I would," he whispered.

A noise disturbed them both. The door opened and a small round-faced man appeared, a stubby and chunky man in a black cape and the undeniable upper-crust linen. He looked Russian, this man, his cheeks so full, his eyes small. One could see the Russian of today in him. He carried a big black cloak over his arm, a fresh garment which he laid down now on a chair. It had a hood to it.

Through small spectacles with silver frames he looked at the young man in the bed, at the girl who didn't even turn to greet him.

"Stefan," he said. He took off his top hat and smoothed back the remaining bits of gray hair that covered his pink skull. "They are guarding the house. They are in every street. And Paganini, they even accosted him in Italy with questions in all this, and the man has denied you, that he ever knew you."

"He had to do that," Stefan murmured. "Poor Paganini. What is that to me, Hans? I don't care."

"Stefan, I've brought a cloak for you, a big cloak with a hood, and some money to get you out of Vienna."

"Where did you get it?" Berthe asked with alarm.

"Never mind," the man said, glancing at her dismissively, "except to say that everyone in your family is not heartless."

"Vera, my sister. I saw her. I saw her when they tried to catch me, she ran in front of them. Oh, my sweetest Vera."

"Vera says you must go away, go to America, to the Portuguese Court in Brazil, anywhere, but go where your hands can be properly set and where you can live, or there is no life! Brazil is far away. There are other countries. Even England, go there—to London, but get out of the Hapsburg Empire, you must. Look, we're in danger, helping you."

The young woman became furious. "You know the things he's done for you!" she said. "I won't give him up." She glared at Stefan, and he tried to stroke her with the bandaged hands but stopped, like an animal pawing the air, his eyes suddenly dull from pain or simple despair.

"No, of course not," said Hans. "He is our boy, our Stefan, and always has been. I only say that it is a matter of days before they find you somewhere. Vienna is not so big. And you with your hands like clubs, what can you do? Why do you stay?"

"My violin," said Stefan in a heartbroken voice. "It's mine and I don't have it."

"Why can't *you* get it?" said the woman to the chubby little man, glancing up at him. She wrapped the gauze around Stefan's left hand still.

"Me? Get the violin?" asked the man.

"Why can't you go into the house? You've done it before. See to the confection tables yourself. See to the special tarts. God knows, when someone dies in Vienna it's a wonder everyone else doesn't die from eating sweets. Come with the bakers to see that all is right with the sweets yourself, it's simple enough, and slip upstairs and into the death room and take the violin. They stop you? Then say, you search for one of the family to beg news, you loved the boy so. Everybody knows it. Get the violin."

" 'Everybody knows it,' " he repeated. It was these words that disturbed the little man who went to the window and looked out. "Yes, everybody knows it was with my daughter he spent his drunken hours anytime he wanted."

"And gave me beautiful things for it, which I have still, and will on my wedding day!" she said bitterly.

"He's right," Stefan said. "I have to go. I can't stay here and endanger both of you. They would think to come here, to watch . . ."

"Not so," she said. "Every servant to the house and merchant to the family loves you, and doted on you, and all those French women, that trash that came with the conqueror, they keep a watch on them, yes, because you are so famous with them, but not with the baker's daughter. But it's true what Father says, you have to go. What have I told you myself? You have to go. If you don't leave Vienna, it is only a few days before they catch you."

Stefan was deep in thought. He tried to rest his weight on his right hand, then caught the error and slumped back against the wooden bedstead. The ceiling was sloped above his head, the window tiny in the thick wall. He seemed so vivid amid all this, too long, too sharpened, too brilliant and fierce for such a small chamber.

The young image of my ghost who walks through great rooms and down broad avenues.

The daughter turned to her father.

"Go into the house and get the violin!" said the daughter.

"You are dreaming!" said the man. "You are brainsick with love. You are a stupid baker's daughter."

"And you, who would be a fancy gentleman, with your fancy café in the Ringstrasse, you don't dare."

"Of course he doesn't," Stefan said with authority. "Besides, Hans wouldn't know the violin from any other."

"It lies in the coffin!" she said. "They told me." She bit the cloth with her teeth, and tore it in two and made another tight knot beneath his wrist. The bandage was already bloody. "Father, get it for him."

"In the coffin!" Stefan whispered. "Beside him!" It was full of contempt.

I would have closed my eyes, but had no such control over any physical body. I held this violin, the one of which they spoke, I had it in my arms, and I thought now, so this thing, this thing we follow through this bloody history is at this time, give it 1825 or more, lying already in a coffin! Has it been sprinkled with holy water, this thing, or will that only happen at the Last Rites, and the Requiem, and will that be beneath a Viennese church with gilt-and-sugar angels?

Even I knew the little man could not get the violin. But he struggled to defend himself, both to them and to his own heart, turning, pacing, lip jutting, glasses flecks of light.

"Why, how, you can't just walk into a room where a Prince in his coffin lies in state . . ."

"Berthe, he's right," said Stefan gently. "It's unspeakable that I allow him to take such a risk. Besides, when could he do it? What is he to do, walk boldly up and seize the thing from the dead man's grasp and rush out with it?"

Berthe looked up; her dark hair was a frame for a white face, her eyes beseeching but clever. She had long lashes and a lush thick mouth.

"There are times," she said, "late in the night when the room will be nearly empty. You know it. When men will sleep. And only a few say their Rosaries, and these even most likely close their eyes. So, Father, you go in to tend the tables. When even Stefan's Mother sleeps."

"No!" Stefan said, but the thought had found a fertile place. He looked forward, absorbed in his plan. "Go up to the coffin, take it from him, it lies with him, my violin. . . ."

"You can't do it," Berthe said. "You have no fingers with which to hold it." She was horror-struck. "You can't go near the house."

He said nothing. He glanced about himself, once again leaning on his hands and then quickly straightening on account of the pain. He saw the clothes that lay ready for him. He saw the cloak.

Then: "Tell me, Hans, tell me the truth, was it Vera who sent the money to me?"

"Yes, and your mother knows of it, but if you ever broadcast this, I will be destroyed; don't brag on this kindness with any other secret friends. Because if you do, neither your sister nor your Mother will have the power to protect me."

Stefan smiled bitterly and nodded.

"Did you know," said the little Hans, pushing his glasses up on his stubby nose, "that your Mother hated your Father?"

"Of course," said Stefan, "but I have hurt her far worse now than ever he did, haven't I?"

He didn't wait for the little man to find an answer. He swung his feet over the side of the bed. "Berthe, I can't put on these boots."

"Where are you going?" She ran around the bed, to assist. She helped him with each foot, and then to his feet. She gave him his black wool frock coat, fresh and clean, supplied no doubt by his sister.

The chubby little man looked up at him, full of pity and sadness. "Stefan," he said, "there are soldiers all about the house, the Russian guard, Metternich's private guards, and police everywhere. Listen to me."

The little man came up to him and put his hand on Stefan's hurt hand, and when Stefan winced and drew back the wounded hand, the little man stopped, apologetic and full of shame.

"It's nothing, Hans. You have done kindness for me. I thank you. God can't look unkindly on that. You did not murder my Father. And my Mother put her blessing on all this, I see. That's my father's finest cloak, lined in Russian fox, you see? How she thinks of me. Or did Vera give it to you?"

"It was Vera! But mark my words. Leave Vienna tonight. If you are caught there will not be a trial for this! They'll see to it you are shot dead first before you can speak or anyone can speak who saw him hurt you."

"I have been tried in here," said Stefan, touching his coat with the wrapped hand. "I killed him."

"Leave Vienna as I told you. Get to a surgeon who can yet mend your fingers. Perhaps they can be saved. There are other violins for one who plays as you play. Go across the sea, to Rio de Janeiro, go to America, or east to Istanbul where no one will ask who you are. In Russia, have you friends, friends of your mother?"

Stefan shook his head, smiling. "All cousins to the Czar or his bastards, every one," he said with a small laugh. It was the first time in this ghostly life that I had seen this Stefan truly laugh. He looked carefree for a moment, and happiness took all the lines from his face and made him, as it customarily does to people, perfectly radiant.

He was full of quiet gratitude for the flustered little man. He sighed and looked about the room. It seemed the unadorned gesture of a man who might soon die and looks at all the simple things with loving regard.

Berthe tied his frills, made his collars peaked and straight against his neck. She knotted the white silk tie in front. She took a black wool scarf and wound it round his neck, lifting his groomed and shining hair and letting it fall down. Long, yet trimmed.

"Let me cut it . . ." she said. More disguise?

"No . . . it doesn't matter. The cape and the hood will hide me. I have no time left. Look, it's midnight. The long deathwatch has probably begun."

"You can't!" she cried.

"But I will! Will you betray me?"

The thought stymied her, stymied her father. They shook their heads, silently and obviously vowing that they would not.

"Goodbye, darling, would I could leave you with something, some little thing . . ."

"You leave me with all I'll ever need," she said softly. There was resignation in her voice. "You leave me with some hours that other women must make up or read about in stories."

He smiled again. Never in any setting had I seen him so perfectly comfortable. I wondered if the bleeding hands hurt him, because the bandages were bad already.

"The woman who fixed my hands," he said to Berthe, sticking to his point, "she took my rings in payment, all of them. I couldn't stop her. But this is my last warm room for the night, my last unhurried moment. Berthe, kiss me and I'll go. Hans, I can't ask you for a blessing, but a kiss, I do."

They all embraced. Stefan put out his arms, as if he could lift the cloak with the clubby hands, but Berthe was quick to get the cloak, and the man and the woman together put it over his shoulders and brought the hood up over his head.

I was sick with fear. I knew what was to come. I didn't want to see it.

☞ 13 ☜

The vestibule of a great house. The undeniable ornament of the German Baroque, gilded wood, two murals facing each other, a man, a woman, in powdered wigs.

Stefan had gained entry, his hands tucked inside his coat, and still spoke sternly in Russian to the guards, who were confused and unsure about this well-dressed man who had come to pay his respects.

"Herr Beethoven is here? Now?" asked Stefan in this sharp Russian. A divertissement. The guards spoke only German. At last one of the Czar's private men appeared.

Stefan played it to the hilt, without removing his bandaged hands, making a deep Russian bow, the cape falling around him on the tiled floor, the chandelier above lighting the dark, near monastic figure.

In Russian, he said, "I have come from Count Raminsky in St. Petersburg to pay my respects." His confidence and bearing were perfection. "And also to convey a message to Herr van Beethoven. It was for me that Herr Beethoven wrote a quartet which was sent to me by Prince Stefanovsky. Ah. I beg you to allow me a few moments with my good friend; I would not at this hour disturb the family, only I was told that the watch was all night, that I might call."

He was on his way to the door.

A great formality descended on the Russian guards and was immediately adopted by the German officers and the wigged servants.

The servants trailed after the guards, then hastened to open doors.

"Herr Beethoven has gone home some time ago, but I can escort you to the room where the Prince is laid," said this Russian official, obviously in some awe of this tall imposing messenger. "And I should perhaps wake . . ."

"No. As I have already explained, I would not have them disturbed at this hour," said Stefan. He glanced about the house as though there was nothing in its regal dimensions that was familiar to him.

He started up the steps, the heavy fur-lined coat dancing gracefully just above the heels of his boots.

"The young Princess," he said glancing over his shoulder at the Russian guard who hastened to follow. "She was my childhood friend. I will come to call upon her at the proper hour. Only let me rest my eyes upon the old Prince and say a prayer."

The Russian guard started to speak, but they had come to the proper door. It was too late for words.

The death room. Immense, its walls replete with the gilded white curlicues that make the rooms of Vienna look so much like whipped cream; soaring pilasters with gilded tracery; a long row of outside windows, each deep in its rounded arch beneath a gilded soffit, its counterfeit in mirrors opposite and far at the end double doors such as those we entered now.

The coffin lay on a great curtained dais of rich gathered velvet, and a woman in a small gilded chair sat on the dais right beside the coffin, her head bowed in sleep. The nape of her neck showed a single strand of black beads, her dress was the high-waisted Empire style but in strict black mourning.

The whole bier was heaped and surrounded by exquisite bouquets of flowers. Marble jardinieres held sprays of solemn lilies and dour roses in profusion all about the room, becoming part of the engulfing decoration.

White-painted French-style chairs were set out in rows, their solemn damask upholstery of deep green or red, in sharp contrast to the clumsy German-made white frames. Candles burned, singly and in candelabra and in the great chandelier above, a massive thing of gold and glass not unlike that which had fallen in Stefan's house, all crusted with beeswax, pure and white.

A thousand flames fluttered timidly in the quiet.

To the rear of the room, a row of monks sat, saying the Rosary aloud in Latin, sotto voce, and in unison. They didn't look up as the hooded figure entered and made his way towards the coffin.

On a long golden couch two women slept, a younger dark-haired woman with Stefan's sharp features, her head against the other woman's shoulder, both of them dressed in rich black, their veils for the moment thrown back. A brooch loomed on the elder's neck. Her hair was silver and white. The younger stirred in her sleep as if arguing with someone but didn't wake, even as Stefan walked past, though some distance from her.

My mother.

The unctuous Russian guard didn't dare to stop the imperious aristocrat who boldly came to the dais.

Servants at the open door stood blind, as if they were waxen dummies in their pre-Napoleonic blue satin and pigtailed wigs.

Stefan stood before the dais. Only two steps above, the young woman slept, in her small gilded chair, one arm in the coffin.

My sister Vera. Does my voice tremble? Look at her, how she mourns him. Vera. And look into the coffin itself.

Our vision took us close. I was flooded with the scent of flowers, deep intoxicating perfume of lilies, other blooms. Candle wax; it was the sweeping swooning scent of my little Prytania Street Chapel of childhood, that capsule of sanctity and safety in which we knelt with Mother at the ornate rail, the rich gladioli on the Altar far outshining our little bundles of lantana.

Sadness. Oh, heart, such sadness.

But I could think of nothing but this before me. I was with Stefan in this attempt, and petrified with fear. The hooded figure quietly climbed the first two steps of the dais. I couldn't bear the heat of my own heart. No memory of mine took first place over this hurt, this harm, this fear of what was to come, of cruelty and shattered dreams.

Look at my father. Look at the man who destroyed my hands.

The corpse looked cruel, but only in a faded dried-up insignificant way, his Slavic features more evident in death, angles hardened, cheeks deeply grooved, nose falsely narrowed by the undertaker perhaps, lips too reddened with cake rouge and turning down, without the breath of life to make them give the quarter smile he'd worn so easily before he was ever angered or brought to this.

Very painted, this face, and his body was excessively dressed with furs and jewels and colored braids and velvet, sumptuous in the Russian style where everything must sparkle to express value. His hands with all their rings lay like dough on his chest, holding a crucifix.

But there beside him lay nestled in the satin the violin, *our* violin, against which Vera's sleeping hand dangled.

"Stefan, no!" I said. "How can you get it?" I whispered in our vigilant darkness. "She is touching it. Stefan."

Ah, you fear for my life as we watch this old tableau. And yet you won't give me my violin. Now watch me die for it.

I tried to turn away. He forced me to look. Rooted in the scene, we would be spared nothing. In our invisible form, I felt his heartbeat, I felt the tight wet tremble of his hand as he turned my head.

"Look," was all he could say to me. "Look at me, during the last few seconds of my life."

The hooded and cloaked figure mounted the last two steps of the dais. He stared down with glazed weary dark eyes at the dead Father. And then from beneath his cloak he reached with his thumbless bandage of a hand and scooped up the instrument and the bow, to his chest, quickly bracing it with the other maimed hand.

Vera woke.

"Stefan, no!" she whispered. Her eyes moved sharply, from left to right, a warning. She motioned desperately for him to leave.

He turned.

I saw the plot. His brothers came from the doors of other chambers. A man rushed to pull away the screaming Vera. She reached out for Stefan. She shrieked in panic.

"Murderer!" cried the man who fired the first bullet which struck not merely Stefan's chest but the violin. I heard the wood splinter.

Stefan was overcome with horror.

"No, you will not!" Stefan said. "No." Shot after shot struck him and the violin. He bolted. He ran down the center of the room, as they pumped their bullets into him. Bullets came now not only from the fancy dressed gentlemen but from guards, bullets shattering into him and into the violin.

Stefan's face was flushed. Nothing stopped the figure that we beheld. Nothing.

We saw his open mouth gasping for breath, his eyes narrowed, the cloak streaming out behind him as he ran down the staircase, the violin and bow safe in his arms, no blood, no blood, save that which oozed from his hands, and now look!

The hands.

The hands were unbound and whole and had no need of bandages. They had once again their long and perfect fingers. They clutched the violin tight.

Stefan bowed his head against the wind as he passed through the front door—I gasped. The doors were bolted and he had not even seen. The crack of guns, the screams, rose in a grating splash of dissonance and then faded behind him.

Down the dark street he sped, feet pounding the shiny uneven stones, only glancing down to see that he had the violin and bow safe in his hand, then giving the run all of his young strength until he had left the cobblestoned center of the town, running, running.

Lights were a blur in the dark. Was it fog that wreathed these lanterns? Houses rose up in unrelieved blackness.

Finally, he stopped, unable to go any further. He rested against a chipped and peeling plaster wall, the cloak fallen back to cushion his head, his eyes shut for a moment. The violin and bow were safe and unscathed in his pale fingers. He took deep breath after breath, and glanced frantically to see if anyone came to follow.

The night was without echoes. Figures moved in the dark but they were too dim to be seen, too far from the lights above occasional doorways. Did he notice the mist that curled along the ground? Was it common for winter in Vienna? Clumps of figures watched him. Were they to him only the tramps of the city night and nothing more?

Once again, he fled.

Only when he had crossed the broad bright Ringstrasse with its string of lights, and its utterly indifferent late-night crowds, and sought the open country, did he stop again and for the first time look down at his restored hands, his hands unbandaged and cured—and at the violin. He held it up by the light of the dim lamps of the city against the welkin to see that the violin was whole, unharmed, not so much as scratched. The long Strad. His. And the bow he had so loved.

He looked up, and back at the city he'd left. From the rise where he stood, the city gave its dim winter lights warmly to the lowering clouds. He was confused, elated, astonished.

We became material. The smells of the pine woods and the cold air, scented by distant chimney smoke, surrounded us.

We stood in the wood not far from him, but too far to ever comfort him, that Stefan of over a hundred years ago, standing there, his breath steaming in the cold, holding the instrument so carefully, his eyes peering towards this mystery he'd left behind.

Something was horribly wrong, and he knew it. Something was so monstrously wrong that he was caught in angst without end.

My spirit Stefan, my guide and companion, gave a soft moan though the distant figure did not. The distant figure held its vivid color, held its vibrant materiality, but it examined its clothes for wounds. It examined its head and hair. Intact, all. Here.

"He's a ghost, he's been since the first shot," I said, "and he didn't know it!" I sighed softly. I looked up to my Stefan and then at the far figure, who seemed the more innocent, the more helpless, the younger only by countenance and lack of poise. The specter beside me swallowed and his lips were wet.

"You died in that room," I said.

I felt such a piercing pain within me that I wanted only to love him, to know him completely with my soul and to embrace him. I turned and kissed his cheek. He bowed his head to receive more kisses, pushing his cold hard forehead against mine, and then he gestured to the distant newborn ghost yonder.

The distant newborn ghost examined his cured hands, his violin.

"*Requiem aiternam dona eis Domine,*" said my companion, bitterly.

"The bullets shattered you and the violin," I said.

Frantically, the distant Stefan turned on his heels and began a trek through the trees. Again and again he glanced back.

"My God, he's dead but he doesn't know it."

My Stefan only smiled, his hand on my neck.

A journey without a map or destination.

We followed him on his crazed wanderings; this was the hideous fog of Hamlet's "undiscover'd country."

I was gripped in a fierce chill. In memory I stood by Lily's grave, or was it Mother's? It was in that suffocating monstrous time before grief begins when everything is horror. Look at him, he's dead and he wanders and he wanders.

Through quaint small German towns with sloped roofs and

crooked streets, he moved and we behind him—both of us bodiless again or anchored only in our shared perspective. He walked across great empty fields and into the light forest again. No one saw him! Yet he heard the rustling spirits gathering: he tried to see what moved above, below, beside.

Morning.

Coming down into the main street of a small town, he approached the butcher's stall, spoke to the man, but the man could not see or hear him. He touched the cook on her shoulder, tried to shake her, but though he saw his gesture plain enough in some deep conflict between will and fact, she sensed nothing.

A priest came in a long black cassock, bidding good morning to the early shoppers. Stefan grabbed hold of him, but the priest could not see or hear him.

He was wild, watching the milling village crowd. Then solemn, trying desperately to reason on this.

Now, with greater clarity, he saw the dead hovering near. He saw what could only be ghosts, so broken and fragmented were their human shapes, and he stared at them as a living being might, in terror.

I squeezed my eyes shut; I saw the small rectangle of Lily's grave. I saw the handfuls of dirt strike the small white coffin. Karl cried, "Triana, Triana, Triana!" as I said over and over, "I'm with you!" Karl said, "My work's undone, unfinished, look at it, Triana, there is no book, it's not done, it's—look, where are the papers, help me, it's all ruined. . . ."

No, go away from me.

Behold this figure staring at the other shades who come as if drawn by his sheen. He feared; he searched their evanescent faces. Now and then he called out the names of the dead he had known in childhood, beseechingly, and then with a twisted frantic look, fell silent.

No one had heard this noise.

I moaned, and the figure beside me held me tight, as if he too could scarcely bear the sight of his own stranded soul, vivid and beautiful in his cloak and shimmering hair, in the middle of a crowd no more or less brilliantly tinted than himself that couldn't see him.

Deliberately he grew calm. The tears hovered, giving his eyes that great lustrous authority that motionless tears give. He lifted the violin and looked at it. He put it to his shoulder.

He began to play. He closed his eyes and gave himself to his terror in a mad dance that would have drawn applause from Paganini, a protest, a lament, a dirge and, slowly, opening his eyes, as the bow moved, as the music ripped through us, he realized no one, no one in the square of this town, no one anywhere near or far could see or hear him.

For one moment he faded. Holding the violin in his right hand and bow in the left, he brought these hands up to his ears and bowed his head, but as the color drained from his shape, he shuddered all over and opened his eyes wide. The air around him swirled with ever more visible spirits.

He shook his head; he brought his mouth back as a child might when crying. "Maestro, Maestro!" he whispered. "You are locked in your deafness, and I am locked out of all hearing! Maestro, I am dead! Maestro, I am as alone now as you are! Maestro, they cannot hear me!" He screamed the words.

Did days pass?

Years?

I clung to my Stefan, the guide in this murky world, shivering though there was no real cold, watching the figure walk again, and now and then lift the violin to his ear and play some frantic series of notes, only to stop in rank rage, his teeth clenched, his head shaking.

Vienna once more perhaps. I didn't know. An Italian city. It might have been Paris. I didn't know. The details of those times were too mingled in my mind from study and imagining.

He walked on.

The sky above became not so much a measure of anything natural but a canopy for an existence apart from nature, a great black fabric snagged with carelessly flung stars like diamonds on a mourner's veil. At morn sometimes, a lowering drape.

In a graveyard of rich tombs, the wanderer stopped. We were invisible again, close to him. He looked at the tombs, he read the names on them. He came to the tomb of Van Meck. He read his Father's name. He wiped the thick crust of dirt and moss from the stone.

Time was no longer fixed to the clock and the watch. He drew out his pocket watch and stared at it, and the face said nothing back to him.

Other spirits clustered in the uneven dark, curious, drawn by his firm movements and bright color. He peered into their faces.

"Father?" he whispered. "Father?"

The spirits shied away, as if they were balloons in the wind, tied on loose string that could be swept to right or left by one blow to the cords that bound them to the earth.

The full realization came over his face now. He was dead, most definitely dead. He was not merely dead, but surely isolated from any other ghost like himself!

He searched the air and the earth for another sentient phantom—as determined, as full of misery. He found nothing.

Did he see it as my Stefan and I saw it now?

Yes, you and I see now what I saw then—what I saw, knowing only that I was dead, and not what it meant that I still walked on earth, what I might do in this wretched perdition—knowing only that I moved from place to place, that nothing bound me or constricted me or comforted me, knowing only that I had become no one!

Into a small church we wandered during Mass. It was in the German style but simpler from the earlier days before the Rococo had covered over Vienna. Gothic arches rose from these rosetted columns. The stones were large and unpolished. The congregation were country folk, and chairs were few, almost none.

His spectral appearance hadn't changed. He was still the sturdy polychrome vision.

He watched the distant ceremony on the Altar beneath the blood red canopy held by Gothic saints, starved, gnawed, venerable, and clumsily positioned there as stanchions.

Before the high crucifix, the priest raised the round white consecrated host, the magic wafer, the miraculously palatable body and blood. I could smell the incense. The tiny bells rang. The congregation murmured in Latin.

The ghost of Stefan looked coldly on them, trembling, as a man bound for execution might on the strangers who watch him walk to the gallows. But there was no gallows.

Out into the wind he went again, walking uphill, walking that walk that I imagine when I hear the Second Movement of Beethoven's *Ninth*, that dogged march. Up and up through the woods, up and up he walked. I thought I saw snow and then rain, but I didn't know. It seemed leaves swirled about him once and he stood in a shower of these yellow falling leaves, and staggered once onto a road to wave at a carriage that took no notice of him.

"But how did it start?" I said. "How did you break through? How did you become this strong tenacious monster that tortures me?" I demanded. In the blackness that shrouded us, I felt his cheek, and his mouth.

Oh, merciless question. You have my violin. Be still, watch. Or give me the instrument now. Haven't you seen enough to know that it's mine, that it belongs to me, that I brought it over the divide and into this realm with my very life's blood, and you hold it, so that I can't get it loose; the gods are mad, if they exist, that let such a thing happen. The God in Heaven is a monster. Learn from what you see.

"You learn, Stefan," I said. I clutched the violin all the more securely.

This brought only helpless need out of him at my side in the pitch dark where we hovered, his arms around me still, his forehead on my shoulder. He moaned as if confiding his pain, in a private code, his own hands covering mine, touching the wood and the strings of the violin but not seeking to pull it loose. I felt his lips move against my hair, finding the curve of my ear, and more so, I felt him pressed against me, urgent, trembling, unresolved. The heat inside me rose as if to warm both of us.

I stared back at the wandering young spirit.

Snow fell.

The young spirit watched it and saw that it didn't touch his cloak or his hair but seemed to fly past; he tried to catch it with his hands. He smiled.

His feet made a crunch in the snow. Was this something he truly felt or merely a sensation he supplied himself through will and anticipation? His long cloak was a dark shadow in the drifting snow, the hood thrown back, his eyes blinking into the white soundless flood from Heaven.

Suddenly a ghost startled him—a filmy wanderer out of the forest, a woman in grave wrappings, evidently addicted to menace, but he fought her off. He was shaken. Though he'd done it with one stroke of his arm, he shivered and he ran. The snow grew thicker, and it seemed for a moment I could not see him at all, and then he appeared, visible, dark, ahead of us.

It was the cemetery again, full of graves both large and small. He stood at the gates. He peered inside. He saw a wandering ghost drifting by, talking to itself like a mad human, a gossamer thing of snaggled hair and wavering limbs.

He reached out and pushed the gate. Was this fancy? Or was he strong enough to make this material thing move? He didn't test it beyond this but merely walked past the high pickets and down the wintry path where snow had not come yet but all the fallen leaves were crisp and red and yellow.

Ahead, a small group of human mourners gathered by a humble grave, its stone no more than a pyramid. They wept, and finally all drifted away but one, one elderly woman, who, walking off, found a place to be seated on the edge of a more richly carved monument, beside the graven statue of a dead child! A dead child! I marveled.

The dead child was marble and held a flower in her hand. I saw my daughter—but this was fleeting—there was no monument for my Lily—and this cemetery of another century—descended once more, with our wandering ghost staring at the distant mournful figure—a woman in a black bonnet with long satin strings, a woman in big full skirts, skirts of a later time than when Vera in her slim gown had rushed across a room to save her brother.

Did the ghost realize this? Decades had gone by? The ghost merely gazed on the woman and walked in front of her, testing his invisibility to her, and shook his head in thoughtful meditation. Was he resigned now to the utter horror of purposeless existence?

Suddenly his eyes fell on the grave round which the mourners had gathered! He saw the single name carved on the pyramid.

I saw it too.

Beethoven.

A cry came from young Stefan's lips that should have waked all from their graves! Once again, clutching instrument in one hand and bow in the other, he pressed his fists to his head as he roared and roared. "Maestro! Maestro!"

The mourning woman heard nothing, noticed nothing. She didn't see the ghost who flung himself into the dirt, digging at it with his hands, letting the violin tumble loose.

"Maestro, where are you? Where did you go? When did you die? I'm alone! Maestro, it's Stefan, help me. Lay my case before God! Maestro."

Agony.

Angor animi.

The Stefan beside me quaked, and the pain in my chest spread like a fire in my heart and lungs. The young man lay before the neglected monument, among the flowers left there by the woman. He sobbed. He beat his fist upon the ground.

"Maestro! Why did I not go to Hell! Is this Hell? Maestro, where are the ghosts of the damned, is this damnation, Maestro, what have I done? Maestro . . ." Now it was grief, pure grief. "Maestro, my beloved teacher, my beloved Beethoven."

His sobs were dry and soundless.

The mourning woman only looked at the stone with the name Beethoven. Through her fingers passed the beads, very slowly, of a simple black and silver Rosary. The somber kind of Rosary used by nuns when I was a little girl. I saw her lips moving. Her face was narrow, eloquent, her eyes half-lidded as she prayed. Gray eyelashes, scantly visible, gaze fixed as though she truly meditated on the sacred Mysteries. Which one did she see before her?

She heard no cries from anyone there; she was alone, the human; and he was alone, the spirit. And the leaves spread out yellow all around them, and the trees thrust weak bare limbs into the hopeless sky.

At last, he drew himself together. He climbed to his knees and then to his feet and he lifted the violin, brushing the dirt and bits of leaf from it. He bent his head in a perfect statement of sorrow.

It seemed an endless time the woman prayed. I could almost hear her prayers. She said her Hail Marys in German. She had come to the fifty-fourth bead, the last Hail Mary, or Ave, of the last decade. I looked at the marble statue of the child beside her. Stupid, stupid, coincidence, or his connivance that he had presented this scene thus to me, with that child in marble and a woman in black. And a Rosary, a Rosary such as Rosalind and I had once torn to pieces in a quarrel after our Mother's death, "It's mine!"

Don't be the vain fool. This is what happened! Do you think I pluck it from your mind, the disasters that twisted my soul and made me what I am? I show you who I am, I make up nothing. I have such agony in me that imagination means nothing; it's overwhelmed by a fate that ought to teach you fear and compassion. Give me back my violin.

"Do *you* learn compassion from this?" I demanded. "You who would drive people mad with your music?"

His lips touched my neck, his hand ground hard into my arm.

The young ghost brushed leaves from his fur-lined cloak, just as a human man might do, and watched in a daze as they fell to the ground. Again, he looked at the name:

Beethoven.

Then he reached down to gather up his violin and his bow, and this time, as he lifted the instrument to play, he began a familiar theme, a theme I knew with my whole heart, the first theme of music I had ever memorized, in my life. It was the lead melody from Beethoven's one and only *Concerto* for violin and orchestra—that lovely, lovely zesty song that seems too full of happiness really to be the Beethoven of the heroic symphonies and mystical quartets, a song even a talentless boob like me could memorize in one night, as I watched an old genius play it.

Softly, Stefan played it, not telling of grief, but only of tribute. For you, Maestro, the music you wrote, this sprightly melody for the violin written when you were young and before the horror of silence came down on you, and wrapped you away from all the world so that you had to make music that was monstrous in that vacuum.

I could have sung this melody with him. How perfectly it rose from the strings, and how the distant ghost let himself drift into it, body scarcely moving, winding in and out of the melody itself to take up orchestral parts and weave them back into the solo, just as he had done with another piece of music so long ago for Paganini.

At last he came to that part which is called the cadenza, when the violinist is to take two themes or all themes and play them together, when themes collide, intermingled in an orgy of invention, and this he let loose—fresh, and lustrous, and full of sweet serenity. His face was smooth with resignation. He played and he played, and gradually I felt my own body grow limp in my Stefan's arms. I felt myself understand what I had tried to tell him:

Grief is wise. Grief does not cry. Grief comes only long after the horror at the sight of the grave, the horror at the side of the bed, grief is wise, and grief is imperturbable.

Stillness. He had come to the end. The note hovered in the air, then died. Only the forest sang on in its usual muted song, of tiny organic instruments too varied ever to be counted—birds, leaves, the cricket beneath the fern. The air was gray and soft and wet and clinging.

"Maestro," he whispered. "May Perpetual Light Shine Upon You. . . ." He wiped at his cheek. "May your soul and the souls of all the Faithful Departed rest in Peace."

The mourning woman, heavy in her black bonnet and huge skirts, rose slowly from her seat beside the marble child. She came towards him! She could see him! She suddenly reached out to him.

In German she spoke. "Thank you for that," she said. "Beautiful young man, and that you played it with such skill and feeling."

He could only stare at her.

He was afraid. The young ghost was afraid. He looked at her perplexed. He didn't dare to speak. She stroked his face with her hand, and spoke again.

"Young man," she said. "So blessed. Thank you for that on this day of all days. I love this music so. And always have. Whoever doesn't love him is a coward."

He seemed unable to answer.

Politely, she withdrew, turning her eyes away to give him his privacy again, and she made her way down the path.

Then he called out: "Thank you, madam."

She turned again and nodded.

"Ah, and this day of all days, my last visit here perhaps. You know they move the grave soon. They will put him in the new cemetery with Schubert."

"Schubert!" he whispered.

He held in his shock.

Schubert had died young. But how could this disconnected counterfeit of a living man know such a thing, roaming in the ether?

It didn't need to be said aloud. We all knew this, all of us—the woman of memory, and the young ghost, and the ghost that held me, and I. Schubert the maker of songs had died young, only three years or less after his visit to the deathbed of Beethoven.

Transfixed, the young ghost watched her leave the graveyard.

"And so it began!" I whispered. I stared at the visible ghost, the powerful ghost.

"What drives this spirit to visibility?" I demanded. "I can take the woman seated beside the marble child, but can you see your dark and secret gift which can cross the divide of death? Do you? Have you ever looked at these lessons before?"

He wouldn't answer me.

✑ 14 ✑

He didn't reply.

The awestruck young ghost waited until the woman was out of sight, and then, walking a pace from the grave, looked up to what he could see of the sky, a Vienna winter sky, almost a soiled gray, then solemnly he glanced back at the tomb.

Around him clustered the disheveled and disoriented dead, more dense and cunning than before. Oh, the sight of these spirits!

Do I see anyone to whom I can appeal? You think your Lily wanders in this gloom, your father, your mother? No. Look now at my face. Look now what recognition brings and isolation solidifies. Where are my fellow dead, whatever their sins and mine? Not even monsters executed for sure crimes come forth to take my hand. I stand apart from all these you see, these wraiths. Look on my face. Look, and see where it began. Look on hate.

"*You* look on it," I cried. "*You* learn from it!"

I saw it only for an instant. The standing figure. The hardened face, the contempt for the wandering formless dead, the cold eyes cast down on the grave.

Twilight.

Another cemetery had risen around us; it was new, full of more grand monuments, more for show, and surely here somewhere stood the monument—ah, yes, to Schubert and Beethoven, their graven statues mounted like friends though in life they had scarce known each other—and before this monumental heap, the young and visible Stefan played a fierce Beethoven sonata, weaving his own work in and out, and a crowd of young women looked on, spellbound, one weeping.

Weeping. I could hear her weeping. I could hear her weeping, and it became mingled with the crying of the violin, the ghost's face mournful finally as her own, and as she clutched her waist in pain, he bled the long notes out, and made the others swoon as they gazed at him.

It might as well have been the worshipers of Paganini in the Lido, here, this magic violinist, nameless no doubt and garbed now completely for the late part of the century, playing for the living and the dead, eyes rising to fix on the one woman who cried.

"You needed their grief, you fed on it!" I said. "You found your strength in it. You stopped your mad zinging crazy dead song and you played a selfless tune and they could see you then."

You're rash and wrong. Selfless indeed. When was I ever selfless? And you, are you selfless now that you have my violin? Is it selflessness you feel as you watch this spectacle? I didn't feed upon her pain, but her pain opened her eyes and her eyes saw me, and those of others opened as well, and the song came out of me, from my talent, my talent born to me in my natural life and nurtured there and tutored there. You have no such gift. You have my violin! You are a thief as surely as my father was, a thief as the fire was that would have burnt it up!

"And throughout this harangue you hold on to me. I feel your lips. I feel your kisses. I feel your fingers against my shoulders. Why? Why tenderness, as you spit hate in my ear? Why this mixture of love and rage? What can I give you that is good, Stefan? I tell you again, attend your own story. I won't give you back an instrument to drive people mad. Show me what you will. I won't do it."

He whispered in my ear.

Does it make you think of your dead husband? When the drugs made him impotent and he was so humiliated? Remember his face, his haggard face and the cold glaze of his eyes. He hated you. You knew the disease was finally on the march.

I don't hold you because I love you. And neither did he. I hold you because you are alive. Your husband thought you a fool with a pretty house he filled with trinkets, Dresden plates, and high-top desks inlaid with fancy figures and crusted with ormolu; he held the crystal from France before your eye, and cleaned the chandeliers; he heaped your bed with pillows trimmed in brocade.

Violin

And you, you, swallowed up with that, and your sense of heroism, that you would marry this sickling man, this fragile man, you let your beloved little sister Faye wander off. You didn't take her to your heart, you didn't stop her. You didn't see her take your Father's diaries and turn and turn and turn the pages! You didn't see her stare the length of the attic to the door of the room where you and your new husband, Karl, lay in bed. You did not see her frailty, displaced in her own Father's house by this new drama, Karl, the rich man, which you fed on as surely as I have ever fed on your misery. You did not see her slip to an orphan beaten down by her Father's written words of judgment, disappointment, condemnation. You didn't see her pain!

"You see mine?" I tried to throw him off. "You see my pain? You claim yours is greater than mine, because you with your own hand struck down your Father? I have no talent for such crimes any more than for the violin. But this we share, this talent for suffering, yes, and for mourning, yes, and the passion for the majesty, the utter mystery of music. You think you can wring from me compassion when you pitch me into forced memories of Faye that I can't endure? You sickened dead thing. Yes, I saw Faye's pain, yes, I did, I did, I did let her go, I did, I let Faye go, I let her go! I married Karl. And it hurt Faye. Faye needed me!"

Crying, I tried to pull loose. I couldn't move. I could only keep the violin from him and turn my head away. I wanted to cry alone. I wanted to cry forever. I wanted nothing but crying, and only those sounds which were eternally and forever the echo of crying, as though crying were the only sound that carried truth or merit.

He kissed me under the chin and down along the neck. His body told of tender need, of pliant patience and sweetness, his fingers caught my face worshipfully, and he bowed his head as if in shame. In a broken voice he said my name:

Triana!

"I see you leapt to strength from love," I said, "love of the Maestro. But when did you start to drive them mad, to make them feel suffering?" I asked. "Or did this turn of events come especially for me, Triana Becker, the unremarkable, talentless woman in the white cottage on the Avenue; surely I wasn't the first. Whom do you serve? Why do you wake me from dreams of the beautiful sea? You think you serve the man whose gravestone brought you such a harrowing pain that you gained material form?"

He moaned as if to beg me to stop.

I wouldn't break off.

"You think you served the God to whom you prayed? When did you start to make the grief if the grief didn't come sharp enough to make you?"

Another scene took shape. Trolleys clattered on their tracks. A woman in a long dress lay on a bed of sensuous curves—call it Art Moderne. The window was framed in that free-drawn leaded design that marked the time. A phonograph stood nearby, its bulbous needle stilled, its turntable dusty.

It was Stefan who played for her.

She listened with glistening tears, oh, yes, the requisite tears, the eternal tears, let tears be as frequent in this narrative finally as any common everyday word. Let the ink turn to tears. Let the paper be soft with them.

She listened with glistening tears and watched as the young man in the short, trim modern coat, sporting his lank satin hair, as if he would not give it up, though surely by now he knew he could change his shape, played the celestial instrument for her.

It was a lustrous song I couldn't name, perhaps his own, dipping into the dissonance that marks even the early music of our own century, a twist, a throb, a thundering protest of nature and of death. She cried. She lay her head against green velvet, a stylish creature, as if painted on stained glass in her frivolous gown, her pointed shoes, her soft ringlets of red hair.

He stopped. He lowered his fine weapons to his side. He looked tenderly at her, and came to her, and sat down on the curved couch beside her. He kissed her, yes, visible and palpable to her as he was to me, and his hair fell down on her as it did on me even now in the airily compassless gloom where we watched.

He spoke now to the woman on the couch in a fresher German more easy to my ear.

"Years ago," he said, "the great Beethoven. He had a grieving friend, a friend named Antoine Brentano. He loved her tenderly, most tenderly, as he loved so many people. Shhh. Don't believe the lies they tell of him. He loved many. And when she was in pain, Madame Brentano, he would come into her Viennese house, saying nothing to anyone. He would play and play for her—on the pianoforte—hour by hour to relieve her pain. These songs would drift up through the floors to her and comfort her and blunt her suffering. And then he would as silently take his leave without a nod to anyone. She loved him for it."

"As I love you," said this young woman.

Was she dead now, perhaps even long dead, or merely ancient?

"Did you drive her mad?"

I don't know! Watch. You don't admit the depth of it!

She reached up with naked arms and wrapped them around the ghost, around something solid and seemingly male and passionate for her, hot for her pampered flesh, for the tears which he licked with his spectral tongue in a gesture so monstrous suddenly that the whole picture went dark for me.

Licking her eyes, her salty tears, licking her eyes. Stop it!

"Let me go!" I said. I thrust against him. I kicked with my heels against his feet. I threw back my head and heard the sound of my skull against his! "Let me go!" I said.

Give me my violin and I'll let you go! Eyes. Are Lily's eyes still in a jar? You let them cut her up, remember, and why, to be sure that you by some negligence or stupidity had not yourself murdered her? Eyes. Remember? Eyes, your Father's eyes; they were open when he died and your Aunt Bridget said to you, Do you want to close them, Triana, and she told you what an honor it was to close his eyes, and showed you how to put your hand . . .

I struggled but couldn't get loose.

There came music, replete with drums, something eerie and savage, yet behind it rose his violin.

Did you even look into your mother's eyes that day you let her go to her death, she died in a seizure, foolish girl, she could have been saved, she was not worn out, she was only sick unto death of living and of you and all her dirty children and her childish frightened husband!

"Stop!"

I saw him suddenly, my captor. We were visible. There was light gathering around us. He stood apart from me. I held the violin and glared at him.

"Be damned with all your visions," I said. "Yes, yes, I confess, I killed them all, I did, I am to blame; if Faye is dead and lying on a slab, I did it! Yes, I did it! What would you do with it if I gave back this violin? Drive someone else crazy? Eat her tears? I loathe you. My music was my joy. My music was transcendence! What is yours but harm and meanness?"

"And why not," he said to me. He stopped close and clamped his hands on my neck, treacherously against my throat. I could scarcely bear to be touched there even by someone I loved, that tender place around the neck, but I wouldn't fall into his trick and try to throw him off.

"Have you the strength to kill me?" I said. "Did you bring that power too, into this void, the power to kill as you killed your Father? Do it then. Maybe we are at the door of death, and you are the god who holds the scales to weigh my heart. Is this the form of reckoning? All made up of things I cherished in my life?"

"No!" But he was shaken, crying again. "No. Look to me! Don't you see what I am? Don't you see what happened to me? Don't you understand! I am lost. I am alone. And anyone who walks in the void at the same pace as I do walks alone as I do! We who are visible and powerful haunts, and surely there must be more, we cannot commune with each other—Bring you Lily? I'd do it if I could! Your Mother? In the snap of a finger, if I knew how, yes, come, comfort her daughter who has mourned her Mother all her life, and so uselessly. And with you, with you, traveling back into this pain, outside my Father's burning house, I saw for the first time the shade of Beethoven! His ghost! He came on *your account, Triana!*"

"Or to stop you, Stefan," I said, making my voice soft. "To school your magic. Yours in some naive and powerful sorcery. This violin is made of wood, and you are flesh and I am flesh, though one is living and the other made by unforgiving greed—."

"No!" he whispered. "Not greed. Never."

"Let me go. I don't care if this is madness, dream or witchcraft, I want to get away from you!"

"You can't."

I felt the change. We were dissolving. Only the violin had form in my arms. We vanished again. We had no selves. The scene descended; the eerie music beat on.

A man was on his knees, hands over his ears, but Stefan the fiddler left him no peace, drowning out the half-naked coffee-skinned drummers who pounded the drums, their eyes fixed on the evil violinist, whom they followed yet feared as they beat the rhythm.

Another moment shone bright, a woman banging his tenacious ghostly shape with her fist as on and on he played, a wailing dirge.

There came a school yard with great leafy trees where the children danced about him in a ring, the fiddler, as if he were the Pied Piper, and a teacher cried out and tried to draw them away, but I couldn't hear her voice over his incessant cantabile.

What did I see now? Figures embracing in the dark, whispers struck my face. I saw him smile and a proffered woman blot out the shimmer of his countenance.

Love them, drive them crazy, it was all the same in the end, because they died! And I did not. I did not. And this violin is my immortal treasure and I will tear you out of life right into this Hell with me forever if you don't give it up.

But we had come to a certain place. The blur was gone. A ceiling ran above our heads. This was a corridor.

"Wait, look, these white walls," I said, thrilled with alarm, with such terrifying déjà vu. "I know this."

Filthy white tile, and there came the demonic taunting of the violin, not music now so much as a rasping, driving torture.

"I saw this place in a dream," I said, "these white tile walls, look, these metal lockers. Look, the big steam engines. And the gate, look!"

For one precious instant, even as we stood at the rusted gates, the great gorgeous beauty of the dream came back, the dream which had had not only this grim cellar passage and its gated tunnel, but the palace of beautiful marble, and before that the gorgeous sea, and the spirits dancing in the foam, who seemed now to me, not wretched like the wraiths we watched in horror, but some free and wholesome thing that thrived on the sheer brilliance and volume of the waves—the nymphs of life itself. Roses on the floor. "It's time."

Yet all that we saw now were the gates to the dark tunnel, and the engines made a droning sound, and he played his violin in there, in the dark tunnel, and no one spoke now, and the dead man, no, dying now, look, dying, bleeding from his wrists.

"Ah, and you drove him to it, didn't you? And this is to teach me that I should give in to you? Never."

I drove his own music out of his head, I drove it out with mine! That became a game as well. With you, I would have driven out the Maestro and the Little Genius Mozart, but you loved what I played. Music was not goodness to you, you liar. Music was self-pity. Music was keeping incestuous company with the dead! Have you buried your little sister Faye in your mind? Have you laid her in a morgue without a name, already preparing for her the noisy rich funeral? With Karl's money you can buy her a pretty box, your sister who was so chilled and alone in your dead Father's shadow, still, your little sister, watching your new husband take his place in the house, a blessed flame that you so easily deserted!

I turned in the invisible grip of his arms. I pushed my knee against his body hard, as hard perhaps as he had kicked his own Father. I shoved at him with both hands. I saw him in a flash.

All other imagery deserted us. There was no white tile or drone of engines. Even the stench was gone, and the music. No echo told us we were enclosed.

He flew back from me, the Stefan who had come to me in New Orleans, as if he were falling, and then he plunged forward again, grabbing for the violin.

"No, you will not." Again, I kicked him. "You will not, you will not! You will not do it again to any one of them, and it is in my hands, and the Maestro himself asked you why! Why, Stefan! You gave me the music, yes, and you give me the perfect absolution for confiscating the origin of that gift."

I lifted the violin and bow in both hands. I lifted my chin.

He brought his fingers up to his lips.

"Triana, I'm begging you. I don't know the meaning of what you say, or what I say. I beg you. It's mine. I died for it. I'll go away from you with it. I'll leave you. Triana!"

Was this hard pavement under my feet? What lucid fantasy would surround us now, what more would be revealed? Dim buildings in the mist. A sting of wind.

"Come at me again with solid flesh and I swear, I'll smash it on your head, this thing!"

"Triana," he said in shock.

"I'll break it first," I said. "I swear it."

I held it up more firmly, ready with the bow, and I swung it at him so that he staggered back in hurt and fear.

"No, you can't," he pleaded. "Triana, please, please, give the violin back to me. I don't know how you took it. I don't know what justice this is, what irony. You tricked me. You stole it from me. Triana! Oh, God, and you, you of all of them."

"Which means what, my darling?"

"That you . . . you have ears to hear such melodies and such themes . . ."

"Indeed you did make melodies and themes and memories too. How expensive is the cost of your entertainment."

He shook his head in helpless frantic denial.

"Such songs for you that there was freshness in them, almost life, and outside your window I looked up and saw your face and felt what you call love, and I cannot remember—"

"You think this tactic will soften me? I told you I have my justification. You haunt no more. I have the violin, as if it were your cock. The rules we may never know, but it's in my hands and you aren't strong enough to reclaim it."

I turned. This *was* hard pavement. This was cold air.

I ran. Was that the sound of a trolley?

I felt the impact of the paving stones beneath my shoes. The air was freezing, bitter, ugly. I couldn't see anything but white sky and dull leafless trees, and buildings like bulking ghosts themselves in their transparency.

I ran and ran. The balls of my feet hurt; my toes went numb. The cold made my eyes shed their first wasted tears. My chest ached. Run, run, out of this dream, out of this vision, find yourself, Triana.

There came the sound of a trolley again, lights. I stopped, my heart pounding.

My hands grew so cold suddenly they hurt. I clutched the violin and bow in my left hand and sucked my right fingers to warm them. Sucked them in my mouth, my lips chapped and cold. God! This was the cold of Hell. The wind went through my clothes.

These were the simple light clothes I'd worn when he stole me away. Velvet tunic, silk.

"Wake up!" I shouted. "Find your place. Get back to your own place!" I screamed. "End this dream. End it."

How many times had I done that, come back through fancy, or daydream or nightmare to find myself safe in the four-poster in the octagonal room with the traffic of the Avenue rushing outside? If this is madness, I will have none of it!

I'd rather live with all its agony than this!

But this was too solid!

There rose modern buildings. Round the curving tracks two streetcars came, sleek, of the present time, linked together, and just in front of me I saw a blazing sight that was no more than a kiosk opening up in spite of the winter, its portable walls hung already with multicolored magazines.

I rushed towards it. My foot stuck in the streetcar track. I knew this place. I fell, and only saved the violin by turning to the side, my elbow hitting the stones instead of it.

I climbed to my feet.

The sign that loomed above read words I'd seen before.

HOTEL IMPERIAL. This was the Vienna of my own time, my own moment, this was the Vienna of now. I couldn't be here, no, impossible. I couldn't wake anywhere but where I had begun.

I stamped my feet, I danced in a circle. Wake up!

But nothing changed. It was dawn and the Ringstrasse was coming to life, and Stefan was utterly gone and ordinary citizens walked the pavements. The doorman came out of the great fancy hotel where such greats have stayed as Kings and Queens, and Wagner and Hitler, damn them both, and God knows who else in its royal rooms which I had once glimpsed. God, this is here. I am here. You have left me here.

A man spoke to me in German.

I had fallen against the kiosk and knocked the wall of magazines askew. We were crashing, all of us, these magazine faces and the clumsy woman in the foolish summer silk with the violin and bow.

Sure hands caught hold of me.

"Please forgive me," I said in German. And then in English. "I'm so sorry, so very sorry. I'm so sorry, I didn't mean—Oh, please."

My hands. I couldn't move them. My hands were freezing. "Is that your game?" I cried out, disregarding the faces gathered round. "To freeze them so they die, to do to me what your father did to you! Well, you will not!"

I wanted to hit Stefan. But all I saw were people too regular and indifferent to be anything but utterly real.

I lifted the violin. I lifted it to my chin and I started to play.

Once again, this time to delve, this time to know, this time to heave my soul upwards to discover if a real world received it. I heard the music, true to my innermost harmless desires, I heard it rise with loving faith. In a blur the real world was as the real world should be in a blur—kiosk, people gathered, a small car come to a halt.

I played. I didn't care. My hands grew warmer from the playing, poor Stefan, poor Stefan. I breathed steam into the cold. I played and played. Wise grief seeks no vengeance from life itself.

Suddenly my fingers stiffened. I was too cold, really, really cold.

"Come inside, madam," said the man beside me. Others came. A young woman with her hair drawn back. "Come inside, come inside," they said.

"But where? Where are we? I want my bed, my house, I'd wake up if only I knew how to get back to my bed and my house."

Nausea. This world was darkening in an ordinary way, I was going numb from the cold, I was slipping from consciousness.

"The violin, please, the violin, don't take it," I said. I couldn't feel my hands, but I could see it, see its priceless wood. I could see lights before me, dancing like lights might do in rain, only there was no rain.

"Yes, yes, darling. Let us help you. You hold it. We hold you. You are safe now."

An old man stood before me, beckoning, directing those around me. A venerable old man, such a European old man with white hair and beard, such a strange European visage, as if from the deep deep past of Vienna, before terrible wars.

"Let me hold the violin in my arms," I said.

"You have the precious instrument, darling," said the woman to me. "Call the doctor at once. Pick her up. Gently, be careful with her! Sweetheart, we have you."

The woman guided me through the revolving doors. A shock of warmth and light. Nausea. I'll die, but I won't wake up.

"Where are we? What is this day? My hands, I need warmth for them, warm water."

"We have you, child, all right, we do, we'll help you."

"My name is Triana Becker. New Orleans. Call there. Call the lawyer of my family, Grady Dubosson. Get help for me. Triana Becker."

"We will, my dear one," said the old gray-haired man. "We will do it for you. You rest now. Carry her. Let her hold the violin. Do not harm her."

"Yes . . ." I said, expecting then that all the light of life would suddenly go out, that this was in fact death itself, come in a tangle of fantasy and impossible hopes and filthy miracles.

But death did not come. And they were tender and gentle.

"We have you, dear."

"Yes, but who are you?"

❧ 15 ❧

The Royal Suite. Vast, white and gold, walls paneled in a taupe brocade. Beige plaster circles above. Such soothing beauty. The inevitable scrollwork in whipped cream along the ceilings, a great cartouche in each corner. The bed itself was modern in size and firmness. I saw galloping gold filigree above. I was heaped with white down counterpanes—a suite fit for the Princess of Wales, or a millionaire madwoman.

I lay in half-sleep, the too exhausted thin sleep, a net of anxiety preventing a luxurious descent, an irritable sleep in which each voice is sharp and rubs the pores of the skin.

The warmth was modern and delicious. Double casement windows kept out the Vienna cold, windows dressed in sumptuous finery. Open the window, and then open the window. Heat droned from concealed or inconspicuous fixtures, filling up the spacious volume of the room.

"Madame Becker, Count Sokolosky, he wants you to be his guest here."

"I gave you my name." Did my lips move? I looked to the side, at a double sconce of gold with two candlelight bulbs burning brightly against the plaster, baubles hanging from the shining brass. "There's no need for the gentleman's kindness." I tried to make my words clear. "Please, if you will, call the man I told you about—my lawyer, Grady Dubosson."

"Madame Becker, we have made these calls. Funds are on the way to you. Mr. Dubosson is coming for you. And your sisters send you their love. They are greatly relieved to discover that you are safe here."

How long has it been? I smiled. There came into my mind a lovely scene from an old film of Dickens's *A Christmas Carol*, Alastair Sim, the British actor, a dancing Scrooge on Christmas morn having awakened a changed man. "I don't know how long I've been among the spirits." Happy, happy ending.

There was a white desk, a chair of midnight blue silk and wood, a soaring plant, the thin sheers parted to let in gray light.

"But the Count begs you to be his guest. The Count heard you play the Stradivarius."

I opened my eyes wide.

The violin!

It was beside me, lying on the bed. I had my hand over the strings and the bow. It was dark brown and shiny against the white linen, nestled in the pillow near me.

"Yes, it is there, madam," said the woman in perfect English made all the more rich by her Austrian accent. "It is by your side."

"I am so sorry to be so much trouble."

"You are no trouble, madam. The Count has looked at the violin, not touched it, you understand. He would not do that without your permission." Softer, the Austrian accent really, than German, more fluid. "The Count is a collector of such instruments. He begs that you be his guest. Madam, it would be an honor to him. Will you take some supper now?"

Stefan was in the corner.

Pale, hunched, faded, as if the color had bled out of him, staring at me, a figure obscured by mist.

I gasped. I sat up, clutching the violin to me.

"Don't fade, Stefan, don't become one of them!" I said.

His face, full of sadness and defeat, didn't change. The image seemed meager, wavering. He lay against the wall, his cheek to the damask panel, ankles crossed on the parquet, resting in mist and shadow.

"Stefan! Don't let it happen to you. Don't go."

I looked to right and left for the lost dead, the dreary shades, the mindless souls.

The tall woman looked over her shoulder. "You are speaking to me, Madame Becker?"

"No. Just to a phantom," I said. Why not be done with it? Why not say it? I had probably registered myself with these kind Austrians as one of the highest rank of the mad. Why not? "I don't speak to anyone, unless, that is, unless you see a man there in the corner."

She looked for him and couldn't find him. She turned back to me. She smiled. Consumed in courtesy, she was uncomfortable and not knowing what to do for me.

"It's only the cold, the trials, the journey," I said. "Don't worry the Count, my host, with all this. My lawyer's coming?"

"Everything is to be done for you," said the woman. "I am Frau Weber. This is our concierge, Herr Melniker."

She pointed to the right. She was a handsome woman, nobly tall, her black hair drawn back into a bun from her young face. Herr Melniker was a young man with ice blue eyes who looked anxiously at me.

"Madam," he said.

Frau Weber tried to delay him with a dip of her head and a rise of her hand, but he pressed on.

"Madam, do you know how you came to be here?"

"I have a passport," I said. "My lawyer will bring it to me."

"Yes, madam. But how did you get into Austria?"

"I don't know."

I looked at Stefan, pale, leaden with despair, his face bleached, only his eyes inflamed as he looked back at me.

"Frau Becker, do you remember perhaps anything that you . . ." The man stopped.

"Perhaps she must take supper now," said Frau Weber, "some soup perhaps. We have excellent soup for you, and some wine. Would you like some wine?"

She broke off. They both stood fixed. Stefan looked only at me.

A thumping noise drew closer and closer. A man with a limp and a cane. I knew the sound. I rather liked it, the thump, the shuffling step, the thump.

I sat straight. Frau Weber hastened to plump up the pillows behind me. I looked down to see I wore a bed jacket of padded silk, tied at the neck, and beneath that, white flannel, very fine. I was modest. I was even clean.

I looked at my hands, then realizing I had let go the violin, I snatched it up and held it.

There had been no hasty movement on the part of my tragic ghost. He had not stirred.

"Madam, you are safe. That is the Count, in the drawing room, would you please to let him in?"

I saw him in the open doorway; the beige doors were leather and thickly padded, and they came in two sets, to seal off all sound perhaps when these rooms were locked apart. He stood there with his wooden cane, the old gray-haired man I had seen on the pavement below, with the white beard and mustache, an old-fashioned figure and pretty, actually, like the venerable old actors in black-and-white films, so divinely Old World.

"Are you well, my child?" he asked. Thank God it was English. He was very far away. How big these spaces were, big as the spaces of Stefan's palace.

Blast. Flames. Old World.

"Yes, sir, I am, thank you," I said. "I'm relieved that you speak English. My German's wretched. I thank you for all your kindness to me. I don't want to be the slightest burden to you."

It was enough to say. Grady could pay the bills. Grady could make everything plain. That's what came with money, that others did the explaining. Karl had taught me that. How could I say I did not need this man's hospitality, his charity? There was some greater, finer point to be made.

"Please do come in," I said. "I'm so sorry, so sorry . . ."

"For what are you sorry, child?" he asked.

He made his limping path towards the bed. Only now I saw the curlicued footboard. And beyond, the chandelier of the other room. Yes, a palace, the Hotel Imperial.

The old man wore some sort of medallion around his neck, and his coat was trimmed in black velvet. It hung unevenly from his shoulders. His white beard looked brushed.

Stefan didn't move. I looked at Stefan and Stefan looked at me. Defeat and sorrow. Even in the angle of his head I saw it, the way he rested against the wall, as though whatever particles were left to him could know fatigue, or knew it even more now, and were knit together ever more precariously. His lips moved just a little as he eyed me, a face speaking to a face, his, mine.

Herr Melniker had rushed to get a big blue velvet fauteuil for the Count, one of the many white and gold chairs scattered about on the inevitable Rococo tiptoe.

He sat at a polite distance.

A pleasant aroma came to me.

"Hot chocolate," I said.

"Yes," Frau Weber said. She put the cup in my hands.

"You are so very kind." I clasped the violin with my left arm. "If you would set the saucer there."

The old man gazed at me in adoring wonder, the way old men would look at me when I was a little girl, the way an old nun had once looked at me on the day of my First Communion. How well I remembered her wrinkled face, and her ecstatic expression. That was at the old Mercy Hospital, the one they tore down. She had been dressed all in white, ancient, and she had said, "You are pure on this day, so pure." I was being taken round to visit as they did it then on the day of one's First Communion. Where had I put that Rosary?

I saw the cup of chocolate trembling in my hand. I looked to the right at Stefan.

I took a drink; it was the perfect temperature. I swallowed the cup, thick and sweet with cream. I smiled. "Vienna," I said.

The old man's brows came together. "Child, that is a remarkable treasure you possess."

"Oh, yes, sir," I said. "I know, a Stradivarius, a long Strad, and this, the bow of pernambuco."

Stefan narrowed his eyes. But he was broken. *How dare you?*

"No, madam, I don't mean the violin, though that is as fine an instrument as I've ever seen, and far more nearly perfect than any I have ever sold or been offered. I mean the gift in your playing, what you played outside, the music that brought us out of the hotel. It was a . . . it was a naïf rapture. That is the gift."

I was afraid.

You should be. After all, why should you be able to do it alone? Without my help? You're back in your own world with the thing? You can't do it. You

have no talent; you rode the wind of my sorcery and now you crawl again.
You're nothing.

"Let's see," I said to Stefan.

The others glanced at one another. To whom did I speak in the empty corner?

"Call it an angel," I said, looking up to the Count and gesturing to the corner. "Do you see it standing there, this angel?"

The Count moved his eyes over the room. So did I. I saw for the first time a fancy dressing table with folding mirrors, such as a lady would love, much finer than mine at home. I saw the Oriental rugs of worn blue and rust; I saw again the thin pale sheers that draped the window beneath deep scallops of brocaded silk.

"No, my dear," the Count said. "I don't see him. May I tell you my name? May I be your angel, too?"

"Perhaps you should," I said, glancing away from Stefan and to the old man. The old man had a large head and flowing hair. He had the same cold blue eyes as young Melniker. He had about him a pearlized whiteness in old age, but a keen expression in his eye, and white eyelashes.

"Perhaps," I said, "I need a better angel in you, for that I think is a bad angel."

How can you tell such lies. You steal my treasure. You break my heart.
You join the ranks of those who made me suffer so.

Again, no movement from the ghost's lips, and the lazy posture didn't change, the lazy miserable air of weakness and lost courage.

"Stefan, I don't know what to do for you. If I only knew the good thing to do, the good thing—"

Thief.

The others whispered.

"Frau Becker," said the woman, "this gentleman is Count Sokolo-sky. Forgive me that I did not make a proper presentation. He has lived here in our hotel a very long time, and is so happy to have you with us. These are rooms seldom opened to the public, so that we may keep them for just such an occasion."

"But what is that?"

"Darling," said the Count, cutting her off but very gently and with the calm unmalicious license of old age. "Would you play for me again? Is that impertinent of me to ask?"

No! Only vain and useless!

"Oh, not now," the Count hastened to add, "when you are ill and need nourishment and rest and for your friends to come to you, but when you feel you can, if you would . . . only a little more for me, that music. That music."

"And how would you describe it, Count?" I asked.

Do tell her, for she will need to know!

"Silence!" I glared at Stefan. "If it's yours, then why don't you have the power to reclaim it? Why is it in my keep? Oh, never mind, forgive me, forgive all this. Forgive this manner of speaking aloud to invented images and dreaming in a waking state—"

"No, it is quite good," said the Count. "We ask no questions of those who are gifted."

"Am I so gifted? What did you hear?"

Stefan sneered with aggressive contempt.

"I know what I heard when I played," I said apologetically, "but if you would, tell me what you heard."

The Count pondered.

"Something wondrous," said the Count. "And wholly original."

I didn't interrupt him.

"Something forgiving?" He went on. "Something mixed and full of ecstasy and bitter endurance. . . ." He took his time, then went on. "It was as if Bartók and Tchaikovsky had walked inside you, and were one, the sweet Moderne and the tragic Moderne, and in your music there was a world displayed to me . . . the world of so long ago, before the wars . . . when I was a boy, a boy too young really for such sublime remembering. Only I do remember that world. I remember it."

I wiped my face.

Go ahead, tell him, you don't think you can do it again. You don't know. I know. You can't.

"Says who?" I demanded of Stefan.

He stood up straight, arms folded, and in his anger flashed a brighter color. "Oh, it's always a matter of anguish, isn't it, petty or great? Look at you, how you blaze now! Now that you drive the doubts into me! What if your very challenge gives me the strength?"

Nothing can give you the strength. You are beyond my power now, and the thing is deadwood in your hands; it's dried wood, it's an antique instrument, you cannot play it.

"Frau Weber," I said.

She stared down at me amazed, anxiously glancing at the seemingly empty corner and then back to me quickly with an apologetic and protective nod.

"Yes, Frau Becker."

"Do you have a robe I might wear, something decent and loose? I want to play now. My hands are warm, they're so warm."

"Perhaps it's too soon," said the Count. However, leaning heavily on his cane, and groping for the hand of Melniker, he was already struggling to his feet. He was brimming with anticipation.

"Yes, yes, indeed," said Frau Weber. She gathered up the garment from the foot of the bed, a simple flaring robe of white wool.

I turned and placed my feet on the floor. My feet were bare and the wood was warm and the gown came down to the insteps of my feet, and I looked up at the ceiling, at all this splendid molding, and ornament and loveliness, this dreamy regal room.

I held the violin.

I stood up. She put the robe over me, and I put my right arm carefully through its loose long sleeve, and then shifting violin and bow, slipped my left arm into the proper place.

There were slippers there, but I didn't want them. The floor was silken.

I walked towards the opened doors. It didn't seem a proper thing to play in the bedroom, to meet either revelation or defeat there.

I entered the spacious drawing room, and turned dazed to see the mammoth portrait of the Great Empress Maria Theresa. Rich desk, chairs, couches. And flowers. Look. All those fresh flowers, like the flowers for the dead.

I stared at them.

"From your sisters, madam, the cards I have not opened, but your sister Rosalind has called. Your sister Katrinka has called. It was your sisters who said to give you hot chocolate."

I smiled, then laughed softly.

"Any other one?" I asked. "Do you remember any other name? A sister named Faye?"

"No, madam."

I went to the center table where the large vase of flowers stood, and peered through the crowded, tumbled blossoms, not knowing the name of a single plant, a single species, not even the common pink lilies with their thick pollen-covered tentacles reaching out.

The old Count had made his way to the couch, with the aid of the young man. I turned around and saw to my right that Stefan had come to the door of the bedroom.

Go on, fail! Dry up. Dry up and blow away. I want to see it. I want to see you give up for shame!

I lifted my right hand to my lips. "Oh, God," I said, more reverently than Frenchmen say *Mon Dieu*. It was a true prayer. "What is the prologue to this? What is the formula, the rule? How do I cast aside what I don't even know?"

Another voice intruded, *"Get on with it!"*

Stefan turned in shock. I saw the fierce anger in his face.

I turned round and round in the room. I saw the dazzled Count, the confused Frau Weber, the timid Melniker, and then the approaching ghost, who was in fact opening the doors to the hall, and this opening of doors the others saw, that I knew, but they couldn't see the ghost, and thought this a draft perhaps.

This ghost came striding in as he had walked in life, they said, with his hands knotted behind his back, filthy as if he'd come from the deathbed, lace stained and ragged, and even with fragments of the plaster of the death mask still on his face.

The alcove stood open to the hall. I saw a gathering of living people there.

Maestro. Stefan's heart broke. His tears came.

Oh, I felt so sorry for Stefan.

But the Maestro was merciless, and dismissive yet intimate.

"Stefan, you tire me, that you bring me back for this!" he said. "Back to this time, for this! Triana, play the violin for me. Simply do it."

I watched the small obdurate figure cross the room.

"Oh, this is splendid madness, I think," I said. "Or maybe merely inspiration."

The ghost took a chair, glowering at me.

"You will actually be able to hear it?" I asked.

"Oh, my God, Triana," he said with a brusque gesture. "I am not deaf in death! I didn't go to Hell. I wouldn't be here if I had." He gave a loud harsh laugh. "I was deaf when I was alive. I'm not alive now.

How could I be? Now play the violin. Do it, do it to make them shiver! Do it, to make them pay for every unkind word that has ever been said to you, for every guilt. Or do it for what you will." He drew himself up. "It doesn't matter, the reason. Fancy injury or love. Talk to God or to the finest part of yourself. But make the music."

Stefan wept. I looked from one to the other. I didn't care about the human beings in the room. I didn't know that I would ever care about them again.

But then I knew it was for them that I had to make this music.

"Go on, play it," said Beethoven in a more commiserating voice. "I didn't mean to sound so gruff. Truly I didn't. Stefan, you are my orphan pupil."

Stefan had turned his head to the door frame, and put up his arm to cushion his forehead. He had turned his face away.

The baffled mortal audience waited.

I took note of them one by one; I tried to see the mortals and not these ghosts. I looked through the alcove at those who waited in the hall. Herr Melniker moved to shut the door.

"No, leave it open."

I began.

It felt no different, this light and fragrant and sacred thing, crafted by a man who couldn't have known what magic he had shaped from the barks of trees, who couldn't have dreamed what power he had loosed from the heated curving wood as he bent it into shape.

Let me go back to the Chapel, Mother. Let me go back to Our Mother of Perpetual Help. Let me kneel with you there in the innocent gloom, before the pain. Let me hold your hand and tell you not how sorry I am that you died, but simply and only that I love you, I love you now. I give you my love in this song, like the songs of the May procession we always sang, the songs you loved, and Faye, Faye will come home, Faye will somehow come to know your love, she will, I believe in this, I know it in my soul.

Oh, Mother, who would have thought that life had so much blood in it? Who would have dreamed, but what we cherish is what we possess; I play for you, I play your song, I play the song of your health and strength, I play for Father and Karl, and in some time to come I'll gain the power to play for the pain, but now it's the evening, and we are in this untroubled sanctuary, among saints we know, and the streets will be filled with tenderly waning light as we make our way home, Rosalind and I skipping before you, and looking back to see your smiling face; oh, I want to remember this, I want always to remember your big hazel eyes, and your smile so filled with pure surety. Mother, it was no one's doing, was it, the undoing of us all, or is there always blame, and is there perhaps some way finally to see beyond it?

Look, look up at these oaks that always clasped branches over my head, all my life, at these mossy bricks down which we walk, look at the sky now purple as it can only be in our paradise. And feel the warmth of the lamps, the gas fire, Father's picture on the mantelpiece, "Your Daddy in the War."

We read now, we snuggle, we sink into the bed forever. It is no grave. Blood can come from many things. I know that now. There is blood and blood. I bleed for you, yes, I do, and willingly, and you bled for me.

. . . And let that blood come together.

I lowered the instrument. I was drenched in sweat. My hands tingled, and my ears were stung with the sound of clapping hands.

The old Count rose to his feet. Those in the hall crowded into the room.

"You write this in the air," said the Count.

I looked for ghosts. There were none.

"Come, we must record this music. This is natural; this is not learned. This is a savant gift and it has not demanded the usual price."

The Count kissed my face.

"Where are you, Stefan?" I whispered. "Maestro?"

I saw no one but the people crowded around me.

Then Stefan's voice in my ear; his breath on my ear.

Not done with you yet, you vicious girl who took it from me! It's not your talent! It's not. It's witchery.

"No, no, you're wrong," I said, "it wasn't witchery, it was something loosed and unwound and unsafe, like the night birds that fly at sunset in a great gust from beneath a bridge. And Stefan, you were my teacher."

The Count kissed me. Did he hear my words?

Liar, liar, thief.

I turned in a circle. The Maestro was most certainly and completely gone. I didn't dare to call him back. I didn't dare to try, that is, because I didn't know how to call him or Stefan in the first place.

"Maestro, help him," I whispered.

I lay against the Count's chest. I smelled his old skin, nice, familiar in its oldness like the skin of my father before he died, and sweet with a clean powder, no doubt beneath his clothes. His lips were wet and soft, and his gray hair soft. "Maestro, don't leave Stefan here, please . . ."

I gripped the violin. I held it with both hands, tight, tight, tight.

"It's all right, my dearest girl," said the Count. "Oh, what you have given us!"

✑ 16 ✎

What you have given us. What was it, this orgy of sound, this out-pouring that became so natural that I had no doubt of it? This trance into which I could slip, finding the notes and cutting them loose in certain strokes of will, with prancing and eager fingers?

What was this gift, to let the song surround me as it unfurled, to see it build and tumble down on me like gentle swaddling for a cradle? Music. Play. Don't think. Don't doubt. And don't doubt or worry if you think and doubt. Just play. Play it the way you want to play it, and discover the sound.

My beloved Rosalind came, quite dazzled to be in Vienna, with Grady Dubosson, and before we left, they opened the Theater an der Wien for us, and we played in the little painted place where Mozart had once played, where *The Magic Flute* had once been performed, in the building where Schubert had lived and written music—the tight, glorious little theater with the gold balconies stacked steeply and dangerously to the top—and after that we played once in the grand gray Opera House of Vienna, only steps from the hotel, and the Count took us into the country to see his sprawling old house, the very kind of country villa once owned by the Maestro's brother, Johann van Beethoven, "landowner," to whom the Maestro, in a letter, had so artfully replied, "Ludwig van Beethoven, brain owner."

I walked in the Vienna Woods, a sweet and mellow forest. I was a living woman with my sister.

At home, scholars reported on Karl's work. The book on St.

Sebastian was in proofs with an excellent publishing house, one that Karl admired. There had been immediate acceptance.

I was freed of that. It was done as well as ever he could have wished it. Roz and Grady traveled with me.

The music was mine and the concerts came one after the other. Grady spent his life on the phone with bookings.

The money flowed into the charities for those who had died unjustly and horribly in the wars. For the Jews, first and foremost, in honor of our great-grandmother, who had cast off her Jewish identity for Catholic in America, but more purely for justice, if not for her, and then for whatever charity we chose.

In London, we made the first recordings.

But there was St. Petersburg before that, and Prague, and the countless random concerts on the street, for which I was as greedy as a dancing school kid who twirls under every lamppost. I loved it.

In every swoon, I told the beads of the Rosary of my early years, the sweet years, drowned in the softest shades of purple and red. I beheld only the Joyful Mysteries. "And the Angel of the Lord declared unto Mary, and she conceived of the Holy Ghost."

It was with the fearless vigor of undefeated and unblemished childhood.

At home, Karl's book went to press at great expense, each color print personally supervised by the finest in the field of such publishing.

I slept at night on fine sheets. And woke to look on splendid cities.

Royal suites became the order of the day for Rosalind and me. Glenn soon joined us. Rolling tables draped in floor-length linen and cluttered with silver covers and heavy forks. Grand stairways and long corridors with Oriental rugs became our wandering ground.

But I never let the violin get away from me. I couldn't hold it eternally, that seemed mad, but I kept my eyes on it when I sat in the tub, staring at it, watching for it to be snatched, for some invisible hand to take it away into a vacuum.

And at night, I lay beside it, violin and bow folded over and over and over in soft baby-blanket wool and bound to me by leather belts which I didn't show to anyone else; and most of every day, I held it, or kept it by my chair.

There was no change in it. Others inspected it, declared it priceless, genuine, asked to be allowed. I couldn't let them play. It was not deemed a selfish thing, but only a prerogative.

In Paris, when Katrinka and her husband, Martin, met us, we bought Katrinka fine coats and dresses—all kinds of pocketbooks and high heeled shoes that neither Roz nor I could have possibly worn. We told Katrinka to do the limping for all of us. Katrinka laughed.

Katrinka sent her daughters, Jackie and Julie, boxes of exquisite things. Katrinka seemed freed from a great and tragic burden. Little or nothing was said of the past.

Glenn sought out old books and recordings of European jazz stars. Rosalind laughed and laughed. Martin and Glenn went off together to the old famous cafés, as if they could really find Jean-Paul Sartre if they looked hard enough. Martin was always on the phone, closing an Act of Sale on a house back home, until I begged him to take over the management of the endless trek for all of us.

Grady was relieved; we needed him as much as ever.

Laughter. Had Leopold and little Wolfgang ever had so much fun? And let us not forget there was a girl child there, a sister who was said to play as exquisitely as her prodigiously talented brother. A sister who had married and given birth to children rather than symphonies and operas.

Nobody could have ever been happier than we were on the road.

Laughter was our natural tongue once more.

They almost threw us out of the Louvre for laughing. It was not that we didn't love the Mona Lisa. We did, only we were so very excited and so bursting with life. We could have kissed strangers, obnoxiously, but we had better sense, and we hugged and kissed one another.

Glenn walked ahead of us, smiling sheepishly and then laughing too because it was too much happiness to disregard.

In London, my former husband, Lev, came with his wife, Chelsea, my sometime friend, and now seeming sister, and the black-haired boy twins, pristine and well behaved, and the tall, blond, beautiful eldest son, Christopher. It made me cry to see this boy, whose laugh did make me think of Lily.

Lev sat in the front row of the concert hall when I played. I played for Lev, for the happy times, and later he said it was like that drunken picnic of years before—only riskier, more ambitious, more fully realized. I was dazed with old love. Or love that is everlasting. He brought his keen academic words to the thing.

We vowed to meet—all of us—again in Boston.

These children, these living boys, they seemed somehow my descendants, descendants of Lev's early loss and struggle and rebirth, and I had been a part of that. Could I claim them as my nephews?

We had room after room at Manchester, Edinburgh, Belfast. The concerts were benefits again for the lost Jews of the War, the lost Gypsies, the struggling Catholics of Northern Ireland, for those who suffered the disease that had killed Karl, or the cancer of the blood that had killed Lily.

People offered us other violins. Would we play this fine Strad for a special event? Would we accept this Guarneri? Would we want to purchase this short Strad and fine Tourte bow?

I accepted the gifts. *I bought the other violins.* I stared at them in feverish curiosity. How would they sound? How would they feel? Could I bring a single note forth out of the Guarneri? Out of any of them?

I stared at them, I packed them and carried them with us, but I didn't even touch them.

In Frankfurt, I bought another Strad, a short Strad, exquisite, comparable to my own, but I didn't dare pluck the strings. It was on the market, and had no one to love it; it cost so much, but what was that to us in our blissful and boundless prosperity?

Violins and bows traveled with the bags. I kept the long Strad in my arms—my Strad—first wrapped in velvet, finally in a special sack with its bow. I would not trust it to a case. I carried the sack everywhere.

I looked for ghosts.

I saw sunlight.

My godmother, Aunt Bridget, came to be with us in Dublin. She didn't much care for the cold. Whether her name was Bridget or not she was soon headed straight home to Mississippi. We thought it so funny.

But she loved the music, and she'd clap and stomp her feet when I played, which made the others in the room—or hall, or auditorium, or theater or whatever it was—rather shocked. But we had this agreement—that I wanted her to do it.

Many cousins and other aunts came to join us in Ireland, and later in Berlin. I made the pilgrimage to Bonn. I shivered at Beethoven's door.

I pressed my head to the cold stones and wept like Stefan had at the grave.

Many a time, I recalled the Maestro's themes, the melodies of the Little Genius or the Mad Russian and plunged into them to open my own floodgates, but critics seldom if ever noticed, so poor was I at rendering anything by anyone else, so utterly beyond control and discipline.

But these were times of unbroken ecstasy. Any fool had to see this for what it was; only the most deranged would have dragged a sorrow or caution into it.

At moments such as these—when the light rain fell in Covent Garden—and I walked in circles beneath the moon, and the cars waited, their lights steaming in the mist as if they breathed as I breathed—all I could do was be happy. Question nothing. Know this for what it is. Know it. And maybe one day, I'll have to remember it from some alien vantage point and it will seem as dreamy and colorful and celestial as those Chapel visits, or lying in Mother's arms as she turned the pages of the poetry book, by lamplight that fended off no menace, because none had come yet to dwell there.

We went to Milan. To Venice. To Florence. Count Sokolosky joined us in Belgrade.

I had a fancy in particular for the opera houses. I didn't need for it to be paid. If they would guarantee the hall, I would come, I would pay myself, and each night it was different, and unpredictable, and each night it was a joy and the pain was safely banked within the joy, and each night it was recorded by technicians running about with speakers and earphones and stringing thin wires across the stage, and I looked out on the faces of those who applauded.

I looked and tried to see each face, not to fail each face, to meet the warmth of each face, when the song was done, not to ever slip back into pain and shyness and cringing as if my past was my shell and I a snail too weak for this ascent, too bound to the old track of ugliness, too full of self-loathing.

A seamstress in Florence made me pretty, loose skirts of velvet, and soft tunics of fine fabric that would leave my arms free in silk balloon sleeves when I played, not hampering the rigor, or ever breaking the spell, yet concealing the weight I hated so much, so that I seemed to myself in the brief films I was forced to see a blur of hair and color and a blur of sound. Glorious.

And when the moment came, and I stepped before the lights, when I looked into the engulfing dark, I knew my dreams were mine.

But there was darker music to come, surely. The Rosary has The Joyful, The Glorious and The Sorrowful Mysteries. Mother, sleep. Lie still. Be warm. Lily, close your eyes. Father, it's over now, say the breathing and the pupils of your eyes. Close them. Dear Lord, can they hear my music?

And I was searching for a very certain palace of marble, was I not, and did I not know from all these opera houses—Venice, Florence, Rome—that the palace of marble in my strange dreams must have been an opera house, did I not know or suspect now from the memory of the central stairs in the dreams, a structure and design I saw repeated in all these regal halls built with pomp and faith, the center stair rising to a landing and then dividing to right and left to climb to the mezzanine for the milling bejeweled crowd.

Where was that palace in the dreams, the palace so full of different patterns of marble that it rivaled the Basilica of St. Peter's? What had the dream meant? Had it been just the leakage of his tormented soul, that he let me see the city of Rio, the scene of his last crime before he had come to me, and found some sharp thorn in my soul connected with that place? Or was it some concoction amended to his memories by my own fancy, along with the frothy, glorious sea that gave birth to countless dancing phantoms?

Nowhere did I see that kind of opera house, that mix of beauty.

In New York, we played at Lincoln Center, and at Carnegie Hall. Our concerts were now broken into programs of varying length. Which means, as time passed, I could go on—unbroken—for a greater time, and the flow of melody grew more complex, and the range greater, and the operation of the lengthy whole more fluid.

I couldn't bear really to listen to my own recordings. Martin, Glenn, Rosalind and Katrinka handled those things. Rosalind, Katrinka and Grady made the contracts, the deals.

They were an unusual item: our tapes, or disks. They offered the music of an untutored woman who can't read a note of music really, except do-re-mi-fa-sol-la-ti-do, who never plays the same song twice, who can't most likely repeat the same song—and the critics were swift to point this out. How is one to value such accomplishments, the improvisation which in Mozart's time could not be preserved unless recorded in pen and ink, but now could be kept forever, with the same reverence given to "serious music"!

"Not really Tchaikovsky, not really Shostakovich! Not really Beethoven! Not really Mozart."

"If you like your music as thick and sweet as maple syrup, you may find Miss Becker's improvisations to your taste, but some of us want more from life than pancakes."

"She is genuine, she is probably technically manic-depressive, possibly even an epileptic—only her doctor knows for sure—she obviously doesn't know how she does what she does, but the effect is, without a doubt, mesmerizing."

The praise was thrilling—genius, spellbinder, magician, naïf—and equally distant from the roots of the song in me, and what I knew and felt. But it came like kisses striking the face, and gave occasional thrills to our entourage, and many quotes were slapped on our packaged disks and tapes, which now sold millions.

We moved from hotel to hotel, by whim, by invitation, by chance sometimes, by sheer caprice.

Grady warned against our spendthrift ways. But he had to admit that the sales of the records had already exceeded Karl's trust fund. And the fund was doubling. And the sales of the records might go on forever.

We couldn't stint. We didn't care. Katrinka felt safe! Jackie and Julie went to the finest school back home, then dreamed about Switzerland.

We went down into Nashville.

I wanted to hear and play for the bluegrass fiddlers. I sought out the young bluegrass genius Alison Krauss, whose music I so loved. I wanted to lay roses at her door. Maybe she would recognize the name Triana Becker.

My sound, however, was not bluegrass anymore than it was Gaelic. It was the European sound, the Viennese and the Russian sound, the heroic sound, the Baroque sound—all that melded together—the soaring flights of the longhairs, as they had once been called before that tag line was co-opted by hippies who looked like Jesus Christ. Nevertheless, I was one of them.

I was a musician.

I was a virtuoso.

I played the violin. It belonged in my hands. I loved it. Loved it. Loved it.

I did not need to meet the brilliant Leila Josefowicz, Vanessa Mae, or my dearest Alison Krauss. Or the great Isaac Stern. I had no nerve for such things. I needed only to think, I can play.

I can play. Maybe someday they will hear Triana Becker.

Laughter.

It rang in the hotel rooms where we gathered to drink the champagne, and we ate desserts full of chocolate and cream, and I lay on the floor at night, looking up into the chandelier the way I liked to do at home, and every morning and night . . .

. . . Every morning or night, we called home to see if there had been any word of Faye, our lost sister, our beloved lost sister. We talked of her in interviews on the steps of theaters in Chicago, Detroit, San Francisco.

". . . our sister Faye, we haven't seen her in two years."

Grady's office in New Orleans fielded phone calls from people who were not Faye, and had not seen her. They could not accurately describe her small beautifully proportioned body, her effervescent smile, her loving eyes, her tiny hands, so strong, and so cruelly marked with small thumbs by the alcohol that had poisoned the dark water in which she had fought to live, so tiny, so sickly.

Sometimes I played for Faye. I was with tiny Faye on the back flagstones at the house on St. Charles, with the cat in her arms, smiling, oblivious, an invincible elf, oblivious to the drunken woman inside, or the screaming fights, the sound of a woman vomiting behind a bathroom door. It was for Faye who lay on the patio, and loved to feel the rain dry up on the flagstones in the sun. Faye who knew secrets like that, while other people quarreled and accused.

There were times on the road that were hard for others. Because I couldn't stop myself from playing the long Strad. I went nuts, said Glenn. Dr. Guidry came. In one place, my brother-in-law Martin suggested I be tested for drugs, and Katrinka screamed at him.

There were no drugs. There was no wine. There was music.

It was like a fiddler's replay of *The Red Shoes*. I played and played and played until everyone else in the suite had fallen asleep.

Once I was even taken from the stage. A rescue operation, I think, because it had gone on and on, and people were clamoring for encores. I collapsed but soon came to my senses.

I discovered the masterly film *Immortal Beloved* in which the great actor Gary Oldman seemed to capture the Beethoven I had all my life worshiped and perhaps in my madness even glimpsed. I looked into the eyes of the great actor Gary Oldman. He caught the transcendence. He caught the heroic of which I dreamed, and the isolation which I knew, and the perseverance which I made my daily office.

"We'll find Faye!" Rosalind said. In hotel dining rooms we replayed together all the good things that had happened. "You've made so much noise that Faye is bound to hear it and she'll come back! She'll want to be with us now. . . ."

Katrinka broke into joke telling and rampant wit. Nothing could chill her now—not the taxes, not the mortgage, not old age, or death, or where the girls would go to college, or whether her husband was spending too much of our money—nothing troubled her.

Because everything in this bounty and success could be solved or resolved.

This was Success Moderne. A success that can only be known in our time, I would guess, when people round the world can record, watch and listen—all at the same time—to the improvisations of one violinist.

We convinced ourselves that Faye had to share this with us, that somewhere somehow she already did, because we reached out for her. Faye, come home. Faye, don't be dead. Faye, where are you? Faye, it is fun in the limousines, and the beautiful rooms; it is fun to push through the crush at the stage door, it is fun.

Faye, the audience gives us love! Faye, it is warm now forever.

One night in New York, I stood behind a stone griffin, I think it was near the top of the Ritz-Carlton Hotel. I looked out over Central Park. The wind blew cold like it had in Vienna. I thought of Mother. I thought of a time when she had asked me to say the Rosary with her, and she had spoken of her drinking to me—which she had never mentioned to any of the others—when she had said it was a craving in the blood, and that her father had it, and his father. Say the Rosary. I closed my eyes and I kissed her. *The Agony in the Garden.*

That night on the street, I played for her.

And soon my fifty-fifth year would be complete. October would come and I would be fifty-five.

Then finally—as I knew it would—the inevitable moment came.

How kind of Stefan and how perfectly impulsive and unwise to have written it himself with his very own ghostly hand, or had he gone into the body of a human being to inscribe these letters?

Nobody in this day and age had a script so perfect as this, in long sharp strokes of a dipped pen, and grand purple ink—on parchment no less, new, of course, but as firm as any he might have chosen in his time.

He didn't keep any secrets.

"Stefan Stefanovsky, your old friend, cordially invites you to come for a benefit concert in Rio de Janeiro, and looks forward to seeing you there. All expenses to be paid for you and your family at the Copacabana Hotel, Rio. Further arrangements and details at your pleasure. Please call the following numbers collect when it is convenient for you to do so."

Katrinka handled the details on the phone. "At what theater? The Teatro Municipale?"

Sounds modern, sterile, I thought.

I would give you Lily if I could.

"You don't want to go down there, do you?" asked Roz. She had had her fourth beer and was mellow and soft, her arm around me. I was dozing against her and looking out the window. This was Houston, a tropical city, really, with a great ballet and an opera, and audiences which had been so warm to and unquestioning of us.

"I wouldn't go there," said Katrinka.

"Rio de Janeiro?" I said. "But it's a beautiful place. Karl wanted to go. He wanted to complete his work on the book. St. Sebastian, his saint, his . . ."

"Academic field," said Roz.

Katrinka laughed.

"Well, that's all done, his book," said Glenn, Roz's husband. "It's being shipped now. Grady says everything is going splendidly." Glenn pushed his glasses up on his nose.

He sat down and folded his arms.

I looked at the note. Come to Rio.

"I can see it in your face; don't go!"

I simply stared at the note; my hands were wet and shaking. His handwriting, his very name.

"What in the name of God," I asked, "are you all talking about?"

Exchange of looks. "If she doesn't remember now, she will," said Katrinka.

"That woman who wrote to you, your old friend from Berkeley, who told you . . ."

"That Lily . . ." I asked, "had been reborn in Rio?"

"Yeah," said Roz, "that's going to make you miserable to go there. I remember when Karl wanted to go. You said you had always wanted to see that place, but you just couldn't take it, remember? I heard you tell Karl . . ."

"I didn't remember that I told him," I said. "I only remember that I didn't go, and he wanted to. Now I have to go."

"Triana," said Martin, "you're not going to find the reincarnation of Lily anywhere."

"She knows that well enough," said Roz.

Katrinka's face was full of dull well-learned misery. I didn't want to see this.

She had been so close to Lily. Roz had not been with us in Berkeley and San Francisco during those times. But Katrinka had been at the bedside, the coffin, the cemetery—through all of it.

"Don't go," said Katrinka in a thick voice.

"I'm going for another reason," I said. "I don't believe Lily's there. I believe that if Lily exists, Lily has no need of me or she would have come to—."

I stopped. His stinging, hateful words came back.

You were jealous, jealous that your daughter made herself known to Susan and not to you, admit it! That's what you thought. Why didn't your daughter come to you? And you lost the letter, you never answered, even though you knew Susan was sincere and you knew how she had loved Lily and how much she believed—

"Triana?"

I looked up. Roz had the old tinge of fear in her eyes, fear such as we knew in bad times, before there was all we wanted before us.

"No, don't worry, Roz. I'm not looking for Lily. This man . . . I owe something to him," I said.

"Who, this Stefan Stefanovsky?" Katrinka asked. "The people I spoke to down there don't even know who he is. I mean the invitation is firm, but they haven't any idea what sort of man—"

"I know him well," I said. "Don't you remember?" I got up from the table. I picked up the violin, which was never more than four inches from me, and had been resting by the chair.

"The violinist in New Orleans!" said Roz.

"Yes, that's Stefan. That's who he is. And I want to go there. Besides . . . they say it's a beautiful place."

Could it be? The place of the dream? Lily would have known to choose Paradise.

"Teatro Municipale . . . sounds dull," I said. Had someone said those words before?

"It's a dangerous city," said Glenn. "They'll kill you for your sneakers. It's full of the poor who build their shacks up the mountainsides. And Copacabana Beach? It was all built up decades ago . . ."

"It's beautiful," I whispered.

The words weren't audible. I held the violin. I plucked the strings.

"Oh, please, don't start playing now, I'll lose my mind," said Katrinka.

I laughed. So did Roz.

"I mean, not every moment—" Katrinka hastened to say.

"It's all right. But I want to go. I have to go. Stefan's asked me to go."

I told them they didn't have to come. After all, it was Brazil, but by the time we boarded the plane, they were eager for this exotic and legendary world, of the rain forest and the great beaches, and this Teatro Municipale, which sounded like a concrete city auditorium.

Of course it was not that at all.

You know it.

Brazil is not another country. It is another world, where dreams take different forms, and humans reach to spirits day by day, and saints and African gods are fused on Golden Altars.

You know what I found. Of course . . .

I was afraid. The others saw it. They felt it. It did make me think of Susan, and not only of her letter, but of what she'd told me after Lily's death. I thought over and over of her, and how she had told me after Lily's death that Lily had known she was going to die. I had wanted to keep that secret always from Lily. But Lily had told Susan, "Guess what, I'm going to die." And laughed and laughed. "I know because my Mom knows and my Mom's afraid."

But I owe you this, Stefan. I owe to your dark assaults the very marrow of my strength. I can't refuse you this.

So I forced the smile. I kept my counsel. To talk of a dead child wasn't such a hard thing. They had long ago stopped asking me how I had gotten to Vienna. They didn't connect any of this with the mad fiddler.

And so off we went, and it was laughter again, and beneath, fear, fear like the shadows in the long brown hollow of the house when Mother drank and babies slept in the sticky heat and I feared the house would catch fire and I couldn't get them out, and our father was off I didn't know where, and my teeth chattered, even though it was warm and the mosquitoes moved in the darkness.

❦ 17 ❧

SLEEPY and sluggish from the long flight south, past the equator, over the Amazon and down to Rio, we were dazed as the vans carried us through a long black tunnel, beneath the rain-forested mountain of Corcovado. That splendor—the granite Christ on the peak with his arms outstretched—I had to see this Christ before we left.

I carried the violin now all the time in a new padded burgundy velvet sack, stuffed with cushioning, and safer to sling from my shoulder.

There was no hurry for us to see all the wonders of this place— Sugarloaf Mountain, and the old palaces of the Hapsburgs who had come here in fear of Napoleon and with reason, as he dropped his shells on Stefan's Vienna.

Something touched my cheek. I felt a sigh. Every hair on my body stood on end. I didn't move. The van jolted along.

As we came out of the tunnel, the air was cool and the sky immense and bountifully blue.

As soon as we plunged into the thick of Copacabana, I felt the chills on my arms, I felt as if Stefan were next to me; I felt something brush my cheek and I hugged the violin in its soft safe sack of velvet, trying to fight off this fit of nerves and see what lay around me.

Copacabana was dense with towering buildings and sidewalk shops, with street vendors, businessmen and -women on the march, slouching tourists. It had the throb of Ocean Drive in Miami Beach, or midtown Manhattan, or Market Street in San Francisco at noontime.

V i o l i n

"But the trees," I said. "Look, everywhere, these huge trees."

They sprang up straight, verdant, spreading out in scalloped umbrellas of large green leaves to make a pure and lovely shade in the pressing heat. Never in such a dense city had I seen anything so green and rich, and these trees were everywhere, rising out of soiled pavements, undaunted by the shadows of skyscrapers, the swarm of those on the pavements.

"Almond trees, Miss Becker," our guide said, a tall willowy young man, very pale, with yellow hair and translucent blue eyes. He was named Antonio. He spoke with the accent I heard in my dream. He was Portuguese.

We were here. We were in the place surely of the foaming sea and the marble palace. But how was it to unfold?

I felt a great warm shock pass over me when we hit the beach and took a turn; the waves were quiet but it was the sea of my dreams, most perfectly. I could see its farthest limits, before us and behind, the arms of mountains stretching out, which marked it off from the other many beaches of the city of Rio de Janeiro.

Our sweet-voiced guide, Antonio, spoke of the many beaches that went on and on south to the Atlantic, and how this was but one in a city of eleven million people. Mountains rose up straight from the earth. Grass-roofed huts along the sand sold cool drinks. Everywhere buses and cars pushed for room, springing free to race. And the sea, the sea was a vast ocean of green and blue seemingly without limit, though in fact it was a bay and did have beyond its horizon other hills we couldn't see. The sea was God's finest harbor.

Rosalind was overcome. Glenn snapped pictures. Katrinka stared with faint anxiety at the endless train of white-dressed men and women wandering on the broad band of beige sand. Never had I seen a beach as wide as this, as beautiful.

There was the patterned sidewalk I had glimpsed in my dreams— the strange design which I now saw was a careful mosaic.

Our guide, Antonio, spoke of a man who had built the whole long Avenue of the Atlantic along the beach, with these mosaic patterns, to be seen from the air. He spoke of the many places we might go, he spoke of the warmth of the water, of the New Year's and the Carnivale, those special days for which we must return.

The car made a left. I saw the hotel rise up before us. The Copacabana Palace, a grand old-style white building of seven floors, its broad second-floor terrace lined with pure Roman arches. No doubt the convention rooms and the ballrooms lay behind those huge arches. And the comely white plaster façade had an air of British dignity to it.

The Baroque, the faint last echo of the Baroque, here amid all the modern apartment towers that had crowded up against it but could not touch it.

Almond trees clustered in the middle of its circular drive, trees with big broad shiny green leaves, none too great, as though nature itself kept them to a human scale. I looked back. The trees spread down the boulevard, they spread in both directions. They were the same lovely trees of the busy streets.

One could not *see* all of this. I shivered, holding the violin.

And look, the sky over the sea, how quickly it changes, how rapidly its vast banks of clouds move. Oh, God, how the sky rises.

Like it here, dear?

I went rigid. Then at once made a little defensive laugh, but I felt him touch me. Like knuckles against my cheek. I felt something tug at my hair. I hated it. Don't touch my long hair. My veil. Don't touch me!

"Don't start having bad thoughts!" said Roz. "This is bee-utiful!"

We moved into the classic circular drive, made the turn before the main doors, and the concierge came out to meet us—an English-woman, her name Felice, very pretty and immediately polite and charming, as the English always seem to me, like a species preserved from the modern obsession with efficiency that debased all the rest of us.

I climbed out of the van and walked back away from the drive so that I could look up the full façade of the hotel.

I saw the window above the main arch of the convention floor.

"That's my room, isn't it?"

"Oh, yes, Miss Becker," said Felice. "It is right in the center of the building, the very middle of the hotel. It's the Presidential Suite, as you requested. We have suites on the same floor for all your guests. Come, I know you must be tired. It's late at night for you, and here we are at midday."

Rosalind was dancing for joy. Katrinka had spied the nearby jewelers, the dealers in the precious emeralds of Brazil. I saw the hotel had arms, with other shops: a little bookstore full of Portuguese titles. American Express.

A host of bellhops descended upon our bags.

"It's damned hot," said Glenn. "Come on, Triana, come inside."

I stood as if frozen.

Why not, darling?

I looked up at the window, the window I had seen in my dream when Stefan first came, the window I knew that I would look out from, onto this beach and the waves, waves now quiet, but which would rise perhaps to create that very foam. Nothing else here had been exaggerated.

Indeed this seemed the greatest harbor or bay I'd ever beheld, more beautiful and vast even than San Francisco.

We were led inside. In the elevator, I shut my eyes. I felt him beside me and his hand touch me.

"So? Why here of all places?" I whispered. "Why is this better?"

Allies, my darling.

"Triana, stop talking to yourself," said Martin, "everybody will think you're really crazy."

"How can that matter now?" said Roz.

We scattered, attended, guided, offered cool drinks and kind words.

I walked into the living room of the Presidential Suite. I walked straight towards that small square window. I knew it. I knew its clasp. I opened it.

"Allies, Stefan?" I asked. I made my voice soft, as if I were murmuring Hail Marys of thanks. "And who would they be, and why here? Why did I see this when you first came?"

No answer but the full pure breeze, the breeze that nothing can soil, flooding past me into the room, over the conventional furnishings, the dark carpet, flooding in from beyond the immense beach and those dark figures moving leisurely in the sands or in the shallow quiet surf. Above, the clouds hung down in glory.

"Do you know *everything* that I dreamed, Stefan?"

It's my violin, my love. I don't want to hurt you. But I must have it back.

The others were busy with bags, windows and vistas of their own; room service carts were brought into the suite.

I thought, This is the purest, finest air I've ever breathed in all my life, and I looked way out over the water, at a steep granite mountain rising sharp from the blue. I saw the perfect shimmering horizon.

Felice, the concierge, came to my side. She pointed to the distant cliffs. She gave names. Below the buses roared between us and the beach. It did not matter. So many people wore the loose short-sleeve white, it seemed the clothing of the country. I saw skin of all colors. Behind me the soft Portuguese voices sang their song.

"Do you want me to take the violin, to perhaps—"

"No, I keep it with me," I said.

He laughed.

"Did you hear that?" I asked the Englishwoman.

"Hear something? Oh, when we close the windows, the room is very quiet. You will be happily surprised."

"No, a voice, a laugh."

Glenn touched my elbow. "Don't think about those things."

"Ah, I am so sorry," said a voice. I turned and saw a dark-skinned beautiful woman with rippling hair and green eyes staring at me, a racial blend beyond the boundaries of imagined beauty. She was tall, her arms naked, her long hair Christlike, and her smile made of blood-red lipstick and white teeth.

"Sorry?"

"Oh, we mustn't talk of it now," said Felice with haste.

"It got into the papers," said the goddess with the rippling hair, holding her hands as if to entreat me to forgive. "Miss Becker, this is Rio. People believe in spirits, and your music is much loved here. Your tapes have been coming by the thousands into the country. People here are very deeply spiritual and mean no harm."

"What got into the papers?" Martin demanded. "That she's staying at this hotel? What are you talking about?"

"No, everyone has expected that you will be at this hotel," said the tall brown woman with the green eyes. "I mean the sad story that you have come here to look for the soul of your child. Miss Becker—" She extended her hand. She clasped mine.

Even as I felt her warm touch, the chills went over me, circuit after circuit. I felt weak looking into her eyes.

And yet in all this, there was something horribly thrilling. Horribly so.

"Miss Becker, forgive us, but we could not stop the rumors. I'm sorry for this pain. There are reporters downstairs already—"

"Well, they'll have to go away," said Martin. "Triana has to sleep. We've been flying for over nine hours. She has to sleep. Her concert is tomorrow night, that's barely enough time . . ."

I turned and looked at the sea. I smiled, then turned back and took the young dark woman's hands.

"You are a spiritual people," I said. "Catholic and African, and Indian as well, deeply spiritual, or so I've heard. What is the name of the rituals, the ones the people practice? I can't remember."

"*Mogambo, Candomblé.*" She shrugged, grateful for my forgiveness. Felice, the British one, stood aloof, disturbed.

I had to admit—no matter what joy we knew wherever we went—someone on the periphery was always disturbed. And now it was this Englishwoman who feared offenses to me which weren't possible.

Aren't they? You think she's here, your daughter?

"You tell me," I whispered. "She's not your ally, don't try to make me think that." I looked down and said it under my breath.

The others retreated. Martin saw them out.

"What do you want me to tell those damned reporters?"

"The truth," I said. "An old friend said that Lily had been reborn in this place." I turned again to the window and to the sweet thrust of the wind. "Oh, God, look at this sea, look. If Lily should come again, which I don't believe, why not in a place like this? And do you hear their voices? Did I ever tell you about the Brazilian children she loved, who lived near us in those last years?"

"I met them," Martin said. "I was there. That family came from São Paulo. I won't have you upset by these things."

"Tell them we are looking for Lily but we don't seek to find her in any one human being, tell them something nice, tell them something that will fill up their municipal auditorium where we're to play. Go ahead."

"It's sold out," said Martin. "I don't want to leave you alone."

"I can't sleep till it gets dark. This is too much, too gorgeous, too perfectly shining. Martin, are you tired?"

"No, not much. Why, what do you want to do?"

I thought. Rio.

"I want to go up in the rain forest," I said, "go up to the top of

Corcovado. Look at the sky, how clear it is. Do we have time to do that before dark? I want to see Christ up there with his arms outstretched. I wish we could see Him from here."

Martin made the arrangements by phone.

"What a lovely thought," I said, "that Lily should come back alive and claim a long life in such a place as this." I closed my eyes and thought of her, my luminous one, bald and smiling, nestled in my arms, the little white collar of her checked dress turned up, so that in her steroid plumpness, her adorable roundness, we called her "Humpty."

I heard her laugh as clearly as if she were sitting astride Lev, who lay on his back on the cold grass of the rose garden in Oakland. Katrinka and Martin had taken us that day. We had that picture somewhere, perhaps it was with Lev—Lev lying on his back, and Lily sitting on his chest, her small round face beaming at the heavens. Katrinka had taken so many wonderful pictures.

Oh, God, stop it.

Laughter.

You can't make it sweet, no, you can't do that, it hurts too much and that you think, perhaps she hates you, that you let her die, perhaps your Mother too, and here you are in the land of the spirits.

"You take your strength from this place? You're a fool. The violin's mine. I'd burn it before I let you have it."

Martin spoke my name. No doubt behind me, he stood watching me talk to nothing, or maybe the wind hushed the words.

The car was ready. Antonio waited for us. We would drive to the tram. We had two bodyguards with us, both off-duty policemen hired for our safety, and the tram would take us up through the rain forest and we would have to walk the last steps to the foot of Christ at the very summit of the mountain.

"Are you sure," asked Martin, "that you're not too tired for this?"

"I'm excited. I love this air, this sea, everything around me . . ."

Yes, said Antonio, there was plenty of time to make it to the tram. It would not be dark for five hours. But look, the clouds, the sky was darkening, it was not such a perfect day for Corcovado.

"It's my day," I said. "Let's go. Let me ride shotgun with you," I said to Antonio. "I want to see everything that I can."

Martin and the two bodyguards climbed into the back.

We had only pulled off when I noticed the obvious reporters, laden with cameras, clustered at the door, one small group in an intense argument with the English concierge Felice, who gave no sign that we were in fact within earshot.

I knew nothing much about the tram, except that it was old, like the wooden streetcars of New Orleans, and it would be pulled up the mountain, like the cable cars of San Francisco. I think I had heard it was dangerous at times to ride it. But none of this mattered.

We rushed from the van to the tram car just as it was about to depart the station. Only a scattering of people were on board, and seemed for the most part to be Europeans. I heard people speaking in French, Spanish and what had to be the melodious angelic Portuguese again.

"My God," I said, "we're going right into the forest."

"Yes," said our Antonio, our guide. "This forest is all the way up the mountain, this is a beautiful forest, this forest is not the original forest . . ."

"Tell me," I said. In astonishment I reached out to touch the bare earth, we rode so close, to touch the ferns lodged in the cracks, to see above us the trees leaning over the tramway.

Others chattered and smiled on the tram.

"It was a coffee plantation, you see, and then, when this man came to Brazil, this rich man, he saw that the rain forest should be brought back, and he had it replanted. This is a new forest, this is a forest only fifty years old, but it is our rain forest of Rio, and it is for us, and he did this for us. All of this, you see, he carefully replanted."

It looked as wild and unspoiled as any tropical paradise I'd ever beheld. My heart was thumping.

"Are you here, you son of a bitch?" I whispered to Stefan.

"What did you say?" asked Martin.

"Talking to myself, saying my Rosary, my Hail Marys for good luck. Glorious Mysteries; *Jesus Rises from the Dead.*"

"Oh, you and your Hail Marys."

"What do you mean by that? Look, the earth's red, absolutely red!" We rose, turning slowly curve by curve through deep gashes in the mountain and then emerging on an equal footing with the soft, dense and drowsy trees.

"Ah, I see the fog coming," said Antonio, smiling sadly, his voice so apologetic.

"It doesn't matter," I said. "It's too lovely the way it is, it's to be seen in all ways, don't you think? And when I do this, ride like this, up and up a mountain towards the sky and Christ, well, I can take my mind off other things."

"Good to do that," said Martin. He had lighted a cigarette. Katrinka wasn't there to tell him to put it out. Antonio did not smoke and did not mind, and seemed in his courtesy surprised to have been asked now by Martin if the smoking was permitted.

The tram made a stop; it picked up a lone woman with several bundles. She was dark-skinned, wore soft shapeless shoes.

"You mean it's like a streetcar?"

"Oh, well, yes," sang Antonio's voice, "and there are people who work up above, and those who come here and there, and you see there is one of a very poor place . . ."

"The shantytowns," Martin said. "I've heard of them, we're not going into them."

"No, we don't have to."

Laughter again. Obviously no one else heard it. "So you're that spent, are you?" I whispered. I pushed down the window! I leant out the open window, ignoring Martin's warnings. I could see the leafy branches coming, I could smell the earth. I talked into the wind. "You can't make yourself visible and you can't make anyone else hear you?"

I save my finest for you, my love, you who took your own bold steps into the cloisters of my mind, even as I played there, singing your vespers to a chime inside me that I myself didn't hear. For you I will be a worker of more miracles.

"A liar and a cheat," I said beneath the rattle of the tram. "Keeping company with ragged ghosts?"

The tram stopped again.

"That building," I asked. "Look, there's a beautiful house there to the right, what is it?"

"Ah, well, yes," said Antonio, with a smile. "We can see it on the way down. In fact, let me call now." He pulled out his small cellular phone. "I will have the van come up to meet us there if you like. It was a hotel once. It is abandoned now."

"Oh, yes," I said, "I have to see it." I looked back, but we had turned the bend. We went higher and higher.

Finally we had come to the end, and to the crowd of tourists waiting to return. We stepped onto the cement platform.

"Ah, yes, well," said Antonio. "Now we climb the steps to Christ."

"Climb the steps!" declared Martin.

Behind us, the bodyguards sauntered side by side, moving their khaki vests back so we and everybody else could see their shoulder holsters and their black guns. One of them gave me a tender respectful smile.

"It is not so bad," said Antonio. "It is many many steps, but it is broken up, you see, and there are places to stop at every . . . how would you say it? . . . stage, and you can get something cool to drink. You do wish to carry the violin yourself? You don't want me to—?"

"She always carries it," said Martin.

"I have to go to the top," I said. "Once as a child, I saw this in a film, Christ with his arms outstretched. As if on a crucifix."

I walked ahead.

How lovely it was, the crowds slack and lazy, and the little shops selling cheap trinkets and canned drinks, and people sitting idly at the scattered metal tables. All so mellow in this beautiful heat, and the fog blew up the mountain in white gusts.

"These are clouds," said Antonio. "We are in the clouds."

"Magnificent!" I cried. "The balustrade, it's so beautifully done, Italian isn't it? Martin, look, here everything is mixed, old and new, European and foreign."

"Yes, it is very old, this balustrade, and the steps, see, they are not steep."

We crossed landing after landing.

Now we walked in perfect dense whiteness. We could see each other and our feet and the ground, but scarcely anything else.

"Oh, this is not Rio," said Antonio. "No, no, you must come back when the sun is out, you cannot see."

"Point out Christ, which direction?" I asked.

"Miss Becker, we are standing at the very base of the statue. Step back here and look up."

"To think we are standing in the heavens," I said.

Like Hell.

"It's all mist to me," said Martin, but he gave me an amiable smile. "You're right, this is some country, some city." He pointed to the right where a great hole had opened up and we could see the metropolis below, greater than Manhattan or Rome, sprawled out before us. The gap closed.

Antonio pointed above.

Suddenly a common miracle occurred, small and wondrous.

The great giant granite Christ appeared in the white mist, only yards away from us, his face high above us, and his arms rigid as they reached out, not to embrace but to be crucified; then the figure vanished.

"Ah, well, keep watching," said Antonio, pointing again.

A pure whiteness covered the world, and then suddenly the figure appeared again, in the obvious thinning of the air. I wanted to cry, and I started to cry.

"Christ, is Lily here? Tell me!" I whispered.

"Triana," said Martin.

"Anyone can pray. Besides, I don't want her to be here." I backed up, the better to see Him again, my God, as once again the clouds opened and closed.

"Ah, it's not so bad on this cloudy day, perhaps, as I supposed," said Antonio.

"Oh, no, it's divine," I said.

You think this will help you? Like pulling your Rosary out from under the pillows that night I left you?

"Are there any cloisters left to your mind?" I barely moved my lips, the words a near senseless murmur. "Didn't you learn anything from our dark journey? Or are you all bent out of nature now, like the wraiths that used to ragtag after you? I wasn't supposed to see your Rio, was I, only the memories of my own for which you hungered. Jealous that I love it so? What holds you back? The strength is ebbing away, and you hate and you hate . . ."

I wait for the ultimate moment for your humiliation.

"Ah, I should have known," I whispered.

"I wish you wouldn't say the Hail Marys out loud," said Martin lightly. "It makes me think of my Aunt Lucy and the way she made us listen to the Rosary on the radio every evening at six o'clock, fifteen minutes, kneeling on the wooden floor!"

Antonio laughed. "This is very Catholic." He reached out, touched my shoulder and Martin's shoulder. "My friend, it is going to rain. If you want to see the hotel before the rain, we should go to the tram now."

We waited for the clouds to break one final time. The great severe Christ appeared. "If Lily's at peace, Lord," I said, "I don't ask that you tell me."

"You don't believe that crap," said Martin.

Antonio was shocked. Obviously he couldn't know how much everyone in my immediate family lectured me daily and eternally.

"I believe that wherever Lily is, she has no need of me now. I believe that of all the truly dead."

Martin didn't listen.

There, once more, loomed our Christ, arms rigid as though he were on the crucifix at the end of the Rosary.

We hurried to the tram.

Our bodyguards, lounging against the balustrade, crunched their drink cans and tossed them into the trash bin and followed along.

The mist was wet by the time we reached the car.

"It's the first stop?" I asked.

"Oh, yes, and we can't miss it," Antonio said. "I have called for the car. It is a very steep drive up, but not so hard down, you see, and we can take our time if you like, and then it won't matter if it rains, of course, I mean I am sorry that the sky is not clear . . ."

"I love it."

Whoever used this first tram stop? This stop beside the abandoned hotel?

There was a parking lot here. Some drove up, no doubt, in powerful little cars, parked here, and took the tram to the summit. But there was nothing else to shelter one here.

The vast ocher-colored hotel was solid, but obviously utterly in neglect.

I stood spellbound looking at it. The clouds did not press so far down here, and I could see the view of the city and the sea that these shuttered windows had once commanded.

"Ah, such a place . . ."

"Yes, well," said Antonio, "there were plans, many plans, and perhaps . . . see, here, look through the fence." I saw a walkway, I saw a courtyard, I looked up at the faded ocher shutters that covered the windows, at the tiled roof. To think, I could . . . I really could . . . if I wanted to . . .

Some impulse was born in me, some impulse I hadn't felt anywhere else in our travels, to stake out some beautiful retreat on this spot, to come here at times away from New Orleans and breathe the air of this forest. There seemed no more beautiful place on earth than Rio.

"Come," said Antonio.

We walked past the hotel. A thick cement railing guarded us from a gorge. But we could see now the great depth of the building and how it was positioned out over the valley. It broke my heart, this loveliness. Beneath me, the banana trees plunged in a straight line, down and down the mountainside as if following the path of one root or spring, and all round the lush growth reached up, and the trees swayed over our heads. Across the road, in back of us, the forest was steep and dark and rich.

"This is Heaven."

I stood quiet. I let it be known. Just a moment. I didn't have to ask. It was matter of gestures. The gentlemen moved away, smoking their cigarettes, talking. I couldn't hear them. The wind didn't blow here as it did on the peak. The clouds were moving down, but slowly and thinly. It was quiet, and still, and below lay the thousands upon thousands of houses, buildings, towers, streets, and then the exquisite placid beauty of the endless blue water.

Lily was not here. Lily had gone, as surely as the spirit of the Maestro had gone, as surely as most spirits go, the spirit of Karl, the spirit of Mother, surely. Lily had better things to do than to come to me, either to console or torment.

Don't be so certain.

"Be careful with your tricks," I whispered. "I learned to play from pain from you. I can do it again," I said. "I'm not easily deceived, you should know that."

What you will see will chill your blood and you will drop the violin, you will beg me to take it, you will let it fall! You will back off from all you have so admired! You're not fit for it.

"I think not," I said. "You must remember how well I knew them all, how much I loved them, how much I loved the sickbed and the last small detail. Their faces and their forms are perfect in my memory. Don't try to duplicate that. We'll be at wits against each other."

He sighed. There was a falling off, a sliding away, a longing that chilled my arms and neck. I think I heard the sound of crying.

"Stefan," I said, "try, try not to cling to me or this but . . ."

I curse you. Damn you.

"Stefan, why did you choose me? Were the others such lovers of death, or just music?"

Martin touched my arm. He pointed. Some distance down the road, Antonio was beckoning for us.

It was a long way down. The bodyguards stood watch.

The mist was very wet now, but the sky was clear. Perhaps that's what happens. The mist melts to rain and becomes transparent.

There was a small clearing before us, and what seemed an old concrete fountain far back, and round in a circle what appeared to be cast-off plastic sacks, vividly blue, simple grocery or drugstore sacks. I'd never seen them in such a color.

"Those are their offerings," said Antonio.

"Who?"

"The *Mogambo* people, the *Candomblé.* See? Each sack has an offering to a god. One has rice in it, one has something else, perhaps corn, see, they make a circle. See? There were candles here."

I was delighted. Yet no sense of the supernatural came over me, only the wonder of human beings, the wonder of faith, the wonder of the forest itself creating this small green chapel for the strange Brazilian religion, so mixed with Catholic saints, that no one could ever untwine the varying rituals.

Martin asked the questions. How long ago had they met here? What had they done?

Antonio struggled for words . . . a ritual purification.

"Would that save *you*?" I whispered. Of course, I spoke to Stefan.

No answer came.

Only the forest lay around us, the sparkling forest as the rain came floating down. I closed my arms tight around the well-covered violin lest some dampness get inside, and I stared at the old circle of strange tacky blue plastic sacks, the stubs of the candles. And why not blue sacks? Why not? In ancient Rome, had the lamps of the temple been that different from the lamps of a household? Blue sacks of rice, of corn . . . for spirits. The ritual circle. The candles.

"One stands . . . you know, in the center," Antonio sought for his English, "to perhaps be purified."

No sound from Stefan. No whisper. I looked up through the mesh of green above. The rain covered my face soundlessly.

"It's time to go," said Martin. "Triana, you have to sleep. And our hosts. Our hosts have some grand plan of picking you up early. Seems they are inordinately proud of this Teatro Municipale."

"But it is an opera house," said Antonio, placatingly, "and very grand. Many people do enjoy to see it. And after the concert there will be such crowds."

"Yes, yes I want to go early," I said. "It's full of beautiful marble, isn't it?"

"Ah, so you know about it," he said. "It is splendid."

We drove back in the rain.

Antonio confessed with laughter that in all the years he had done such tours he had never seen the rain forest during the rain, and this was quite a spectacle to him. I was wrapped in beauty, and no longer afraid. I figured I knew what Stefan meant to do. Some thought was taking shape that almost seemed a plan.

It had begun in my mind in Vienna, when I had played for the people of the Hotel Imperial.

I never slept.

The rain teemed on the sea.

All was gray and then darkness. Bright lights defined the broad divisions of Copacabana Boulevard, or the Avenida Atlantica.

In a pastel bedroom, air-conditioned, I dozed perhaps, watching the gray electric night seal up the windows.

For hours, I lay peering at what seemed the real world of the ticking clock, in this the Presidential bedroom of the suite, peering through thin closed eyelids.

I put my arms around the violin, curled against it, holding it as my mother held me, or I held Lily, or as Lev and I, and Karl and I, had snuggled together.

Once in panic I almost went to the phone to call my husband, Lev, my lawfully wedded husband, whom I had so stupidly given away. No, that will only cause him pain, both him and Chelsea.

Think of the three boys. Besides, what made me think he would come back, my Lev? He shouldn't leave her and his children. He should not do that, and I should not think of it, or even wish for it.

Karl, be with me. Karl, the book is in good hands. Karl, the work's done. I drew the haggard confused figure back from the desk. "Lie down, Karl, all the papers are in order now."

There came a loud banging sound.

I woke up.

I must have been asleep.

The sky was clear and black beyond the windows.

Somewhere in the living room or dining room of the suite, a window had blown open. I heard it flapping, banging. It was the window in the living room, the window in the very center of the hotel.

In sock feet, the violin in my arms, I walked across the dark bedroom and into the living room, and felt the strong push of the cleansing wind. I looked out.

The sky was clear and studded with stars. The sand was golden in the electric lights that ran the length of the boulevard.

The sea raged on the broad beach.

The sea rolled in, in countless glassy overlapping waves, and in the lights, the curl of each wave was for an instant almost green, and then the water was black and then there arose before me the great dance of foaming figures.

Look, it was happening all up and down the beach, with every wave.

I saw it once, twice, I saw it to the right and to the left. I studied one great chorus after another. Wave after wave brought them rising with their outstretched arms towards the shore or towards the stars or towards me, I couldn't know.

Sometimes the stretch of the wave was so long and the foam so thick that it broke into eight or nine lithe and graceful forms, with heads and arms and bowing waists, before they lapsed back and the next band came rolling after them.

"You're not the souls of the damned or the saved," I said. "Oh, you are only beautiful. Beautiful as you were when I saw you in prophetic sleep. Like the rain forest on the mountain, like the clouds crossing the face of God.

"Lily, you are not here, my darling, you are not bound to any place any longer, not even one as beautiful as this. I could feel it if you were here, couldn't I?"

There came that thought again, that half-finished plan—that half-conceived prayer to fight him off.

I drew up a chair, and I sat down by the window. The wind blew my hair back.

Wave after wave brought the dancers forth, no one ever the same, each company of nymphs different, as were my concerts, or if there was a pattern to it, only the geniuses of chaos theory knew it. Once in a while, one dancer came so tall as to have legs that seemed ready to leap free.

I watched it until morning.

I don't need sleep to play. I'm crazy anyway. Being crazier still could only help.

The dawn came and all the rapid traffic, and the milling people below, the shops opening their doors, the buses rolling. Swimmers were in the waves. I stood at the window, the sack of the violin hanging over my shoulder.

A sound disturbed me.

I turned, jumped. But it was only a bellman who had come in, and in his arms he held a bouquet of roses.

"Madam, I knocked and knocked."

"It's fine, it was the wind."

"There are young people down there. You mean so much to them, they have come so far to see you. Madam, forgive me."

"No, I want to do it. Let me hold the roses and wave to them. They'll know me when they see me with the roses and I'll know them."

I went to the window.

The sun glared on the water; in an instant I found them, three slim young women and two men, scanning the face of the hotel with shaded eyes, then one saw me, saw the woman with the brown bangs and brown hair holding the red roses.

I lifted my hand to wave. I waved and waved. I watched them jump up and down.

"There is a song in Portuguese, a classic song," said the bellman.

He was fussing about with the little refrigerator right near the window, making certain of the drinks and the temperature.

The kids down there leapt in the air. They threw kisses.

Yes, kisses.

I threw them kisses.

I drew back, throwing kisses until it seemed the moment had reached its fullest, and then I let the window close. I turned to the side, the violin like a hump on my back, the roses in my arms. My heart was pounding.

"The song," he said. "It was famous in America, I think. It is 'Roses, Roses, Roses.'"

❦ 18 ❧

It was the corridor with the Greek key mosaic in the floor, the deep thick scrolls of gold, the brown marble.

"Very beautiful, yes, oh, God," said Roz, "I've never seen such a place. All of this is marble? Look, Triana, the red marble, the green, the white . . ."

I smiled. I knew. I saw.

"And this was in the cloisters of your memory?" I whispered to my secret ghost, "and you didn't mean for me to see it? Rushing to my bed?"

It must have sounded to the others like humming. He didn't answer me. A terrible sorrow overcame me for him. Oh, Stefan!

We stood at the foot of the staircase. To left and right stood the bronze-faced figures. The railings were a marble as green and clear as the sea in the afternoon sun, the balusters squared and thick, the stairway branching as it does in all such opera houses, it seemed, and behind us, as we mounted the stairs, the three doors of leaded glass with spoked fanlights above.

"Will they come in this way tonight?"

"Yes, yes," said the slender one, Mariana, "they will come. We are sold out. We have people who are waiting now. That's why I took you in the side door below. And we have a treat for you, a special treat."

"What could be grander than this?" I asked.

All together, we climbed the steps. Katrinka was suddenly stricken and sad. I saw her eyes meet Roz's eyes.

"If only Faye were here!" she said.

"Don't say that," said Roz, "you'll only make her think about Lily."

"Ladies," I said, "rest your minds, there is no waking hour when I don't think of Faye and of Lily."

Katrinka was suddenly shaken and Martin had come to put his arms around her, to make her stop carrying on, to shame her somewhat, even as he pretended to comfort her, the disciplinarian.

As we turned and went up the left side, I saw the great mezzanine and I saw the three magnificent stained-glass windows.

Mariana's soft voice told me the names of the figures, just as she had done in the dream. Lucrece, the darling woman beside her, smiled and commented too, on how each figure had its meaning in music or poetry or theater.

"And there, down there, are murals in that far room," I said.

"Yes, yes, and in the one at the other end, you must see . . ."

I stood still, the sunlight pouring through these painted pictures in glass, past these buxom, half-naked beauties with their raised symbols, surrounded by their garlands and their drapery.

I looked up and up and saw the paintings far above. I thought my soul would die in me in quiet, and nothing mattered now but what had mattered in the dream—not whence it came to me or why, but only that it was, this place, that someone had made it out of nothing and it stood, still, this place, for us, in its spectacular grandeur.

"You like it?" Antonio asked.

"More than I can ever say," I answered with a sigh. "Look, up there, the round plaques on the wall, the bronze faces, that's Beethoven."

"Yes, yes," said Lucrece graciously, "they are all there, the great opera composers, you see Verdi, ah, you see Mozart, you see there the . . . the . . . playwright . . ."

"Goethe."

"But come, we don't want you to be tired. We can show you more tomorrow. Let's go now, for our special surprise."

Laughter all around. Katrinka wiped her face, glaring angrily at Martin.

Glenn whispered to Martin to leave her alone.

"I lie awake all night," Glenn whispered, "wondering about Faye. Just let her cry."

"Don't draw attention to yourself," Martin said.

I took Katrinka's hand. I felt her hold tight to me.

"Surprise?" I said to Mariana and Lucrece. "What is it, my dears?"

We went down the splendid stairs together, the brilliant glass, the shining marble, the streaks and streaks of gold all melded in a canopy of glorious harmony—a man-made thing that seemed to rival the very sea with its tossed and leaping ghosts, the very forest in the rain, where the banana trees plunged down and down and down into the glade.

"This way, all of you, come this way . . ." Lucrece led. "We have a strange surprise."

"Yes, I think I know," said Antonio.

"But you see it's not just that."

"What is it?" I asked.

"Oh, the most beautiful restaurant in the world, and it's here under the opera house."

I nodded and smiled.

The Persian palace.

We had to go out to come in, and suddenly we found ourselves surrounded by the blue glazed tile, and the columns with the bulls, their hooves gathered and bound at the top, and Darius in the fountain slaying the lion, and all those étagères filled with sparkling glass, so like the cabinets of Stefan's burning palace.

"Now let me cry if you will," said Roz. "It's my turn to cry. Look, you see the Persian lamp? Oh, God, I want to live here forever."

"Yes, in the forest," I whispered. "In the old ruined hotel one stop down from the foot of Christ."

"Let her cry," said Martin, crossly, staring at his wife.

But Katrinka was brightening.

"Oh, this is magnificent," she said.

"It was meant to be the palace of Darius, you see."

"And look, amid all this," said Glenn softly, "people are eating, look at the tables, people are having coffee and cake."

"We have to have coffee and cake."

"But first let us show you the surprise. Come this way." Lucrece beckoned. I knew.

I knew as we went past the old carved wood bar and down the passage. I heard the huge engines.

"These run the cooling and the heating for the building," she said. "They are very old."

"God, there's a bad smell here," said Katrinka.

Then I heard nothing. I saw the white tile; we passed the metal lockers. We walked round the big engines with their giant old-fashioned screws like the engines of the old ships; we walked on and on, and the talk was soft and agreeable around us.

I saw the gate.

"Our secret," said Mariana. "It is an underground tunnel!"

I laughed with appreciative delight. "Really? It is truly that? Where does it go?" I drew near the gates. My soul ached. Darkness back there, beyond these rusted spokes of iron on which I laid my right hand, getting it filthy, filthy.

Water gleamed on the cement floor.

"To the palace, you see, the palace is just across the street and in the old days, when the Opera house was first built, they could come and go through the secret tunnel."

I pressed my forehead against the pickets.

"I adore this, I'm not going home," said Roz. "Nobody's going to make me go home. Triana, I want the money to stay here."

Glenn smiled and shook his head.

"You can have it, Roz," I said.

I stared into the darkness.

"What do you see there?" I asked.

"I don't know!" said Katrinka.

"Well, it is wet and damp, and there is something leaking there . . ." said Lucrece.

So none of them saw the man lying with his eyes open, and the blood pouring from his wrists, and the tall black-haired phantom, arms folded, leaning against the dark wall, glaring at us?

No one saw this but mad Triana Becker?

Go on. Go ahead. Go on the stage tonight. Play my violin. Display your wicked witchery.

The dying man climbed to his knees, confounded, fuddled, blood streaming on the tile. He rose to his feet to join his companion, the ghost who'd driven him mad, driven out his music, just before coming to me, with these vivid memories his soul, this ghost, his tissue-thin soul that overflowed with all this, unwillingly.

No. It had a hint of panic.

The others talked. There was time for cake and coffee and rest.

Blood. It ran from the dead man's wrists. It ran down his pants as he staggered towards me.

No one else saw.

I looked beyond this stumbling corpse. I looked at the agony in the face of Stefan. So young, so lost, so desperate. So afraid of utter defeat again.

✑ 19 ✑

I WAS always quiet right before the concert. So no one noticed.
No one said a word. There was so much kindness and richness here—
old dressing rooms, baths of handsome Art Deco tile, murals and
names to be explained—the others were gently borne away.

A stillness came down on me. In the great impossible palace of
marble, I sat with the violin. I waited. I heard the great theater begin
to fill. Soft thunder on the stairs. The rising hum of voices.

There came the thump of my vain and eager heart—to play.

And what will you do here? What can you do, I thought. And then
again there came that thought, that image that perhaps I could lock in
my mind, lock as one locks upon a Mystery of the Rosary, to fight him
off—*The Crowning with Thorns*—and nothing he could do could
weaken me, but what was this terrible, aching love for him, this terrible sorrow, this pain for him that was as deep and bad as any pain for
Lev or Karl, or any of them?

I lay my head back in the velvet chair, let my neck roll on the
wooden frame, held the violin in its sack, gestured No to water and
coffee and things to eat.

The auditorium was now filled, said Lucrece. "We have received
many donations."

"And you'll receive more," I said. "It is a magnificent place; it must
never be allowed to fall into decay. Not this, not this creation."

On and on Glenn and Roz talked, in their soft muted compatible
voices about the mingling of the tropical color and the Baroque scale,

the fleeting sophisticated European nymphs combined with a forbidden indulgence in the range of stones and patterns and floors of
parquet.

"I love your . . . velvet clothes, what you wear," said kind Lucrece,
"this is pretty velvet that you wear, this poncho and skirt, Miss
Becker."

I nodded and whispered thanks.

It was time now to walk across the immense dark shadowy rear of
the stage. It was time to hear our feet clopping on the boards and look
up, up, into the ropes and pulleys, the curtains high above, the ramps,
and the men peering down, and children, yes, even children up there,
as if they had been sneaked into the place, and to the right and left the
awesome wings full of great operatic scenery. Painted columns. All
that one could see, for real and true in stone, painted again.

And so the sea is green when the wave curls, and the balustrade
of marble looks like the green sea, and there is painted the green
balustrade.

I peered through the curtain.

The first floor was filled, each red velvet armchair held its eager
occupant. Programs . . . mere notes on how no one knew what I would
play or how or just when I would stop and all that . . . fluttered in the
air, and jewels caught the light of the chandelier, and three great balconies rose one atop the other, each overflowing with figures struggling to their seats.

There were those in formal black, and gay gowns, and others high
up in workman's clothes.

In the boxes to the left and right of the stage sat the officials to
whom I had been presented, never remembering a single name, never
having anymore to remember, never expected to do more than what I
meant to do, and what I alone could do:

Play the music. Play it for one hour.

Give them that, and then into the mezzanine they'll pour, talking
about the "savant sophisticate," as I had come to be known, or the
American Naïf, or the dumpy woman who looked too much like a pre-
maturely aged child in flaring velvet, scratching at the strings as if she
fought with the music she played.

No hint before of a theme. No hint of a direction. Only that
thought in my mind, a thought begun somewhere else in music.

Violin

And the admission in my secret self that it was scattered within me, the Rosary Beads of my life, the splinters of death and guilt and anger and rage; it was in broken glass I lay down each night, and waked with cut hands, and these months of music making had been a dreamlike respite that no human being could ever expect to last, that no human being had any right to expect of Heaven.

Fate, fortune, fame, destiny.

From behind the edge of the huge stage curtain, I stared at the faces in the first row.

"And those velvet shoes, those pointed shoes, don't they hurt?" asked Lucrece.

"It's a hell of a time to mention that," said Martin.

"No, it's only an hour," I said.

The roar of the house swallowed our voices.

"Give them forty-five minutes," said Martin, "and they'll be delighted. All the money is going to the foundation for this place."

"Boy, Triana," said easygoing Glenn, "you sure do get a lot of advice."

"Tell me about it, brother," I laughed softly.

Martin hadn't heard. It was all right. Katrinka was always shaking at this moment. Roz had settled back in the wings, straddling a chair like a cowboy, with the back in front of her, her legs spread comfortably in her black pants, her arms folded on the back of the chair, so she could watch. The family receded into the shadows.

It seemed a calmness had settled over the technicians.

I felt the cooling driven by the engines far below.

Such beautiful faces, such beautiful people, ranging from the fairest to the darkest, with configurations of features never ever seen by me anywhere before, and so many of the young, the very young, like the ones who had come with the roses.

Suddenly, asking permission of no one, giving no warning, having no orchestra below me to alert, having no one to find me now but the light man with his spot high above, I walked out to the center of the stage.

My shoes made a hollow sound on the dusty boards.

Slowly, I walked, giving the spot time to descend and fall on me.

I walked to the very lip and looked down at all the faces ranged before me.

I heard the quiet fall over the house as if the noise had been urgently dragged away.

In coughs, in final whispers, all sound finally died.

I turned and lifted the violin.

With a shock, I realized I wasn't on the stage at all, but in the tunnel. I could smell it, feel it, see it. The bars were right there.

This would be the great struggle. I bowed my head against what I knew was the violin, no matter what the spell that kept it from my eyes, no matter what the charms that drew me to that filthy tunnel and its dank water.

I lifted the bow that I knew had to be in my hand.

Ghost things? The playthings of a spirit? How do you know?

I began a great downward stroke, falling into what had become for me the Russian mode, by far the sweetest and the one which made the most room for sadness.

Tonight it would have to enlarge and carry the dark tide, and I heard the notes clear, shining, falling like coins in the dark.

But I saw the tunnel.

A child was walking towards me through the water, a child in a country dancing dress with a bald head.

"You are doomed, Stefan." I didn't move my lips.

"I play for you, my beautiful daughter."

"Mommie, help me."

"I play for us, Lily."

She stood at the gate, she pressed her small face to the rusted iron pickets and clutched them with her small chubby fingers. Her lip jutted. "Mommie!" she cried in heartbreak. She clabbered as babies and young children do. "Mommie, without him I would have never found you! Mommie, I need you!"

Evil, evil spirit. The music descended into protest and riot. Let it go, let the anger go.

It's a lie and you know it, you idiot spirit, it's not my Lily.

"Mommie, he brought me to you! Mom, he found me. Mom, don't do this to me, Mamma!

"Mamma! Mamma!"

The music rushed forward, though I stared wide eyed at a gate I knew was not there, at a figure I knew was not there, so heartbreakingly perfect I felt my breath cease. I made myself breathe. I made the breath come with the stroke of the bow. Play, yes, for you, that you would be there, yes, that you could come back, yes, that we could turn the pages, that it would be undone.

Karl appeared. He walked softly towards her. He laid his hands on Lily's shoulders. My Karl. Already thin with disease.

"Triana," he said in a hoarse whisper. His throat had already been hurt by the oxygen tubes he so hated, and finally came to refuse. "Triana, how can you be so heartless? I can wander, I'm a man, I was dying when we met, but this is your daughter."

You're not there! You are not, but this music is real. I hear it, and it seemed I had never risen to such a height, charging the mountain as if it were Corcovado and looking up through the clouds.

But still I saw them.

And now my father stood beside Karl. "Honey, give it up," he said. "You can't do it. This is all evil, it's sinful, it's wrong. Triana, give it up. Give it up. Give it up!"

"Mommie." My child grimaced in pain. The country dress was the last dress I had ever ironed for her, for the coffin. My Father had said they will—

No . . . the clouds come now across the face of Christ and it matters not if He is the Incarnate Word or a statue made lovingly of stone, it matters not, what matters is the stance—the outstretched arms, for nails, or to enfold, I will not—

In astonishment, I saw my Mother. I slowed the pace; was I pleading with them, was I talking to them, was I believing in them, and giving in to them?

She came to the iron gate, her dark hair pulled back the way I loved it, her mouth touched with the barest lipstick just as if she were real. But there was a lurid hatred in her eyes. Hate.

"You're selfish, you're vicious, you're hateful!" she said. "You think you fooled me? You think I don't remember? I came that night, crying, frightened, and you, scared, clung to my husband in the dark and he told me to go away, and you heard me crying. You think even a Mother can forgive that?"

Suddenly a startled sobbing broke from Lily. She turned and raised her fists. "Don't you hurt my Mamma!"

Oh, God. I tried to close my eyes, but Stefan stood right there before me with his hands on the violin.

He couldn't move it, or jog it, or make one note fall short of the mark, and on and on I played, of this chaos, this hideousness, this . . .

This truth, say it. Say it. It's common sins, that's all, no one ever said you bashed them with a weapon, you were no criminal hunted in dark streets, no wanderer among the dead. It's common sins, and that's what you are, common, common and dirty and small, and without this talent you stole from me, you bitch, you whore, give it back.

Lily sobbed. She rushed up to him and beat on him. She pulled on his arm. "Stop it, you leave my Mommie alone. Mommie." She threw up her arms.

At last I stared straight into her eyes, I stared straight into her eyes and I played of her eyes and I played, regardless of what she said, and I heard their voices and saw them moving, and then I lifted my gaze. I had no sense of time, only a sense of the music shifting.

I saw not the theater I wanted so desperately to see. I saw not the party of ghosts he so desperately presented before me; I looked up and beyond and I envisioned the tropical forest in its celestial rain, I saw the drowsing trees, I saw the old hotel, I saw it, and played of it, and played of branches reaching the clouds, and of Christ, his arms outstretched, and of the arcades of the old hotel, the windows with their yellow shutters stained by rain and rain and rain.

I played of this, and then of the sea, oh, yes, the sea, no less wondrous, this mounting, tossing, glossy, impossible sea with its phantom dancers.

"That's what you are! Oh, if only you were real."

"Mommeeee!" She screamed. She screamed as if someone was hurting her unbearably.

"Triana, for the love of God!" said my Father.

"Triana," said Karl. "God forgive you."

She screamed again. I couldn't sustain it, this melody of the sea, this summoning of the triumphant waves, and now it melted again into anger and loss and rage; oh, Faye, where are you, how could you leave; oh, God, Dad, you left us alone with Mother, but I will not . . . I will not . . . Mamma . . .

Lily screamed again!

I would crack.

The music surged.

The image. There had been some thought, some simple half-formed thought, some little thought, and it came to me now, came to me with an ugly vision of the glittering blood on the white napkin lying by the blazing heater, the menstrual blood, the blood swarming with ants, and then the gash in Roz's head when I smashed the door, after the Rosary broke, and the blood they drew over and over and over from Dad and Karl and Lily, Lily crying, Katrinka crying, the blood from Mother's head when she fell, the blood, the blood on the filthy napkins and on the mattresses when she wore nothing at all and bled and bled without cease.

And it was this.

You can't deny the wrongs. You can't deny the blood that's on your hands, or on your conscience! You can't deny that life is full of blood, pain is blood, wrong is blood.

But there is blood and there is blood.

Only some blood comes from the wounds we inflict on ourselves and on one another. That blood flows bright and accusing, and threatens to take with it the very life of the wounded one, that blood— and how it glistens, so celebrated, that sacred blood, that blood that was Our Lord's Blood, the Blood of the Martyrs, the blood on Roz's face, and the blood on my hands, the blood of wrongs. .

But there is another blood.

There is a blood that flows from a woman's womb. And it is not the signal of death, but only of a great and fertile fount—a river of blood which can, when it would, form whole human beings out of its substance, it is a living blood, an innocent blood, and that was all it was on the napkin there, beneath the swarm of ants, in squalor and dust, just that blood, flowing and flowing, as if from a woman letting loose the dark secret strength in her to make children, letting loose the powerful fluid that belongs to her and her alone.

And it was this blood now with which I bled. Not the blood of the wounds he inflicted on me, not the blood of his blows and his kicks, not the blood of his scratching fingers as he tried to get the violin.

It was this blood of which I sang, letting my music be this blood, flow like this blood; it was this blood that I pictured in the chalice raised at the Consecration of the Mass, the wholesome sweet and female blood, this innocent blood that could in the right season form a receptacle for a soul, the blood inside of us, the blood that makes, the blood that creates, the blood that ebbs and flows, without sacrifice or mutilation, without loss or ruin.

I heard it now, my own song. I heard it, and it seemed the light around me had swelled impossibly. I didn't want such bright light and yet it was so lovely, this light that rose up to the beams I knew to be above.

And, opening my eyes, I saw not only the great hall filled with rows and rows of faces, but I saw Stefan, and the light was directly behind him, and yet he reached out at me.

"Stefan, turn!" I said. "Stefan, look! Stefan!"

He did turn. There was a figure in the light, a short stubby figure, beckoning to Stefan in great impatience, Come. I gave the music one last thrust.

Stefan, go! You are the lost child! Stefan!

I could play no more.

Stefan glared at me. He cursed at me. He made his hands into fists. Yet his face changed. It underwent some complete and seemingly unconscious transformation. He gazed at me with wide and frightened eyes.

The light behind him faded as he drew close, a dark shadow, fading even as he hovered over me, a gloom no more substantial than the shadows in the wings.

The music was ended.

I saw the audience rise en masse. Another victory. How so, God? How so? Three tiers and they reward this din that is my only tongue.

The hall roared with applause.

Another victory.

There was no sight or sound of those contrived ghosts.

Someone had come to take me from the stage. I stared out into the faces, nodding; do not disappoint, sweep the hall with your eyes, all the way to the right and to the left, look up at the topmost balconies and then at the boxes, don't raise your arms in vanity, merely bow, and bow, and murmur thanks and they will know, thanks from my bloody soul.

In one last dim flash I saw him, close to me, confused, bent, near invisible, fading. A wretched miserable thing. But what was this bewilderment? This strange wonder in his eyes. He was gone.

I was held by others once again, oh, lucky, lucky girl, to have such kind and helping hands. O Fate, fortune, fame, and destiny.

Stefan, you could have gone into the light. Stefan, you should have gone!
Backstage, I cried and cried.

No one thought it the slightest bit unusual. The cameras flashed, the reporters wrote. I knew no doubt within my heart of peace for those I'd lost—except for Faye . . . and Stefan.

❧ *20* ❧

I went to the Teatro Amazones in Manaus because it was a singular place and I had seen it once in a movie. *Fitzcarraldo* had been the name of the film, made by a German director, Werner Herzog, now dead, and Lev and I in the hellish time after Lily's death had spent a calm night with each other at the show, actually together.

I didn't remember the plot, only the opera house, and the stories I had heard of the rubber boom and the luxury of the theater, and how splendid it was, though nothing on earth would ever compare with this palace in Rio de Janeiro.

Also I had to play another concert immediately. I had to. I had to see if the ghosts would come back. I had to see if it was over.

There was a little controversy before we left for the state of Amazonas.

Grady called and insisted that we go back to New Orleans.

He would not tell us why, but went on and on that we must come home, until finally Martin took the phone and, in his subdued abusive way, demanded to know what was Grady's meaning.

"Look, if Faye is dead, tell us. Just say so. We don't have to fly home to New Orleans to hear the news. Tell us now."

Katrinka shivered.

After a long moment, Martin covered the phone. "It's your Aunt Anna Belle."

"We love her," said Roz, "we'll send lots of flowers."

"No, she's not dead. She claims that Faye called her."

"Aunt Anna Belle?" said Roz. "Aunt Anna Belle talks to the Archangel Michael when she's taking a bath. She asks him to help her not to fall and break her hip again in the bathtub."

"Give me the phone," I said.

We all came together.

It was as I suspected. Aunt Anna Belle, now past eighty years, thought she had received a call in the middle of the night. No phone number given. No place of origin.

"She said she could hardly hear the child, but she was sure it was Faye."

The message? There was none.

"I want to go home now," said Katrinka.

I questioned Grady over and over. A garbled voice, supposedly Faye, no content, no origin, no information. What about the phone bill? Coming soon. But then the phone bill was cluttered up because Aunt Anna Belle had lost her card and somebody in Birmingham, Alabama, had run up a whole mess of calls on it.

"Well, get somebody to be right there," said Martin. "By Aunt Anna Belle's phone and the phone at home, in case Faye does call."

"I'm going home," said Katrinka.

"To what?" I asked. I hung up the phone. "To sit there and wait day by day in case she ever calls again?"

My sisters looked at me.

"I know," I whispered. "I hadn't known before, but I know now. I am so very angry with her."

Silence.

"That she'd do this—" I said.

"Don't say things you'll regret," said Martin.

"Maybe it was Faye," said Glenn. "Listen, I'm pretty piqued myself, I'm ready to go home, I don't mind going back to 2524 St. Charles and waiting for a call from Faye. I'll go. You all go on. But I don't think I'm up to keeping company with Aunt Anna Belle. Triana, you go on to Manaus. You and Martin and Roz."

"Yes, just that last place," I said. "We've come so far, and I love this land so much. I'm going to Manaus. I have to go."

Katrinka and Glenn went on.

Martin stayed to manage the benefit concert in Manaus, and Roz went with me, and nobody forgot about Faye. The flight to Manaus was three hours.

The Teatro Amazones was a gem—smaller, yes, than the grand marble creation in Rio, but very splendid, and very strange, with the coffee leaves right in its iron, and the very velvet seats that I had seen in the film *Fitzcarraldo*, and murals of the Indians, and a general embrace of the native art and lore wound up with the Baroque by the bold and crazy rubber baron who had built it.

It seemed that everything in this country, or nearly everything, was done—as it was in New Orleans—not by any group conscience, or group force, but by some single and mad personality.

It was a thrilling concert. No ghosts came. No ghosts at all. And the music now was directed, and darkening, and I could feel the direction of its flow, rather than drowning in it. I had a current. I didn't fear the deeper colors.

There was a church to St. Sebastian on the square. I sat inside for an hour while it rained, thinking of Karl, and thinking of many things, and of how the music had felt and that I could now actually remember what I'd played, or at least hear a dim echo.

The next day, Roz and I walked along the harbor. The town of Manaus was as wild as the opera house itself, and it reminded me of the port of New Orleans in the forties when I was a really little girl, and our city had been a true port, and there had been ships like this at every dock.

Ferryboats carried the hundreds of workers home to their villages. Street vendors sold goods from sailors' pockets, flashlight batteries, cassette tapes, ballpoint pens. In our day back then it had been cigarette lighters with naked women on them. I remembered that the trashy item you could buy down there by the customs house was a cigarette lighter with a decal of a naked woman.

No call came from the States.

Was it ominous? Was it good? Did it mean nothing?

In Manaus, the River Negro ran before us. When we flew back to Rio, we saw the joining of the black and the white waters that make the Amazon.

When we walked into the Copacabana Palace, there was a note waiting. I opened it, fully expecting to read some tragic news, and felt suddenly weak and sick to my stomach.

But it was not concerning Faye.

It was in the old fancy script, the fine eighteenth-century script, firmly written.

I must see you. Come up to the old hotel. I promise you, I will not try to hurt you. Your Stefan.

Baffled, I stared at this. "You go on up to the suite," I said to Roz. "What's the matter with you?"

There wasn't time to answer. With the violin in the shoulder sack, I had to run down the curved drive to catch Antonio, who had just brought us from the airport.

We went on the tram alone, without bodyguards, but Antonio himself was a formidable man and afraid of no sneak thieves and we saw none. Antonio called on his cell phone. One of the bodyguards would come up the mountain to meet us at the hotel. He'd be there in minutes.

I rode in stiff silence. Over and over I opened the note. I read the words. It was Stefan's writing, Stefan's signature.

Good God.

When we reached the Hotel stop, the next to last, we got off and I asked Antonio if he would wait for me on the bench, right by the track, where the waiting passengers sat, and I told him I wasn't afraid to be alone in this forest and he could hear me shout if I needed him.

I walked uphill, step after step, remembering suddenly with a tight smile, the Second Movement of the Beethoven's *Ninth*. I think I heard it in my head.

Stefan stood at the cement barricade over the deep gorge. He was dressed in his nondescript black clothes. The wind was blowing his hair. He looked alive, solid, a man enjoying the vista—the city, the jungle, the sea.

I stood, some ten feet from him.

"Triana," he said. He turned and only tenderness came out of him. "Triana, my love." His face was as pure as I'd ever seen it.

"What trick is this, Stefan?" I asked. "What now? Has some evil force given you the very tack to take it away from me?"

I had hurt him. I had struck him right between the eyes, but he shook it off, and I saw again, yes, again, tears spring to his eyes. The wind blew his long black hair in streaks and his eyebrows came together as he bowed his head.

"I am crying again too," I said. "I thought laughter had become our language, but now I see it's tears again. What can I do to stop it?"

He beckoned for me to come close.

I couldn't refuse, and suddenly felt his arm around my neck, only he made no move for the velvet sack which I brought down gently in front of me.

"Stefan, why didn't you go? Why didn't you go into the light? Didn't you see it? Didn't you see who was there, beckoning, waiting to guide you?"

"Yes, I saw," he said. He stood back.

"What then, what keeps you here? Why this vitality again? Who is it who pays now for this with memories or sorrow? What do you do, raise your educated tenor voice, no doubt tutored in Vienna, as fine as your violin style. . . ."

"Hush, Triana." It was a humble voice. Serene. His eyes were only quiet and patient.

"Triana, I see the light continuously. I see it always. I see it now. But Triana—" His lips quivered.

"What is it?"

"Triana, what if, what if, when I go into that light—?"

"Go! God, can it be worse than the purgatory you revealed to me? I don't believe it. I saw it. I felt its warmth. I saw it."

"Triana, what if, when I go, the violin goes with me?"

It took one second for the connection to be made, for us to look into each other's eyes, and then I saw this light too, only it was not part of anything around it. The late afternoon kept its radiant glow, the forest its stillness. The light clung only to him, and I saw his face change again, transcending anger, or rage, or sorrow, or even confusion.

I had made my decision, after all. He knew.

I lifted the sack with the violin and bow and I reached out and put it in his hands.

He raised his hands to say no, no. "Perhaps not!" he whispered. "Triana, I'm afraid."

"So am I, young Maestro. And I'll be afraid when I die too," I said.

He turned and looked away from me, as if into a world I couldn't possibly measure. I saw only a radiance, a swelling brightness that made no assault on my eyes or my soul, but only made me feel love, profound love and trust.

"Goodbye, Triana," he said.

"Goodbye, Stefan."

The light was gone. I stood on the road in the rain forest above the ruined hotel. I stood staring at stained walls, and the city of towers and hovels down below, going on for miles and miles over mountains and valleys.

The violin was gone.

The sack in my hands was empty.

🎵 21 🎵

THERE was no point in calling Antonio's attention to this, that the violin was gone. Our bodyguard had come with the van.

I held the sack as if it contained my violin. We rode down the mountain in silence. The sun came pouring through the open windows of the lofty green leaves, it threw down sanctifying shafts on the road, and the cool air touched my face.

My heart was brimming, but I couldn't name the feeling. Not completely. Love, oh, yes, love, love and wonder, yes, but more, something more, some fear of all that lay ahead, of the empty sack, fear for myself and fear for all those I loved and all those who now depended upon me.

I thought dim rational thoughts as we sped through Rio. It was near dark when we reached the hotel. I slipped out of the van, waving to my loyal men, and went inside, not even stopping at the desk to see if there was a message.

My throat was tight. I couldn't speak. I had one thing to do only. That was to ask Martin for the violin we carried with us, the short Strad we had bought, or the Guarneri, and see what happened.

Oh, bitter small things on which the fate of a whole soul hangs and with it the whole universe known to that soul. I didn't want to see the others. But I had to see Martin, had to find the violin.

When the elevator doors opened, I heard them all shrieking and laughing.

For a moment I couldn't interpret this sound.

Then I crossed the hall and hammered on the door of the Presidential Suite.

"It's Triana, open up!" I said.

It was Glenn who pulled back the door. He was delirious. "She's here, she's here," he cried.

"Darlin'," said Grady Dubosson. "We just put her on the plane and brought her down, soon as they stamped that passport."

I saw her against the distant window, her small head, her small body, a tiny waif of a being, Faye. Only Faye was that small, that delicate, that perfectly proportioned, as if God loved as much to make elves and small gentle children as he did to make grown things.

She wore her faded jeans, her inevitable and characteristic white shirt. Her auburn hair was cut short. I couldn't see her features in the twilight glow from the window.

She ran into my arms.

I closed my arms around her and I held her. How very very small she was, perhaps half my weight, so little that I might have crushed her like a violin.

"Triana, Triana, Triana!" she cried. "You can play the violin. You can play. You've got the gift!"

I watched her. I couldn't speak. I wanted to love, wanted to welcome, I wanted a warmth to flow from me as it had come with the light to Stefan on the road in the forest. But for the moment I only saw her small bright face, her pretty gleaming blue eyes, and I thought, She is safe, she is not dead, she is in no grave, she is here, and she is unharmed.

We are all together again.

Roz came booming over, throwing her arms around me, lowering her head and her voice. "I know, I know, I know, we should be angry, we should scream at her, but she's back, she's all right, she's been on some dangerous adventure, but she's come home! Triana, she's here. Faye is with us."

I nodded. And this time when I held Faye, I kissed her thin cheek. I felt her small head, as small as a child's head. I felt her lightness, her fragility and also some terrible strength in her, born of the black water of the womb, and the dark house, of the stumbling mother, of the coffin lowered into the ground.

"I love you," I whispered. "Faye, I love you."

She danced back. How she loved to dance. Once when we'd been separated and all came together in California, she had danced in circles and leapt in the air just to see us all united, the four of us, and so we were now, and she frolicked around the room. She leapt up on the wooden coffee table—a trick I'd seen her do before. She smiled, her small eyes flashing brightly, her hair red in the light from the window.

"Triana, play the violin for me. For me. Please. For me. For me."

No contrition? No apology?

No violin.

"Martin, would you get the other instruments? The Guarneri. I think the Guarneri is strung and ready to play and there's a good bow in the case."

"But what happened to the long Strad?"

"I gave it back," I whispered. "Please don't argue with me now. Please."

Grumbling, he went out.

Only now did I see Katrinka, wrung out and red-eyed, sitting on the couch. "I'm just glad you're home," she said in a raw and tortured voice. "You don't know." How Trink had suffered.

"She had to go. She had to wander off when she did!" Glenn said in his gentle drawl. He looked to Roz. "She had to do what she did. The point is, she's home. She made it."

"Oh, let's not do this tonight," said Roz. "Triana, play for us! Not one of those horrible witches' dances, I can't stand another one of those."

"Aren't we the critic!" said Martin, closing the door. He had the Guarneri violin. It was the nearest to what I had had.

"Go on, play something for us, please," said Katrinka in her broken voice, her eyes dazed and hopelessly hurt and relieved as she looked at Faye.

Faye stood on the table. She looked at me. There seemed a coldness in her, a hardness, something that could not say that she had any care for us, something perhaps that said, "My pain was greater than you knew," the very thing we feared when we had called morgues in dread and given out her description over phone lines. Maybe it was only "My pain is as great as your pain."

Here she stood alive.

I held this new violin. I tuned it quickly. The E string was very slack. I wound the peg. Gently. This was not as fine as my long Strad, not as well kept, but it had been very well restored, as they said. I tightened the bow.

What if there is no song?

My throat tightened. I looked at the window. In a way, I wanted to go over there and just look out at the sea, and just be glad she was here, and not have to learn yet how to say it was all right that she'd gone away, or talk of whose fault it was, or who was blind, or who didn't care.

I'd especially like to *not* know whether or not I could play.

But events such as these have never come to me at my choosing. I thought of Stefan in the forest.

Goodbye, Triana.

I tuned the A string, then the D and the G. I could do it now with no help. In fact, I'd been able to arrive at near perfect pitch even from the beginning.

It was ready. It had responded to me this much, and I remembered from the day it was first shown to me, played for me, that it had had a lower, more lush sound than the Strad, a sound that was a little akin to the large viola, and perhaps it was larger. I didn't know such things about this kind of violin. The Strad had been the object of my love.

Faye came to me and she looked up.

I think she wanted to say things, but she couldn't, any more than I could. And I thought again, You are alive, you are with us, we have a chance to make you safe.

"You want to dance?" I said.

"Yes!" Faye said. "Play Beethoven for me! Play Mozart! Play anybody!"

"Play a happy song," Katrinka said, "you know, one of those pretty happy songs you play."

I know.

I lifted the bow. My fingers came down rapidly, pounding away on the strings, the bow racing, and it was the happy song, the gay and free and happy song and it came unstintingly and bright and fine out of the violin, so fine and so loud and so new in my ear from this change of wood, that I almost danced myself, pivoting, dipping, turning, yanked by the instrument, and only dimly out of the corner of my eye seeing them dance: my sisters, Roz and Katrinka and Faye.

I played and I played. The music poured forth.

AND THAT night, when they slept, and the rooms were quiet, and the tall willowy women for sale walked the boulevard, I took the violin and the bow and I went to the window in the very center of the hotel.

I looked down at the spectacle of the fantastical waves. I saw them dance as we had danced.

I played for them—with surety and ease, without fear and with no anger—I played for them a sorrowful song, a glorious song, a joyful one.

The End

finished: May 14, 1996
1:50 a.m.
second run: May 20, 1996
9:25 a.m.
last run: Jan. 7, 1997
2:02 a.m.

Anne Rice

A NOTE ON THE TYPE

This book was set in Janson, a typeface long thought to have been made by the Dutchman Anton Janson, who was a practicing typefounder in Leipzig during the years 1668–1687. However, it has been conclusively demonstrated that these types are actually the work of Nicholas Kis (1650–1702), a Hungarian, who most probably learned his trade from the master Dutch typefounder Dirk Voskens. The type is an excellent example of the influential and sturdy Dutch types that prevailed in England up to the time William Caslon (1692–1766) developed his own incomparable designs from them.

Composed by Creative Graphics, Inc.,
Allentown, Pennsylvania
Printed and bound by Quebecor Printing,
Fairfield, Pennsylvania
Designed by Virginia Tan